THE
FAR-BACK
COUNTRY

Kate Lyons was born in 1965 in outback New South Wales. She has had her short fiction and poetry published in a range of Australian literary journals. Her first novel, *The Water Underneath*, was shortlisted in the 1999 *The Australian*/Vogel's Literary Award and was published by Allen & Unwin in 2001. Her second novel *The Corner of Your Eye* was published by Allen & Unwin in 2006. *The Water Underneath* was shortlisted for the Nita B. Kibble Literary Award (Dobbie Award) and the Fellowship of Australian Writers Melbourne University Press Literature Award, and was a notable book in the 2001 Pan Pacific Kiriyama Prize. She holds a Doctor of Creative Arts degree from the University of Technology Sydney and was the New South Wales Ministry of the Arts Writing Fellow in 2006. Kate lives in the Blue Mountains, New South Wales.

KATE LYONS

THE FAR-BACK COUNTRY

ALLEN&UNWIN
SYDNEY·MELBOURNE·AUCKLAND·LONDON

Thanks to Les Murray for permission to use an extract from his poem
'The Wilderness' on p. vii.

 Recipient of Government Arts NSW 2006 Writer's Fellowship
funded by the NSW Government in association with Create NSW

Allen & Unwin
83 Alexander Street
Crows Nest NSW 2065
Australia
Phone: (61 2) 8425 0100
Email: info@allenandunwin.com
Web: www.allenandunwin.com

 A catalogue record for this
book is available from the
National Library of Australia

ISBN 978 1 76063 283 0

Set in 12.2/18.6 pt Goudy by Bookhouse, Sydney
Printed and bound in Australia by Griffin Press

10 9 8 7 6 5 4 3 2 1

MIX
Paper from
responsible sources
FSC® C009448

The paper in this book is FSC® certified.
FSC® promotes environmentally responsible,
socially beneficial and economically viable
management of the world's forests.

For Ada

. . . my childhood was in danger
So I preceded you, in all but spirit,
To the far-back country
Where all tar roads end.

'THE WILDERNESS', LES MURRAY

CHAPTER ONE

DECEMBER 2006

Ray was on the edge of things when Delly died. He'd been out there six days. The only sign of life the odd goat or derelict windmill, the tracks of his ute girdling the creek. Now and then, shadow of an eagle, high, hefty, circling, rippling cruciform across the stave of his fence.

The rest was dust, scrub, gibber. Along old wash lines, blue bush, black oak, old man saltbush. Tired green tracing lost water, petering to low mallee, dead mulga. Sly wink of desert varnish, haloes of salt. Beyond that, across thin hills and iron ridges, more gibber, great ribs and drifts and spines of it, stepping a glittering distance, and him with it. Wire falling, hand to horizon, all the way from north bore soak to the edge of the old mine workings, where no stock grazed, no fence ruled.

When he stopped for a breather, he could see every taut and shining hour. Could feel it running through him, a brutal architecture. Leaving this gaunt shadow at his heel.

He bent along it. Stepped a run, laid his string line, checked his level. Stepped it out again.

⁓

If his memory of high-school history was correct, this creek he'd been following all morning was one of Sturt's. He'd tried to pin it to history, with ducks and diaries, maps and scurvy. Water like boiled black ink, he'd written, the image slipping bright down lines of faded copperplate, along the curve of Ray's pick, out into the shadow of his hat. Eyes shut and body braced, he could almost see it, almost feel it. Sweat braiding between his shoulderblades, a cool ribbon in this sea of stone.

Then he struck, the force shattering up his arm, finding every leak and tributary in the muscles of his back. History had sailed on. The only trace of water now the step and rim of ancient crab holes, what old-timers called dead men's graves.

Ephemeral, these creeks. He rolled the word round his head as he worked, letting its fey shape and liquid rhythm carry him, hand over fist, toward the final ridge.

Halfway there, his line met a low stone well. Necklace of goat bones round the old pulley. Shadow at the bottom, hair, teeth, horn, but long gone, like the water. Just the ghost of a smell.

Beyond that, a miner's hovel, all tumbled sandstone and orphaned doorways, the inside evil with barbed wire, broken glass, toilet paper. A black mass, alive with flies. Plotting a wide arc to avoid it, he crossed trails of other lives. Camel rib, ore bucket. Horseshoes so ancient, they crumbled underfoot. A wide leather miner's belt, notched almost to the point of death.

In the last stretch before the drop-off, in a bend of dry creek where shade and water might have grown, his pick hit a grave railing. The tiny mound was embroidered with paddy melon, no stone or cross. Instead, like some strange offering, a fossilised thong.

Digging post holes along the spine of the ridge, he spotted it finally. A white stone chimney topped with a ram's skull, marking the limit of Sam's new land. In better weather, with decent equipment and a proper offsider, about three hours' slog away. But the last fly-by-night had downed tools well short of the boundary and this was jump-up country, no flesh to it, what earth there was flayed with flint, ironstone, mine tailings. Nothing to work with, not even the bones of a fence. And now the sun was a hammer overhead.

For an hour, just the ring of his spade, the crunch of his boots. The sounds shaken out of him, helpless and thorough. Every thump of the post driver darkened the dirt with sweat. The dog's claws ticked back and forth across the ute tray, a ragged metronome to the heat. Whenever he turned to look at it, he found it staring back, all ribs, ears, hot toffee-coloured eyes. He'd considered letting it loose for a bit, but it was too young, too stupid to even get under the tarp he'd rigged from the cabin to give it a bit of shade. One sniff of roo and it'd be off, down into the badlands. If it fell through one of those old mine shafts, that would be that.

Standing up to swig some water, the red world yawed boot-wise, shuttered black for a while. He breathed deep, bent down, worked on. Moving slow as an astronaut, pitting sweat, energy and his remaining water, against the torn muscle in his back, the weight of the sun, the distance to the skull.

Stupid to slog through the worst of it, for a job like this. No feed this far out, so no sheep except dead ones. Putting a fence here was like planting a flag on the moon. But this was Sam's new land and he wanted to mark it and Ray had promised he'd do it, and just this once he'd been paid ahead. And there'd be no second chance. By this time tomorrow he aimed to be as far from here as half a tank of petrol would allow. He wanted clean clothes, cold beer, food that wasn't heat-slimed or reconstituted. Water that didn't taste of ute. Wanted to walk into a room where he recognised nothing and was responsible for no one. Order a meal he wouldn't have to cook.

That reminded him of the shed. All that meat stuffed into those unreliable fridges. All those flies. Between midday dinner and a motley mob of contractors, stock hands and pig shooters, a Pommy grog artist who'd be drunk by afternoon smoko and a fourteen-year-old ginger nut who seemed incapable of washing his hands. Last time Ray left Mick in charge, he had every man down with salmonella and the rissoles not fit for a dog.

Should have cooked some stuff for the freezer. Should have left him a note. But there was no time when it came upon him, the way it always happened. The feeling rising with first light, formless, grey then silver. The urge running through him like a fuse.

By two pm, big heat, dead heat. Heat so vast, it felt solid, some mineral-toothed prehistoric thing.

He was too far out for radio here, so no news or music. Just the work, the dog, his book. Couldn't see to read once the sun went, torch was going, but he had a good memory, for songs and stories, poems and fables. Anything with a shape to it, an outline to bestow on a place without boundary, except the one he was making, with sweat and fists.

When it got too hot for words in one place not another, it was lists of lost cities and dead languages. Grand Latin names for tiny desert plants. For half an hour, up and down the rigging, all the sails on a seventeenth-century ship of the line. When words failed, scrambled by sun, it was maps, old ones, folding and unfolding, tea brown and intricate, all those spidery, puffing latitudes that had entranced him well before he'd learned to read. When he could, even their names were a sort of magic, to a small boy, alone in the dark. Ptolemy, Ribero, Anaximander. A chant against the void.

In that boyhood atlas, his mind falling open now to those big central plates, he traced Australian river systems, their broken calligraphy. The sepia routes of failed explorers, in glossy fade. On page 42, a certain nest of creek bends like the bud of a tiny fern. So small that when he'd put his childish initials there, he'd erased the home they enclosed.

When he was too tired to see pictures, it was words again, but old ones, those curled so deep, they required no memory, only obedience. Hymns, Bible stories, other fairy tales. Recipes. Cup of this, pinch of that. Mam's voice in his head. Cream butter and sugar until light and white. Flour, eggs, vanilla, ratio two to three, wet to dry. Proper butter, not marg or lard, and get it soft first but don't leave it out all night. Under that tin roof, it'll be soup by dawn.

When the loneliness arrived, finding a man and his dog under relentless sun, it was poetry that returned, rising like the contours of a river revealed by drought. It told the day in new order. Snake shimmer, lizard scuttle. Bright angles, tiny agitations. A world all gleam and shift, himself airy and askance. When he was absent from it, this place made its own kind of sense.

There was dusk, a ruffled blue moment when earth released its grip on the heat. There was sunrise, that same heat blooming from a low spine of hills. There were stars wheeling frozen round the hinge of his firelight, the only certain thing. Even the hardest hottest day out here held the ghost of a curve to it, in the long glitter of a week. A red mouse. A purple flower. Two nights ago, in the middle of the desert, the sound of the sea. Looking up, he'd seen, by starlight and torchlight, a vast tide of cockies, flying a wind of their own making, flowing east. So many, they blotted the moon.

Seeing that war-shaped underbelly, hearing them cry one to the other, ragged, urgent, looping the darkness, gathering it like a wave, he knew he was alone. And it was enough. To feel time passing and him with it, riding that thready edge of change.

Even this fence wasn't straightforward, although it was as plumb as he could make it, following boundaries worked by other men, accompanied by other dogs, long dead. But no matter how careful he was with string line and spirit level, earth here followed its own rhythm, the wire bending through what was missing, an undulation so slight it could be heat mirage. Beneath his feet, the secret mutter of the old mine workings. Old rock falls, ancient exclamations. Caverns so deep and dark no voice or rope would reach the end. Tying off, he felt the echo of it. Held the shape of absence in a palm.

Somewhere out there, another fence joined this one, but right now, it felt improbable, the place eating up any certainty except the horizon itself. This wire might loop on and on until he met himself again.

You'd go mad if you thought about it like that. If you stared long enough against the heat of midday, you'd start to see camel trains, sailing ships, company coming when there was none to be had. Better to stick to the job in hand. After a while, the heat, the sweat, that web of skin between thumb and forefinger which took all the punishment, everything slipped away.

There was this patch of dirt banded with the shadow of four wires. Crows were black notes creaking across it. There was your own shadow, simple as a cave painting on the ground. There was this moment, no other. Your hands took hold of it, wrestled it into place.

Fold in the flour. That's the hard part, you're not making cement. Bit like bathing a baby, swoop and cradle, an easy balance between precious substance and greedy air. Can't say how, words won't hold it. Like cupping water, something vital always slips away. A knowledge whorled into gut and brain and fingertips, like the image of someone standing in such bright morning sunlight, their outline glows even when you close your eyes.

They'll stay there forever, kettle steaming, sun pouring like melted butter through a window. Radio murmuring stock prices, a dusty incantation. Flour dappling the fine hairs on a freckled arm.

⌒

Late afternoon, no amount of water seemed to replace the sweat he was losing. On the far horizon of heat haze, a man wavered toward him, bearing a spear.

With the skull in spitting distance, he was forced to pack it in. Heading back along the creek bed, he rocked the ute through dust fine as cornflour, careful to stick to the tracks he'd made on the way in. One careless turn here and you could end up buried in one of those hot black arteries underground. A finely calibrated safety, like walking in small bare feet on top of someone else's big steel-toe boots, back and back, toward some familiar yet frightening place.

Near the chimney, a little gum gave a bare nod to shade. He tied the dog to it, doused his head and strung the tarp. Sat beneath it, smoking and sweating, while the kelpie, bug-eyed with frustration, tried to wrench the sapling from its roots. To make up for the long hot day it had endured, he threw it the tail of the roo he'd shot the day before. Stupid thing tried to swallow it fur and all. He recognised that, how ravenous you could be, for some rare sweet chunk of life, lived on a grand and momentous scale.

He had a sudden memory of Tilda, aged three, squatting bare-bottomed behind the wood pile, intent on something between her legs. Odd kid Tilly, always peeing al fresco, always taking off all her clothes. When he'd got closer, he'd seen she'd somehow got hold of Mam's special biscuit tin, the one with the young Queen on it, her rouged cheeks and faded diamonds nibbled by scars of his old disappointments, all those nights spent dragging a chair across the kitchen, standing on tiptoe to reach the shelf above the fridge. Thinking, just one, no one would notice, not if you rearranged the layers, only to find Dad had sealed the lid shut with an iron fist.

Tilda hadn't bothered with any of that. She'd just bashed the tin with a rock, got her little fingers under the rim. By the time Ray caught up with her, she'd eaten nearly all the biscuits Mam had baked for Mrs Tangello up the road, who'd had a baby or whose husband had died, he couldn't remember which. Delly McCullough was famous for her biscuits. Won all the local shows.

Wasn't Tilly's fault. Too young to know. And they'd all loved those cockle biscuits, better than sponge cake or even lamingtons. All that butter and sugar, that terrible richness on the tongue. Special occasions only, Christmas or birthdays, or swimming training, when Urs got up with the alarm and did some stealing of her own. Four am, way early in the season, sun not up, brown ice on the river and Ray nursing a middle ear infection but Father O'Reilly wanted that Regional Schools Trophy and nothing would stand in his way. A cold wobble on top of the town bridge, big priest face looming, boiled red as football leather. Stink of old whiskey and stale tobacco, a phlegmy bark of breathe and blow. The whistle like an electric shock. The dive a clear, brief moment, the whole town laid wide, silo to highway, crystal at dawn. Then fierce brown water, the jerk and rasp of the ankle rope. Nut-clenching cold.

He swam for hours against the current, until his arms felt nerveless as tripe. But after, there was always Urs, with her thermos and blanket and royal biscuits. Nothing tasted so good, even mixed with mud-flavoured snot.

Dad caught up to him of course. Had a nose for trouble, Dad reckoned, and though he meant Ray when he said it, what Ray imagined was Dad himself. Standing on the front verandah, one foot on the railing, one hand in his pocket. Head high, nose flared, sniffing Ray down. Dad reckoned he could smell trouble on Ray before Ray did anything, before the thought of doing anything had even crossed Ray's mind. Something in the blood.

Tilly threw up behind the wood pile, where Ray made her hide. Ray vomited too, in time with Dad's belt strokes, shame and acid fizzing in his throat. The salvation of those biscuits, the very idea of them, ruined forever. Stained by sour disappointment and too much self-sacrifice. Keen as an oversharp vinaigrette.

In his stints at shearing sheds and pub kitchens, he'd tried over and over to recapture the taste of those biscuits. Did everything the way Mam used to, even down to putting a fork mark in the batter and sticking a silver gee-gaw on top. Couldn't make them as dainty as hers were of course. Would have been laughed out of town. Had to make them thick and shearer sized, like big yellow pikelets. Maybe that's why they never tasted the same.

No treats tonight, but he had two beers left in the esky and the rest of the roo. It was ponging a bit, because he couldn't run the car fridge without running down the car battery, but those explorers he'd spent his childhood with had eaten all sorts, hadn't they? Sheep's eyes and spoon-soft rabbits, shoe-leather soup. He'd just chuck on lots of chilli, hold his nose and close his eyes.

⁓

Six o'clock. Still too hot to light the fire. Even the kelpie had given up, lying spatchcocked in the shade of the tarp. He lay down beside it, comforted by the yeasty smell of warm dog. Watched the sun begin its long slow slide to where he'd come from, plumping ridges, softening old creek bones, gibbers glowing like round pale flesh. Night would arrive in a lash of shadow beneath that rib of sand.

He closed his eyes to wait it out. Was twelve years old again, Christmas morning, sun just up, sky through sailing ship curtains already brassy with heat. At the end of his bed, the second-hand Brittanicas Urs had smuggled in at midnight, as if she was Father Christmas and he wasn't awake and still believed. Stacked so high, they threatened to topple if he moved. Kill him with love and words.

He wet an imaginary finger, opened the very first volume for the very first time. Could almost taste it, the dense and serious joy of those old pages, and while he dozed, he dreamed, in a place still holding fiercely to the day's heat, of frozen tundra, avalanching mountains, husky liver stew.

CHAPTER TWO

JUNE 2007

There wasn't much. What there was could have fitted into the fruit crate provided by the landlord. If they'd arrived half an hour later, if Ursula hadn't insisted on a taxi not a bus from the station after what had happened with Tilda on the train, the crate would have been packed and waiting for them outside room 22.

What little they found would have been reduced to what they saw when it was all over. A narrow hallway, bent and bright. A raw pine box bearing the stamp Sunraysia Oranges, his name picked out by a shaft of light from the upstairs verandah, where a lonely cocky spent his days in a too-small cage.

'No one said nothing,' the landlord complained as he led them up a staircase smelling of cat. 'Far as I knew he was still in hospital. Who'd you say you were again?'

Ursula's face swam up in a wall of mirror tiles, bloated with fluorescent, shifty with dust.

'Friends of his.'

The cocky squawked in dull outrage. Tilda gasped, baulked, blocking the way like a bulky cork.

'Close friends. We've come for his things.' Ursula prodded her sister in the vicinity of her ribs until she turned, continued up the stairs.

'How long you gonna be? Big footy comp on tomorrow. I need the room.'

There was something unreliable about the man, with his sketchy mullet and little red elbows. When they first arrived, he'd been halfway up the stairs, crate in hand. Jumped a foot when they rang the bell in his front bar.

'But I told them. When they rang, the second time. Urs? I did.'

'We're here, that's what matters. Mind your step.'

The stairs seemed to go on forever, precipitous and gloomy, performing awkward corkscrews where the old stone pub had been spliced with a jerry-built extension, spawning errant landings, stray hallways, a warren of oddly shaped rooms. In the corners, shapes blacker than ordinary darkness, and Ursula was reminded of that rhyme Dad had taught her, in some rare soft moment, one which she'd taught Ray and he'd taught Tilda, all of them passing it on like some form of congenital weakness. That little riddle which was supposed to be funny but which contained at its heart something darker, tangling and seeding. Surfacing later, at night, when you were alone. It knotted sheets, sculpted monsters from school clothes hanging on a chair. That man who wasn't and wasn't and was never there. His terrible, thirsty yearning, like staring at a sky full of country stars, trying to believe the universe had no end.

As they reached the top, stood blinking in sudden glare, something brushed past their ankles and Tilda screamed.

'Till. Settle down. Just a moggy. See? Like Harry's cat, back home.'

It wasn't. This thing was feral, cock-eyed, with a weeping stub for a tail. Ursula stamped her foot until it fled down the hall. Taking her sister by the elbow, she steered her over rolling humps of lino to where the landlord was fiddling with the door to room 22.

'Did you know him? Had he been here long?'

'Eh?' The landlord was bent over the lock, swearing softly as he tried key after key. 'Who?'

Ursula braced herself against giddy waves of floor.

'Your guest. Mr McCullough. The man in this room.'

'Oh. Right. Nuh. Month or so. Wife does all that. Travelling sales, fertiliser or some such. Or so she said.' The door swung open and the landlord peered in, wrinkling his nose. 'On the turps, I'd say. We get a bit of that round here.'

Dazzled by the sun in the hallway, Ursula could see nothing at first. Dust motes, curtains, in a pink and breathing rhythm. The windowpane was cracked. The rest was darkness, cradling denser outlines, like something seen on the inside of a squeezed eyelid, glowing, pulsing, sidling quickly out of sight.

She tried the switch. Of course the light didn't work.

'Listen, there's not much to worry about. Just a few old clothes. And all them papers. Ambos took the rest.'

The curtains shifted. Objects gathered shape and heft. An iron bedstead, a hoop-backed chair. A single boot, fallen sideways under the bed. In one corner, a skew-whiff shadow, like a tall man with a broken neck. A skittering somewhere, so faint it could be leaves on the roof, curtains blowing across the broken floor.

'Bus'll be here soon. I need to clean.'

Ursula stared. Dust was so thick in here, they'd left footprints up the hall.

'Papers? What papers?'

'Yeah. That's how we found him. Or the wife did. Musta knocked them over when he went down. Bloke next door reckoned we had rats.' He looked back at the room, shaking his head. 'Good thing it's no smoking up here.'

She put out her hand. 'Thank you. We'll take it from here. I'll lock up when we're done.'

He was about to protest but when he saw the look on her face, one which had struck the fear of God into countless classrooms without Ursula having to say a single word, he handed the key over, shuffled off down the hall.

'Urs? Why'd you say that?'

She was grateful at least that it was the wife and not that bloodshot mess of a man who'd been the one to find him. To see the place the way Ray had left it, not that there was much to see. Same buckled red lino as the hallway, squares missing, floorboards showing through. Rust-coloured curtains, worn thin as tracing paper, hemmed with safety pins. A narrow bed of chipped white iron, covered in orange chenille. Next to it, on the bedside table, a folded newspaper, a pair of reading glasses, a Bible, two books. Under the window, a sink streaked red from years of dripping taps. Beside and beneath it, along every available patch of wall, newspapers, in teetering piles. The tallest one in the corner, the shadow with the lopsided neck. In the middle of the floor, a dead cockroach, folded gently in upon itself. It was the same colour as the rust stains and the orange curtains, echoing in its husky sheen the cheap varnish of the tallboy in the opposite corner, the door of which creaked open even as they stood there, from the weight of their bodies on the uneven floor.

She put on her glasses. Waited for her eyes to adjust, her heart to slow.

'Urs? Why'd you tell him that? Why'd you lie?'

Nothing, nothing. A coat, some empty hangers, the mate of the boot under the bed. An oblong of tarnished mirror which gave them back to themselves, silvered with dust motes, as if they were the ghosts here, not Ray.

'I don't know. Didn't like the look of him. And we don't need to tell everyone our business, Tilda. Not every minute of the day.'

They stood for a long time on the threshold. Even Tilda seemed unwilling to disturb the scant order of that room. It had the mute rebellion of museum tableaux, something set up to show how kings or miners once lived. The narrow bed, the clot-coloured curtains, the plastic crucifix above the sink. Ordinary objects labouring under the weight of history, giving off great thrums of loneliness, all intersecting in the burnished light from the window, and she was reminded of a toy she'd once made for Ray, four nails hammered into the end of a cotton reel, around which he'd looped wool unpicked from one of her old jumpers, producing the endless finger of a non-existent glove. Something missing though, some useful purpose or final conclusion. Leaving this. A room humming on its bones like the skin of a drum.

The bulb in the ceiling came on, flickered, went out again.

'Come on. Let's get this over with. It'll be dark soon and this light's on the blink.'

There wasn't much. The coat, the shoes, the books. The glasses she didn't know Ray had worn. The coat was old, black, faded, a cheap polyester blend. The shoes, buffed to a shine on the uppers, were ingrained with years of red dirt at the sole. In a drawer, two pairs of underpants, a greying singlet. No trousers. He must have been wearing them. Must have only had the single pair. The wardrobe smelled musty, the creaky leathery scent of things hollowed out by too much ownership, not enough love. The taint of St Vincent de Paul.

Something rose up but she swallowed it down. Put the glasses in her handbag, the shoes at the bottom of the crate.

'Hey, Urs. There's a dog out there. It's lying right in the middle of the road.'

While Tilda stuck her head through the curtains, peering out at the last things Ray might have seen, Ursula went through the pockets of the coat. Didn't need to see it, that wide country street framed by curly iron and dust haze. It was just a street in a town like the ones he had grown up in, empty of incident, crowded with hours.

The pockets were empty except for a drycleaning receipt. The hospital had taken his wallet, for identification. A nurse had shown it to Ursula, sealed up in a bag like a murder clue. The details from his Medicare card had been recited to her, laboriously, adenoidally, every digit, every initial in that ridiculous string of names. Is this your brother, the nurse had asked? Ursula just demanded they hand it over, in her most imperious voice. But there were rules, procedures, forms the doctor had to sign. The nurse was young, keen, none too bright. Ursula knew the type, from years of teaching. A plodder, a mouth-breather. At school, she would have been a decorator of pencil cases. An inveterate raiser of the hand.

'It's exactly like that one Ray used to have, except not white and blue. Urs? Can we take it home?'

'No.'

Old, the wallet, cracked and creased, the calfskin worn thin. Oily dents on the billfold, where his fingers must have returned to emptiness, again and again. But decent quality, at one time, so at some point he must have had the money to buy it, if not to put in it. She held hard to that fact, a talisman of sorts.

Over this, she'd surprised even herself. When the nurse had been distracted by a ringing phone, she'd just reached across, slipped the plastic bag in her pocket, strolled off toward the waiting room as casually as her arthritis would allow. She hadn't had time to go through it yet. Didn't want to do it in front of strangers, or in front of Tilda. And at the time she'd thought there'd be more important things to see, beyond the green rubber doors. But when she'd gone to walk through, another nurse had blocked her way. Older, this one, no nonsense, with the bandy legs and bumptious strut of a bantam. There'd been a bus accident, out on the highway. The body wasn't ready for viewing yet. The body, she'd called it, in her squashed Adelaide vowels.

'This is boring. I'm hungry. And I need the toilet.' A familiar rising note in Tilda's voice. Something was about to tip loose, whatever had been building since the train.

'In a minute. Check under the bed. He might have left something. Lost something. Money maybe. You know what men are like.'

This wasn't strictly true. Tilda claimed to know all sorts of people, some of whom were men and some of whom were real. But the sort Tilda made a habit of collecting, on railway platforms and in dank alleyways behind early opener pubs, weren't the type to own a bed, let alone anything to leave under it, and they certainly weren't the sort of men Ursula would care to know. At least her sister was distracted again, head under the bed, vast bum in the air.

The sun was dipping low through the curtains now, shadows crawling from the corners of the room. Ursula worked faster, rummaging through the bedclothes, flicking through the books beside the bed. The first was a gilded pot boiler, spine uncracked. Could have belonged to anyone except the boy she'd known. The other one, thin-papered and bound in blue leather, looked more promising, a collection of Paterson's poems. But when she turned to the flyleaf, looking for Dad's rampant copperplate, she found instead a page of date stamps and a little cardboard sleeve.

'Yuk.' Backing out from the under the bed, Tilda dislodged a stash of empty port bottles, sent them rattling across the floor.

'Jesus, Till, be careful. Don't break anything. I'd never hear the end of it.'

'It stinks down here.'

'Nearly done. Check those drawers.'

'You did it already.'

'I might have missed something. Go on. Never know. You might find a clue.'

While Tilda swore and sighed, wrenching tallboy drawers in and out, Ursula hesitated over the Bible. Must belong to the pub, although it didn't seem the sort of place to run to such luxuries. Then again, Ray had never been religious, she'd made sure of that. But as coat hangers clattered to the bottom of the wardrobe, a thin and final sound, she realised she didn't know that, did she, any more than she knew whether he'd conquered his fourteen-year-old aversion to custard and peas. All she had to go on was that little pile of possessions in the crate. Full of meaning but resisting any grammar. She might as well try and make sense of the hoarded contents of one of Tilda's plastic bags.

The newspaper was local, almost three weeks old. When she picked it up, paper fluttered out like confetti. That's when she noticed them, little drifts and trails of paper, littering the floor, lining the windowsill. Thick as mice droppings underneath the bed. Oddly tidy though, the mounds in rows, each mound bearing the imprint of cupped hands. As if Ray had left a giant puzzle for her to solve.

That rustling noise again. She spun toward it, jarring her hip. Horrors breeding in her mind. But what sort of rat could survive the cat she'd seen on the stairs?

'Got it!'

Taking a sandal off, holding it high above her head, Ursula advanced toward the pile of papers in the corner of the room.

'Urs? I found it!'

'What?'

'The clue.'

'Oh. Good. Rightio.'

Lunging forward, she kicked the pile until it toppled, jumped back. The stink of mice and desperation was overwhelming now, even above the abiding smell of port.

'It's all numbers, but really small and all mixed up. Reckon it's a code.'

Edging forward again, Ursula saw the newspapers were all ancient, the ones from the bottom a urinous yellow, the most recent she could see at least two years old. All different, all local, from tiny, far-flung places, bearing grand mastheads like *The Truth* or *The Tribune*, front pages no doubt breathless with council squabbles and school fetes. Couldn't tell. Each one was folded open to the funeral notices. Every page had been cut to lace.

She backed off, sat down on the bed. Trying to see him here, crouched on this dirty floor. Swigging his rotgut, wielding his scissors. Making tiny order from random bits of death.

'Is it? Urs? Do you reckon? A code?'

'For pity's sake, Tilda. *What?*'

Tilda let go of her sleeve. Sat down next to her, far too close, her breath sour on Ursula's cheek. Dropped something in Ursula's lap.

'See? Why are they all pointy? I don't understand.'

21

It was an old beer coaster, advertising the doubtful joys of a country pub like this. Turning it over, Ursula saw line upon line of numbers, arranged in a sort of pyramid, dribbles of something brown down either side. Looking closer, she saw they were actually the same numbers, repeated over and over, in sets of two and four and eight, like a square dance performed by ants. With each new line, a fresh number had been added or another subtracted, the lines forming blurred steps to the base of the triangle, like a bird trying out a tune, in descending trill. Or maybe it was the other way around, the song becoming half-hearted as the climb proceeded, a thing working itself toward memory, before resolve faltered, hope failed, sense tattered away. Precise only in its meaninglessness, like Tilda finding Jesus in the stock results, writing Bible verses all over the living-room wall. Ursula threw it down on the floor.

'It's nothing. Just rubbish. Leave it there.'

But Tilda had snatched it up again. Was staring urgently, lips moving, as if trying to burrow beneath the lines. The landlord chose that moment to stick his head round the door, mutter something about a bus.

'We know! You told us. Just fuck off!' The man almost fell backwards into the hall.

'Matilda McCullough! That's enough.' Yanking her sister upright with one hand, she smuggled the coaster into her pocket with the other, then pointed at the crate. 'Right. Take that outside while I do a final check. And don't forget your coat.'

As Ursula turned to take a last look at that room, the smell of which, old sweat, old clothes, old booze, would stay with her for days and days, she noticed a drawer in the bedside table, hidden beneath the drape of a doily someone had placed there in a failed attempt to cheer things up. Inside the drawer, a little velvet pouch, clinking tinnily in her palm. A child's trinket probably, some rubbish from Woolworths. Nothing to do with Ray. But she slid it into her pocket. Didn't want to add to the coiling silence of this room with another lost and broken thing.

'Remember these? We had ones like these, didn't we? When we were small.' Crate forgotten, Tilda was back on the bed. Lying down on it, legs sprawled, eyes dreamy, idly fingering nubs of chenille. 'Yours was blue. Mine was pink. I don't remember Ray's.'

She couldn't possibly remember that. Far too young. She must have seen a photograph, although Ursula didn't recall one, and anyway, why would anyone have taken a photo of Ray's old room?

'His curtains had sailing ships and there was a blue rug on the floor.'

Someone must have told her. Mam probably, at the end of things, ranging far and wide on morphine. So far gone by then, she'd thought her daughters were her long-dead sisters come to visit and she herself a girl again, waving her father off to war. Even then, with a mind fallen to cobweb, Delly McCullough could weave the lace of family like nobody else. After days of silence broken only by the rattle of lungs, the blip of machines, a clear sentence, falling into that high white room like a stone. Mam retrieving from some stray brightly lit corner what she'd worn to a second cousin's wedding. Shantung silk, a pillbox hat, a collar of broderie anglaise. That big wedding, the one with the food, where so and so's niece married that Greek fellow, the one who played the violin.

'His was green. I remember now. And he had boxing gloves and all those books and a map of Australia on the wall.'

Despite herself, Ursula felt a thrill at her sister's flat reportage, the absolute nature of her make-believe. Sometimes she almost had Ursula convinced of her radio waves and other-worldly messages, as if her illness was a wildly waving antenna that now and again and despite itself picked up the dying light of other people's thoughts.

'It was just like this one though, wasn't it? Except not orange. Wasn't it? Urs?'

'A lot of people had bedspreads like that, didn't they? Back then.' Despite the lump in her throat, the old habit of dealing with Tilda surfaced seamlessly. Noncommittal agreement, followed by a careful statement of fact at some harmless angle to the truth.

'Come on. His Lordship's waiting. Time to go.'

But Tilda just kept lying there, hand straying toward the pillow. If Ursula had to watch her lay her head there, erasing the scent and hollow of the last head that had been there, she felt she wouldn't be able to staunch the howl that was growing in all the threadbare places of herself.

⌒

They waited in the hallway while the landlord changed the sheets, showed the floor a broom, then locked the door. Two locks, a bolt and a Yale, even though the door itself was plywood you could put a boot through and despite the fact that room held nothing anyone would want to steal.

'We'll need a room. Just for tonight.'

The man jumped. Seemed astounded to find them still standing there.

'You'll be lucky.' As if it was the bloody Ritz. Tilda started to insist that she wanted to stay here, in Ray's room and no other, until the landlord pointed out, logically enough, that there was only one bed. Lezzos, you could see him thinking. Lezzo sisters, no less.

Clutching the crate, Tilda looked ready to dig in her heels.

'Listen, why don't we just leave that here for now? We'll have to bring our bags up anyway, before tea.' Ursula stared hard at the landlord, who sighed, said he'd see what he could do.

'What about fish and chips? Like you wanted on the train.'

Tilda dropped the crate, raising a puff of dust. Which was why as they walked away, Ursula felt she'd deserted Ray yet again. The sun falling low and deft through the verandah windows, haloing the black fruit stamp, the raw splinters of his name. Or perhaps it was they who remained, stuck fast in dust motes, while he receded, etched sharp in detail, leaving no trace. Travelling some landscape known only to him.

CHAPTER THREE

Sunset carved deep, long planes of rust, silver, purple. Old mine hills tender blue. Saltbush cauled with shadow, each stone and tree released. Things becoming what they were, no more.

To celebrate his last day out here, he allowed himself a second beer. Felt guilty about not finishing that last stretch but he would have had to chuck it in soon anyway, his back the way it was. One false move with the post driver and he'd be frying with the dog in the back of the ute. No one to notice, not really. He'd given Sam only the vaguest idea of when he'd be back. There was Barb of course, covering his shifts at the bistro and not happy but, then again, Barb never was. Freda would be expecting him to do the cook-off for her birthday but it could go on without him. He'd made all the arrangements, digging a hole for the fire pit, rigging a kero drum for the spit roast, even baking her a cake in the shape of a handbag, stippling grey icing with a matchstick to resemble crocodile skin. If Freda couldn't have the bag she'd seen in the window of Myer, she could at least have the cake.

He felt bad about Charlie. He'd promised to visit after Saturday's pensioner lunch. Charlie never attended, because of the bingo and the drinking, but Ray usually took him a bit of the apple crumble or lemon delicious he'd made to go with Freda's dry-as-dust pasties or her incinerated roast. Sometimes a new cowboy novel or a spare cardigan. Charlie felt the cold, even in summer. Silly bugger never ate enough. But if he could be distracted, if Ray listened patiently as Charlie trawled through his newspapers, making arcane patterns from birth dates, death dates, the number of letters in a surname against the addled numbers of the funeral date of the son he'd killed, as if Charlie was a toddler and Ray was playing aeroplanes with the spoon, the old man might be persuaded into a mouthful of something sweet.

Yet all the time he was making plans and promises, pinning himself to various points along some imaginary string of time, he'd known that well before the lunch or Freda's birthday or his next shift at the pub, he'd be leaving Sam's tools by the chimney. Driving far from fences and obligations. No note. Nothing much to say.

It was a recurring sickness, this, and the only way to treat it was with doses of absence, cold and pure. Four months in one place was good going, six at a pinch. His current set-up, out the shed for shearing or shooters, in at the pub for weekends and holidays, cooking bacon and eggs, steak and eggs, chips and steak, had lasted longer than most. Didn't like the pub. Too many people, too many dark and dirty rooms. Didn't like taking orders from a man like Pete, in whose sudden bursts of rage against keg or wife or bar stool he recognised something of his father and therefore something of himself.

The shed was better. Quieter at least, between meals. Even at fever pitch it was orderly chaos. Breakfast, smoko, dinner, smoko. Tea, a beer, then bed. Between these, long stretches of hot silence broken only by the shrill of the oven timer, the tick of a cooling roof. At night, the radio and his book of poems. In this way he parcelled time into pockets of ordinary meaning, gave himself a reason to move from one moment to the next. The rules and habits by which other people carved up their lifetimes let him breathe in the spaces they created, like pressing his shadow flat to pass through the wires of a fence. Days out the shed held few surprises, as long as the fridges and ovens held up. In town, he kept his eyes down, his fists open and elbows up. Kept plodding through the mire created by other people, pouring their beers, cleaning their carpets, frying their stodge, smell of beer and piss and pig rising until he couldn't get rid of it, even in the shower. Until his own skin felt disgraced.

That was always the beginning, his scalp starting to crawl. At the shed, rising at dawn to set bread and jelly, put cheap meat to braise on hot afternoons, he kept to gaps, edges, small allowances. A walk in the bush, a night in the desert. He did what was expected, what was required. Yet all the time some part of him floated above it, aghast, unscathed. At some point he could never put his finger on, significant only in retrospect, could be some ordinary morning or an afternoon of faltering routine, this feeling would start, tick in the brain. Work failing to soothe him, and the mere sight and sound of other people—Sam with kicks to dog, sheep or apprentice; Pete's bloodshot trembles; Suzy's wrinkled lipstick as she sucked down her break-time rum and coke—everything started to rankle and itch.

Worst were big nights at the pub. Saturdays, paydays, Melbourne Cup lunches that went on until the small hours. Or sometimes just the opposite—days when nothing happened, time falling heavy, fermenting in the beer carpet, building muscle. When trouble started, Ray's job to sort it out. But Pete didn't know who he was asking, and it wasn't always enough, was it, Ray's steady eye and boxer's stance. As hats came off and chests went out, Ray couldn't help but feel a corresponding weather, a tremble in the blood.

One morning he'd wake to his alarm clock shrilling in its metal bucket, find once again what he knew to be true. That whatever life he'd cobbled together, in whatever place he found himself, was just a thin icing on something denser. It had the weight of dead planets, black holes. Lying in some room above some pub, watching a square of light grow at the window, fluttering through curtains someone had hung there at some point in the seventies, once pink flowers on an orange background, now the colour of old smoked salmon and speckled with flies, a day ordinary at bedtime would have become by dawn trackless, weightless, ruthless, and him useless against it, frail as the plywood walls of his room. Things that had anchored him for weeks and months beforehand, all those days graphed by cleaning, chip frying, beer pulling, being a ready sponge for other people's boasts and griefs, on that day, it just wouldn't be enough.

That's when he had to get in the ute, drive in a random direction. Find a fence with nothing to meet it, before the needle spun off the dial.

⁓

When the fire died down, he scavenged for wood, keeping to the circle of footprints he'd made around the tent. Didn't trust this place, not in the dark. Earth too thin, too friable. Air so dry, it gave him nosebleeds, dripping onto dirt the same colour, instantly absorbed.

As a boy there'd always been the sense and smell of water, even in bad times when the river dried up. At home earth was the colour of milk chocolate, tinged with rust. Rich and biddable, it sprouted wheat, kids, yellow box. Unearthly crops of granite, sly rumours of gold. Sheep so fat, they looked like anchored clouds. Trees in richer people's gardens, giving luxuriant puffs of European green.

When he longed for home, it was never for the house itself, its wide-hipped roof and bone-pale verandahs circling rooms kept dark by curtains, by some indelible secret at its heart. His dreams were set there of course, the relentless geography of childhood sniffing him down. Bad dreams, in which he was always running, from front door to kitchen door to laundry door and back again, and he'd been swimming and he was naked but it wasn't a game and he wasn't a child. Heart thudding, feet snapping out a syncopation, urgent smell of bushfire somewhere and Tilda calling, Urs calling, but he couldn't seem to break the rhythm, the skin of it. Corners sliding him in wide arcs of tree, sky, paddock, his own past trying to shake him off. Each door locked, each bearing its cross of white wood.

No, when he thought of home, it was always of the river. Green grey, black brown, cholera coloured at flood time. Swirling curds by moonlight, like off-milk tea. River red gums standing sentinel for all its homeward flow. Old lady faces carved from bark by the roo light, grainy sheaves of hair. Ray's job to hold the death beam steady as they rode the fence boundaries, the truck bumping and lurching and almost tipping as Dad cut wide then sharp through the dip where the creek crossed the property, flushing stragglers, pushing the old Ford right through floodwater sometimes, skirting boulders, barbed wire, drowned sheep. Dad never faltered, the truck never stalled, Dad never missed a shot.

At the last gate, where the creek joined the river, straightening suddenly, tacking off at an urgent angle, as if it had changed its mind about the McCulloughs and was leaving them for dead, they'd stop for tea, if dawn was close. Light a fire under the old white gum where Dad had carved all their names as they were born. Ursula and Matilda on one side, Ray on the other, all by himself. Ray, not Raymond. So faint, it might have been insect scribble in the bark. No surname, all his saints' names flayed away. A name without flourish or foothold, bald as a cough.

Ray once dared to ask Dad why. Dad made a sound like Ray's name, a harsh little bark. Went back to coaxing the fire, with rough hands and smoky breath.

Ray got to sleep the way he always did on nights like these. Rolled up with the dog in his sleeping bag, he thought himself back and back, until he was lying in the crook of his father's arm, in a way he never had. Homesickness like this lay in wait sometimes, even when there was no home to run to or away from, when even the idea of home was ruined, a roofless thing in fog.

Here, on the brink of yet another escape, he could almost forget why he'd started running in the first place. Why he kept going. Dumb muscle by now. Tick in the brain.

Couldn't be avoided this feeling, only navigated, through days strung on a hum of fence wire. Dull mirror to these strings of stars.

CHAPTER FOUR

'Those shoes. They're too small. And too brown. They're not his.'
Dinner was something dark and wet from the bain-marie.
Fish was off, according to the landlord, although a footballer at
the next table had some and it was microwaved frozen nuggets,
as far as Ursula could tell.

'We should call the cops.'

Ursula spat a lump of gristle into her serviette, took a large gulp
of wine. Tried to explain, for what felt like the umpteenth time.

'The police had nothing to do with it, Tilda. He died in the
ambulance. Of natural causes.' She drained her glass, refilled it
from the bottle she shouldn't have bought. 'The nurse told us,
remember? That's what the doctor's going to write on the form.'

Tilda snorted so loudly the footballer dropped his fork.

'Yeah, right. Doctors are full of shit.'

She leaned urgently across the table, scarf trailing in her gravy.
So close, Ursula could see shreds of meat between her front teeth.

'They said they couldn't find his wallet, right? That's because they nicked it. They do it all the time. Take all your stuff and steal your shoes and give you clothes from dead people. Then they pretend you're someone else.'

Her plate now empty, Tilda reached for the remains of Ursula's roast. At the age of thirty, her sister still ate like a four year old, all bared molars and avid elbows and puffs of humid-smelling wool. Under the army greatcoat she'd kept on despite the fug of the bistro, she wore a fisherman's jumper, her favourite Rabbitohs jersey, a pair of leopard print leggings and a trailing pink petticoat, everything that didn't fit into her collection of plastic shopping bags, it seemed.

Ursula knew it was the medication which, in the space of six months, had turned her sister from someone all bones and angles to a woman so bloated her eyes were like currants in a bowl of porridge, as if it was helium not lithium in those little pills. But watching Tilda's jaws work on the soft mess of meat, it was hard not to think of some grazing animal, a blind lump of appetite which might turn nasty at any moment. Ursula stared hard at the tablecloth, counting plastic flowers. Willing herself not to turn away.

'See? Do you get it now? Do you understand?' Each question hammered in with the butt of a fork. 'If they nicked his shoes and his wallet, that's a crime. So we do need the cops.' She clicked her fingers in Ursula's face. 'Give us your phone. They can meet us there.'

'Where?'

'The hospital of course.'

For the first time in years, Ursula wished for a cigarette.

'But the hospital's miles away, Tilda. We caught a cab remember? Anyway, it's far too late.'

'You can't close a hospital. Or a police station. They're open all the time.'

With both plates wiped clean, Tilda started fiddling with her serviette, twisting it round and round her little finger until the tip turned red. When the paper broke, she proceeded to roll the shreds into little pink balls.

'If you've finished for now, it's time for your pill.'

Ursula put it on the table, small and pink as the little balls of paper, one of which Tilda tried to swallow instead. So Ursula made her open her mouth and put the pill on her tongue, watching carefully while Tilda drank it down with her shandy, which was mostly lemonade, Ursula having supervised the barman, but it was still a mistake, because by the time Tilda's ice cream had arrived, she'd lost interest, which was saying something, and the old agitation was back. Feet tapping, knees jiggling, fingers pecking at hair, throat, coat buttons. A tendon shrilling out in her neck. Every so often she whipped round to stare behind her, as if Ray might be hovering there in his too-small shoes.

'Listen, why don't we go upstairs? There might be something on TV.'

'We don't have a TV.'

'Not in the room, but there might be one somewhere else. In the lounge or something.' She wished fervently that there was a lounge and that it contained a TV. 'Or we could play a game. Cards. You like cards.'

Wrong thing to say.

'And that card thing. The clue. That wasn't his either, because I know his writing and it wasn't like that. Too small. Just like the shoes.'

She was shouting. Heads turning at the bar. Bloody doctors. They must have got the dose wrong, yet again.

'And his feet were bigger than that. Feet can't shrink.'

'Till, I told you. I really don't remember.'

'I fucking do!' Tilda slammed her fist on the table, upsetting the glass of wine. Ursula watched the thick purple river heading toward her lap. Couldn't seem to move.

'You don't *listen*. I told you like a billion times. It was that really hot Christmas, when he came for lunch and cooked for me and Harry, that creamy bitey shit. You weren't *there*. He should have taken his shoes off because that's the rule and there was dust all up the carpet and he wrote his name on the wall, like I used to, when I was sick, with the Bible, and he gave me that cake mixer thing that I didn't like, that red one you broke. And that other time, when I was little and he gave me that big blue kitten? You were at work or something and Dad was out or maybe Mam was there but she was asleep and he had a big brown hat on, just like the second time, and I couldn't see his face, only his beard but his boots were big and *really* brown. And one of his thumbs was bleeding, because maybe he hit it with a hammer, like Dad did that time except that was an axe, and it was his foot and remember it wouldn't stop bleeding and Mam wrapped it in a towel and the blood got stuck and we had to soak it off in the bath? And there was blood on that note too, that he pinned to the kitten, *for Tilda* it said, and remember how I thought the blood should be blue not red? And that was blood on that card too, that brown stuff, but the writing was too small and pointy. Wasn't his.'

She was off then, on a rampage of remembering, hats and boots and blue kittens all knitted up with bikes and horses and heatwave Christmas dinners, the only thread holding it all together was Tilda's voracious appetite for near disaster. Fire, flood, snakes, axes. Wild pigs, rogue tractors, other lethal bits of farm machinery. A steady motif of gouged eyes, severed limbs, cracked skulls.

Most of this was pilfered from Tilda's memory of other people's memories. From stories told by Ursula, to distract her sister from voices, doctors, approaching needles. From stories told by Mam at the end of things, riding high, ranging deep, fetching up now and again against hard little toeholds of grief. Travelling memories so old and dark, they were passing with her, out of time. Hour after hour she kept dredging them up, thickly, painfully, all those old bad-days tales about the things that went wrong when people turned their back on fate and rivers, dogs and God. Stories meant to frighten, shame or chasten, which Tilda lapped up and made her own. It was Mam, not Tilda, who had viral meningitis at the age of two. Mam's brother who shot himself in the middle of a drought. Mam who walked barefoot to school in country winters, heels blue with frost.

Some of these stories came straight from Dad. Never a reliable source at the best of times, less and less so after Ray left, and now, with Mam gone, sunk in his monstrous nostalgia, not at all. To hear Dad tell it, the farm never failed, he and Mam never fought, his long-lost brother Len had come to lunch one day and Ursula was just some busybody from the government, out to steal his pension. If Ray's name was mentioned, Dad just gazed out an available window. As if by sheer force of will, he could cut Ray out of the family history, leave a convenient hole.

Ursula had the photographs though. The proof. The family photo album was one of the few things she'd managed to salvage from the sale of the homestead, along with Grandad's war medals, Ray's Brittanicas, a few of Mam's old clothes. Wasn't even an album, not really, just a cardboard box into which Dad had stuffed random handfuls of dog-eared time. Whiskers and whalebones, boob tubes and bee hives, all mixed up with hand-tinted portraits of milk-faced soldiers off to war. On the verandah of some dreadful bush shack in the middle of nowhere, a Victorian woman looking noosed by her collar of lace. Great-Great-Grandmother Someone or Other, from the grim-eyed, big-chinned Irish side of things. And running through everything, the land itself, giving off its dreary wheat-coloured hum. The land being bought, land being sold, land being harvested or grazed upon or built over, land drowned in a flood or burnt to a crisp. Always summer back then, in that dirty orange Polaroid glow. Sometimes, in an empty corner, like an afterthought, a woman sweeping, a woman leaving. A woman waiting. Right at the bottom of the box, floating up like a heart stammer, Mam's wedding photo, her stolid face carved to elegant planes by the artist's brush. Impossibly creamy. Impossibly young.

There were lots of Ray, taken by Ursula. Ray in the family christening gown, although he'd never actually made it as far as the church. Ray cooking with Mam, barely high enough to reach the table, his blond hair pale with flour. Ray on a quarter horse, at the Agricultural. Ray digging the trench for the new homestead sewerage, circa 1971. Ray winning the eight hundred metres at the local pool. Ray as a four year old, growing backwards, learning how to swim. Those hands under his shoulders, distracted, disembodied. Too loose, too careless. Too young.

There was only one photo of Ursula, thanks to Dad and his scissors. She was sixteen, standing in front of Uncle Len's old Holden, brand new back then. The dress she was wearing also new, run up from Mam's old dining room curtains in time for the school dance. Even now, despite the glaring overexposure, her face a hectic blob in Polaroid drought, she could still feel the shame of that lush red velvet against hot bare skin.

She'd worn that dress just once before she'd grown too stout for it and Mam had put it in the suitcase along with all the other clothes Ursula had made for her doomed trip to Sydney. Dad had locked the suitcase up in the shed, which was probably what he would have liked to have done with her. As if those clothes, with their modest hems and sweetheart necklines, were somehow to blame.

Sometimes, between Mam's absence, Tilda's lies, Dad's rapacious forgetting, those photographs were all she had. Now she didn't even have these to call her own. A week ago she'd come home to find the box of photos upended on the living room floor. Tilda crouched over them, scavenging what she could.

'Urs! Remember this? This was my favourite. It was all floaty and stuck out like a ballerina's when I turned around.' Tilda waltzing down the hallway, the photo of Ursula clutched to her chest.

Ursula could have stood for fantasies of ponies and rabbits and coming-out balls. It was the way Tilda flooded those modest little memories with such lurid detail, inserting herself into every eye line, bursting history at the seams. Nothing was safe from it, that insatiable remembering. The past ravaged, dismembered, tacked back together, waxed moustache to diseased cleavage, toothless crone to newborn baby. Ursula's life turned inside out like a sock.

Now she found herself listening to an account of the time Mr Finlay from the garage had to cut Tilda out of the milk urn she'd climbed into one Christmas, to get away from Dad. With perfect pitch her sister recalled the embarrassed swelling of her five-year-old body, the cheesy feel of old milk on sunburnt shoulders, the whine of Finlay's saw. Every detail vivid, febrile, accurate, except that all this had happened to Ursula before Tilda was born.

'Yes. You were very brave. Come on. Let's get some sleep.'

Their room was vast and chilly, a sort of bunkhouse for itinerant shearers. Five beds, same torn lino, a row of tall windows overlooking the verandah. No curtains at all this time. Ray's crate sat under yet another dripping sink. Only thing available, according to the landlord, and Ursula had wanted to say, if you're so short on space, why put us here? But she was too tired.

It was one o'clock by the time Tilda had chosen a bed according to the position of windows and the moon. Two-thirty before footballers stopped retching in toilets and stampeding up and down the stairs. Nearly four before Tilda began to wind down like a watch.

When all seemed quiet, Ursula gathered the crate, her hip flask, a rough horse blanket from one of the beds. The window screeched as she forced it and she froze, one leg hooked awkwardly over the sill. But her sister snored on, breath condensing like a thought bubble above her head.

The cocky was huddled in a corner of his cage. No one had thought to cover him up. As she went to throw her blanket over, she got a whiff of sweat, dust, old lanolin. A country smell, childhood smell, the layered grease and dumb terror of the shearing shed back home. And when the bird's beak snapped inches from her finger, what she heard was the sound of a dog's teeth deciding against her, a work dog chained and cowering in a pool of shade. She saw her father's steel toe stepping on that dog's paw, over and over, teaching it to heel. The same dog had taken the tip of Ursula's little finger off together with the sausage she'd been holding out to it, and even now she was flooded with the hot shame of it. Watching as Dad's belt descended, over and over, on that brindled map of skin and bone.

She found a fold-up chair in a corner of the verandah. The moon cast faint gloss on the floorboards, making stark sculpture of ordinary things. A leaning broom, the iron railing. The thin marble of her own hands. When clouds scudded over, there was just the pollen glow of streetlights, the stuttering neon of the Chinese takeaway. Beyond that, a darkness more absolute than any city night. She knew it well, how you had to draw thick curtains against it before settling down to sew or pray. How in that action, arms wide to a depthless eye of country, you both opened yourself up and made yourself small. Devil eyes at a window, possum claws on an old iron roof. Just the cocky shuffling along the bars of his cage.

Not enough light to see by now but she had her torch. Always travelled with it, her bladder being what it was. She unpacked the crate. The coat, the trousers, the boots. The glasses were cheap plastic ones from a chemist, mended at the bridge with electrician's tape. They felt too modest in her palm, too intimate, as if she'd walked up to a stranger and stroked his skin. She steeled herself with a swig of whiskey. There should be some ceremony to this. Something to echo the staunch refusals of that room.

The wallet was a disappointment. Three TAB receipts, a tattered Lotto entry and an old bus ticket, date and destination worn away. No money. Someone would have seen to that, the landlord or that screechy little nurse. No driver's licence, not even a library card to account for the book of poems. Everything looked like it had been underwater, even Ray's name on the Medicare card with a drowned and distant look to it, the embossing scoured to white. The initials on it, R.A.A McCullough, looked too formal, too alien. Sounded like a banker, a whiskery endower of monuments. Raymond for a roguish great-great-grandfather. A for Alfred, after Mam's father, proud bearer of the family chin. Bookish, toothless, always smiling, always gentle, Alfred Flanagan, even after two World Wars. The other A was for Aloysius, Mam's favourite saint. Patron of teenagers or pestilence, Ursula couldn't remember which. She and Mam had fought like alley cats over that. But in the end, after what Ursula had done, what could she possibly say?

While Mam knelt on the bathroom tiles, cupping water and muttering strings of Latin, Ray blinking up at her through globs of shampoo, Ursula had just stood there, helpless with rage and love. Between them, they'd somehow cast a spell. Doomed a little boy to ricochet forever between the repelling poles of their desire.

Taking a deep breath, she went through the book of poems more carefully this time. Her father used to quote reams of this stuff, the dusty doggerel taking on the rhythm of fence stringing or wood chopping, all flying sweat and chesty grunts. As a girl she'd hated it. Dad in declaiming pose on the front verandah, gaze fixed on some heroic distance, vowels all swollen with hubris. Even his accent changed when he did poetry, went all BBC. No one but Ursula seemed to notice. No one seemed surprised by the fact that the men in Dad's poems didn't resemble her father in the slightest. Where they were stoic, brave and resourceful, Dad was irritable and sly; where they did things, rode things, made things, suffering in silence, Dad lost things and broke things, farms, horses, promises. When things went wrong, he lashed out, at whatever animal, child or cupboard was within reach.

Seemingly harmless, those poems of Dad's, all pantomime glitter, like Grandad donning a Hitler moustache at Christmas and popping his teeth to scare the kids. But underneath, alchemical. Denying something, changing something. A greasy sleight of hand.

Riffling through the Paterson, looking for a letter or a postcard acting as a bookmark, the volume fell open at Ray's favourite.

Someone had dog-eared the page. Someone else had scored urgent furrows under the famous lines. Anyone could have done that though, a bored student, a nostalgic pensioner. There was marginalia as well, but so tiny and spidery, she couldn't tell whether the writing resembled the numbers on the coaster. The words too small, the torch too faint.

Even before she'd realised it was a library book, she should have known it wasn't Dad's. Too new for a start, and Dad's had a red cover not a blue one, and the spine was cracked in a way Dad would never have allowed. Books were precious, frightening, singular, retrieved from a locked cupboard as if from a tabernacle, doled out in that wafer of time between Sunday tea and early bed.

That reminded her of the Bible, still at the bottom of the crate. Like everything else, it was scurfy with water damage. Pickled in port, by the smell. The printing so ant-like, the paper so thin, the words were as indecipherable as the beer coaster or the graffiti Tilda used to scrawl on railway tunnel walls. At the back, more underlining, more of that feverish annotation. Whole verses had been filleted, just like the newspapers. Couldn't tell what was missing. Despite the nuns' best efforts, her knowledge of the Old Testament was sparse. But she trained her torch on it anyway, because it was all she had to go on, the random leavings of someone who might have been drunk or mad or both. She was among strangers, either way. The man who'd lived his last hours in that room and the man she'd been searching for, both lost. And what she yearned for anyway, uselessly and always, was the boy.

He was a tough little boy, wiry and sun-speckled, with upstanding blond hair. Tireless with axe or hammer, he could swim any river, sit almost any horse. Had a way with dogs and words. By fourteen he'd developed a passion for boxing, ancient history, learning Chinese. A quiet boy, a taker apart of radios, toasters, family history, always putting them back together in unexpected ways. A boy who liked poetry, who loved that colt from old Regret and who could recite the whole thing, along with scores of others, who could just as effortlessly recall the taxonomy of ancient Mesopotamian languages and the death dates of famous Celtic warriors and the Roman numerals attached to momentously forded rivers, as if he had swallowed every volume of his Brittanicas, as if all those tiny certainties were printed on his skin. If this boy became a man who in last extremis had turned to the Bible, something she'd tried to banish from his life along with other forms of barbarism, what else might have been possible, in such a room, at such a time?

Her little circle of light shivered with her as wind raked the verandah. The torch was just a glimmer now and the spare batteries were back in the room. Seeing herself there, crouched in cold and dark, scrambling after mouse tracks in ink and time, she threw the Bible down in disgust. The binding gave way and thin yellow pages fluttered under the railing, down to the street.

A line of grey on the horizon. A deep breath. The boots.

These were R.M. Williams, badly resoled and unevenly worn. If she was Sherlock Holmes, Ray's hero at the age of twelve, when he'd read the whole of Dad's Conan Doyle compendium in a single weekend, she might, with the help of the magnifying glass she now needed to do the cryptic, deduce that the man who'd owned them was poor, of short stature, had one leg shorter than the other and smoked roll-your-owns. This last wasn't a feat of deduction. She'd found three wizened roll-ups hidden in the toe.

Tilda was right about one thing. Ray was tall, nearly six foot by the age of fourteen. Then again, he had small feet for a boy that size. The Flanagans were known for small feet, Mam always boasted, as if to separate herself from the galumphing Highland rabble on the other side. Instead of being proud of how all those indestructible little Irish women had dealt with drunk husbands and no money and far too many children, what Mam remembered was their feet. Except for Ursula, of course, who had feet like canoe paddles at the age of twelve. When she'd found out at school that her name meant she-bear, she wasn't surprised, although Mam had always insisted she was named for the saint. Predictably, a virgin, martyred by Huns.

Picking up the coat again, she held it up against the scant light from the street. Even allowing for wear and stretch on such cheap fabric, the shoulders were broad. Yet the trousers were short and the shoes were small. What an oddly proportioned man he must have been. When exactly did feet stop growing? She wasn't sure.

Her eyes were scratchy with tiredness now and she was so cold she could barely feel her toes. In desperation she went through the coat pockets again, sticking the feeble torchlight into each and every fold. Nothing except the drycleaning docket, three greenish coins, a packet of Lifesavers and a load of lint. When she opened the lollies, they crumbled to multicoloured dust. Then the torch flickered and went out.

She took a slug of whiskey. With expert hands, she retraced every inch of the coat lining. Always a secretive little boy.

Even in the dark, with fingers stiff with cold, the old knowledge flowed seamlessly, the language of hems and facing and working to bias, the patience needed to tame a devious bolt of silk. She could tell, down to the last seam and buttonhole, exactly how that jacket had been made. Not very well, by all accounts. Shoddy seams, shoulders baggy, back panels all seated, lapels out of whack. Unpicking it in her mind, spreading the raw makings out on a remembered dining-room table, she read it all in smooth reverse. Imagining how crisp paper wedges, careful tacking and a decent pair of scissors might have overcome this poor fabric and corrupted nap. Trimming and turning, pinning and sorting, she fitted it back together in her mind. Shoulder to collar, underarm sleeve to sleeve opening, wrong side of facing to wrong side of jacket, feeling again a tidy pleasure at how something so discarded and unpromising—curtain remnants, bits of old ball gown, the bolt ends from the makings of richer people's clothes—could be transformed. How with enough skill you could hide the ugly truth of things. Make something into which love and hope could be poured.

There. Along the bottom of the pocket. A hole. Inside the lining, a lump of sorts. She shivered again, perhaps from cold, perhaps from finding a lump like that in the lining of her own skin, years ago. Could just be careless sewing, a bit of fabric doubled up when they did the seam. But it was too solid, too separate, the bulge sliding around between her fingers, and there were smaller lumps inside the bigger one. What she really needed was some proper light and her nail scissors, but they were back in the room along with the spare torch batteries and she couldn't risk waking Tilda, who, before she'd finally dropped off, had started in again about the man on the train.

'I'm telling you! Why don't you believe me? It was him!'

It took the threat of missing breakfast to get her into bed. But nothing would shake her sister's conviction that the old man in a cheap sports coat like this one, emerging from the toilet and struggling to do up his fly against the sway of the train, was the same man Tilda claimed had followed her five years ago to the foyer of her housing commission apartment, who had somehow scaled ten storeys to stare in at her bedroom window, an elderly human fly. At the time she'd been just as convinced that this was the same man wanted by police for attacking three women in the city while they slept. To prove it, she'd cut out the identikit picture from the newspaper. Shoved it under the nose of neighbours, shopkeepers, librarians, everyone she met.

Tilda followed that poor man for weeks, to his pub, his golf club, his place of work. Stood at midnight in his front garden, screaming out her truth. Ursula saw the man in the waiting room of the police station when she went to pick up her sister, to try and explain, with the support of a thick folder of hospital documentation, that this sort of thing always happened when Tilda went off her medication, always at the same time of year. How it didn't matter that the man Tilda had been harassing—late middle age, ruddy complexion, thinning ginger hair—bore no resemblance to the description of the rapist—youngish, olive-skinned, heart-shaped tattoo. Neither of them looked anything like Ursula's ex-partner Simon either, who was ash-blond, tall, with pale grey eyes. Didn't stop Tilda from splashing turps across his artworks, stealing his shirts for the sniffer dogs, nicking his photograph from Ursula's wallet and pinning it to the local library noticeboard, the word rapist slashed across it in bright red crayon. On certain days, in Tilda's universe, everything and nothing was true.

Dawn was the colour of her fingertips, ice blue. In this light, objects felt rarefied, as if strained through muslin, each milky floorboard, each grain of dust. Yet nothing stood revealed.

She drained the last of the whiskey. Lit one of Ray's rollies, the stale tobacco making her cough. With hands still strong with the memory of sewing and bread kneading and pastry making, all that useless history rising up, she ripped at the coat lining until it gave. Tucked inside was a little hanky, tied at the corners, like something a bald Englishman might wear on a grey shingle beach. She fumbled at it, cursing her clumsiness, Ray's Boy Scout knots, his Russian doll secrets, out loud, for anyone to hear.

What tumbled out were teeth, rattling like seed pearls in her palm. She counted them, counted them again. All there, five of the seventeen that had come through in a child of four. Those remaining were protected from sugar and accidents and brushed religiously by Ursula. Those still to come, sleeping in raw red gums, Tilda being a late starter even at something so elemental, had surfaced in the weeks and months after Ray left home. The hot swelling soothed by Ursula with a thumb dipped in honey, the earache rocked away in Ursula's bed. Now, against all odds and despite years of neglect and countless Mars Bars and hospital pap, Tilda's teeth were white and strong.

She shook her palm. The teeth blurred, multiplied, posing more questions. The day dense with them, no horizon in sight.

Before climbing back through the window, she opened the door of the cocky's cage. The stupid thing just cowered there, regarding her with one gnarled eye.

CHAPTER FIVE

D awn. A day all his. Light like cream.
Piling Sam's tools beneath the wrecked chimney, he checked the ute from tray to glove box but everything else, including the fool of a dog, belonged to him.

At the last minute and because he was in that sort of mood, he aimed a gibber at the sheep skull. Got it down second go. Tying an old blue oil rag around it like a bandanna, he propped it on the handle of the shovel. Left it watching there, grim and jaunty, as he got in the ute and backed away. When an old pay slip fluttered down from the dashboard, he paused, engine running, his precious petrol ticking away.

Leave a note. The right thing to do. Wish Freda happy birthday, ask her to look in on Charlie, maybe give him the old clothes he'd left out the shed. He could also point out to Sam, who'd go into orbit when he realised he was minus a cook, that by rising at three this morning and working by hurricane lamp and car headlights, he'd done what no one else had managed in a year. He'd finished the fence.

In the end, his pencil stayed cocked behind his ear. No note. No point. No sign he'd ever been here, except this wire twanging off in the rear view, spare and true. A job worth doing. Dad in his head. The rhythm of that voice, gravelly, ponderous, keen as the wheel ruts he was following between creek bed and mine workings, rocked him slowly toward solid ground.

⌒

By seven am, he was on back roads, crossing other properties. At each gate he checked his bearings. Sam's place was northeast, the old mine northwest. The place he used to call home roughly south. Always his pole star, flinging him wide and away.

Keeping to fence runs and stock trails, he plotted east below the border, avoiding the main drag in case of meeting someone from Sam's. It was the long way round, and with all the gates, slow going, on tracks little better than overgrown goat runs, rubbly grooves that petered out entirely sometimes, and he was forced to drive through long grass, flushing roos, emu rocking like stately bustled ladies in front of the ute. When he was far enough away, he'd loop down and join the road proper. Head for one of those drop-offs Charlie was always going on about, drawing his mud maps on stray bits of newsprint and pressing them urgently into Ray's hand.

Before the car accident which had killed his son and turned him from drink to God, Charlie had haunted the corner of these three States in a wild haze of money schemes and whiskey fumes.

Every few weeks he'd call the feed company he worked for, lie elaborately about blown tyres and missing parts, then hole up in a pub. Charlie had stashes of petrol and water everywhere round here, or so he said.

After the top-up, Ray's map was blank. Could cross the border at Hungerford. Always work up north, even at this time of year. After that, if he found he was in the mood for buildings, water, people, he could strike west then south, head to Adelaide the long way round.

For now it was enough to be on the move again, to be alone again, travelling tracks called Dry Lake Road, Dead Horse Road, heading to places called Dotted Lake or Garden Vale, dry grim jokes. With every lurch and bump, he felt his old life shaking free. A small dot behind him, receding and unregarded, the cook, the fencer, the barman, mopper-up of beer and dreams.

In tune with his abdication, the land shed height and colour as he went. Sage green, blue green, grey green of saltbush, blue bush, mulga and mallee, sudden yellow of late blooming Dead Finish, everything growing more muted and exhausted the further he travelled from homesteads, bores, proper roads. The place scouring, flensing, paling to snake colour, bone colour. Something seen through old lime wash, grown stubbornly back through.

Green just a tired rumour here, in this dry and final closing down.

⌒

At the last gate before the highway, in a place so drought and fire ravaged, earth was the colour of steel wool, he smelled burnt hair. A lamb, collapsed in the shade of the post. Tiny, blackened, earless, too far gone to move or bleat, it regarded him through one boiled-looking eye. Next to it, the ewe, unrecognisable, architectural. Black ribs, crisp whorling of fleece, already collapsing back to earth.

It was only while he was rummaging in the ute tray for his shovel, wishing for something quicker and cleaner, that he remembered Sam's gun. He'd hidden it so well, wrapped in a pillowslip and stowed beneath his seat, that he'd missed it when he was packing up. He swore, batting down the dog. Didn't have a licence for the rifle. Had only taken it so he could have some fresh meat while he worked.

Too far to go back now. Not enough petrol, not without the top-up. And he couldn't have left it by the chimney anyway, he now realised. Wouldn't have been safe. Although it wasn't loaded, the bullets were locked in his strong box. He'd heard enough of Dad's stories to know not to travel with a loaded gun. Men shooting mates, men shooting pets. Kids shooting fathers, farmers blasting their wives to bits over the Weetbix. Guns going off in cupboards, all by themselves. And there was always Uncle Len.

Ray had heard that story ever since he was old enough to sit up. It had been told so often, at Christmas and funerals and family gatherings, that by the time he was thirteen, the facts had been worn to nubs in a swamp of detail, and those were a moveable feast. Sometimes it was high summer, sometimes spring flood. Sometimes banks or politicians were to blame. Once, it was a nagging woman that sent Len out to the far paddock, at dusk, all alone. Shocked silence and nervous titters round the kitchen table at that. Eccentric, that's what they called Dad's sense of humour, back then.

Sometimes it was dawn, but mostly sunset, and Len usually lived until they got him back to the homestead, and there was always a death scene in the bedroom, Mam and Aunty Sheila crying on Dad's shoulder, neighbours collecting like awkward flotsam on the front verandah, everyone useless and hopeless and helpless, except Dad. It was always Dad who found him, Dad who braved heat or creeks or rampant bushfire, Dad who ran shoeless, hatless or waterless to call the doctor and fetch the truck. Aunty Sheila mad with grief, Dad's shirt soaked with the dying man's blood.

The facts of it were simple enough. Out checking stock, code in hard times for shooting the last of his cows, Len had crawled through a fence while trailing a loaded gun. Somehow managed to shoot himself in the head. Careless, stupid, but not criminal, not sinful, not compared to the other stories Ray had heard while hidden under the kitchen table as a child. The bank debts, the gambling, the mortgage foreclosures. The children lost down wells or locked in fridges, the women dying in childbirth while some black sheep cousin drank himself senseless in a pub. Against all these, Len's fate seemed ordinary, almost innocent, at least in the dense ledger of fate, penance and retribution the family history entailed.

Yet there was something about this story. The angle of it peculiar, too intimate. Dad's telling of it lacking his usual bluster, tinged always with a hangdog air. Seemingly doomed to repeat it at every family gathering, like some figure in a myth. With every retelling, changing something, shifting something, moving the story in tiny, irreversible degrees further from the truth. By the end, a story so layered with contingency, it seemed unrecognisable, even to Dad himself. Every detail so deft yet so changeable, as if Dad was telling the beads of the story in ordinary daylight while letting the texture of it fall, amorphous with dust motes, into that twilight world under the kitchen table. A landscape of clenched knuckles and ticking feet.

Shorn of plot, dates, reliable weather, only the images remained. These had the rimy glow of half-awake dreams. The gun-metal light of a winter sunset. A man gaunt as his fences, hollow-eyed as cattle. So thin by then, their hipbones had shuffled through the hide. Like broken umbrellas, Dad said once, planting a picture that never went away.

When he was too big to sit under the kitchen table, bored too with the talk there, always more concerned with wheat and weather than the wilder terrain Len's story gestured toward, he'd avoid the house altogether, slam out the back door. Taking Dad's gun from its hiding place in the wood box, he'd sit for hours on the chopping block, drawing trajectories in the dust. Trying to winnow the bones of it. Drought, dusk, gun. For the first time, he began to realise how words could describe some tiny and untenable corner between what had happened and what was true.

At sunset, the hour when, if he averaged Dad's retellings, Len had most often died, he'd head for a section of fence hidden from the house. He tried everything, crawling forwards on his belly, shuffling backwards, twisting himself to unnatural poses, even hanging his head upside down. Never quite worked. When he was older, he would come to understand it, that particular arrangement of gun, dusk, dying landscape. Not then.

In the end he used the shovel on the lamb. Felt more honest to look the poor little bugger in the eye.

⌒

He'd hit the road proper and a rare patch of bitumen and he was fiddling with the radio, looking for weather, finding only strung-out country and western, a pastel sadness swelling and fading between low-slung hills, so at first he didn't see the figure up ahead.

When he did, he thought he'd imagined it, the way he kept seeing wildlife crouched in bushes by the side of the road. Even when he'd shot past and pulled up in a flurry of dust, while he sat there waiting, engine humming, watching in the rear view what had looked like a grown man in heat haze shrink to a lanky, knock-kneed boy, he still refused to believe it. There were lots of kids in baseball caps and baggy jeans, lugging skateboards, wires sprouting from their ears. Just didn't expect to see one all the way out here. Then the boy reefed off his cap and Ray saw the red hair, the freckles standing out like flares.

He drew level, and Ray had time to see the layer of dust and sweat on him, the skin of his cheeks scalded with sun, before he walked right on by.

'Oi! Mick! Wait. It's me.'

Even after he'd edged the ute forward and cracked the passenger window, Mick just kept staring straight ahead. Didn't seem surprised to find Ray way out here, in a place where neither of them should be.

'Mick? You all right? What's going on?'

He mumbled something. Got chucked, is what Ray thought he heard, above the engine noise. No way he was going to turn her off, with the petrol getting low.

'Why? Who's out the shed?'

Mick shrugged. Even through petrol fumes, Ray could smell him. Breathed out beer, pungent weed. And still his foot hovered over the accelerator, as if he could pretend he was still travelling, had never stopped at all.

'How'd you get all the way out here?'

'Got a lift.'

It was like pulling teeth. Reluctantly, Ray killed the ute, praying he could get her started again.

'And?'

'Bloke was drunk. Nearly had an accident. I made him let me out.' Without the shudder of the engine, Ray realised it wasn't the ute but Mick who was swaying. Face burnt, eyes red, from crying, dope or dust, couldn't tell.

'Ray, you got anything to drink?'

Ray wanted to shout, what sort of idiot gets himself stranded way out here, with no car, no food, no water, no hope, except that someone like Ray might come along? Instead he started up again, opened the passenger door.

CHAPTER SIX

'Here. Ever heard of these?'

Mick's sleeve was silver with snot. He used the hanky but five minutes later he was sniffing again, a dreary punctuation to the disintegrating road. After Ray gave him some water and stale biscuits from the glove box, it was crunch, slurp, sniff.

'You got a permanent cold or what?'

Allergies, he snuffled. Allergic to work, Ray reckoned, as the truth came out, in dribs and drabs.

The night before, Mick had gone to town with one of the men. Headed for the pub, where, on strict orders from his mother, Sam had forbidden him to go. No problem once there. Barb never bothered to check ID. He'd spent all his pay, then rolled in at dawn with the same twit who'd given him the lift. Turned up late to morning shift again, still drunk or stoned or both. That smell of stale beer round him, those lobster-coloured eyes. He'd spewed in the shed sink. Couldn't help it, been spewing all morning. Must have a bug. Ray said nothing, just lit a cigarette.

Of course, the drain had arced up, what with Sam's ad-hoc plumbing, and then the whole system went down. Also Mick's fault. Always sticking tea leaves down the sink. With the contractors on site and his new shed half-done, Sam had to drop everything, get down there with his electric eel. And then, because that Pommy cook Sam had hired to do the dinners was work to rule, there was no one to fix breakfast. No one except Freda, who had enough to do, with three kids, five horses, her superannuated chickens, her B&B business and that vegetable patch of hers which kept dying in the heat.

Mick didn't say any of that last bit of course. Just whined on about his stomach. That's why he'd needed to have a smoke behind the shed. His mum swore by it, apparently, when you were crook in the guts. Ray, steering silently round craters and sink holes, thought about Mick lounging around with a lighter near all that LPG. What with the drains and the salmonella and the bits of money that kept going missing from the office, the whole day put off Sam's tense calibration, it must have been the final straw.

'OK. Let's get him on the blower. He's probably calmed down by now.'

But when Ray reached for his phone, Mick knocked his hand away.

'Nuh. Don't. He hates my guts. And I gotta go home. To Bourke.'

Anger battled it out with Ray's own reluctance to speak to Sam. 'Yeah, well. I told you. I'm not going that way. Turning off before that. Heading out there.' He pointed out toward some unnamed track heading to some other horizon he hadn't decided on yet. Another border, yet another fresh start. That new minted feeling he'd had this morning already leaking away.

'It's me mum, Ray. She's in hospital. She's really crook.'

In the six months Ray had known Mick, his mother had been sick at least once a fortnight and at least five of his grandparents had died.

'Isn't your place somewhere this side of town anyway?' No answer. More sniffing. 'Well, Sam said it was. So the turn-off's got to be somewhere round here.' Mick rolled his window down and stared out. 'Easiest thing, I'll drop you home. You can sort it out from there.'

Mick shrank down in his seat. Didn't speak again for half an hour.

The fuel gauge had started blinking yellow, the warning light. Ray worried about muck in the tank, a blocked line. Prayed it was just dips in the road. Trying to winkle the details of Charlie's drop-off out of memory, recall the shape of the little map Charlie had drawn for him on a bit of newsprint still marking a place inside one of his books back at the shed, he drew a blank. What had the old man said? Dry creek, third bridge after the first junction, a track bearing left. Dead tree, red rag, pile of painted stones. But he'd been so distracted by the kid that he'd hadn't been paying attention. They'd passed a junction but that was way back, and since then, no cairn of rocks, no trees at all. The threads in Charlie broken long ago. Now and again though, and without warning, elaborate memories rose to the surface, finely layered, entire to themselves. Floating free, like intricate scabs of rust. At the core of Charlie's particular madness Ray believed there might be a single can of fuel.

'Ray? Pull over. I'm crook in the guts.'

Ray didn't need to be told. The air in the cabin was foul.

'I can't stop now. Might not get her started again.' Place was atomic with heat now, bare of anything except the odd termite mound. Maybe they'd gone over the third bridge already, or was it only the second? There'd been lots of little bridges. This road kept crossing the same dry creek.

'Stick your head out the window. You'll be right.'

Mick answered by spewing all over his own lap. The stink was unbearable, chunks on the dashboard and halfway up Ray's leg. He pulled over in a flurry of swearing and dust.

While Mick lay on the ground, too far gone to even kneel, Ray tried to clean up with a rag and some radiator water when what he really needed was a hose. The dog whined, flies buzzed, the kid moaned like a stuck cow. Ray felt a wave gathering in his own stomach, but he couldn't let it break, not yet.

He changed his trousers, cranked all the windows, gave the dog some water and a rare rough pat.

Mick was dry-retching now, just bile. Ray considered for the first time that he might really be sick. Boy knew nothing about cleaning or cooking, was always leaving chicken to defrost without a cover or even a plate. Sam only took him on in the first place because his dad was a cousin or something. Mick knew next to nothing about sheep, couldn't ride a motorbike, and horses brought him out in hives.

'Jesus, what have you been drinking? More you lean over, more you'll keep going. Try and sit up.'

Half-carrying him to the ute, Ray propped him in his seat. Wiped his lips with a wet hankie, too afraid to give him a proper drink. Dry toast and Vegemite, that's what Urs used to recommend. But that was later. When it was this bad, you just had to grit your teeth and ride it out.

Trouble was, Mick had no grit to him. Mick Jones sounded like a tough nut, like one of those boys Ray had gone to school with, rough boys who'd grown into rough men of hard fists and few words. The sort of men he'd known in pubs and sheds and down the mines. Didn't suit this piece of ginger ectoplasm, his head juddering bonelessly against the window as Ray started up, third time lucky. No answer to Ray's request for directions but Sam had said Mick's dad owned a small acreage this side of town. Ray knew most of the big ones around here. Not that track to the right, that was part of another station, and the last side track he'd seen was an hour ago and that led in the wrong direction, north toward the border he'd hoped to cross this morning. No chance now. Not today.

Taking a punt, he took the next left. Hoping his petrol lasted, that by some miracle this might also be the turn-off Charlie had talked about, that the little dirt furrow actually led somewhere, wasn't just a rabbit run. Grinding his teeth in lieu of a cigarette, he scoured the distance for a glint of sun on roof, something resembling a driveway, a mailbox perhaps. Crossing a cattle grid over a dry culvert, they passed a tin sign propped against the stock guard. In dripping red paint, in the hand of a psychotic preschooler, *Privet, No Trespassing. Thieving Abo Skum will be Shot.* Nice. The gun under his seat rattled as they bumped across. What sort of bloke was this Mr Jones? He glanced over to ask but the boy was lost to his own misery, hiccupping with every hole in the road.

The fuel light had settled to a steady yellow glare. No turn-offs for the next thirty ks. No more signs, no trees even, just ribbed sand and rusted car shells, the empty bellows shape of a rotted roo. The ute hit a mound of dust. A warning cough from the engine as he tried to rev through it, his back wheels floating, hitting, skittering wildly across gravel, crunching through the dip and gouge of yet another nameless creek. No bridge though, no pile of white rocks. Knowing Charlie, that drop-off could be a hundred ks either direction from the spot he'd marked on his little map. Probably off some other road entirely, in some other State or decade. Some other life.

Just as he was about to give up, turn around, Ray spotted two faint wheel marks climbing steeply toward an eroded ridge. Sun twinging off metal up there. A fence in the distance. A squat thing that might have been a mailbox, up a track where no postie in his right mind would ever go.

'Oi. Wake up. This it?'

The kid might have nodded or his head might have just knocked against the seat. Sighing, Ray started crawling along the soft shoulder, sticking his head out the window, negotiating deep corrugations, chunks of rock larger than his head. Reaching behind his ear for his last cigarette, the one he'd been saving for when he was alone, he lit it one-handed, but Mick started retching again, so he put it out.

At the point where the track petered to a slew of dust and gibber, he found an old milk can propped drunkenly on a pile of bricks. More rust than metal, the letters J and O scrawled in that same dull red paint used on the previous sign. The rest indecipherable. Didn't bode well. Where Ray came from, your mailbox said something about you. No matter what was happening, and even if it was just something your dad had knocked up from old bits of tin, looking like a smaller version of the house it belonged to, even down to a tiny verandah to stop the rain that never arrived from getting in, you made sure your mailbox was in good nick. Keeping up with the Joneses, Mam used to call it. From the look of it, these Joneses were on their last legs.

The kid had his whole head out the window now, panting like a dog. The driveway so peppered with boulders, Ray feared the chassis would be ripped from the wheels. God knows how they got up it in the wet. Then again, with that topsoil blowing in steady curtains across the windscreen, every fence in tatters and the only dam he'd seen bone dry, it hadn't rained round here in quite a while.

By the time they got to the house, he knew what was what. He'd seen places like this before. In bad times, in good times, when bad people were in charge. A slow cancer had crept in from that yellow stubble, consuming everything worth growing or tending, rotting car innards, scouring weatherboards, eating every bit of metal to a lace of rust.

He pulled up beside a shed housing a disembowelled tractor. No sign of a working truck or car. The shed itself was just two walls and a roof propped at a stray angle to the earth. And everywhere, the dust, rising, swirling, advancing in a low hum from bare paddocks, forming knee-deep mounds around the verandah posts. He thought of Urs, after a dust storm, sweeping the front verandah. Women took dust so personally, were always in battle with it, armed only with their cranky determination and their twiggy little brooms. It was the earliest sound he could remember, the scrape of yellow straw over old wood.

'You called, right? Let 'em know?'

The kid picked at a hole his jeans. Ray forced his voice to go softer, like he was talking to a skittish horse.

'Listen. Don't need to say what happened, with Sam. Just tell 'em you were crook.'

No answer. No footsteps sounding inside as he mounted the front steps and knocked. Just the silence of air long undisturbed. He peered through the only window not strung with sheets, but the dust was so thick, all he could see was himself. A brick red colour growing at his neck. Just the heat. The sun was dipping lower, but according to an old thermometer nailed to the verandah post, still forty in the shade.

He walked round the side. A bedroom window had been smashed. The back door was boarded up, layer upon layer of fence palings, nailed at furious, overlapping angles. Something wrong. Some frantic fear entombed behind those criss-crossed boards. As he came full circuit and climbed the verandah steps again, he felt the world tipping sideways and he wondered if he was coming down with whatever bug Mick had before he realised it was the verandah itself. The foundations were so leached of moisture, the whole thing was lurching away from the house at a horrified lean.

He knocked again on the front door, harder this time. Knowing it was useless. Then he just stood there, flies feasting on his hat. The wind got up again, the screen door banged. A big dent where it met the boards, like it had been doing that for years. Wouldn't have taken five minutes to fix it. All it needed was a screwdriver. Broken spring, that was all.

It wasn't the bad road, the falling-down verandah, the ravaged paddocks, the poor excuse for a shed, but that final tiny dereliction that sent him in a sudden burst of fury toward the ute.

Mick, seeing the look on Ray's face, wound his window up. Ray kept tapping until he wound it down again.

'It's no good. No one here.'

'Yeah, I can see that.' Ray heard his voice go all clipped and reasonable, the way it did when he was just holding on. 'You've got a key though.'

Mick shook his head.

'Forgot it. Lost it. I left it at the shed.'

'Which is it?'

Another shrug.

'Your dad then. He in town? Shopping or something. What's his number? Let's give him a ring.'

But when he walked round to the driver's side and got his phone off the dash, he saw it was out of juice. And when he found his charger, it was on the floor, and he'd trodden on it while driving and the business end was clogged with dust and spew. Couldn't risk starting the ute up just to charge the phone, even if he could get the engine going again. And Mick wasn't volunteering any information. He was just sitting there, picking at his jeans.

Ray took his time walking back round to the passenger side. Hoping the slow lope through heat might calm him down. When he got there, he stuck his head through Mick's window, taking the full force of the puke smell in the face.

'Right. What's the story?'

At least this time Mick had the sense not to shrug.

'Spit it out. Or I'll leave you here to rot.'

The boy started crying. Ray couldn't believe it. Not just snivelling, really crying, in great wet gulps, like a toddler. Not even trying to cover it up. Just sitting there, leaking like a jellyfish, waiting for some stray bit of life to pick him up and smash him on a rock. The wave in Ray's blood finally crested and broke.

When he wrenched the door open, Mick, leaning on it and taken by surprise, fell out. Just lay there, in the dirt, T-shirt all rucked up. The skin of his stomach white as milk. Milk belly, fish belly. No hair, no balls. No spine. Ray had never been a jellyfish, not at Mick's age, not since. He'd learned early that weakness like that made the hum in other men's bloodstreams thicken and roar. Made retribution fast, smooth, unthinking and unquestioned, deft as primed muscle. Everything correct, due, accounted for. The boot, the belt, the fist.

'Get up.'

The kid just gaped at him, like his brain had fallen out of his mouth along with the spew.

'I said, get up.' He heard himself pleading. Get up, before I do something I'll regret.

Instead of grabbing him by his long red hair as he longed to do, Ray got a handful of shirt. The fabric tore, he kept pulling, Mick squeaking in fear. When he had him upright, it all came out, in tearful gulps and snotty bursts. By then, Ray didn't need to hear it. It was an old story, a country story, the syllables engraved here long ago, in dry dams and starving animals and makeshift curtains, in dust and rust. A story of bad luck and bad faith, of giving up and giving in. So old, it had told itself to silence, was already weathering away. The sort of story which might have been Ray's to inherit, if he hadn't left home when he did.

'Your mum. She's in hospital, you said. Or are you lying about that as well?'

Mick shook his head, then nodded, his head going in circles while he wiped his nose on his arm.

'And your dad?'

'Queensland. Went for work, ages ago.'

'What about family? There's got to be someone. An aunty or something.'

'There's Cheryl. Dad's sister. But she hates my guts.'

'Yeah. It's going around.'

Ray turned to look at the house. The windows stared back, blind with sun.

'She's got to have a phone number, your aunty. And you've got to have a phone.'

'Nuh. I lost it. I told ya. Someone nicked it. It wasn't my fault.'

Ray played with the dog's ears, whistling tuneless country and western. Trying to drown out the throb in his head.

'In the house, dickhead. There's a window broken round the side. I'll knock the glass out, you climb in, ring Aunty Whatserface. OK?'

Predictably, the kid was shaking his head again.

'The phone's cut off. We couldn't pay the bill. And anyway, I can't. She'll tell Dad about Sam. Dad'll kill me.'

Not if Ray got there first.

'Did you let Sam know about all this before he sent you home?'

But Mick was staring at his feet again.

Ray turned away. Sat down on a tree stump, staring out at the horizon, smoking the rest of his last cigarette. It was getting late, the sun low, even by daylight-saving time. Earth with that warning purple hum to it, light gone soft and sly. Roos would be swarming soon, looking for feed beside the road. If it was up to him, if the kid wasn't sick and homeless and clueless and apparently parentless, he'd have risked it, dusk, wildlife, lack of sleep.

He remembered the petrol and groaned. Looked around, but it was hopeless. No other sheds, just the one with the tractor, and that didn't even have an engine, let alone a tank. No use going back to find Charlie's stash. If it was anywhere near where Charlie had said it might be, it was probably about the same distance to town by now.

He heard a trickling sound, startling in all that dryness. When he looked round, he saw Mick, with acres of drought to choose from, pissing up against the ute. Swivelling his hips, trying to write his initials on Ray's dusty duco, leaving wet scrawls all over the tyres.

Ray stared down at his own patch of dust. Letting it saturate all his layers. Blood colour, rage colour, drying, hardening, until his pulse slowed down.

CHAPTER SEVEN

Mick chose that moment to pipe up. 'Hey Ray. I forgot. Saw that mate of yours last night. That old bloke. The priest.'

It took Ray a moment to twig. Then he remembered the worn black coat he'd given Charlie last winter, when the old man just couldn't seem to get warm. The black stovepipe trousers of Sam's that Freda had offered to go with it, sixties slim, laughably small for Sam with his beer belly but short enough in the leg to fit Charlie, almost. They formed a sort of mismatched suit which Charlie wore religiously, teaming it with a new white shirt Ray had bought him, the cardboard stiffener from the collar worn around the top button, blacked out except for a square at the throat. Father O'Reilly, in faded priest black, self-ordained. Hand raised in benediction outside the pub and the TAB. Absolving sinners, splitters, drinkers, gamblers. Forgiving everyone but himself.

'Charlie?'

'Yeah. He was in the pub. He gave me something. To give ya, if I saw ya. Just a sec.'

Mick started rifling through his pockets, retrieving a yo-yo, a packet of Tally-Hos, a suspiciously thick wad of notes. Retrieving something small and white, he held it up, flapping it at Ray.

'Charlie was in the pub?'

'Yeah. He was looking for you. Kept going on about something he saw in the paper, and when you weren't there, he wanted to ring ya and he asked to use my phone but I didn't have one, because I lost it. I mean, it got nicked. And so he tried to use the one behind the bar and that fat chick, the one with the hair? She got the shits. Something bad.'

Even making allowances for Mick's tall tales, Ray could believe it. Barb behind the bar, ropeable because she'd been left in charge of both pub and bistro, while Pete was at his Saturday night drinks, at the only other pub in town. Then old Charlie coming in, upsetting people with his talk of God. Waving his bits of paper announcing the death of strangers, someone he imagined was his sister or his cousin or his long-lost father. The dates on them circled, because they bore a secret coded message from his wife. After thirty years, giving Charlie permission to come home.

'I took care of him, don't worry. She gave us free beers because I got him away from the bar. We had a bet on the trots.'

Looking proud of himself, Mick walked over, handed Ray a beer coaster from Pete's pub. The back was covered in numbers. Ray squinted against the glare, couldn't make head nor tail.

'Charlie was drinking?'

'Yeah. So? He was in a pub.'

Ray could see that too. Barb giving schooners to an arch alcoholic and a stoned fourteen-year-old boy. Charlie, trembling, rheumy, staring at the beer like it was the holy grail. Mick leading him toward the betting tables, right off the edge of the abyss. The smell of beer and the gabble of race calls stripping years of rectitude away. Poor Charlie trying to raise his wall of numbers against it, his frantic voodoo of Scripture notations, saints' birthdays, papal Roman numerals, funeral dates, engraved here on this coaster in what looked like the eyeliner Barb kept in her pocket for quick repairs.

Ray tried to drop the coaster but it clung to his fingers. It was sticky with beer.

'He kept going on about this message I had to give ya. Something about a phone number and a funeral, in the paper. I promised to do it. If I saw ya.' Mick had picked up the coaster, was frowning over it, like it was one of those newspaper puzzles he was always doing instead of washing up.

'Whose funeral?'

'I dunno. Made no sense. He just said to say your mam was dead and to ring your mum. Mad, eh.'

Mick was still smiling, still talking. Setting his yo-yo going now, trying to walk the dog. To Ray, he was frozen, voiceless, a blank cut-out against the sun. No sound at all except the steady pounding of his own blood.

He walked over, snatched the coaster, headed for the ute. It seemed to start by the fury of his will alone. Mick only just managed to scramble in as he floored it, passenger door flapping, careering back along the driveway and down the track.

⌒

On the way into town, Ray didn't trust himself to do anything but steer. He drove so fast, the ute fishtailed from verge to verge, the dog nearly strangling on its rope. Mick, after all that shrugging and sulking, had developed verbal diarrhoea. Yarning away like some old-timer on a verandah while laying out a game of patience on the glove-box lid.

Everything had kicked off with a bout of hooky, apparently. A few days off school. Then he'd been caught driving his father's truck on the road at the age of twelve. Had to, it was an emergency. His mum was sick. Not his fault. At thirteen, he'd stolen a car. Not his idea. Wrong crowd. Easily led. The excuses made by his deluded mother flowed like oil off his tongue. Got chucked from school, more truancy, a bit of dope, some money missing from another kid's bag. Wasn't him, never did it, teachers had it in. Then the police started hassling his mum. She was really sick by then, and his dad was off work. Bad back. His dad a drinker. Started hitting his mum. Hit Mick too, that time he nicked the car, before his dad left and he got sent to Sam's, last chance. Nearly broke his arm.

Mick stuck his elbow into Ray's line of sight. A tiny crescent there. Probably a burnt-off wart. The kid waited, looking hopeful. Expecting sympathy, admiration. Ray just knocked his arm away. Kept his eyes on the road, his hands on the wheel. Gripping so tight, he later found indentations in his palms.

Twenty k from town, crossing yet another dry creek on the red grooved ghost of yet another bridge, he spotted a scrap of faded rag fluttering above a pile of white stones. Right where he wouldn't have been if he hadn't met Mick, in exactly the opposite direction to the spot marked on Charlie's map.

Throwing the ute toward the ditch, Mick yelping as he banged his head on the roof, Ray slammed out, fetched his funnel and shovel from the tray. Hiking over, he dug until metal hit metal. An old jerry can, so rusted and battered it looked like it had been through World War Two. When he shook it, a flurry of dust and the faintest splash.

It was almost all fumes. But he decanted what there was and, with a few rough coughs, got the engine going again. The kid finally had the sense to shut up, except for the odd startled appeal.

'Ray? Something wrong?'

But Ray was lost to everything now except the hum of his tyres, the spool of the road, the judder of the grids.

On the final stretch, he really put his foot down. One twenty, one forty, the ute shaking so much he could hear rivets working their way out of his door. But no matter how much he floored it, still he felt like a tiny ant crawling over a vast red picnic blanket, pulled tight by hands unseen. As he got closer to town, he checked the mirror for cops. Would have welcomed it. Something to rage at instead of this boy. All this time, while Ray had been rescuing him from drunk truckies and thirst and heat stroke, while he'd been wiping up his spew and serving him biscuits and taking him here and there like a fucking butler, that thing had been in his pocket. And he'd never said a word.

He stopped at the first motel he saw, a set of fibro boxes on the outskirts of town. Mick had gone to sleep. Ray half-walked, half-dragged him across the car park to their room, dumped him in the double bed. He'd take the single. He'd move it to the other side of the room. He'd drag it out to the car park if he had to. Anything to be alone.

Standing in the motel phone box, coins hot in his palm, he stared at the coaster, little numbers dancing like eye motes in the glare. Could be anything, race numbers, birthdays, the magic digits from ten years' worth of losing Lotto entries. Charlie had his wires crossed. Charlie in his cups. Yet Mick reckoned he'd started on all this before he'd even touched a beer. Then again, Ray only had Mick's word for that. Charlie might have gone off the deep end with cheap port before he even got to the pub.

Get it straight. No harm in that. He tried to remember the number of Charlie's boarding house and failed. There was a phone book but it was local and it was a Yellow Pages and of course some joker had ripped half the pages out.

He'd put a coin in and dialled directories before remembering you didn't need a coin for that. Too late, bloody thing wouldn't give it back. As he hit the coin return, a mechanical voice asked for a name and his mind went blank. He realised he didn't know Charlie's last name and even if he did the old man wouldn't be listed. No phone of his own, no fixed address. The dosshouse was attached to some church or other but he must have got the saint's name wrong, because the voice said no such listing. No point in any case. No one ever answered the phone in the hallway there. Wasn't that sort of place.

He could try the pub, see if Barb knew anything. But then he checked his watch and saw it was after five o clock. They'd be well into happy hour by now. He imagined the phone ringing in

Pete's office, everyone in bar or bistro, the sound stifled by the tinny carnival of the pokies and the footy on TV. And even if Barb did hear it ring, it would probably be too much trouble to haul herself off a stool.

The voice was insistent now, repeating its electronic question. He found himself asking for J. and A. McCullough, Twenty Bends Road. That was how they were always listed, on official bills. No idea whether they were still there of course. They could have sold up and moved to town, to a retirement village, for all he knew. Although he couldn't see it, Mam and Dad drinking sherry on a balcony, doing the crossword, taking sunset hobbles by a fake lake. And anyway, if they were still there, at home, he didn't need to ask for the number, did he? It was engraved on his brain.

How many times over the last thirty-odd years had he stood in a phone box just like this, on some servo forecourt, on the sun-blasted main street of some one-horse, one-silo town, coin in hand, receiver raised yet unable to dial? An old fear, this one, deeply grooved. And if he did manage to push the buttons, each digit clicking over like a step toward a cliff, how many times had he hung up at the first ring, afraid of hearing that voice on the end of the line? Leaving him with the hollow roar of his own blood, against a silence dense as antimatter. Fragile as the bones of a young skull.

No listing for that address. His hand was shaking. He cupped the receiver between ear and shoulder, lit a cigarette.

Could ask for U. McCullough. But where? She wouldn't still be in town. She'd wanted to get far away from sheep and tractors as soon as she could. Probably to the city, like she'd always wanted, or maybe even to Europe. She could be driving one of those little white sports cars like the ones in those old movies she used to like, scarf round her hair, cat's eye sunglasses, the whole thing in Saturday afternoon black and white. Or the nuns might have got to her, their patient seeds of guilt and shame taking root in the hot air of somewhere wretched and far-flung. Africa. That's where the starving children on the side of the Project Compassion box were from. Those stylish skirts of his sister's could be covered in stray bits of leper for all he knew.

He'd waited so long, the plastic voice had given up. Disconnected. Coin wouldn't come back, no matter how many times he hit return. The old anger thundered through, pure as oxygen, a sheer relief. He bashed the receiver on the shelf, once, twice, three times, until the handset cracked and he saw the old biddy at reception staring at him above the rabbit ears of her little TV.

He burred the wheel of the lighter round and round, letting it burn his finger. Bring him back to himself, such as he was.

With his last coin, he dialled the homestead. Freda might know. She might have seen Charlie in town, might have talked to Barb at the pub. The thought of Freda calmed him somehow. Solid, square, reliable Freda with her seamed face and strange buried passions, her boiled-looking hands. She had her own secrets, Freda, deep as old splinters. Freda would know what to do.

He listened to the phone ring, echoing along the dark tongue and groove hallway, the walls lined with pictures of Sam's heavy-whiskered forebears, the sideboards heaving with their elaborate silverware and pewter, all the squattocracy heritage Sam was fast squandering through bad management, bad stock, overgrazing, get-rich-quick schemes. All the stuff Freda had inherited and which she had to shoulder, polish and tend. Drowning, like Ray, under the useless weight of the past.

He let the phone ring five, seven, nine times, long enough for her to stop hanging washing or weeding the garden. To stand up, hand to back, cursing her lazy children and the distance to the phone. He imagined the screen door slapping, its lonely echo as she ambled blue-veined up the hall. At just the moment she might conceivably answer, he hung up. Couldn't have told you why.

⌒

After the glare of the phone box, the street felt almost cool. He stood in the car park, blood humming. Couldn't go back to the room, not yet. Didn't trust himself inside those four walls, not with this blackness grinding itself to red. Like so many times before, he fell into the rhythm of doing things just to keep a grip.

Fetching the kero can and the funnel from the ute, he untied the dog, looped the rope around its neck, let it drag him up the street. He'd never bothered with a collar for it. Wasn't even really his dog, he'd just rescued it from an unwanted litter Sam was going to sell or drown. For now though, he'd pretend. Be an ordinary man taking his dog for a walk.

Stopping at the servo, he filled the jerry can with petrol. At the newsagent he bought a phone charger. At the chemist, some salts for Mick, some Panadol for himself. When the lass behind the counter asked him how he was, he kept his eyes fixed on the glucose lollies. Old habits, rising fast, whorling deep. At times like these he was unrecognisable, even to himself.

The supermarket next, just as they were about to close. Bread, butter, dog food, Vegemite. He had tea and coffee in the ute and there was a kettle in the room. No toaster, but there was a gas BBQ out near the pool. Fucked if he was going to pay for a continental breakfast. What was continental about stale cornflakes and cold toast?

He'd passed the pub twice now. Third time the charm. Before he could think too much about it, he ducked inside, dog and all. The man behind the counter started to arc up until he saw the look on Ray's face. Lucky he couldn't carry any more than a sixpack, what with the petrol can and the groceries and the dog lunging at every municipal tree. He considered stepping on its paw, teaching it some manners. Shouldn't have bought the beer. Even the thought of it, the cold chink chink against his thigh, was loosening action from consequence, the tide in his blood swelling fast. The street ahead with its last-minute shoppers and languid cars and pointless chats between men in hats, everything pulsed in a sea of red.

While the boy slept through dinner and the sun set in a fever of pink and orange, he drank his beer by the pool. It was empty except for a puddle of red water at one end. The dog writhed between his legs, gulping its Pal. Wasn't supposed to have it there of course. Signs all over the place. No pets, no smoking, no running, no diving, no eating, no glass bottles. Can't do this and mustn't do that. He was waiting, just waiting, for that old boiler with the curlers to come out and have a go. He needed a target, something better than the deflated plastic sea monster he was lobbing his empties at. He was afraid of hurting the boy.

He stayed out there most of the night, even though he had change in his pocket now and his phone was charged and Freda would be in the house for sure, folding clothes or helping with homework while she cooked dinner, some burnt offering which Sam would refuse to eat. Awful cook Freda, everything either muddy with Gravox or riddled with uncooked flour. All that meat Sam kept killing, day after day, just so she could grill or boil or bake it to within an inch of its former life.

He turned his back on the phone box, that little oasis of light. Fixed himself out toward the highway, where brightly lit semis were travelling, out to places he might have been. Then he turned his back on that as well, lay down on a banana lounge, shutting his eyes against the unblinking yellow gaze of the dog. Kept drinking, until all the beer was gone and he was on to the brandy in his first aid kit. He drank until the stars wheeled toward their last trajectories, his blood cooling and hardening in the watery light of dawn.

When he finally went inside, he found the boy sleeping peacefully, sprawled across the double bed. Ray collapsed on the single. When the dog stopped clawing his chest, it at least went to sleep.

CHAPTER EIGHT

They walked through three carriages before Tilda found the right seats. Something about windows and easterly directions. More of Harry's feng shui nonsense, no doubt. Ursula bit her tongue, kept on plodding. It was important Tilda stayed calm, at least until the train pulled out.

Once Tilda had chosen two seats bearing no relation to their tickets, when she'd settled herself into a nest of coats and sandwiches, had popped her can of Coke and opened her copy of *New Idea*, Ursula told her she was going to the toilet. Wouldn't be long.

'But you can't, not when the train's stopped. That's the rule.'

'There's a ladies on the platform. Plenty of time.' Five minutes by the station clock. Fortunately Tilda wasn't really paying attention, was already deep in knitting patterns and pudding recipes, as if in vital research for some other life she still planned to have.

'Have you got your ticket? The man might come while I'm gone.'

She had to wait then while Tilda rummaged through her carry bags, unearthing ancient shopping catalogues, more sandwiches, a pile of scarves, two blackened bananas. A vast bra which Ursula blushed to see thrown on the back of the seat.

'You wanted to carry it, remember? Look in your coat.'

When the ticket was found and then stuffed back into one of Tilda's many pockets, never to be seen again, Ursula hurried as fast she could toward the sliding doors. But as she got there, Tilda yelled out, startling the old lady across the aisle.

'Urs! Get some more chippies. Not those skinny ones. The normal sort.'

Ursula had tried to explain that there'd be plenty of food on the train. That there'd be a little cafe or a little buffet or someone with a little trolley. For such a big woman, Tilda was a fan of little things. With as much enthusiasm as she could muster, Ursula had promised lunch in some dining car she wasn't sure existed, at a little table with a little red lantern on it, watching for emu while they ate the much longed for fish and chips. But the thought of being caught without food or drink had filled Tilda with such nervous aggression that Ursula had bought enough plastic-covered sandwiches and tubs of coleslaw to last them across the Nullarbor, let alone the eight hours to Sydney and the cafe near the taxi stand.

As she hurried out the station exit and down the street, she told herself it would be all right. Tilda had her ticket, if she could ever find it again. There was fifty dollars in her wallet and Ursula had pinned the wallet to the lining of Tilda's coat. They'd make her get off this train at Central because it terminated. It was the time in between she worried about. All those lonely, weedy platforms they'd passed on the way in, marking tiny dusty towns with long and melodious names. What if Tilda took a liking to one of them, decided to get off? Found herself stranded in the middle of nowhere as the sun went down?

And there was always the rightful owner of Tilda's seat. There might be a scene. Worse still was what might happen when the sandwiches ran out. She saw Tilda leaning across, helping herself to the old lady's lunch. Tilda stealing wine dregs from the buffet car. Tilda running through carriages, awash with alcohol and chemical tears. Tilda taking all her clothes off, forcing the train doors open. Tumbling, vast, pink and victorious, into chilly country air.

And even if she did manage to last all the way to Sydney, would she be able to navigate all those tunnels and escalators leading from the country platform to where the buses came in? If she got lost, Ursula was banking on another kiosk. Tilda couldn't walk past a shop without wanting to buy something. She'd go looking for her wallet and find inside it, next to the fifty dollars, the note Ursula had left her, detailing directions to the bus stop, numbers of buses, the location of payphones in case of emergencies, Harry's mobile number, the pot plant hiding spot of the spare house key, contact numbers for two cab companies in case of a transport strike. Also, a letter addressed to Harry explaining, however disingenuously, what Ursula intended to do. Tilda would open it. She could never resist a letter not addressed to her.

If all else failed, Ursula comforted herself with Tilda's habit of talking to complete strangers on public transport. If she somehow lost both her ticket and her wallet, surely someone would help, as soon as they realised who they were dealing with, this middle-aged woman with flecks of ham sandwich between her teeth. As long as the person wasn't bad or mad themselves. As long as Tilda didn't start going on about God on the radio, didn't get out Dad's old transistor, start trying to tune him in. As long as there were no men on the train who fitted in with God's increasingly vicious predictions and the pill Ursula had given her this morning lasted all the way home.

By the time she'd figured out the remote locking on the rental car, shattering the quiet of the country street with a series of squawks and alarms, she'd convinced herself it was the only thing she could have done. She wouldn't have been able to cope with Tilda, not on top of everything else. And Tilda would never have understood.

By the time they'd woken up this morning, Tilda had had her own version of events. Didn't matter that it was the exact opposite of what she'd believed the night before. As far as she was concerned, Ray was dead, and might as well have been already buried, with no flowers and little ceremony, in this stark red ground. All she could talk about at breakfast was getting back to the city in time to see some BBC drama she'd been watching on TV. And then she'd been so excited by the renting of the shiny little Toyota that she'd forgotten why they were driving to the hospital in the first place. Hadn't even asked Ursula what she'd seen behind those green rubber doors.

The bantam had been on duty again. She'd handed Ursula another plastic bag. Inside it, things they'd found in his trouser pockets. No apology that these had been mysteriously mislaid the day before. A diver's watch, expensive looking. Didn't go with the cheap coat or the worn-out boots. The missing money from the wallet, ten dollars and some change. More grimy TAB receipts, a Ventolin inhaler. A wedding ring, the gold band frail as sucked barley sugar. A set of rosary beads which slithered, chilly and familiar, through Ursula's hands. But when Ursula had gone to take them, the nurse had grabbed the bag back again. More questions, more forms to sign. Ursula had fought an urge to stick her own palm out, collect the gum with which the nurse was smacking the end of each dreary vowel.

Then the doctor who would sign the death certificate had appeared. Plump, officious, he had one of those little hair verandahs gelled into the front of his head. He'd said he was sorry for the long wait and for her loss, although he didn't appear to be. Like the nurse, he didn't really look at her, seemed more interested in his sheaf of notes. If she could just confirm some details. Wouldn't take long.

'You're Mr McCullough's sister, is that right? Mrs McCullough?' Ms, she corrected him. 'On these Medicare records you're listed as next of kin. But his details were out of date. We had quite a job tracking you down.'

He paused, biro hovering. What did he want, a round of applause?

'There are a few things we'd like to check. Circumstances suggest a chronic heart condition. I presume you know your brother had a pacemaker installed?'

So young for heart trouble. Her own kept thumping, reliably, painfully, against her ribs.

'Problem is we've had trouble finding any record of the operation or of any ongoing treatment. Your brother's last visit to a medical practitioner appears to have been in Queensland, over fifteen years ago. Not for his heart. For a broken arm. He'd also had all his teeth out, quite recently. He seems a little young for that.'

She thought of baby teeth, rattling in a palm. Of a small boy's white teeth, with a big gap in the front, just like hers. Of a small heart, light and fast as a bird's, beating against hers.

'Would you happen to know the details of any of his health professionals? His GP? Even his dentist would do.'

She shook her head. Refusing to open her mouth, reveal her own crumbling remnants. To say, this and this. This is the least of the things I didn't know.

She stood for what seemed like hours in that corridor, jostled by trolleys and drip-fed patients, straining to hear what the doctor was saying over the yakking of nurses, the shrieking of phones. Like so many young people, the man seemed to swallow his sentences, and she was forced to keep saying, excuse me, can you repeat that, like some old dame with an ear trumpet. How serious was her brother's asthma? Was he a smoker? She nodded, thinking about the rollies in the shoe. What about drinking? Not to her knowledge. She blushed, remembering the stink of port in that room above the pub. His jaundice suggested otherwise. The little hair verandah waggled side to side.

'The thing is, Mrs McCullough, your brother appears much older than his records would suggest.' He was speaking very slowly and loudly now, as if she was stupid as well as deaf. 'That's not unusual, though, if he was sleeping rough. Was he indigent, do you know?'

'Indigenous?'

'Indigent. Homeless.'

'Thank you. I do know what it means.'

At one point she tried to push past him but he put an arm out, as if herding geese. They weren't ready yet, because of the bus accident. She hoped it wasn't a school bus. That it was a small white bus favoured by drunk footballers. That there were no small broken bodies beyond the green rubber doors.

'Just one more thing, for our records. Would you know your brother's most recent permanent address?'

She'd been forced finally to admit that she hadn't seen Ray in over twenty years. The doctor frowned and scribbled, and she'd drawn herself up, summoning the authority of those old women who used to rule her, as if a rosary rested against her own sternum, a large wooden cross hooked like an extra pelvis around her waist. Tapped the clipboard until he was forced to look her in the eye.

'I won't know anything for sure until I see him. And I'd like to do that now. My sister's waiting. She's not well.'

By the time she got in there, she was almost expecting it. After the Bible and the teeth and the newspapers, the fancy diver's watch and the rosary beads, she was so caught between clashing versions of the man on the trolley, each one leaching steadily at her memory of the boy, she felt doubled also. One version of her stood in the small green room, looking at a too-small body covered by a sheet. The other floated somewhere up near the fluorescents, for some reason bearing the John Lennon glasses and craggy nose of Sister Ignatius, the steeliest of the convent nuns. Ignatius had taught physics and sewing with equal rigour. Abided no sloppy science, no crooked hems. Ursula remembered Sister lighting a match with her dry, nunnish fingers, levitating a floating lemon slice within an upturned glass. Observe Ursula. What can you infer?

Had it been another nun, Ursula would have said a miracle and earned a holy card. But it was truth or nothing with Ignatius. Truth, or Sister's fist grinding into the tender part of your spine.

'Take the sheet off please.'

'Oh. Right. I'm not sure. The paramedics . . .'

'There should be a scar. If you want me to be sure.'

She found if she looked in quick snatches, like amputated, oddly angled photographs, she could just about manage not to faint. Rabbity thighs, suffering Jesus ribs. Chest hair like something sprouted in a cellar. Purplish feet, small as the boots. A sad little pot belly, pale as a fish. She remembered a boy fresh from the river, sleek as a seal. This flesh had rarely seen the sun. The body had been washed of course but she believed here and there she could see the shadow of ancient dirt.

'Mrs McCullough? Should I get a chair?'

'Not unless you need one.' Stand up straight, Ursula. Pay attention. What's the difference between what you see and what you know?

She forced herself, against fear and disgust, to take her time. Tiny hands, chalky nails, telltale blush on the palms. She knew what that meant, having done voluntary work in an old man's hospice, long ago. Couldn't touch those hands, didn't want to, but knew if she did, they'd be soft as a girl's. She noted too, the weedy arm muscles which had never wielded axe or hammer, the mole on the left shoulder. The absence of a scar on the stomach, near the thigh and across the hip, that long flare of skin stitched up by Dad with a darning needle soused in brandy and heated on the stove. Instead, a strange brown splotch on the right collarbone. A trail of splats, like dried gravy. Maybe just dirt.

Across the breastbone and rib cage, big bruises, in the shape of paddles or powerful hands. Somewhere beneath that skin, a faithless nest of wires. She imagined it as red, plastic, heart shaped. A child's toy, in need of batteries or winding up.

No matter how hard she tried, she couldn't bring herself to look at the middle of things, as if the groin bore one of those criminal blackout squares. Couldn't bear the idea of the sad wrinkled greyish objects she might see. Anyway, the last time she'd seen Ray unclothed was in the bath at the age of ten. Always a secretive little boy.

'Mrs McCullough?'

Finally she forced herself to look at the face.

'Is this your brother?'

And because he wanted her to say yes and because he was a man in authority all strung about with ballpoints and name tags and stethoscopes, and such was the old habit of obedience, as if she was kneeling beside someone in stiff carapace stinking of incense and tobacco, asking her to swear to mysteries beyond her own brain and eyes, she almost started to nod. The bulbous nose, the pinched little jockey face, the undershot jaw. Cheeks scrawled with plum-coloured capillaries, skin cured to leather by wind and rum. No forehead to speak of, eyes too close together. Didn't they realise how beautiful Ray had been?

'No.'

'Take your time. You said it had been a while.'

She turned away. The room swung back to its correct angle. Became just a dingy space with a dead stranger in it. She buttoned her coat.

'I told you. It's not him. However, I would like to know how he came to possess Ray's things.'

She was using her teacher's voice, her nun's voice, but it was just habit. Didn't mean it, didn't really read the forms they handed to her to sign, all the new bits of paper she'd somehow generated, attesting to this or certifying that. The body sliced free again, even from what little had held it, to that room above the pub.

Tilda had been right, for the wrong reasons. Now the police would have to be called. Back at reception, the doctor told her they would want to talk to her and any personal effects she'd found in the room must be handed over straight away. She heard herself promising to make herself available, to deliver to reception, as soon as possible, the things in the crate, now stowed in the boot of her car. First, however, she had to check on her sister, who needed to take her medication and because of this they had to get something to eat, from the cafeteria. After that, she'd be back. Within the hour, if required.

She'd felt guilty of course, as she'd tugged Tilda down the nearest fire exit and hurried her past the foyer gift shop, ignoring Tilda's fervent desire for a pink and silver 'It's a Girl!' balloon. Breaking speed limits, she'd driven straight to the station, Ray's crate rattling forlornly in the boot. While Tilda bought supplies at the kiosk, she'd written the letter to Harry. Lying again. At some point, in some clear, untangled future she couldn't yet imagine, it would have to stop.

Driving out now toward the highway, she promised herself that as soon as she could she would sort out, to the best of her knowledge, what was Ray's and what had belonged to that poor man on the trolley. Whatever she didn't have a right to she'd post back to the hospital. Nothing else for it. She'd wasted nearly two days already and she couldn't bear the idea of another night in that mice-infested pub. If the police were involved, she'd have to prove somehow that she had a right to those things in the crate. And she had no proof, just the Medicare card, a library book which may or may not bear Ray's handwriting. Tilda's teeth.

How on earth would she go about explaining those? She saw hours and days of it, waiting around in long green corridors, all those questions without answers, opening back and back. Her mouth closing and closing on things she wouldn't tell, couldn't say, didn't know.

She fixed her mind on those things in the boot. Something connected them, fragile as a fossil in a rock. Even those bits and pieces that didn't belong to Ray might have something to tell her. But any inkling she had would disappear under the harsh gaze of waiting rooms and hospital lights.

She'd been stupid last night. Too tired, too sentimental. So lost in empty pockets and secret codes she hadn't seen what was staring her in the face. The drycleaning docket, the library stamp on the book of poems. Both from Bourke. Ray's name on that Medicare card. The first sign she'd had of him since he'd left home over thirty years ago. Not much to go on. A coat, a name, some teeth. A feeling. Faith, maybe, after all this time.

Have faith, Harry was always saying. But in what? Faith itself? Faith was sly. Faith was blind. In turn, it blinded you, with spells and beads and bits of marble. You might as well hug a statue and expect it to hug you back. And while you were staring at your shoes, giving thanks for having feet, you could be run over by a bus.

She swerved to the gutter, earning a blast from the semi behind. Did what she'd been dreading all morning. Rummaging through the glove box for the new mobile Harry had insisted on buying her after her old one had been stolen by Tilda and thrown from the window of a bus, she dialled the only number in it. Harry had programmed himself in.

It rang so long she began to hope she could just leave a message. When he did pick up, it sounded like he was standing in the rain.

'Harry Fredericks speaking.'

He always answered the phone like that, as if he was already running the natural therapies clinic he was always just about to set up.

'Hi. It's me.'

'Sorry? Who's that?'

She wound the window up.

'It's me, Ursula. What's that noise?'

It sounded like he was sitting under a waterfall. Maybe he was on one of his meditation retreats.

'Oh, thank God. Where are you? Are you all right?'

'Yes. Why wouldn't I be?'

'Well, your note . . . is Tilda with you? Is she OK?'

'She's fine. I can't hear you though. Is there something wrong with your phone?'

'Sorry. I was just about to get in the shower. Give me a moment. Don't hang up.'

She waited, listening to traffic rumble and her shower drip. Imagining Harry in her bathroom, one of her pink towels wrapped around his waist. Or worse, no towel at all. She was always coming home to a glimpse of his defeated buttocks through the bathroom steam. He always seemed to forget to shut the door. Because she and Tilda weren't there, he'd have his clothes laid out in her lounge room so he could get dressed by the heater. He was always complaining about the cold in his room. One of his vintage suits probably, it being his day for band practice, maybe the one with the pinstripes, and that bilious ruffled shirt he liked, something a real estate agent might have worn to a wedding in the seventies. Salmon pink, rosy and bulbous as Harry himself.

Teamed with socks, sandals and not quite enough irony. She blamed the Marist Brothers herself.

'Hello? I'm back. I'm here. Ursula, what on earth's going on? I've been so worried. I tried ringing, but your phone was off.' She saw them now, six missed calls. She'd had the phone buried at the bottom of her bag. 'Actually, someone did ring here last night, on the home line. But you know I don't answer that any more. Was it you? There was no message. Sometimes the message bank plays up.'

There was no earthly reason she should have rung him, no reason she should feel guilty, but this was Harry's special talent, this vague, oily reproachfulness. It seemed to seep through the phone, covering her in irritable sweat.

'No. I didn't ring. Listen Harry, I'm driving, so I can't talk long. I need a favour.'

'Driving? I thought you caught the train.'

'I did. And now I'm driving. I hired a car. Are you home tonight?'

'We could have taken mine. I could have driven. I did offer, remember?'

He had. The very thought of it. Harry beside her, all the way there, all the way back. Harry driving at his regulation ten ks below the speed limit, treating her to long disquisitions on Aboriginal place names or the evil of GM crops. Harry grilling the pub landlord on the provenance of his frozen vegetables and his white sliced bread. The thought made her wind the window down again, fumble around in her handbag for the dead man's last rollie, start peeling off the No Smoking sign on the dash.

'Anyway, you're coming home now, aren't you? How's your dad, by the way?'

'Sorry?' Then she remembered the note she'd left. 'Oh. Yes. He's fine.'

A long, priest-like pause. 'It wasn't your dad, was it? It was that other business all along.'

She had the rollie in her mouth, the book of matches at the ready, before remembering those tan-coloured teeth, the little blue lips. She spat the cigarette out, threw it out the window, into the slipstream of a passing truck.

Harry sighed.

'I knew it. All those phone calls. You know, you really can't keep doing this Ursula. It's not good for Tilda. She's getting worse. She needs some proper therapy.'

Ursula stuck her whole head out the window. Got a face full of truck fumes so she pulled it back in.

'I wish to God you'd never put that notice in the paper. Offering money, that's just madness. I did warn you, didn't I? Many times.'

So many times, she'd wanted to bash her head against her bedroom wall.

'It was a hospital who rang, Harry. Nothing to do with the paper. They weren't after money. They asked me to come. I could hardly say no.'

'I really can't believe this is still going on. Now we'll have to change our number again.'

Our number. Her phone. She should ask him to move out. Should never have invited him to move in in the first place.

But when he'd appeared at her front door one afternoon, having seen the notice for a lodger she'd put up on a telephone pole, taken one of the little scraps of paper and rung her, telling her he was a quiet, mature man looking for a quiet place to live, he'd seemed a solution of sorts. To her lack of money. To Tilda. With all his courses and therapy and phone counselling, he'd appeared unfazed when she explained about Tilda. And with all his night sessions and volunteering, he'd be at home during the day, could keep an eye on Tilda when Ursula was at work. And with all those jobs, she'd thought he'd be out when she was in. She hadn't banked on a bunch of alcos and ex-addicts and mad people collecting like flotsam in her lounge room every weekend. People like Tilda really, but worse, because they kept finding God behind her sofa cushions. A stink of incense and chemical delusion greeting her at the front door every Friday afternoon.

'So what happened this time? Another dead end I suppose.'

'No. Not really. Listen, I don't have time to explain. Why I rang. I'm going away for a bit. I've put Tilda on the train, so she can make her next appointment. I was hoping you could pick her up.'

Another pause, a stunned one this time.

'On her own? Really? Was that wise?'

'Probably not. She gets to Central around eight. I told her to wait where all the buses come in.'

'But I've got that course tomorrow. I told you. I'll be away.'

'Well, if you can't do it, just ring the clinic, get them to send someone. I can pay. Use the cash in my bedroom drawer.'

'But where are you going?'

'Tilda's got a letter in her coat. It explains everything. And if she causes any more trouble, just take her to the doctor early. She needs a new prescription, not more therapy.'

She started up the car, turned the blinker on. 'Thanks Harry. I've got to go.'

'Wait though. When are you going to be back?'

'Not sure. I'll ring again.' She turned the phone off while he was still talking, threw it in the glove box. Pulled into the stream of traffic, heading west.

CHAPTER NINE

It got easier once she'd left the town where the man who wasn't Ray had died. As if the place had a rubber band attached, the fraying knot of a stranger's days and habits, singing with electricity. Just the hum of new tyres on potholed road.

Only when she'd passed the last pub and street sign and hit real country, cotton, cotton, wheat, more cotton, did she feel free. Not happy but on her own.

Stopping for coffee and petrol in the town where two of the TAB slips had come from and where that old Lotto ticket had been bought, she found the pub and garage open, the newsagent closed down. Couldn't face the pub, the dusty beery gloom of it and, anyway, what would she say? Whether a man short or tall, blond or greying, nearly old or almost young, had once placed a bet there, two months ago?

At the service station, a soupy love song was in full cry over the outside speakers. Near the bowser, a fat Labrador that someone had once pampered, mournful now, a weeping sore on its head.

She turned her back on it, trying to block the music out, trying to find the catch for the petrol cap. Everything sealed in plastic in these brand-new cars. She didn't know how to check the oil or water either, or even if you had to. Hadn't driven a car in years.

A man at the next pump watched her fumble for a while. Then he walked over, took his hat off, bent down, worked some invisible lever until the petrol cap popped up. Put his hat back on, walked back to his truck. Didn't say anything, didn't look at her. As if he'd been waiting there just to perform that small service. As if even he, a stranger, knew she was somehow less than a real person, having left, in this latest of so many leave takings, some vital part of herself behind.

Going inside to pay, she saw, in the sliding glass doors, what he must have seen. A woman shorn of ballast, features. A tall, nun-like woman in a bunchy black coat. Standing there, a banana in one hand, a box of Milk Tray in the other, she urged herself to hurry, to choose something healthy after all the stodge and whiskey of the last few days. But perversely, now she was on the brink of it, she felt capable of no momentum at all. People moved around and behind and through her reflection, carrying loaves of bread and tins of cat food, jangling their keys. People with somewhere and someone to be.

So are you, Ursula. So are you. She forced herself to join the queue at the till.

She should be good at this, having done it so many times. She'd seen her escaping self clearly since she was fifteen years old. In her mind's eye, with the ruthless clarity of childhood, she'd been a girl in crisp relief moving through a self-effacing landscape, teachers, boyfriends, angry fathers, mad sisters, even the rambling brutal landscape of childhood, everything diminished by an unerring aim and determined velocity, scattering neatly out of her way. In turn, she'd believed she would become a woman bound by no compass, with no fixed destination, no organising thread.

Real life was more complicated. You trailed it behind you, leaking things you couldn't afford to lose. At fifteen, she'd thought she was taking everything that mattered, all those evening dresses and race-day outfits copied from the pages of waiting-room magazines. Thought that the angle of a hat or the fit of a jacket was somehow more important than what she was leaving behind or the spotty youth she was running toward. Where on earth she'd thought she was going in all that Melbourne Cup finery, God only knew.

In the end, that first escape had imprisoned her, for years and years. With shame, with lack of money. With silence and lies.

At twenty-nine, the skin of things had seemed less important than shedding those layers of silence that had accumulated during those last years at home. Mam sick for the first time; Dad in a rage, at drought, debt, a world that wouldn't, despite all his fury, bend to his will. Tilda beginning her long slide to incoherence. Ray gone, the fatal hole at the centre of things. All that silence, festering in hot curtains and dark rooms and beneath the steep angles of roof and verandah, summoned, creeping out, seeping in. Threatening to make her soft and insubstantial as Mam, a thing which Dad could batter himself against. By then all she'd needed was a clean space, a way to look bare-faced at some gaping absence in herself. Clothes didn't matter at all, as long as they didn't lie or constrict.

She'd left home a week after Ray took off. Took off was how Dad put it, consigning Ray to another footnote in the family history, one of the lost McCullough boys. All those fourteen, fifteen or sixteen year olds beguiled by shearing or circuses or boxing tents, who'd strode off into some version of Dad's heroic distance, never to be seen again. Never disappearing entirely. Lingering, at dusk, in the faltering space between stories, gates and margins, invoking a sort of greedy dread in those left behind.

Ursula was too angry, too frightened by then to be fobbed off with another of Dad's tall tales. When pressed, he admitted there'd been an argument, down by the creek. Which was how Tilda had been knocked unconscious, lost most of her teeth. Ray's fault of course. Dad's voice getting louder as he told it, the story growing colour, filling in its own blanks. Ray had stolen money, the pay Dad got for working on the roads. Working his fingers to the bone. But why would Ray steal money? He never had before. And what would he spend it on, seeing he didn't drink or gamble, and he didn't care about bikes or clothes or cars, only books and horses, and he had a horse, she'd bought him one. And there wasn't a bookstore in town and he could get any book he wanted at the library. And what about school? His exams.

Gone shearing probably, Dad told her, as if it was an explanation. Or fencing, or fruit picking, depending on which time of day Ursula asked. Then he was doing a bit of work with a mate of a mate, on a property out west. But where and how did he get there and for how long? And without saying goodbye?

Dad went back to chopping wood, although it was Christmas and nudging a hundred in the old currency. He'd be back, Dad reckoned, when he'd sorted himself out. Be the making of him. The making of what exactly? A man like you? Axe raised, face purple, Dad turned but she stood her ground. When he lowered the axe, deep into the heart of a log, she walked off, through thick, unbearable silence, toward the house. As if a boy of fifteen, in the space of a single afternoon, could decide to become a man.

In Ray's room, she sat on the bed, looking at his open cupboard. His winter coat still hanging in there, his good pair of trousers folded on the chair. His knapsack and work boots were missing, along with his blue heeler puppy, his poetry book and all the housekeeping money from the pantry tin. A hollow in his pillow, smelling of peppery sweat. A hollow in her heart.

Retrieving the key to the back shed from its hiding place in the flour tin, she unpacked her old suitcase, left all her fancy dresses to moulder along with the rats. While Dad raged and Mam stood in her bedroom doorway, crying, in silence, great gouts of it, as if silence was leaking out of her, etching funnels between nose and chin, Ursula packed a pair of sandals, two cardigans, three old shifts. At the last minute, she grabbed Ray's photograph off her dressing table, leaving behind the silver frame.

Then she walked off down the driveway, leaving Dad shouting on the verandah, Mam in half-shadow behind the front screen door. Didn't turn around, even when she heard the patter of feet behind her, Tilda howling as she caught her fingers in the slammed front gate. The first bend, then the second, and she saw herself disappearing into the elbow of the road. Joining the ghosts, out there on the fringe.

She walked next door, a three-hour slog. Using the bit of money she'd made from dressmaking and her job at the chemist, she bought the ancient ute Tangello had for sale in his front yard. Drove to town, first to Old Alf's shack and the footy oval and the feed barn, then to all three of Dad's favourite pubs. Men turning, hat brims shaking before she'd even finished asking. Nuh, haven't seen him, hasn't been in. Hasn't bought a drink or asked for work or thumbed a lift.

After that, she went to every property within walking distance. Bothered gruff men on tractors, knocked at screen doors where other women stood in shadow, faded and worn as Mam. No one reported stolen food or money, no signs of someone dossing in a shed. Back in town, she was told at the police station where she tried to file a report that she hadn't waited long enough, hadn't suffered enough. Not yet. Boys his age do this sort of thing all the time, she was told. He'll turn up, when he gets hungry or runs out of money. They always do. Except for those who don't. All those lost McCullough boys.

By the end of that first day, she'd given Ray's description to so many people and so many times that even to her, even then, he'd started to recede. Young, blond, tall, blue heeler puppy, scar on his thigh. In the face of so many blank faces and shaking heads, he'd already started to seem like someone she'd made up.

At dusk, at the last garage on the edge of town, she filled up the old ute with petrol, bought a map. Drew a circle on it marking towns a week's hitchhike from home. She drove that circle three, four, ten times, arriving in towns just like the one she'd just left. A wheat silo, a Royal Hotel. Peering into pubs and shop windows, trying not to think of Ray in Dad's old blue shirt, in his worn-out boots, plodding those empty roads she'd just travelled, without coat or money or even food for his dog, she talked to every housewife or farmer or schoolchild she came across, made a nuisance of herself at little weatherboard police stations and truck cafes. One fat-bellied cop watering the lawn outside his little weatherboard police station started waving when she drove by. Every second day, she'd ring to see if Ray had come home. If Mam answered, a trembling silence. If it was Dad, she just hung up.

When those first places came up blank, she drew new circles, wider and wider, until her map resembled a scribble of failed orbits, a string of black holes where Ray hadn't been. Another phone box, another pub. Another blue heeler dog. She'd followed one for an hour once, trying to see if it had a kink in its tail. Got a nipped finger in return. In sun-addled milk bars, she ordered grey hamburgers and drank an early form of cappuccino, Nescafe shaken with milk. Poring as she ate over local newspapers, until the list of people born, married, sick, dead or dying formed a knot in her throat along with dry lumps of mince.

On hot afternoons, when no one knew anything, everything was shut and she was at a loss as to where to go next or what to do, she sat clutching Ray's photograph on town park benches, in the shadow of stone memorials boasting in imperial measure of stolen land and long-dead sheep. Began to know the desolation of empty civic spaces. Their thin sandstone light.

The old ute got to her to Sydney before it died. Thinking to lose herself in a boil of people who weren't Ray, she got a job working weekends at a pub, another at a wedding outfitters, making alterations to richer people's clothes. Keeping to small detail and even stitches, returning at night to her little flat by the railway line, where she tried not to wait for the phone to ring, watch the TV news. Tried not to spend money, to save it against the day she found Ray even though she told herself she wasn't looking any more.

She'd been stupid enough to think it was over. Didn't know that like some sort of tropical fever, this would recur for years and years. That she would continue failing to see him, at cafes, in rest rooms, on beaches and trains. A boy jostling ahead of her through morning rush hour, a head taller than the crowd. A brown nape of neck, on the back seat of a disappearing bus. A boy with a lope, a hat, an earring, a blond boy dyed dark, with a sly spring to his knees. A boy sleeping rough in a King's Cross doorway, in a string T-shirt like a shopping bag, his pale flesh like unripe fruit. Too young. Too old. Not Ray.

Her answer was to run away. For a while, she changed schools and jobs like they were hairstyles, men like they were jobs. After she got her degree and did her teacher training, she lived in seven different cities in as many years. Sydney, Melbourne, then Brisbane and Perth, then three months in London, followed by six months in Europe with a teacher friend. Ray in every suntanned blond backpacker, in every homeless or lost-looking boy.

Back home, she left again, almost immediately, heading as far west as you could without falling off. In schools where there were more flies than children and where in summer the thermometer rarely fell below a hundred degrees, Ray's ghost grew younger. A gap-tooth smile, brown skin, a shock of white blond hair. In Sydney, during a brief stint of unemployment and an even briefer and more aimless love affair, she saw Ray at the cinema. Something about the ears, the earnest Adam's apple against the flicker of the screen. As he got up to leave, she climbed over the knees of the man she was with, raced up the aisle and into the foyer, only to find someone too old, too drunk. Too sad.

There were other near misses, other failed escapes. Other men. At fifty-five, she should have known better. Being such a getaway artist herself, she should have seen Simon's packed suitcase on top of the wardrobe in the spare room for what it was. But she'd believed him when he told her they were old things he was taking to the charity shop. Love made you stupid, enclosed you in some sort of warm-breathing tunnel, and at the end all you found was some blinking, blinded, junket-pale version of yourself.

Six months ago, with Mam gone and Simon gone, with Tilda so far gone she was almost out on the other side, she'd barely escaped filling her pockets with stones, leaving for good. But she didn't. Couldn't. Too much to do. The funeral arrangements. Real estate agents, solicitors, contracts, phone calls. Dad had decided to sell the property, out of the blue. She had to clean things, sell things, throw other things out. Find a rental place for Dad while the sale went through. She drove that long road home in

Simon's old Volvo, on Christmas Eve. On the way she stopped at Kmart, bought Dad some new clothes. The nurse she'd hired after Mam got sick for the last and shortest time informed her he'd let himself go. His shirt buttons all missing, his trousers covered in jam.

In the end she failed to leave, because of small things, minor irritations. Lack of pills, the impossibility of finding an open chemist, in a country town, on Christmas Eve. The town in drought, Twenty Bends Creek just a chain of muddy pools. The homestead oven electric now. In the end, because she was too stubborn, because she wasn't a coward. Because there was still a tiny bit of hope, even if she'd created it herself.

Before the funeral and the trip home, she'd gone into Harry's room, what used to be the spare room before Simon came, then the room where Simon kept his painting things and his empty suitcase and his spare clothes, then the room he retreated to when he was up late painting or didn't want to disturb her, then finally the room where he slept alone. A room once white and monk-like, smelling of turpentine and clean astringency, now littered with the arcane and the fuzzy and the nearly useless. Harry's belongings, nearly all of it second-hand. Bit like Harry himself.

Digging through the mess of ethnic doodads on Harry's desk, she unearthed his laptop, which he'd tried to rusticate with greenie stickers and a scree of joss-stick ash. She didn't own a computer. She used one of course, at work or in the library, but refused to have one in the house. Because of Tilda, she told herself, reasoning she had enough on her hands without letting her sister loose on the web. But really, because of herself. Because she was afraid that if she reopened that old black hole of longing, it might swallow her whole.

The password was easy. The Dalai Lama smiling beatifically from a poster on Harry's bedroom wall. After that, a few choice words, a few clicks and there they were. The lost and the missing, the longed-for and sought-after, still waiting, still gone, but multiplied now, a millionfold. She recognised a few, from her obsessive scouring of local papers and police reports, years ago. Men with jug ears and flamboyant sideburns and wide lapels. Girls with blue eye shadow and mushroom perms, wearing boob tubes and butterfly shorts. Young boys never to grow into raw cheekbone or jawline, their Adam's apples tender in a pale stalk of neck. Caught forever in their terrible grainy buck-toothed ordinariness, with their poignant haircuts and shark-grin braces, some missing since 1954. The glare of history and cheap photo stock bleached out freckles and identifying scars. Leaving only sadness, even that fading beneath the crisp language of the police reports.

Last seen wearing, last seen walking, last seen driving. Last heard calling from a payphone in 1975. Disappeared from school, from a bus stop, at a beach, while buying milk or cigarettes. Last dressed in a blue bikini, an orange headband. Leaving a shoe, a baby. A car abandoned beside an outback road.

Watching herself as if from above, she clicked faster and faster, going deeper and deeper, digging into scrubby forests or holes in sand dunes behind some isolated beach. The serial killer with his baker's dozen, heads and hands cut off. Young boys, their bones jumbled up with those of their pet dogs, buried in shallow graves.

And beyond that, out past the newspaper stories and official reports, like some giant dating service gone horribly wrong, the others. Those who were searching. People like her, who'd lost someone and were therefore endlessly missing from themselves. On badly designed, lurid-lettered, long-scrolling websites, they uttered their plangent, ungrammatical little cries for help. Searching for, I need to contact, need to know. I have stomach cancer, I have liver cancer. My aunt, my stepfather, his adopted son. All those random missed connections, a lost letter or a late train, imploding down the years. Her name was Rhonda, she used to work at Myer. My grandfather, a baker by trade. He liked ballroom dancing, cryptic crosswords and antique clocks. Looking for me mate, bloke called Jug, his dog called Jot. A gun shearer, nicknamed Eskimo. Last seen in Cunnamulla or Auckland, last met drinking in a pub in Gulargambone. Long grey hair, gold tooth, six foot four. A heart-shaped, a dragon-shaped, a woman-shaped tattoo.

That's why it was easy, in the end. In a world awash with loss, her private grief seemed confederate, inconsequential even. Easy to tell herself it wouldn't matter, because no one would notice, and that, at the same time, it mattered urgently, to join the chorus, leave a trace. Something more than that old picture she'd come across on one psychotic-looking web page, linking back to the archive of Ray's original missing person's report.

Male, fourteen years old. Blond hair, olive skin, three-inch scar on left thigh. Six foot tall. Last seen wearing a blue shirt and grey trousers, accompanied by a blue heeler dog, in the vicinity of Twenty Bends Road, 19 February 1972.

The photo, reproduced so many times was fuzzy, sun wrecked. Useless. Creeping in from one corner and despite all her efforts to excise them, the fingers of someone else's hand.

A few extra words in the funeral notice, one missing name. That was all it took. Adelia McCullough, wife of Jim, mother to Ursula and Matilda, grandmother to Ray. That, and a phone number and the offer of reward money for information on Ray McCullough, missing from home since 1972. Not much money but enough, all that had been left to her in Mam's will. And even as Harry told her it was a mistake and she was asking for it, as he fielded all the mumbled phone calls and she read all the badly written letters that arrived, accompanied by photos, of tall men, thin men, fat, short and bald men, men with scars and hare lips and missing digits and missing teeth, she didn't regret it.

She'd done something. Broken the silence of over thirty years.

～

She'd reached the front of the queue. The service station attendant tapped irritably on the counter. Didn't look at her as he punched numbers into the till. Perhaps she really was invisible. Was still asleep and dreaming in that room above the pub.

She had a sudden urge to turn, drive off, retrace her steps. Insert this rented car over the grease stains left by Simon's old Volvo in the garage at home. Climb inside the wardrobe where his clothes used to hang. Curl up in the familiar scent of him being gone.

Instead she bought maps along with the petrol, a whole stack of them, covering nearly every State. Unfolding their dry concertinas on the car bonnet, she found crease upon crease of familiar crisp green absence. All those places Ray might not be.

The old dog was still waiting patiently by the bowser. Following an urge to do something wild and unexpected and beyond the confines of any map, she opened the passenger door.

CHAPTER TEN

They got lost trying to find the ward. Every second corridor ended in a lace of scaffolding or a No Entry sign. Place seemed half-built. Ray begrudged every lost minute, every wrong turn. Hated these places, the cream green hush of them, that smell of organised death. When his time came, he wanted a wall of water. A bullet to the head.

In a corridor where the blue line they were following petered and then disappeared, Mick rattled to a stop. Flipping his skateboard into his arms, he tried to lounge casually in a doorway for a moment, then launched himself bodily toward the woman in the bed.

'Jesus. Look what the cat dragged in.'

'Micky? What on earth?'

In for tests was the least of it, Ray could see that now. So thin, her body barely broke the sheets.

'Love? What's wrong? Everything OK?'

In answer, Mick buried his face in his mother's chest.

'Michael. Get off her. You'll pull out the drip.'

The blonde in the chair had to be Cheryl. Sam's cousin. Same nose, same Rottweiler jaw. She was knitting, her lap full of hairy pink wool.

'Love, it's great to see you, but what are you doing here?'

'And who's this?' Cheryl snapped her gum.

Mick's mother turned to look at Ray and he saw how beautiful she might have been. Broad cheekbones, dark eyes, a mass of thick black hair. With the flesh of her cheeks fallen away, the skin mazed by weather, like a brown paper bag which had been folded and reused too many times, she looked like a rapidly ageing girl.

Mick mumbled something into his mother's neck.

'Is that right Mr . . . ? You work with Mick?'

Like he was the boy's navvy or something. Ray took his hat off, craving a cigarette.

'Ray McCullough. Yeah. That's right. I gave him a lift.'

'Really? All that way? Hope he didn't put you out.'

'That's OK. I was heading here.' First lie of the day. 'No problem, Mrs Jones.'

'It's Lily.'

She smiled, and he was so startled by the high beam of it, so embarrassed by the way Mick was snuggling into his mother's body, he had to look away.

'But listen, love. Aren't you supposed to be at work?'

Mick sniffed something about being worried, a phone call. Christmas, Ray heard. His mother was trying to prise the boy off her chest but he was stuck fast, fingers tangled in her hair.

Ray stared at his shoes, then at a vase of sickbed roses, then at Cheryl. She shot him a look of blank hostility which he returned.

'I'm fine, love. See? Really. Just a bit wobbly when I rang, from the drugs, that's all. Feel much better today. Come on. Sit up.' Mick did, reluctantly, and she stroked his forehead, smoothing away his sweaty red hair.

'You feel a bit clammy. You sick?'

Mick nodded, staring mournfully at Ray. Ray cleared his throat. He was still unsure how he'd come to be here, reporting on the boy like he was his nanny, his teacher. Mentally he was still measuring the distance to the door.

'Yeah. He was a bit crook. Earlier on.'

'The hay fever again? Are you taking your pills?'

A doleful shake of the head from Mick.

'I ran out. And Sam wouldn't let me go to town. And I'm broke.'

'Oh, stop the presses. Mum's got cancer but you caught a cold. And you had enough to buy a new skateboard I see.'

Mick shot Cheryl a look of pure hatred across the top of his mother's head. Cheryl stared back glassily, still knitting, needles strutting in and out of the bright pink wool. Ray was reminded of a crow pecking roo guts by the side of the road.

'Cheryl. I bought him that. Early Chrissie present, wasn't it? Glad it got there in time. The man in the shop said it was the best kind. For tricks and things.'

Mick, ungrateful little bugger, gave one of his all-purpose shrugs.

'Maybe we could get some knee pads for your birthday.'

'Might want to pay some bills first, Lily. There's the specialist, and I told you the electric got cut off, out home.'

Mick buried his face again in his mother's hair. So dark and thick and glossy, at first Ray had thought it was a wig. But Mick was pulling on it, kneading at it, like a baby does when suckling, and Ray was so repulsed, he had to turn his back, walk off toward the window. While Mick and Cheryl erupted into a slanging match, conducted in the low sharp tones people reserve for hospital rooms, he stood staring down at the car park. Somewhere out there, in a sea of sparkling windshields, was his ute. His dog. He would have parked in the shade, if there was any. Car park was new. No trees. Should have left the dog in the tray. He hadn't thought he'd be in here this long. Never meant to come in at all. He'd intended to post the kid at reception like a redirected letter, and he would have if there hadn't been that confusion about the name of the mother and the ward she was in and what she was in for, and if the boy hadn't looked so shocked when he heard the word oncology. If he hadn't gone so quiet.

Not quiet now though. Get fucked, you been drinking, I can smell it, sick my arse. Fuck off, you're not my mum. Don't tell me what to do. Lily pleaded with both of them, in a tired, useless little descant. Mick, don't swear. Cheryl, give the boy a break.

So hot. Sweat springing in a butterfly shape on his back. He tried the window but of course it was sealed. The air stitched tight in here, with women, sickness, perfume, dying flowers. Female smells. Maybe he was coming down with Mick's bug.

~

It had all seemed so simple this morning. Waking from his scant hour of sleep, Charlie's numbers, listened to slantwise, through the skin of eyelids, gauzy sunlight, fretful dreams, danced, reformed, fell quietly into place.

While Mick rode his skateboard up and down the motel driveway, leaving a trail of beheaded pansies in his wake, Ray drank three strong coffees in a row. The motel women waddled out from her den, curlers bristling, but Ray turned his back. He had only so much energy this morning and he wasn't wasting it on either of them.

Looking at the coaster in bright morning sun, he saw it now. Two sets of four numbers, repeating. The first four digits, phone numbers in his home town. The rest, in varying patterns of four, not anything he recognised, but repeating, scrambled, lost in a static of booze, loneliness, the numbers of races on the pub TV.

He tried every combination he could think of but the numbers didn't exist. Then he tried directories again, because he'd been out of it yesterday, not thinking straight, but there was still no listing in his home town for a J. and A. McCullough or an A. and J. McCullough or even a D. and J. McCullough, in case Mam had used Delly, the name everyone except the local priest knew her by.

Something wrong. He tried plain J. McCullough. Got a listing. Dad, if it was him. On his own. Ray felt sick. An address too, Frederick Street, out beyond the bridge, near the old tip. Heart pounding, he rang it. No answer, and so he tried again. It rang and rang, until it disconnected. Might not be him. Still, he fetched his pen, wrote the number down on his forearm. He would try again. Later on.

What now? The name of Charlie's hostel floated up as coffee and adrenalin took hold. He tried it, no answer, then rang the presbytery at the church which ran the charity which ran the hostel. A cleaning lady told him the priest was hearing confession after early mass.

Plan C. He checked his watch. Should be safe enough. Sam would be hounding contractors or feeding stock, in what passed for the cool of the day.

This time the homestead phone answered first ring. No voice, just the crackle of a bad line, then buzzing.

'Freda? It's Ray. You there?'

But instead of Freda's lady-in-a-hat telephone voice, an ominous growl. More buzzing, followed by a rattling cough.

'Who's that? Fucking thing.'

A loud thump and Ray jerked the phone away from his ear. Stupid, stupid. Sam, in a strop already, and only eight am. Ray thought about hanging up, but he'd promised himself that today wouldn't be like yesterday. That he would face what must be faced.

'Oi. Speak up. Phone's on the blink.'

Another thump, and the line cleared. Sam's voice suddenly so loud it was like his hairy bulk was squeezed beside Ray on the step of the empty pool.

'Sam. It's Ray.'

A long breath, rich with choler and phlegm.

'Oh. Is it. 'Bout bloody time. I been trying to get hold of you for days. You were supposed to be back yesterday. You done? Heading in? Better be. Got five kinds of hell breaking out round here.'

Ray didn't ask. There was always something. Sick stock, bad fences, shonky contractors, silly wives. Rising irritation, followed by slow simmering anger and a full-scale explosion. That was the normal weather of Sam's day.

'Yeah. Not really. Something came up. I'm in Bourke.'

It was on then, for young and old. Sam yelling so loudly and so continuously, Ray expected spit to fly out of the phone. Contractors useless, new shed roof still not finished and everything costing an arm and a leg. Shed pipes were rooted, hundreds of bucks on an emergency plumber, and that Pommy cook had walked off, citing no help, no water. Would you credit it? A week's worth of meat left out of the fridge to go bad. Then to top it all off that waste of space apprentice had done a runner, along with half the petty cash. All Ray's fault of course.

Ray put the phone down on the pool step while he found his smokes. Even at a distance he could hear Sam's voice buzzing through the receiver like a furious fly. Good thing it wasn't shearing time and it was only shooters and contractors going hungry. Good thing he hadn't had time to mention he wasn't coming back at all.

When he picked up again, Sam had worked himself to a crescendo over the mine boundary fence. No other bugger to finish it and what about his tools, and Ray could bloody well pay back his advance.

Ray waited for him to draw breath, descend into another lung-cracking cough. Then he reported clearly and calmly, down to the last roll of wire, the work he'd done.

'Tools are out near the old chimney.' He decided not to mention the missing gun. 'And, point of fact, mate, I reckon you owe me. A day's work, over and above. Listen, though, a few days off and we'll call it quits.' Another lie, that he was coming back at all. But right then, Sam didn't deserve the truth.

'Oh, you reckon so, do you? And what about that other section I told ya needs starting, out north? Who'll be doing that? Muggins I s'pose. I told ya, I need it done this week, got stock going in there. And that other bloke who woulda done it, well he's pissed off, hasn't he? On another job. Because I told him you'd be doing it, for double pay, if I remember right, and now what? I'll tell ya. I'm up shit creek.'

Closing his eyes against the glare from the empty pool, Ray pointed out that with travel time and at holiday rates, that other bloke would have charged triple what Ray had been paid and no way he would have done it before Christmas in any case. No one but Ray would be mad enough, at this time of year, in this kind of heat. He got a mutinous grunt in response.

'And another thing. What do I do for a cook? These gold-plated fuckers out here come all the way from Bourke. That's double time, mate, and they're here another three days. They're expecting a feed. Part of the deal.'

'Yeah. Well. Mick'll be back.' Third lie. From the corner of his eye he saw the woman from the office had managed to collar Mick mid-rampage, despite her size. She was waggling her finger and pointing to the wreckage of her flower garden. Mick was looking down at her, oblivious. His earphones still in.

It took a while for what Ray had said to dawn on Sam.

'And just how would you know? About Mick?'

'Oh. Yeah. I bumped into him, on the road, after you gave him the shove. Good thing I did. He was pretty sick. He wasn't lying about that.'

'He'll be a lot bloody sicker when I get hold of him. Little bastard tell ya he nearly blew up my shed?'

And he was off again. Ray peeled the label from one of his empty beer bottles, then stuck it back on. Imagining Sam, standing by the phone table in the homestead hallway, his bull neck mottled purple, his hands itching to punish something and, in the absence of Mick or Ray, finding one of his wife's dried flower arrangements, some spiky, dead-looking thing Freda had crafted painstakingly on the advice of some five-year-old home and garden magazine. Hours of work, crushed to dust. Another mess for Freda to sweep up.

'And I didn't give him the sack! That little shit couldn't lie straight in bed. I just told him to rack off for a bit.'

How to explain, to a man like Sam, who went at everything—food, sheep, wife, dogs—as if all the world was made of the same harsh, inhospitable substance as himself, that, for a dreamer like Mick, a few words might be all it took. That the final shove, slap or telling-off, no different to all those that had gone before, might be enough for you to find a pattern, take the world at its word. That in the face of things that wanted to beat you down, bend you over, pummel you into something as dead and blank as itself, running away might seem the best and bravest thing to do. And that once you'd started, there might seem to be no option but to keep going, keep running. That you could do it for years and years before you realised no one was behind you. No one waiting. That, without noticing, you'd somehow left the person you thought you were behind.

In the end, he just cut across Sam's tirade by shouting louder.

'Hey. Listen. Why I rang. Just to let you know I done the job and I'm heading off for a bit. I need some time off. It's Christmas. I've got family stuff. If that's no good for you, fine by me. I need a word with Freda. She around?'

'Nuh.' Sam's tone murderous, sulky. Feeling guilty no doubt, about the boy. Never admit it of course.

'Where is she?' Except for church on Sunday and the pensioner lunch, Freda was always there. Part of the landscape, like the weathered floorboards and the leaking roof.

'Mixin' martinis. Where do ya think? She's down the shed. Doing your bloody job.'

Ray's turn to feel angry now. Sam could have hired someone else when the cook walked off. Freda could have insisted. Could have put her foot down, instead of letting Sam wipe his size twelves all over her. But Freda had suffering down to an art. Had done it for so long, she'd taken on its contours, like a tree warping round a rock.

'You know if she saw Charlie yesterday? At the lunch in town?'

'That wacky old priest of yours? I dunno.'

'Or maybe he rang. Left a message. I gave him your number, for emergencies.'

'Oh. You did. Great. Just what I need. A dropkick like that ringing me up.'

Ray's temper was a bulge in his chest now, moving to his throat. He flicked his lighter on and off, bringing it close to his wrist.

'Did he ring?'

'How would I know? Not your bloody secretary. All I know is Freda got back late and my tea wasn't ready and then she was on the blower to Barb for half the night, because Barb was looking for you. But that's OK, we've got nothing better to do.'

'What did Barb want?'

'Fucked if I know, mate. You probably, back at work. Suppose you're standing them up as well? Excellent. Sterling job all round.'

Ray singed a hair off his forearm, watched it flare and curl away.

'Did Freda say anything about Charlie? About Barb seeing him at the pub?'

'Nuh. Hardly a headline, is it? Drunk spotted in pub.'

Ray moved the lighter onto his skin. The smell of burning hair. He thought of the lamb, its crisped ears and anguished eyes.

'Oi? You there?'

'Yeah.'

'Look. All I know is, Freda said Barb had a message for you. She tried your mobile but you didn't pick up, just like you didn't pick up when I rang five fucking times yesterday to find out where you was.'

'What message?' Even now he was still hoping it was all a mistake, that Charlie or Mick had got it wrong.

'Something about your mum. Thought you said your mum was dead.'

Ray imagined his fingers closing on that thick red neck, squeezing and squeezing, until the bones crumbled, dry as Freda's flowers. Bandy legs kicking, fat frog eyes popping out.

'Anything else?'

'Nuh.'

'OK. Tell Freda I rang. Tell her to ring me back.'

'Tell her yourself. And you'd better be back soon, mate, or that's us square. And bring that little bugger with you, I don't care if he's bleeding from the ears. Promised his dad I'd keep an eye. Right?'

'Right.'

'Right.'

But neither of them hung up. They just stayed there, listening to each other's white-hot breathing, as if they were chest to chest, nose to nose. That buzzing noise again, then the line went dead.

⁓

'Is that right, Mr McCullough?'

It took him a while to realise she was speaking to him. When he turned, she was smiling at him uncertainly. Those big dark eyes. He found himself trying to work out what colour they were. Not brown or green, something in between. River colour, creek colour, tannic water over rock.

'Sam gave Mick a few days off? For Christmas?'

'He did. Didn't he? Ray?

Mick looked pleadingly at Ray across the top of his mother's head. Now he was being asked to lie yet again. But it seemed a small price to pay to get himself out of here and on the road.

'Yeah, for Christmas. And because he was crook.'

'That's odd. Freda knew I'd be in here.'

Mick's mother looked done in, playing tiredly with the boy's long curls.

'Well, I don't know where he thinks he's going to stay. There's no room at my place, Lily. I got the whole lot coming to me for Christmas. With you in here, I gotta do everything this year.' With a sigh, Cheryl stuck another stick of gum in her mouth and the slap of fresh chewing was added to the clank of needles, the clatter of bangles and rings.

'I'll just stay here. With Mum. I'll sleep in a chair.'

'Can't. Against the rules.' Cheryl cast off victoriously and a tiny pink jumper arm fell into her lap.

'Then I'll stay out home.'

'Told you. The electric's off.'

'I don't care. Don't need it. I'll use a torch. Or I can go back to that motel, where Ray and me stayed last night. It's right near here. It was OK. Wasn't it, Ray?'

'Oh, right. And your mother's just made of money. Let's chuck it around.'

Mick was getting off the bed now, face vibrant as his hair. Ray watched, fascinated, as Cheryl tied a knot, broke the wool with small white teeth, then cast on again, all without taking her eyes off the boy. A thin smile on her bright orange lips.

Despite his longing to be gone, he didn't like leaving the boy to the mercies of a vulture like this.

'I'll go where I want. Fuck all to do with you.'

'Micky. Don't swear.' Lily tried to pull him back to the bed, but he shook her off, fists clenched, knuckles white.

'Listen, love, I'm really sorry about Christmas, but Cheryl's right. You can't stay out home, not without lights or a phone. How would you get back and forth? And they won't let you stay in here.'

'I'll sleep in the waiting room. They won't even notice. And you'll be coming home soon anyway. And I got money.' He fumbled in his jeans pocket, pulling out Sam's petty cash. 'Maybe they'll turn the electric on again, if I pay a bit.'

'Thought you said you were broke. Where did that come from? You on the rob again?'

'Shut up.' He turned his back on Cheryl. 'Mum? We could just go home, for Christmas, if I pay the bill. I could cook and stuff.'

'Oh, she'll be in here for a while yet. Spewed all night last night. Can't keep anything down.'

'It's just for a few days, Mick. While they sort out the dose.'

Mick started crying for real now, shoulders shaking, that toddler-like gulping again. Ray rummaged in his pockets for his keys.

'And, anyway, you've got your job. Freda told me last time you were doing really well. And if you work hard and get your reference then you can come home next year, and get a job in a restaurant, like you wanted, after you finish school . . .'

'Not going back there. It's shit.'

Ray had edged round the wall and was nearly out the door, when Lily spoke to him again and he froze.

'Mr McCullough? Sorry. Before you go. If you're heading back to Sam's and it isn't too much trouble, could you give Micky a lift? If you're heading that way. I've got some cash somewhere. I can pay something toward the petrol.' She opened the drawer of her bedside table, fumbling around, then fell back, defeated by tubes and sheets.

'Yeah. Sorry, Mrs Jones. I'm going south now. Heading home.' He'd said it as another lie, then realised it was true.

'Oh. For Christmas? That's nice.' She closed her eyes, face greenish beneath her tan.

'See? I'll have to stay here.'

'You'll do as you're told. Lily, if he was mine—'

'Well I'm not, you stupid bitch.'

'Lily? Did you hear that? If his father was here . . .'

Ray could stand no more. 'OK. Look. Easiest thing is, he comes with me. For a few days. Until you get out.'

He regretted it as soon as he said it. But they were all staring at him now and he was caught, between Mick's red face, Lily's big eyes, Cheryl's gimlet stare.

'But your family. We don't want to impose.'

'One more won't matter. My sister always cooks too much.'

Having conjured up this fake family Christmas with its groaning tables and scores of relatives and a sister cooking turkey, he was stuck. He found himself saying he'd be heading back this way anyway, on his way to Sam's, for a job he didn't have any more. That it'd be no trouble to drop Mick off at home for a visit, if that's what she wanted, before New Year.

'Really? That's very nice of you.' She fiddled with her sheets. 'If you're sure. I'll be back home by then. Do you want some money for Mick's food, or petrol . . .'

'Not to worry. Fix me up later. We better get going though. My dog's out in the car.'

Once outside, he rounded on Mick so fast, the boy dropped his skateboard in shock.

'Right. Listen up. Here's what's going to happen. First, you're gonna ring Sam, apologise for nicking money and for running off. Then you're gonna promise to pay him back, every cent. OK?' Mick nodded miserably, not meeting Ray's eye. 'Second, when I get you back to your mum, you're going to tell her you're going back to work at Sam's, after New Year. That's if he agrees. Either that or go back to school. Last thing. No more lying, no more drinking, no more nicking or smoking dope. And I'm telling you, mate, if you steal from me, there won't be any cops involved.'

Ray turned on his heel, walked toward the ute. In the glittering fish-bowl windows of the new cafeteria, he saw a tall man, striding fast and furious, a boy trailing behind. All the fizz gone out of him, like an empty balloon.

CHAPTER ELEVEN

She wasn't sure what she'd been expecting to find at the drycleaners. Certainly not herself. Not in some credulous, Harry-type way, but literally. Here in her hand.

At first she'd thought there'd be nothing at all. When she handed the docket over, the girl behind the counter just stared, as if no one had ever walked in and asked for their clothes before.

'Two items. This doesn't say what they are, although it should. They've been paid for however. In full.'

'This is old.'

The girl dropped the docket on the counter, looked bored. She had purple hair, sharp black fingernails with lightning strikes painted on them. The shop smelled powerfully of her musk deodorant and cigarettes.

'Yes, I realise that. But according to your sign, you keep unclaimed items for six months. And see? This is dated two and a half months ago.'

The girl just goggled at Ursula through her sticky-looking fringe. Even years after retirement, teenagers like this could still manage to enrage. The way they drooped and dripped through life with their pants falling off. Ursula had an urge to walk behind the counter, deliver a nunnish jab between the shoulderblades. Stand up straight, stop chewing, you're not a cow. Buy a belt, use a hairbrush. Go back to school.

'And they've been paid for. So I'd like you to check. Today, if possible.'

With a sigh, the girl slouched off. Was gone so long, Ursula decided she must be sitting out back somewhere, blowing smoke through that languid-looking fringe.

She circled her neck, tired from driving. Tired too of this caustic stranger who kept taking over her mouth. As she waited, she peered out the window, curious to see this place famous for its riots and racism, but she could see very little, having mislaid her glasses again. From what she could see, it looked like every other town she'd driven through today. Empty of people, bloated with fast food. Like her, Ray must have been passing through.

She was about to go and look in the back room herself when the girl appeared, bearing a suit in a plastic sleeve. Ursula pressed it flat, feeling greedily across the breast and hips. Nothing there.

'Was there anything left in the pockets, do you know? Things put aside?'

The girl shrugged, too dim to think Ursula might be accusing her of something.

'That's ten dollars.'

'What? It's been paid for. I told you.'

'Prices have gone up.'

Too tired to argue about the logic of this, Ursula handed the money over and walked out.

She didn't want to look at it on the street or in the car. It felt like a private thing. Buying a coffee full of froth and chocolate, she drove to a park out of town, sat in a picnic shelter out of the wind. Fed the dog half her doughnut and put some Savlon on its head. Its sore was weeping yellow stuff and it needed a bath. It occurred to her for the first time she'd have to find somewhere to stay. Most motels wouldn't allow pets.

Laying the suit out on the table, she ran her fingers over it again, but the pockets remained flat and empty as the day. The trousers were big, she could see that even without taking the cover off. Much longer in the leg than the pair in the crate. The coat was broad in the shoulder and long in the sleeve, about the same size as the cheap black one from the pub. This was better quality though. There was a faded label on the collar, advertising a men's outfitters in Sydney, long defunct.

It had been tailored, this suit, by someone special, for someone special, long ago. Good fabric, too. Good feel to it as she removed the plastic shroud. Proper heft to the tweed, generous cuffs, finely stitched buttonholes and the inside was expertly lined. Too high in the waist and flared at the calf to be fashionable, but it had a stern sort of elegance. She could imagine a grandfather wearing it to a wedding, a christening. A funeral even, it was sober enough. Soft grey with that fleck of purple, a classic pattern. Barleycorn perhaps.

Looking closer, she saw it wasn't part of the pattern, that tidemark on the lapel. It was a stain.

She felt enraged, out of all proportion. Wanted to storm back to the drycleaners and shake that girl until her nose ring fell out. Two months and two payments and they hadn't even bothered to clean it. Just left it to moulder, like the stuff in that room above the pub.

Fingers trembling, she gathered the fabric up, pressed it to her nose. Faint sweat, stale tobacco, the autumnal smell of once-damp wool. Hint of sherry or aftershave. No stink of port.

It was only four o clock but the sun was already dipping low over the oval goalposts. Grass gone silver, a chill rising from the stone bench. She'd put the coat back on the hanger and slipped the cover back on, when she remembered that other coat, the hole in the lining. Tilda's teeth.

Tearing the plastic off again, she pulled both the coat and the trousers inside out. Pored over the lining, inch by inch, until she found a sort of old-fashioned secret slit for money or fob watch, deep inside the breast pocket. And there it was, folded to a tidy square.

Turning the letter over and over in her hand, she marvelled at how round and confident her writing had been back then, considering everything else that was going on. The envelope was grubby, a tea ring disfiguring the head of the Queen. By the date on the postmark, this would have been the last in that long line of letters she'd sent to Dad after Mam died. Couldn't remember what was in this one. Not much by the feel of it, just a single page. And she still couldn't find her glasses, and it was too dim inside the shelter now anyway. Probably just some practicalities about agents and solicitors, a list of things scavenged from her clean-up at the homestead, all those stacks of ancient tractor repair and feed invoices, the yellowing paperbacks and flyblown butter covers, the remains of Mam's wedding china. Her spare dentures. Her mass-going coat, still with her cameo brooch on the lapel.

This was how she and Dad communicated after Mam died. Lists of who owned what, who owed what, who did what to whom and when but never why. Never saying what should be said, never showing the real intent. Just vicious little paper cuts, delivered back and forth, the family history rewritten in poisonous, slightly worded decrees. Both of them scavenging over what remained. Teeth and cups, rings and bones.

There'd been that one final explosion, after the funeral but before his move to the nursing home. Dad at Frederick Street, rocking, shouting, going on about the funeral notice in the paper. How dare she, dirty laundry, all out there, in black and white. The shirt off his back, his house out from under him. The teeth from her own mother's head. Selfish, greedy, useless. The words pinged harmlessly in the dark little lounge room. She'd grown some armour by then. Tough as old boots, or so she'd thought. Impenetrable as a nun.

After that, nothing. Her letters to him went unanswered. After his move to the home, he wouldn't come to the phone, even for emergencies with Tilda. According to some woman with a silly name who answered the phone at the reception, he was at lunch, or swimming, or shopping. Playing bowls. Dad couldn't swim, hated shopping and he'd never played bowls in his life.

She'd thought, right, if that's how you're going to be. She'd hauled everything she'd saved from the clean-up out of the garage, sold anything sellable, arranged for a few of the uglier but more valuable bits of furniture to be shipped back to Dad's rental place. Kept only Mam's sewing machine, her recipe books. The photographs. Then she'd sent all the remaining clothes off to Vinnies, along with those stupid old ball gowns from the back shed. No time for sentiment. Slash and burn.

After that, she'd rung the real estate. Told them not to wait for Dad's fantasy price, and not to worry about his daily calls saying he'd changed his mind, that he didn't want to sell any more. To just say yes to the first buyer who came along.

Out near Simon's shed, she'd made a bonfire. A funeral pyre. To Dad's old books, his work hats, his vast collection of belts, she'd added the family Bible, the one he'd kept asking for in his letters. She stood watching the family tree on the frontispiece curl and blacken, first Grandad's stoic copperplate, then Mam's frail cursive with its listing of wobbly old saint's names, then Ursula's own branch, dead, black, gone. Ray's name had been written there, by Mam, but unattached, out on the margins, like an immaculate conception. Dad had tried to obliterate it with a biro, rubbing so hard, he'd worn a hole in the paper. Genesis bleeding through.

Selfish, greedy, lazy. Useless. But not completely useless. She'd left Ray a clue, which in turn had become a clue for herself, disappearing and reappearing, like the alphabet she used to write for him on his little Magic Slate. Like a coded message on one of those treasure hunts she used to devise for him when he was little and she was teaching him how to read. It was a thing Dad used to play with her, when she too was small and loveable, but that seemed unlikely now. She only remembered the game, little rhyming notes hidden under mailbox or birdbath or verandah step, clues about history or science or geography, a trail of breadcrumbs leading a little boy from inland seas and perished explorers past unknown cities and famous rivers, following rumours of great books yet to be discovered, stories yet to be told. Coaxing him, step by step, from ignorance to knowledge. To herself in the kitchen, waiting with a glass of milk and a cockle biscuit. Reliable as the old wood stove.

Codes. Secrets. Pockets. She remembered the little red velvet bag, still in her own pocket. She hadn't even opened it. Inside was a jeweller's receipt, from a jewellery shop in her home town. Like the drycleaning docket, dated two months ago.

Wrapped inside the receipt, the ring itself. Small, a single diamond. So dainty, it fitted only the pinky of her own big-knuckled hands. She thought of the man on the trolley, his frail little wedding ring. But this ring was new and flawless and polished and his ring had been so worn and old. Codes, secrets. Treasure. A map, of sorts.

It would be dark in an hour or so. But the route looked straightforward, on the map at least, on decent road. She was so flushed with the letter, so buoyed up by the smooth hum of the Toyota, she broke every speed limit on the way out of town.

In her mind, a little boy, smiling up at her, a rim of milk around his mouth. Waiting patiently for her to work it out.

CHAPTER TWELVE

He left Mick with the dog in the town park. Dog was in heaven but the boy was in shock, his body sodden with it. Arm lifting, the dog trembling in anticipation, the tennis ball dribbling away. Mick hadn't asked where they were headed and Ray hadn't told him. He was only one step ahead of that underwater feeling himself.

Trick was to do, not think. He went through his usual routine when he was in a town. Post office for banking, bills, forwarded mail. Supermarket, essentials only, a surgical strike. But it was Christmas and the place was clogged with shoppers, angle parkers, herds of prams. In the post office, seeing the long queue of people, he dodged through the crush to the table of directories, collecting one from every State. At his side, a fat woman was wrapping a doll, her flesh rubbing clammily against his arm.

Perth, Brisbane, Adelaide. Urs had never really talked about going there. As a child, he remembered her pointing them out on a map but like all the other places beyond Twenty Bends to which he'd never been, they'd seemed theoretical, improbable, big black dots holding down the great swathes of space.

Melbourne. Theatre. Books. Racing week, in the *Women's Weekly*. Lots of McCulloughs there, but none with the initial U. She could be using her middle name but then she'd always claimed she didn't have one, that having a name like Ursula was quite enough. And she'd always had a thing for Melbourne—the fashion, the floaty dresses and silly race-day hats. Always reckoned she could make dresses twice as good for half the price.

As for Sydney, he wouldn't know where to start. McCulloughs everywhere, a sea of possibilities. But Urs had always wanted to see the sea. Mam and Dad had gone once, on their honeymoon, and Mam had said the Opera House looked a bit yellow. The idea had made Urs giggle. Mam up there with her sponge and Ajax, giving the sails a scrub. Dad had lots of stories, scalloped bays and slippery oysters, fine white sand and sailing boats, telling Ray about them out there on the hot verandah, in the middle of a drought. The briny smell of the harbour, jellyfish trailing the ferry wake like plastic bags. Fist-sized bridge rivets, hailstones big as grapefruit, that white pointer at Curl Curl which swam straight between a man's legs. A shark in the aquarium that spat a man's arm out, complete with watch. Old stories, borrowed stories, tall tales, urban myths, pub furphies, wild rumours gleaned from tabloid newspapers, all weaved seamlessly into the family history, spawning new and exotic forms of truth.

As a little boy sitting by Dad's knee, he'd waited for those repetitions and elaborations. Even the lies were part of the magic, a coda to the rough dry rhythm of a voice bearing waves of salt, vinegar, seaweed. Memory. Shark, rivets, jellyfish. Grapefruit hail. Beneath the dry sigh of an iron roof and the sound of Dad's voice, he could almost smell it, almost taste it. The dusty rhythm of Dad's voice swelling them both to salty tides and wave-tipped horizons, somewhere beyond the verandah eaves.

Problem was, all these things had already happened, or they'd never happened, or if they had, it was a long time before Ray came along. And if he asked about them, wanting to hear about singing whales and river dinosaurs, and if his father realised who was asking, who was listening, Dad would clam up, start folding those stories back inside himself. Sentences shed words, words shook off flesh. Silences growing longer, until all that remained was a starved line of facts. Sea, boat, sand. If you kept asking, that fist in Dad's lap, big as a bridge rivet, might come your way.

After a while, you stopped asking and he stopped telling, and it was as if he'd never been to Sydney. As if those stories and the stories you'd told yourself about those stories had never happened. And when you tried to remember, not even the words, just the feel, the old rhythm of telling and untelling, trying with a boy's poor stock of experience to embroider Dad's angry silence with blue and gold blandishments, a city by the sea, everything receded to strangled jump cut and wan sepia, like those old black and white newsreels in the cinema. Puffs of smoke rising snappily from troop trains, a man dancing like a jerky puppet, kissing a woman and doffing his hat. Until even the idea of it, I once went to Sydney, had been eaten away.

Ray shut the directory with a bang, startling the doll woman, who gave a fat person's wheezy huff. Useless. Urs could be anywhere. Could be married, or divorced, for all he knew. Women were always disappearing under a silent wake of fathers and husbands, when all you wanted was for them to stay where you'd left them. Standing on a verandah, hand cocked to a forehead. Waiting for you to come home.

⁓

In the supermarket, it was a smell that did it, like so many times before. Whiff of horse leather, rain on hot tin. Scent of a flowering plant that grew near the baths at home, what he always thought of as swimming pool bush. One sniff and he'd be lost, buried deep in some wood-smoke scented version of the past.

Turning a corner from frozen goods, it hit him. Spice, soused fruit, boiled booze. At first he thought they must be pumping it in with the music, but a woman was peddling bits of warm pudding from a tray. Cinnamon, nutmeg, the plump smell of her deodorant, and he could almost hear the cricket on the radio, smell chemical steam wafting off a raspberry jelly, Mam's face gone the same colour as she stirred and sifted, the turkey sizzling in an oven which had been on since dawn.

In an aisle where he'd intended to get bicarb and batteries, he found himself loading up on dried fruit, almonds, custard powder. A family packet of Swiss rolls. Trifle. He'd make it, if Mam was ill. Baking paper. He wondered if they sold muslin. Brown paper would do. He could help with lining the cake tins and wrapping the pudding, if he got there in time. Before the check-out, curry powder, coconut milk. He could tell Urs how to make the curry that Thai bloke had shown him once, in a logging camp long ago. Of course she'd be there, if Mam was sick. How could she not be, that brown tall sister of his, solid and cranky as the old Kooka stove. Mam would be dubious, curry at Christmas time, and Dad wouldn't eat it, but Urs would be game. She was always making things up from old mutton and tinned pineapple, conjuring spaghetti bolognaise from soft tomatoes, a pound of mince and a bottle of chemist-bought olive oil.

On the way back to the car, he spotted a table of last minute gifts outside a charity shop. Tatt, most of it, soap shaped like rosebuds, coat hangers embalmed in crochet, but in the middle, a bright red food processor, still in its box. Just the thing. He could chop the onions and turnips for pasties, Mam could mix the cake and pudding without dislocating a shoulder or having to call in Dad.

It wasn't until he had it in the ute, all wrapped up in reindeers and with a stupid bow on top, Mick asking over and over, what's that, is that a present, is that for me, that he realised it was way too late. Mam would have made the cake and pudding months ago, if she'd made them at all. If they existed, these imaginary flummeries, they would have had a dozen doses of brandy by now. The pudding would be hanging in the linen cupboard, biffing Dad on the head every time he went for a tea towel, the muslin deep brown, pebbled with fruit and coins. As for Urs, what with all those planes and hats and sports cars, she probably didn't have time to cook, if she was there at all. And if she was, if she'd never escaped the place, never got to London or Paris or

Melbourne, she'd probably married some great lump of a farmer like Sam. Become someone like Freda, so ground down by drought and sheep and children, she'd resorted to buying roast dinners at the supermarket, as a treat. Beef and gravy and spuds each in their own little compartment, just like on an aeroplane. Freda had never been on an aeroplane. The frozen aisle at Coles was as close she'd ever got.

Still, he rushed toward it, this concocted future of his, negotiating a slew of red lights and stop signs while Mick worried at the present, upending it, shaking it, picking roughly at the ribbon. Hearing the lonely rattle of cheap plastic attachments, Ray thought of the fragility of what he was offering against all those things for which he had to make amends. Desertion, years and years of silence, years of running away. When Mick dropped the present on the floor, crushing it with his boot, Ray lashed out, meaning only to cuff him on the shoulder but Mick had dived down to pick the box up again and Ray's hand connected hard with the boy's cheek. An angry mark. Mick's freckles standing out in bright relief.

They spent the rest of the day in silence. The hum of tyres, fuzz on the radio, until Ray turned it off. The sun descended, hovered behind in the rear view, was extinguished like a wick. Now and then Mick snorted back tears. Ray stared ahead, popping No-Doz, drinking thermos-tainted tea. He stopped once or twice, the kid getting out wordlessly, squatting miserably with the dog under a tree. Ray stayed where he was, engine humming, eyes on the waiting white line. Running on pure adrenalin by then.

When it grew too dark for the game of patience Mick was laying out on the glove-box lid, Mick slammed it shut, spinning the wheel of his skateboard in the dashboard glow. A dull, angry, grating sound. In the dark, Ray felt his mouth try and fail to find the shape of sorry. Before he could manage it, Mick huddled down into his hoodie, as far from Ray as he could get. Went to sleep.

Ray drove all night, dodging roos and thoughts and road trains. The dark soothed him, a long blind curve into nothing, the moon thin and yellow, keeping pace. If he could just keep moving, keep going through the motions, keep following blind rules and grim proportions, like a man beating egg whites or kneading bread dough, if he could resist the urge to turn left or right at random, veering like quarry on one of those wild detours of his, maybe he could make this right.

Dawn came up, sharp and red. Slamming down the visor, he punched the accelerator, amoeba shapes pulsing at the edges of his eyes. No time to stop. Sunday today, Christmas Eve. Mam would be awake already, wondering about how many potatoes, how much pumpkin to peel. Dad would be swearing as he tried to find the one bung bulb in a tangled nest of fairy lights. In an hour or so, Mam would be at early mass, in that little stone building already harvesting the day's heat. Fanning herself with the hymn sheet, turning slow and heavy on some old priest's dry words.

That's where he was, behind the veiny stained glass of his eyelids, when he hit the roo. He braked too hard, too fast, wrenching the wheel away from what was already a mound of fur and blood. A tyre went out and the ute skidded into the path of an oncoming truck. The truck horn sounding both loud and somehow far away.

After what felt like a lifetime of spinning, the ute hit the ditch, coming to rest tipped sideways, vaguely balanced on two wheels. The semi roared past, shaking them with slipstream. Didn't even bother to stop.

He tried to breathe. The seatbelt banded like iron across his neck. A dripping noise and he sniffed. Not petrol. But when he turned, he saw blood on Mick's forehead. The glove box had popped open, pinning him at the stomach. The boy's eyes wide but blank. No seatbelt. He must have taken it off while he slept. A black stain was spreading across his jeans. Reaching over, Ray dabbed at it with his hand. Not blood.

'Mick? You OK?' The boy's eyelids fluttered. 'Stay awake. Don't move.'

Ray's buckle was jammed. Manoeuvring out of the noose of his belt, he cracked his door and squeezed out, staggering around on hands and knees for a while before finding his feet. Walking round to Mick's side, trying to leverage the door open against the roadside bank, he saw how lucky they'd been. If they'd tipped the other way, Ray would have gone out his open window. If they'd tipped further to Mick's side, if the bank hadn't caught the roof, they might have gone right over, and the kid would have been crushed by the car. If they'd hit the verge just a few metres over, they would have hit that tree. And if they'd been going any faster the kid could have been sliced open by the glove box which had left a blossom of dark red below his ribs.

Ray felt gingerly around Mick's belly, the boy flinching a bit. Just a graze, just bruised, as far as Ray could tell, but he couldn't be sure. Shouldn't move him, not really. Should call an ambulance, but then he thought about the paramedics and the police and the fact that he wasn't the boy's father. The gun he didn't own still hidden in the tray.

'Can you move? Your neck all right?'

Mick shook his head. His neck worked at least. A dripping sound again. Nothing else for it. Ray carried him out carefully and propped him against the tree. The scratch on his forehead wasn't deep but it was bleeding a lot. A whimpering noise. He'd forgotten all about the dog, still hanging by its rope from the tilting tray. He got it free, put the rope in Mick's hand, but it flopped out of the boy's open palm. At a loss, he gave them both some water in his hands, the dog lapping it up, Ray murmuring it's okay. But it wasn't. A few inches left or right.

Keep going. Keep doing. He got the jack from the back, found the tyre lever, propped stones under the wheel, leveraging the weight with a branch. With four grunting rocks, he got the car upright. Miraculously, no real damage that he could see except a dent to the passenger door and the shredded tyre. After he'd changed it and he was back on the bitumen, creeping along and hugging the verge, he swore he'd take the boy straight to hospital, if the car got him as far as town. Swore that he'd be a better man than this.

At the next roadhouse, he pulled in, paid the sleepy attendant double and a half to check the fuel line and hammer out the wheel. Going inside to buy the boy a Coke, he was the only customer. The lass at the counter wished him Merry Christmas in a frightened sort of way. When he got to the toilet, he saw why. Blood on his shirt. Blood on his face. That look in his eyes.

He thought of that woman in the hospital bed. Of her boy, grey as mould under his freckles. What sort of man did these sort of things? A man like him. A man doing this thing and then that thing and the next thing, piling them up and calling it a life.

He changed into his only clean set of clothes, the old suit he'd bought at a charity shop years ago, for a mate's funeral in Sydney and which he'd not worn since. While the boy was waiting in emergency, he stood in the hospital car park, sweating, trying the number written on his forearm again. Thinking, please. Mam's voice, and all this might be a bad dream.

It rang and rang. He started freewheeling then, trying all the possible number combinations on Charlie's coaster, swapping digits furiously, as if this was the key to all else. On his sixth attempt, it rang through. Random luck, like Charlie's Lotto balls.

'Good morning. Riley and Sons.'

'Sorry? Who?'

'Thomas Riley. Riley and Sons Funerals. How can I help?'

CHAPTER THIRTEEN

In the dark before dawn, something cold and damp stroked her cheek. Whiff of lavender, old vase water, mildewed silk. Scent of the grave.

She reared up, clawing away the bedspread, then had a sneezing fit. Like everything else in the room—the swarming tartan cushions, the bowls of potpourri, the commemorative royal teaspoons marching round the picture rail—the bed wore a pelmet of dust.

Ordinarily she would have run a mile from a place called the Heather Brae B&B. Would have preferred some anonymous red brick motel along the highway, but after what happened yesterday, on a lonely stretch of road, she no longer trusted herself behind the wheel.

⌒

The hitchhiker had been a mistake. She'd known it even as she pulled over, in a gully steep with white gum, the road etched with leaf shadow. Dusk had arrived early there. The day gone sepia with cold.

But when she'd seen that figure on the verge—tall, blond, thin, canted fanatically against altitude, his hat demented with corks—the car seemed to lose speed of its own accord. He seemed to have arrived for her alone, totemic in a claustrophobia of trees.

'Thank you, my dear. Much obliged.'

He brought that greasy courtesy and the smell of old shoes into her car. Up close, she saw his hair wasn't blond at all but the colour of ash. When he grinned at her through her window, his teeth were yellow and curved as the dog's. But it was too late by then. He was already opening the back door, climbing in, settling his suitcase across his knees. A little brown suitcase, like kids used to take to their first day at school.

'God bless. On my last legs back there. Where you headed? Off to Coona myself.'

Winding down her window despite the cold, she glanced at her map. Told him she was only going as far as the next place, which was half an hour away. Decided she wouldn't be able to stand the smell any longer than that.

'I'm visiting family,' she told him, in case he had any ideas. 'They're waiting for me. I'm running late.'

This was true and untrue, in various ways. But according to Harry, lying by omission was the same as lying itself. For Harry, there was the broad easy path, paved with good intentions, and the narrow, dull-shining way. Trying to sneak between them, you stepped a treacherous tightrope, like the single floorboard traversing the cat-pee dirt of her half-renovated front hall. No room in Harry's universe for the twisting dead ends she kept finding herself on, the trackless wastes where Tilda weaved her elaborate make-believe.

'Nice day for it.' She nodded, though the sky was the colour of iron, and with the sun on the wane, it was cold as sin.

He leaned forward, stuck his head between the front seats. So close, his big beard bristled against her neck. Beside her, the dog growled. Putting a hand on its collar, she felt a tremble in the fur.

'We should give thanks. Another day God gave.'

Just her luck. A bloody holy roller, what Dad would call a creeping Jesus, like the tambourine Christians who used to haunt the riverbank back home.

According to a sign, there was an intersection coming up. No name on it, just a farm track or fire trail, but it would do. She'd drive a little way up, wait for a while, until someone else with even less wit and no sense of smell had picked him up. While she waited, she'd eat that box of Milk Tray she'd bought at the service station for no good reason. She wasn't visiting someone in hospital. And she'd been on a diet for the last thirty years.

She shouted above the wind rush that she needed to go a different way, needed to turn off. No answer. In the rear view, she saw he was fossicking around inside the suitcase, his face hidden by the lid.

'Did you hear? I said I'll have to let you out. Just up here.'

He started throwing things across her back seat. Shoes, hats, dismembered paperbacks. A hail of greyish underwear. In the warmth of the car, the stink got stronger, the shockingly intimate aroma of a hot iron meeting the armpit of an unwashed shirt.

The dog was growling in earnest now. She kept one hand on its scruff, one eye on the rear view. A wooden coat hanger, what looked like a Bible. A rusty bread knife. How could one little suitcase contain so much?

She'd reached the turn-off and had started to pull over when he clamped a hand on her shoulder. Startled, she punched the accelerator and the car swerved back into the middle of the road.

'Wait! I've got a message for you.' And she realised then what he was. An omen. A harbinger, in Harry's universe. Some vengeful ghost of an old habit, fashioned from dusk, sticks, shadows, the small stone of her own longing, on this bleak stretch of road. Even as she'd first seen him, even as she'd told herself he was too short, tree shadows having distorted his figure on the road, and too old, his face a travelled maze of purplish leather, the colour of bodies found in bogs, part of her had been cutting the cloth to fit. The pop of his hat corks, that jaunty dip to his knees. His red scarf and blue shirt, coin bright against pewter landscape. The crude old-fashioned lines of him, as if he'd stepped out of some simpler, more softly tinted history, the faded world of those old Polaroids. And the outdoor life could do terrible things to you, couldn't it? Just witness the man from the pub.

'Have you met the Lord? Have you taken him into your heart?'

She hit the brake and a plague of pamphlets erupted from the back seat.

'Wait! You're going the wrong way!'

She said something stupid like, I thought you were going to Coonabarabran. 'Evils of the flesh,' she thought she heard, thighs chafing against her slacks. The dog's growling rose a notch. The car was spiky with warnings now.

'Listen, I've just remembered. I've forgotten something.'

It was infectious. She was talking in bloody parables now.

'I have go back, the other way. You'll have to get out.'

Beneath the stench of unwashed body, she smelled it, that salty bitterness men give off when aroused. Then everything else was obliterated by the smell of entrenched halitosis as he stuck his mouth right next to her face.

'God sees, you bitch. He knows what you do.'

Thank God or whoever for the dog. With an agility she wouldn't have given it credit for, it lunged backwards, went straight for the old man's throat. With similarly surprising speed, as if a much younger man was hiding beneath that ragged disguise, he opened his door, tumbled out. She floored the accelerator, back door still swinging, steering with one hand while grabbing behind her with the other. Finding the handle of his suitcase, she heaved it sideways. In the rear view, she saw his medieval curses fluttering gaily across the road.

For just a moment, she felt fifteen again. As if instead of finding a broken ghost of Ray by the side of the road, she'd discovered some looser-limbed, more flamboyant version of herself, swaggering single-handed round those icy curves.

⌒

The feeling had deserted her now.

She should get up. All this tartan was giving her a rash. Should comb her hair, wash her face in ye olde ewer. Ring the rental place and arrange another car. But it was still early and her mobile was out in the glove box, and in the spirit of all this faux Victoriana, no phone in the room. There'd been *incidents*, according to a stridently punctuated notice on the bedside table, and all non-local calls from reception must be paid for *prior* to checkout, which was 10 am, *on the dot!*

The dog started whining so she fed it a chocolate. Watched it slobber in arthritic circles, distributing strings of drool. Convinced herself no one would notice, given the hectically swirling carpet. She couldn't just keep calling him the dog. Bloodshot eyes, saggy jowls. Winston. That would do.

She could hear his stomach rumbling from across the room. Shouldn't give a dog chocolate, she remembered. Shouldn't have it in here at all. The author of all this elaborately patterned discomfort also objected to children, vegetarians and the wearing of shoes upstairs.

When the dog started to retch, she turned the radio on. Another sugary love song, then an ad for tractor parts.

⌒

After the accident, after the car hit the guard rail and came to rest, leaning like a curious sightseer over the drop, she'd stepped shakily out. The dog remained sitting bolt upright in the front seat, still staring straight ahead. She was starting to wonder if he was quite all there. The car itself she hardly dared look at, a twisted lump of metal where the front numberplate should have been. When she opened the door to get the dog, the smell of Holy Roller lingered. Walking around the layby to calm herself, she found one of those awful God pamphlets stuck to her heel.

At the edge, a sign pointed down a flattened tunnel of grass. A lookout, some world-famous waterfall. Pushing past a cluster of Closed and Danger warnings, that same little man they always used, toppling over and over from a cliff, she found herself on a slim finger of sandstone hanging over the darkening blue. She sat down on the bench provided, closed her eyes. Listened to the dreamy tick of insects, the rustle of treetops like a woman's skirt.

You should stay away from high places, Harry used to warn. As if there weren't pills and ovens in the world. This was after she'd told him about her daily visits to the cemetery, how she'd climb over the safety barrier, walk along the cliffs, head right to the edge. Balanced there above a chaos of surf and rocks, she'd close her eyes, lean out, try and see what Simon had seen, in his paintings of this place. Instead of a curve of blue littered with gulls and sailing boats, that whiteness which had eaten all his work towards the end. A vacuum outlined by an emptiness, like the tool silhouettes in her garden shed. As if his inner landscape had been nuclear blasted, leaving only the blind certain shape of what he was not.

I see, Harry had said, steepling his fingers, sunlight picking out the bald patch behind his ponytail. I see, he kept saying, while seeing nothing at all. Yet he'd seemed so unshockable and sponge-like in his home-made jumpers, she'd told him everything. Well, not everything. In the air of humid intimacy Harry carried with him like weather, even the bones of the truth had stuck in her throat. In the end, it had been a mistake to tell him anything at all. On top of his kindness about Simon, she'd then had to endure him being kind about Ray as well. It was such a burden, Harry's kindness. Delivered in big, moist servings, in lumpen daily doses, it was impossible to fend off, digest, absorb. Always lurking in hallways or crawling up phone lines, waiting to obliterate her outline, like the Blob in that movie which had scared her witless as a kid.

And Harry wouldn't have understood. All that talk about opening to grief and gaining closure, like she was a cupboard or something. You could tell he'd never been in love. When she'd told him how her partner of six years had just left one day, had taken his suitcase of spare clothes from the spare room and just walked out, through the back door and out the back gate, disappearing forever into the white-hot point of a Sydney summer afternoon, and how she'd been looking for him ever since and, worse, finding him, in every rangy, white-haired, blue-eyed man, Harry's solution had been to take a course. A great believer in courses, Harry. Always on one himself. One week rebirthing and car maintenance, the next flamenco guitar. As if there was a course he could take which would make him into a man she might want. How could you want someone whose violin-patterned socks poked through the toes of their orthopaedic sandals? Who, when the buckle broke on those sandals didn't swear like a normal person, just smiled beatifically and tied them up with string? A man who used the word bloke in invisible inverted commas, as if it was a passport to some club he wanted to join.

The thought of Harry propelled her off the bench, right to the edge of the cliff. Bracing herself against the smelly bulk of the dog, she hung her head over, waiting either for the swell of terrible freedom she used to feel after Simon left, or for the lurch of terror she'd felt as her car teetered against that guard rail, heading for the abyss.

She found she felt nothing. Vaguely hungry, despite the chocolates. Faintly curious about this famous waterfall, which she couldn't see, only feel. A fine spray on her cheek, as if God was spitting on her head.

Something had shifted, without her permission. Perhaps when she realised Simon wasn't coming back and wasn't dead either. She'd seen his name in the paper, some art exhibition, Melbourne or somewhere. He'd just slipped sideways from the outline she'd allotted him, leaving her mooning over seagulls, a cliché on a cliff. Left her with Harry and his unravelling jumpers and his endlessly unravelling feelings, his relentless picking over her feelings, like she was a bag of fabric remnants he was determined to make into something else.

Perhaps when Mam died, another sinew to the past torn away. Where once she'd thought she was still that woman at the cemetery, someone who, if she believed her own propaganda, should have been brave enough to throw herself off the edge of things, she wasn't that woman and in fact had never been. If she was, she should have welcomed that hitchhiker's rusty knife with open arms. Should have wished for a breath of wind, a crack in the guard rail, something to disturb the hairsbreadth balance of the car as it hung over the drop.

In the end, she was too bloody-minded. As Mam used to say, stubborn as a root. How else to explain all those hairpin bends she'd taken with such spinsterish diligence, all those semitrailers she could have driven into, all that icy road she'd negotiated between abandoning the hitchhiker and that moment when, blinded by the last rays of sun through a dirty windscreen, she'd seen him, ahead of her again. Rebuilt from guilt and ether, his little suitcase bursting with mysteries and mildew. Thumb cocked, waiting for her by the side of the road.

CHAPTER FOURTEEN

He got all the way to the Twenty Bends turn-off before it dawned on him. Then just sat there, in the middle of the highway, a sitting duck for any P-plater roaring round the curve. Aghast at himself, his cow-eyed addiction to the old rhythm of things.

All those times he could have turned right toward the tip and the industrial park and the turn-off to Frederick Street, and he'd kept on, slipping through possibilities like a fish. After the hospital, where Mick got the all-clear on his X-ray and some Panadeine for his head, instead of taking the bypass over the rail crossing, circling the racetrack and the grain silo, he'd driven straight through. At the feed-barn corner, where Dad always had a debt to settle and where he should have turned right, across the bridge where he'd first learned to swim, he'd sat at the lights, in the middle lane, hypnotised by the past. Smell of chaff and shame and horse leather through the open window, all mixed up with the river mud, bags of blood and bone. After that he must have sailed unseeing along the whole three blocks of the Memorial Park, its grey Spitfire erected in honour of some war hero not his father, flying nowhere over the monkey bars.

At some point he didn't remember, he must have circumnavigated the footy oval where at twelve he'd broken his nose in a ruck and played straight through. Hadn't noticed. Too busy obeying some other, more potent architecture. Beneath those flaking wooden stands, gone now probably, old Chinese Alf had taught him to box. An unlikely assassin, five foot nothing, old as Moses and skinny as a root. But deft, deadly, silent, his narrow face wizened as one of his roast fowls. Ducking and weaving, relentless, in board-filtered light.

'Ray? Reckon I'll head home. I got money. I'll be right.'

Past that mailbox he was staring at, through the gate and up that winding track, inside the house he couldn't see but which, from the sign out front, had just been sold, had lived the man Alf had taught him to defend himself from. A big man, twice Ray's height. Hands so strong, they could bend fence wire without pliers, break another man's fingers with a single squeeze. At fourteen, Ray had thought that if he could only make himself as strong and big, his anger and muscles just as hard, he'd be all right. Didn't realise that fists were no defence against things you couldn't see or name.

'Ray? I gotta head back. Get the house ready, for when Mum gets home.'

The old milk can mailbox had seen better days. The name barely visible, just a faded M from McCullough, the white ghost of the J&A, the rest of it held together by rust and paint. The top gate was goose-winged against deep furrows, the road Dad had made with Mr Tangello's grader mostly potholes now. The driveway was so overgrown with Paterson's curse, the white stones marking it had all but disappeared. Some wanker had taken a pot shot at the real estate sign. The metal post all dinged up.

'Ray? You listening? If you drop us in town, I'll get a bus.'

Could have kept the mailbox up. Least they could have done.

'No buses out your way, not from here. And I can't. I promised your mum.'

'Yeah, well. Don't reckon she'd be too keen.' Mick lifted his shirt, flashing the bruise where the glove box had got him, a blue-green shadow below his ribs.

'Just drop me in town, eh. I'll work it out from there.'

'Shut up for a bit.'

A puff of dust was coming off the track. Heading down to the road.

'Who lives here anyway? You know them or something?'

The dust materialised slowly into a shiny white HiLux, bristling with bull bars and aerials. Could afford to trick their ute up like Christmas, but couldn't be bothered to paint a mailbox or fix a gate.

Ray wrenched the ute in a savage uey, headed back into town.

⌒

Didn't need to look for the house number on Frederick Street. He spotted the plump white curves of Eddie's Holden even from the corner, such was the generous sprawl of new bitumen, the burnished arc of heated air.

What was Dad doing here? If he'd sold the old place, surely he could afford something better. Yet the man at the funeral home had confirmed the address. Always the rough side of town, this bit near the tip and the wreckers' yards. The desolation had spread now though, a welter of car parts, old tyres and rusted caravans. One house roofless, another with a hole in its front wall. But this new road had nothing to do with them. At the top, behind a chain-link fence, bulldozers were grinding away, flattening piles of stink. A billboard promised something called Whispering Pines. Not a pine tree in sight, just their dead counterparts, little timber-frame boxes all up the hill. So cheek by jowl, you could spit from your kitchen window, hit someone next door.

'I'm starving. Is there a Maccas?'

'Probably. I dunno.'

'Mate. I want a burger.'

'Mate, how about I just take you back to Sam's?'

Mick subsided, picking at a hole in his jeans.

Ray pulled up well shy of the driveway. No matter if it never went further than the front yard, you could never park Eddie's Holden in. As a boy, Ray had hated that car, the smug shiny chrome of it, the fleshy curves and female bulges, the fins swooping like Brylcreemed hair. All those Saturday afternoons he'd spent washing and buffing it, just so Dad could drive it back into a shed and cover it with a tarp.

'Wait out here. I won't be long.'

'But it's boiling! And I'm thirsty. And it's boring out here.'

'Yeah? You reckon? I'd take boring any day over what's in there.'

Why did he say that? He didn't know that. Not any more. Knew only the old pattern, hot tedium to raging explosion and back again, as if Ray was cold water and Dad was caustic soda and they were shaking themselves together, over and over, inside the four walls of a house.

'Why? Who lives there?' Mick was gazing curiously at the house.

'None of your business. Look, use the hose if you want, and while you're at it, give the dog a drink. But don't forget to wind it up again. And whatever you do, don't touch that car.'

Why was he issuing these frozen little Saturday afternoon rules? Weren't his rules, had nothing to do with Mick. Nothing to do with this little stone house, gleaming like a bone on its treeless block. A single rosebush languished beside the fence. The front yard was concrete edging a single square of grass. The tiny patch of yellow buffalo was so infested with water-filled soft drink bottles, not even the bravest dog would have risked it, or so it seemed to Ray. The hose coiled with iron precision, the rosebush pruned to within an inch of its life. Not a piece of driveway bluestone out of place. Nothing to show the disarray of grief.

Yet there was something, wasn't there, in the way light was falling, so clipped and sheer across the modest wrought iron of the gate. A thin light, resonant with chores all done, life rushed through, hours finished far too early and folded away. By late afternoon it would slant through half-closed venetians, bounce dully off clothes long dry on a line. Bring time and its passing into shallow focus. Make even a mean old bastard stifle a sob.

That bit of pity was the only thing moving Ray forward when everything in him wanted to run the other way. As he squeezed past the Holden, he knocked some bluestone off the driveway. Bent to put it back. His shadow gone apelike on the ground.

He ignored the front door. At home, the back door was always the front. Round the side, he tried to peer in at a window but the venetian blinds were thin-lipped. Out back, a big garage and a Hills hoist took up most of the yard. Dad must hate that, how small it was, all these fences around him, curlered heads poking over to count his empties or check the state of the washing on his line.

The back door was open. The TV was bellowing, a hardware ad. Maybe he was in the garage. Ray listened for the sound of the axe. But it was the height of summer and a glimpse through the shed window showed enough split ironbark to last a homestead through a dozen winters.

'Hello?' The flyscreen rattled under his knock. 'Dad? It's me.'

Me. Stupid. After all this time.

When there was no answer, he pushed the screen door open, walked in.

Dark in there. Hot too, and musty, the smell of egg grease and nylon carpet funnelled by looming furniture, close wood-panelled walls. The combustion fire glowered from a corner, although it had to be thirty-five degrees outside. The curtains were all drawn, so the sun didn't fade the carpet, one of Mam's old rules. The only bright spot was her old linen tablecloth, shining pearl-like in the centre of the room.

He almost fell over his father before he saw him. Then froze, legs straddled. Thinking, I'm too late. Then he heard a faint rustle, saw the newspaper on Dad's chest rise and fall.

His father lay at an awkward bucking angle in his rocker recliner, his glasses askew. A little pot belly overflowed his stained trousers. Rivers of pigment on his skull. Wasn't right, seeing him like this. Yet Ray stayed there, balanced between his father's feet. Remembering everything, noting everything, each hard shaved and peppery bristle. Shoring himself up against this new defencelessness. Firelight stippling things in.

Dad woke like a lizard. No movement, just tense awareness. Flicker of nerve through skin.

'Oh. Right. You're here.' Dad batted his newspaper, stuck out his hand. Like Ray was a plumber who'd dropped by to fix the loo.

'Better late than never. Come far?'

Ray managed a brief touch of his father's hand before it snapped away and Dad spun around to glare at the clock. Same old spiky copper one from the homestead kitchen. Same old dinosaur skin on Dad's hands.

'Gone two. I'll get the kettle on.'

He rose so abruptly, Ray had to jump out of the way. Was left stranded next to the recliner while his father rushed toward the kitchen. Just as he used to, always rushing from one job he didn't want to do toward another one where something would go wrong. But there was something different, some articulation gone awry. An awkward shuffle to his Dad's walk, a panicky cant to his stride. His legs failing to spring from the thigh as they used to, as if he was always just about to mount a horse.

'Took yer bloody time, I gotta say.' Dad was yelling above the sound of water drumming into the kettle. 'Almost gave up. Even tried the cops, or the wife did. Useless though, of course.'

The wife. Not Mam, not Del. Ray peered round the doorway to the little kitchen, afraid of finding some stranger at Mam's old kidney-shaped table. But there was just Dad, rushing between bench, stove and fridge, as if someone had inserted a key.

'Come far? How's the car?'

The teapot was smashed down on the draining board, the knife drawer wrenched out. Cutlery tossed like salad, sugar fell in a shining rain all over the floor. When Ray was a kid, this terrorising of objects was a warning to sneak out one of those doors leading off the verandah. Head down the creek until things had calmed down.

'Dad?'

His father snorted through a haze of kettle steam.

'Dad? What's that old bastard got to do with anything? Long gone and good riddance. I woulda let ya know but didn't know where to find ya.' Dad was shovelling tea into the teapot now, four, five, six tablespoons, as if it was the big urn at the homestead and he was navvy, doing smoko, except it was just Mam's little teapot, more china ornament than working object, the one she used to store loose change, old buttons, spare keys.

'Half the town came. Wouldn't credit it. Pity ya missed it. We could have had a knees-up on the grave.' Ray stood mesmerised by that shaky relentless spoon. Seven, eight, the pot brimming with leaves by now. His father wheeled round, tea caddy in hand. The old glare in his eyes.

'Bit of a mongrel act, that. Just pissing off. You coulda rung. Dropped us a line at least.'

Something wrong. Not just the words, which made almost no sense, or the anger, which was par for the course and to be expected after all this time, but the way his father seemed to be addressing someone else, on some other, distant horizon. His whole body cocked toward it, tuned to some agitation going on over Ray's shoulder, beyond these four walls.

'Yeah. Dad. I'm sorry.' What else to say? Every word felt unreal, ludicrous, after so long. 'It's been a while. I'll try and explain. Can we go and sit down though? Forget the tea. I'm right.'

But Dad had locked into his groove again, was sprinting past Ray with the teapot, slamming it down on the lounge-room table, heading back, piling a plate with biscuits, sliced white bread, half a piece of fruitcake. Back to the lounge room, then back to the kitchen, because he forgot the cups. Ray stood and watched, pressed helplessly against the wall. Like his father was in a film that had been speeded up, going faster and faster, and Ray was a painted tree, a cardboard stone.

'Well, come on. Hurry up. Tea's getting cold.'

Dazed, Ray walked back to the lounge room, sat down at the table. Dad was pouring, tea bouncing off the cups. A wet ring spread on Mam's tablecloth. Her old cosy on the old teapot, but Dad had jammed it on with such speed and force, it was all askew, the spout sticking out from where the handle should have gone, the way a little kid will stick its arm through the neck hole of a jumper then just stand there, blinded and helpless. Funny for a grown-up, frightening for a child. The world turned upside down and inside out.

'Dad. It's me. Ray. I probably look a bit different, eh. It's been a while. Done a few things since I seen you. Been working, up Queensland, out west. On the mines. Had a few adventures. Got a few stories to tell.' He was gabbling desperately, trying to snare his father's attention with some facts. Find some toehold on reality, for himself. Avoid saying what he had to ask. Despite what the funeral man had told him, it hadn't sunk in, not yet. Seemed unreal as the man before him, piling sugar in his tea, ferrying a Scotch Finger to his mouth with a shaking hand.

'Listen, Dad. I was real sorry to hear about Mam.' Nothing. His father dunking his biscuit, over and over, until the end fell in. 'I would have come earlier. Or got in touch. But I only just found out.'

'Here.' Dad jabbed the plate of fruitcake in Ray's face. 'Go on. What ya waiting for? You always loved a bit of sweet.'

At a loss, Ray took some. The cake was stale. He was trying to wash the lump down with some of the mouth-puckering tea when Dad swore, banged the table, and Ray jumped, spilling tea all down his front.

'Forgot the marg.' And he was off again.

Ray sat staring at the tea cosy. Wanting to take it off and fix it, sweep up the crumbs, whisk off Mam's tablecloth. Set it to soak, before the stain set in. As if in doing these things he could fix all else.

Instead he got up. Paced, four steps one way, to the kitchen wall, six steps the other, until he hit the living room wall again. Too jittery, he sat down again, in Dad's rocker recliner this time, something he would never have dared to do in childhood, but it was as far away as he could get from this meal of the past. Too close to the fire. The leather arm of the rocker was all split with heat. Cost a bloody fortune, that chair. Special delivery, all the way from Bathurst. All those levers and headrests and viciously unfolding foot stools, a hundred different ways to sit, none of them right. Dad forever fiddling and banging and swearing at it, his body jumping to contorted angles, which would have been funny in another house, another family. Not theirs. That sense, faint but unmistakeable as the smell of burning rubber, that something was about to break.

Dad stomped back, without the marg, carrying another plate of cake. Asking about the trip, the traffic, what type of car, did it go OK, while sugaring his tea all over again. Ray sat smoothing the burst leather of his armrest over and over, trying to mend it and failing. Trying to bridge the gap between what he knew and what was coming out of his father's mouth.

'And what about the car?' Insistent now, brows lowered, spoon clicking furiously against his cup as he stirred the sugar in.

'Fine. Good. A Landcruiser.' So hot in there. His shirt was soaked with sweat. Ray wrestled off his suit jacket which he'd put on because the occasion had seemed to demand something. Tea all over his lapel.

'Jap car? You're joking. Holdens are the go. You taught me that. Remember when I bought that Toyota from that wog up the road? Piece of junk, you said, and you were right. Now your old girl, that's a car. She got a knock in the engine a while back but I changed the sparks and now she's right. Good as the day you left.'

It dawned on him, belatedly. Dad thought he was Eddie, his long-lost older brother. Eddie of the shiny suits and the failed businesses and the flash car, who ran off when Ray was ten, leaving a wife and three kids and a load of gambling debts. Who wrote Dad begging letters over the years, asking for money to invest, money he promised to pay back. Money that should have gone to his family. Money Dad never had.

'Maybe we could take her for a spin later. Down the river road. Like old times.'

Did he look like Eddie? There used to be a photo on the mantelpiece at Twenty Bends. Same dark blond hair, Eddie's oiled up in a quiff. Gold signet rings, a gap between his front teeth. Something about the ears. Ray looked down at his hand gripping the armrest. Felt himself shuttling through realities. His fingers seamed with dirt, horny and work ravaged, just like Dad's. Who thought he was Eddie. Who'd be in his nineties by now, if he was still alive.

'Dad, where's Urs?' Surely, despite everything, she hadn't left her father here on his own. Not like this. 'Is she around?'

'Oh, her ladyship! Don't talk to me about her.' And Dad was up again, gathering plates and cups. 'Her and her bloody doctors. All those tests. It was tests did her in!'

Ray sat helplessly while Dad performed the frenzy of a few moments ago, but in reverse. Whisking off Ray's half-drunk tea, bashing bread and butter plates together, the stain on the tablecloth spreading. The tea cosy wrenched off, used to mop it up.

'Nothing they could do, according to madame,' Dad yelled from the kitchen, above the sound of water running, into the sink this time. Ray sat sewing chair leather together with his fingers. Mending brokenness, over and over, while the fire crackled and china kittens smirked at him from the top of the TV. A small relief. Urs was in touch. She was alive, at least. He wanted to ask where and how to get hold of her but when he walked into the kitchen, the gas on the stove was flickering, a tea towel smouldering beside it, and Dad was filling the kettle, preparing to start the whole joyless cycle of refreshment again.

'No more tea, Dad. I've had enough.' He took the kettle off him, doused the tea towel under the tap. His father grunted, started swilling things around in the sink.

'Of course she knows best. Always did.'

'Tell me what happened. With Mam. What tests?'

'Oh, don't ask me. I don't know anything apparently. She only went downhill once the doctors got their hands on her. All madame's doing of course. It was all panic stations and let's call the specialist and never mind what muggins thinks. I told her, I know far more about Delly McCullough than you'll ever forget.'

Dad was washing up without scraping plates. Bits of cake floating in the sink. And now he was on about the car again, the trip, the Holden, the traffic. Word soup. Mam gone, Urs somewhere, Eddie back from the dead. The sky gone purple, trees growing upside down.

'Dad, please. Stop,'

And he did, suddenly, a plate held in mid-air. His eyes fixed somewhere past Ray, toward the front of the house. Ray realised it had always been like this. Ray off to the side. Dad listening to something only he could hear.

'What's that?'

Ray could hear nothing but the tick of the copper clock.

'What?'

'Bloody little shit.'

Dropping the plate with a crash, Dad ran out of the kitchen, his fury giving him the speed of a much younger man.

'Oi! Get out of it. Bugger off!'

When Ray reached the front room, he found Dad squeezed beneath the bunched-up venetians, rapping furiously on the window. More china kittens, shivering on the sill. The little room was hot, dark, moribund with looming furniture, all that old heavy stuff from the homestead. Oak dressers, mahogany sideboards, the wood clotted with carved lions and scrolling grapes. As Dad knocked at the window, his elbow caught a kitten and it smashed on the fireplace surround.

'Shit. Where's the key?'

As Dad rummaged through his trouser pocket, Ray could smell his father. He smelled like Charlie. Dirty clothes, stale tea, old sweat.

'Oi!' Dad rapped at the window again. 'Get off my lawn!'

When Ray got the blind up, he saw Mick had collected all the bottles from the little square of lawn, lined them up along the fence. He was picking up another handful of bluestone from the driveway. Raising his arm, squinting thoughtfully, his tongue stuck out.

'Little mongrel! I'll show you.' In the slatted light, Ray saw with horror that his father was undoing his belt. Same old belt, same grooves in it, worn pathway of his days and ways. Still supple though, the buckle thick and ponderous, capable of a whining flick, that tense silence before it buried itself in flesh. The mark it left more shameful than the beating itself. Only way through was to say nothing, do nothing. Be nothing. Bring silence to bear.

A bottle went flying, gravel pattering against the side of Eddie's car.

'Oi!' Dad had picked something up from the mantelpiece, raised his own arm, preparing to throw it, before Ray grabbed his fist. 'Ray! Do that again, and you won't know what hit yer. Get inside!'

And although the belt was still at Dad's waist and the little figurine in his father's hand weighed nothing and Dad was only doing violence to the window, still Ray thrilled to it, the power coursing through that old brown muscle. Through his own fingers and up his arm.

'Dad. Stop, OK? Calm down. I'm Ray. I'm here. And it's all right. The boy's with me.'

A horrified look on his father's face, fleeting visions of drunk barmaids, welfare cheats, little bastards. Like Ray himself.

'I'll fix it. Don't worry. Go and sit down.'

Dad gazed out the window then back at Ray, looking very tired and old.

⌒

By the time Ray went out the back and up the driveway, squeezing himself past the hulk of the Holden, Mick had shied another bottle off the fence.

'And what the fuck did I say?'

He'd let the dog off as well. It was squatting next to the rosebush, a look of dense concentration on its face.

'They're just rubbish. What's the big deal?'

Ray tightened his grip on Mick's arm until he dropped the stone. 'Get inside.'

Ray picked up the gravel and the dog mess, tied the mutt up to the tap. Going back in, he found Mick at the table, kicking chair rungs. Dad was back in his recliner, batting his newspaper, eyes trained on the boy.

'Dad. This is Mick.'

'Yeah, we done all that. Shouldn't he be at school?'

'He's not at school right now. He works with me.' Ray blocked Mick's leg mid-kick. Mick, looking sulky, scuffed at the carpet instead.

'I'm starving. When's lunch?'

'Too late. Past two. You'll ruin yer tea.'

Dad shook his newspaper out, disappeared behind it. Too rough, too fast, one corner folded over like a puppy's ear too big for its head.

'I'll make you a sandwich. Dad? You want something?'

'Ate already. Anyway, no bread.'

A relief to have something to do. Checking the fridge, Ray found half a tomato, a heel of cheese. Two eggs in a carton, well out of date. No fresh stuff, nothing in the fruit bowl, a snow drift of crumbs in the bread bin. Dead cockies in the cutlery drawer. He worried about what Dad had been living on. Stale fruitcake and treacle tea. Still a big man, but he'd lost weight and height.

The old belt cinched tight, the freckles on his head, and that little pitching scuttle to him when he walked. He remembered an old photo, wintery, golden, a tracery of branches, a big animal, hanging. A big man, casting a long shadow. He shook his head. Scrambled, not poached, if the eggs were old. No butter. Marg would have to do.

Dad came in just as he was tipping the eggs in the pan. Started rushing around in those eddying circles again. More tea leaves on top of the dregs in the pot, dirty spoons filed back in the drawer. Something building, the old tension in the air. And any dull pride Ray might have had in scrambling the eggs just so, not too wet, not too dry, splash of milk, touch of salt and pepper, no herbs to be had, the ancient shadow of oregano dust in a jar, was gone.

His father was right up next to him suddenly. Voice spitting in his ear.

'Why'd you have to bring him here? I looked after it all, didn't I? I never told her. Never said a word. I got enough little bastards to cope with. With Ray.'

What shocked Ray was not the words but the fear in Dad's voice. He switched the stove off and took his father by the arm. The muscles felt slack as string.

'It's OK. We'll get out of your hair soon. I'll make the tea. You go and sit down.'

Shaking his head slowly, his father shuffled off again.

By the time Ray delivered the food, Dad was fast asleep. But his bum must have contacted the remote. The football bellowed out. Ray turned the TV off, putting his fingers to his lips. Mick nodded through a mouthful of egg. Even he seemed to sense the dangerous unreality in the air.

Starting in the lounge room, then the little bedroom and the kitchen and finally the front room, Ray searched, carefully at first, sliding drawers out slowly, trying not to wake his father. Hearing a loud snore, he worked faster and more carelessly, rifling through piles of old newspapers and paperbacks, faded pizza flyers, ancient bills. Finding only a harvest of dust, cake crumbs and flaked-off skin. In one drawer, there was a year's supply of TV guides.

Finally, in a drawer of the hulking upended sideboard in the front room, the thing resting precariously on its mirror, so he had to get down on his belly to wrench it open, he found, amid a mulch of half-used candles, dead batteries, receipts for fertiliser and scribbled recipes for sponge cake in Mam's wavering hand, a letter which wasn't a bill, addressed to Dad. Months old, according to the frank.

He recognised the handwriting straight away. Rounded, solid and plain. A return address on the back, the front pristine except for a ring from a teacup. It hadn't even been opened. The depths of the old man's bitterness could still surprise him, even now.

Tucking the letter into an inside pocket of his coat, he touched Mick on the shoulder, pointing toward the back door. The old man didn't stir, even when Mick let the flyscreen bang.

CHAPTER FIFTEEN

The jeweller had moved. Still this side of the river, the cabbie had told her. Before the post office, past the cathedral, behind the Scottish restaurant, in that brand-new arcade. When she confessed she didn't know it, he showed a country person's astonishment that she wasn't familiar with every kink and wrinkle of his home town.

Ten minutes drive. But she didn't have a car. The rented Toyota had died on the outskirts, the new one wouldn't be ready for hours yet, the jeweller closed at one o'clock, and out here, at midday, in the back blocks, not another cab in sight.

Picking her dress out of her armpits, she let Winston tow her along the gutter, avoiding mirrors, windows, the up and down motion of kerbs. She'd almost forgotten it, the strict rules, the curt sun and bluff shadow of a country town on a Saturday afternoon.

Not many people about, thank God. Outside the Lutheran, a gaggle of what Mam used to call splitters, fresh from a wedding or a christening, all shaking hands and nodding hats. Pushing past them to spit blood in a bin, she scattered women and children like fish. Only the men's frank disapproval let her know she was home.

She seemed to have lost her bearings here, in a place she'd lived for a quarter of her life. There were landmarks of course. The lolly pink police station, the town oval, blond with drought. Some of the old shops struggled on, under sun-struck facades. Minnie's Haberdasher, the Town and Country Auctioneer. The Imperial Coffee Lounge, still unable to spell cappuccino, still having a bet both ways.

But these were nouns without a sentence, arriving in facets, skittering away. The rest was fast food, frothy coffee, lurid discount stores. There'd been an outbreak of nail salons. In front of the Council building, in a town known for sheep and bushrangers, a day's drive from any sea, palm trees and beach umbrellas. A lot of lumpy public art.

The place felt dizzy, skittish. Like her, on the verge of something but whether terminal progress or slow decline, it was hard to tell. Either way, an incomplete disease. Between the bright scabs of modernity, shuttered pubs and browned-out awnings, murky shades of her childhood bleeding through. Outdated even when she was young, those dirty reds and distempered yellows. Faded now to pale butterscotch, ute-rust brown.

The Royal Hotel was still there, peeling grandly on its hill. Along with a grain silo, nearly every town around here had one but theirs was the oldest and biggest, according to Dad. Fastest, tallest, biggest. These were his yardsticks, the way he sliced up the world. At ten, she was small and slow and plump. At twelve, tall and strong. While Dad weaved the main street looking for her, his temper rising, her name cracking dangerously against yellow sandstone and moribund heat, she'd be scuttling across that top verandah, hearing snores and cries and worse from the rooms upstairs. A quick shin-up the posts, a flying leap via railings and drainpipe to the hot, hidden world behind the parapet, where shadows on a tar-paper roof announced, in scrolling reverse, that the Royal was built in 1836. And there it was, the whole town laid out, just for her. Suddenly the tallest girl in town.

To her left, the long green sigh of the Memorial Park, unlikely in all that dun and terracotta. To the right, the cathedral, looking like just another outcropping, complete with belltower, of the granite that pushed like grey molars through the earth round here. And running through everything, the town writhing along it, streets shooting off at panicky angles as if eager to get away, the river. Thick, brown, muscled looking, yellow and murderous at flood time, breaking lives and levees. In bad years, sulking deep inside its own history. A secret world down there, the bed fine-grey and furrowed as the moon.

In the distance, past the racetrack and the feed barn and the grain silo, where the river veered sharply round the twin boulders known locally as the Bushranger's Balls, the scoured paddocks and tannic coils of Twenty Bends Creek. Her far horizon at the age of twelve.

That road in had been familiar at least. Plump hills, flabby corners, old mile posts whited out now but still mouthing their ghostly distance, the leisurely proportions of simpler days. Spotting the twenty-mile mark, she'd realised the rented Toyota must have broken down not far from their old driveway, thinking she was home. Whipping round to stare out the back window of the cab, she'd caught a glimpse of faded red roof. The old water tank, a chunk of rust on stilts. But the cab was going way too fast round those sick-making corners, the tow truck in front was kicking up too much dust.

For an old-fashioned mile along the road, the remains of the old orchard, all but one of the apple trees cut down. Frost on those branches so thick sometimes, it resembled snow. How Ray used to long for it but, like rain, mostly it passed them by. Just once, when he was little, a scatter like icing sugar on the river paddock slope. They'd gone down it on a piece of roof tin, Ray's solid little body clamped between her legs. They'd leapt off just before they hit the water, black under its skin of ice. Urs, Urs, can we do it again?

Her leaping and shinning days were long over. Climbing the stairs of the Royal at old dog pace, she stepped under the curly iron awning, into complicated shade. Counting blocks back toward the river, she tried to unravel in memory that tangle of alleys, side streets, and old dunny lanes, all tending by ragged degrees toward the bridge and the highway out. Here and there, between buildings, a slice of river, tamed here to sullen lakes and khaki wetlands, home to cycle paths, fitness circuits, overfed ducks. On the far side, the barbed wire and broken bottles of the waste ground under the feed barn bridge.

That was all she could see without actually getting on the roof. A new housing estate had colonised the town tip hill. A rash of raw-looking villas blocked her view of the silo and the boulders, even jostling out the cathedral spire, always a compass for the corrugated backside of town.

It would be dark in there. Cool, at least. She could light a candle, just for the old yellow glow of it after all this glare. Behind dusty red velvet, someone would be kneeling, posting three sins exactly through the mesh. In return, the droning penance of a curtained priest. I'll give you something to cry about, like Dad used to say. If she still believed in any of it, she'd kneel there herself. She'd cut her left breast off for the offertory plate, crawl naked up the aisle. Do anything, say anything, if it meant finding Ray.

Who was she kidding? She'd never make it up that hill. And anyway, the last time she'd gone to mass, one Easter over twenty years ago, she hadn't recognised anything. The church looked like a Scandinavian office block. It was all peace signs and floaty dancing by then, nuns with ambitions and out-of-tune guitars. She'd spent the whole hour in a sort of sniper's crouch, unsure whether to sit or kneel, even which direction to face. Had no idea where this shinier, smilier, more streamlined version of God was supposed to be. No real altar, just a stripped pine table. No proper cross, not that she could see. Just Jesus rising from the dead on a bedsheet, drawn by preschoolers. Simpering, crayon-coloured. Harmless as an egg.

She'd reached the end of the street now and still no arcade. Something called a Homemaker's Centre now took up the whole two blocks before the highway and she couldn't for the life of her remember what was there before. A whole chunk missing from memory, like the ragged hole in her gum.

All this must have been here last time. The place couldn't have changed that much in six months. But last time she was here, to clean out the property and arrange the sale, she hadn't been paying attention. After all the sorting through and throwing out, she'd gone straight to the bank and the solicitors, then to the real estate, to sign the papers, then out to Frederick Street, to tell Dad about the account she'd opened in his name. The proceeds from the sale would pay all his bills at this new retirement place he'd been so keen on, the one they were building on top of the tip.

But in the two months since his last letter, she'd found he'd rewritten history yet again. Dad in his recliner, glaring, rocking, spitting biscuits and bile. What bloody retirement place? Never heard of it. Never catch him in one of those places, no fear. Full of conmen, chancers. Thieves like her. This time she'd stolen fifty dollars from his bedside table, Mam's dentures from the bathroom cupboard. His house out from under him. The teeth from her own mother's head.

After that she'd taken the bypass straight out of town. Blind with grief and rage.

She felt dizzy suddenly. Almost fell down the steps into the path of the main road's only car. Crossing to the Memorial Park, she headed for a bench in the shade. Sat down to catch her breath.

Perhaps just the anaesthetic, the way everything, the band rotunda, the wintry stubble of the floral clock, had gone hollow and glassy. The edges of her slipping and folding between flat slices of autumn light. As if she'd been cut out of some blurrier, dirtier history than this, then badly superimposed.

The cabbie had warned her, when he'd found out she'd been born here. Won't know yourself. New golf club, new abattoir, new civic centre. World class this, state of the art that. A new B&B, out at that old place near the creek. A luxury health retreat. Boom times apparently, despite the drought and falling wool prices, something to do with sausage casings and the Japanese. Winding the window down to escape his provincial boasting, she'd stuck her head out, let cold wind drill across the nerve in her bad tooth.

A smell of horse as the taxi idled at the rail crossing. A float waited between her cab and the tow truck, a shiny, muscled, racehorse bum. How Ray had loved horses. How he'd nagged and nagged her about getting one, but they had motorbikes for the sheep. Waste of time, waste of money. Waste of feed. To defy Dad and please Ray, she'd worked extra Thursday nights and Saturday mornings at Dymphna's the chemist, doling out hernia trusses and enema kits and other things made of queasy brown rubber, just so she could buy that big black gelding Mr Tangello had for sale. She knew nothing about horses. Didn't realise the brute was unmanageable, that's why it was so cheap. Knew only that Ray had a way with animals. When he'd climbed into the saddle, his little legs stuck out like flags.

The second time Ray rode that horse, it threw him straight at a fence. Where the star post got him, a three-inch gash in his stomach, barbed wire embedded in the muscle of his thigh. She'd had to cut the trousers off him, blood and skin peeling away with the denim while Ray tried not to cry. So brave, so full of the need to be, as if it was a test and of course it was. No hospital, not on a Sunday, not for a McCullough, not unless it was snakebite or heart attack. Too dark, too late, too many roos and the truck headlights were playing up.

And of course Dad had seen worse. Dad always had. Mud, blood, bitten bullets. The man from Snowy River, Uncle Len and the shotgun, Grandad's war medals. The Battle of the Bulge, the fucking Kokoda Trail. Ray so full of Dad's stories that he didn't realise the man who was telling them, no matter how strong and tall, was just a shadow puffed up with retailed heroism, second-hand dreams. His image no more real than the monsters Ursula used to make with torch and fingers on Ray's bedroom wall. And she'd had to stand and watch while this big man, with heated needle and impatient fingers, stitched up her little boy like he was so much tent canvas. Swearing and grunting, like Ray was some bit of farm machinery that had failed to work.

That was why when they'd first hit town and she'd seen the arid patchy gloss of it, she'd asked the cabbie to strike right then left, burrowing deep along one of those old narrow winding side streets, home to a tyre repair place and the backside of a Chinese restaurant and yet another nail salon. This was the town she remembered: dead tyres, overflowing rubbish, squalling cats. The unpicked seam of things.

Above the Chinese restaurant that used to be a milk bar, a familiar rickety wooden staircase. A cracked red lamp. When the cabbie realised where she was headed, he'd offered to take her to the new medical centre out on the highway. State of the art. But she'd waved him off. Tying Winston to a railing, she climbed the stairs and rang the bell.

Even as she saw the tray of dirty-looking instruments, the big polyester belly looming over her, felt the man's rampant chest hair tickling her arm through the missing buttons on his shirt, guilt kept her in the chair. An old fault this, the lineaments of it familiar yet distant, like looking at a photo of some long-dead relative you'd never met, under glass. It felt right somehow, this grubby intimacy. It was where she belonged, what she deserved.

While he jabbed her mouth three times with the needle until everything but the nerve in question was numb, she'd examined that guilt from all angles, worrying at the small, stubborn outline of it, like it was a communion wafer stuck to the roof of her mouth. Trying for the shape of it, the moment behind the habit. Finding only the fact, hollowed out. So old by now, the rest of her had grown around it, like a foot in an ill-fitting shoe.

When her molar had shattered under his pliers, the dentist stopped pretending. Climbing on the chair, he braced a knee against her shoulder. Went at her as if wielding a crowbar. She'd closed her eyes, feeling boneless, riding tides of pain. They rang her clear as cathedral bells.

This was familiar. He was a man and she was a problem to be solved.

CHAPTER SIXTEEN

By the time she found the jeweller, in a little alley behind the McDonald's car park, it was shut. Scottish restaurant indeed. One of those country jokes. If you didn't get it, you weren't from here.

Without much hope, she wrote her name and number on the back of one of the dead man's receipts, slipped it under the door.

At the nursing home, the receptionist looked startled when she walked in. In the mirror behind the counter, Ursula saw why. Lip huge, jaw swollen, a knee-shaped bruise blooming on her chest. She looked like a beaten wife. An old beaten wife. A beaten-up spinster, in fact.

The woman's nervous smile disappeared as soon as she heard the name.

'Oh. Right. Jim's daughter. We've spoken on the phone.' Brandy, Mandy or something. The one who kept telling her Dad was shopping, swimming, bowling. Couldn't come to the phone.

'I tried down at the unit but there was no one there.'

'No. Your father has been moved to managed care. Quite some time ago. He's had some problems. His doctor thought it was best. We tried to contact you, many times, but the number you gave us didn't exist.'

They'd had to change the phone number at home. Harry had insisted on a silent one, because of all the calls. All the men, young, old, mad, bad, drunk and greedy, ringing up, pretending to be Ray.

'You know we do rely on relatives to keep their contact details up to date. We thought you would get in touch. Earlier than this.' The woman frowned, shuffling papers crisply, not meeting Ursula's eye.

'Problems? What problems?'

'A fire in his kitchen, for a start. There was quite a lot of damage to the unit above. And he started wandering. We found him out on the highway once, in the middle of the night. Anyway, you'll see for yourself. If you've got time, of course.'

Ursula stood tall, gathering her cardigan across the bruise on her chest.

'Which room is he in?'

'It's Saturday. He'll be down at the pool.' Dad. At a pool. 'I'll take you through.'

In silence, she followed the woman's stiff pink back down a maze of pink hallways, emerging in a glassed-in courtyard tropical with heat. A spa pool steamed luxuriantly in the corner, empty except for a pair of yellow floaties. Beyond the picture windows, a rock garden, a Japanese bridge, a circle of raked white sand. No plants. They were all in here. Palms and vines and fleshy-looking flowers, sprouting and furling, in almost indecent abundance, and among them, parked at random angles, people in walkers or wheelchairs, staring at the pool, the windows, the wall. A water feature dribbled somewhere. Must be murder on the bladder. Hers ached in sympathy.

She'd walked right past him before she realised the woman in pink had stopped. Was leaning down, patting someone gently on the arm.

'Jim? It's Shandy.' Shandy. That was it.

'You've got a visitor. See? It's your daughter. How about that? After all this time.' She shot Ursula another thin-lipped look before turning back, all smiles.

'How about I get you both a hot chocolate? Then you can have a chat. OK? Back in a tick.'

Ursula didn't recognise the man in the chair. He'd shrunk a little, which was to be expected. A bit paunchier round the middle, paler too, his seemingly permanent outdoor tan receding, although his cheeks were hectic. No wonder, it was like an oven in here. Balder on top, although he'd more than made up for it with what was going on below the ears. Snowy hair snaked down from his bald spot, curling luxuriantly on his collar. White tufts peeked through the mismatched buttons on his pyjama shirt.

It was all of this and none of it. Mostly it was the smile he turned on her. Big, beaming, blue eyes all crinkled up. The way he leaned forward, almost falling out of his chair in his eagerness to take her hand.

'I knew you'd come. I told them you would.'

Her father wanted to hold her hand. Never one for touching or hugging, even when she was little and, when he did, there was usually something—gloves, wood, leather—between his skin and your own. She touched his fingers quickly, drew back. Sat down opposite him, wiping her own hand on her dress. His palm so moist and soft.

'Hi Dad. How you doing?'

'Lovely. Long trip? Come far? By train?'

'Yes. No. I mean, I came by car.'

'How'd it go?'

'Here we are. Careful, it's hot.' Shandy settled two mugs of hot chocolate on the little table between them along with a plate of biscuits.

Ursula wanted to ask what had happened, why she almost didn't recognise him, but all she could come up with was, 'His hair.'

'Blood pressure meds,' the woman said briskly, tucking a curl behind Dad's ear. 'It's a side effect.' As Shandy knelt down to rearrange a travel rug around Dad's knees—all that wool, in this heat—she murmured in Ursula's ear. 'They like to be touched you know. You're only the second visitor he's had since he came in.' Ursula was about to ask who the other one had been but the woman bounced upright again.

'How's that? All good, Jimmy?' Dad grinned. Jimmy. Dad was always Jim. James sometimes, in official documents, McCullough to other men. Never Jimmy.

'Now, I'll be back soon and then we'll have a rest and then we can go for a swim. Careful with that, all right? Let it cool down first.'

'Swim? I have to get changed.' He started trying to lever himself out of his chair. Dad, who hated swimming, hated water, because of the creek and the river, its receding fortunes and swelling disasters, either drowning sheep or coughing them up as a dusty pile of bones. Never seen Dad in a pair of bathers. Never seen him smile so much.

The nurse pushed him gently back into his seat. 'No, Jim, not right now. Later. Ursula's here now, see? Your daughter. I'll let you catch up.'

With a final warning glance at Ursula, she walked off, leaving Ursula alone with the stranger in the chair.

'I told her you'd come.'

'Sorry? Who?'

'Ursula. I told her. She comes by train. Did you come by car? How'd it go?'

Playing for time, she took a sip of chocolate, which was lukewarm and horribly sweet.

'Dad. I'm Ursula. See? I'm here.' Although she couldn't be entirely sure of that right now. That dizzy slippery fading feeling again. Maybe the codeine she'd taken on an empty stomach. Or the heat, the bleach stink of the pool.

'She likes chocolate. Shouldn't really. Size of her.' Her father slurped greedily, froth on his lip. 'Lovely stuff.' Lovely. Her father never said things like that. Things were either buggered or OK. 'Here.' He was holding the mug out, hand shaking, chocolate dribbling down the sides.

'No thanks, Dad. I've got some.'

But he was shaking his head, sticking his tongue out, waggling it, and it took her a while to twig. Leaning forward cautiously, avoiding fingers, knees and fronds of hair, she blew on his chocolate quickly, sat back. Watched him lap away like a cat while her own chocolate formed a skin.

How dare he. The snowy guileless glow of him against the white of his shirt, the blue zing of the pool, the nursery pink of the walls. After all this time. Smiling and smiling, like bloody Father Christmas or a rosy-cheeked gnome. Just when she needed something hard and dark and definite to brace against, he'd slipped his traces, shifted the territory. Changed the rules.

'Long trip? By car? How'd it go?'

She should find a tissue, wipe that silly froth off his lip. Should work out how to do this, how to knock him back into a shape she could deal with. Find the thing she knew was still lurking beneath the ice-cream colours, the fairy-floss hair.

'Yes. I came by car. It was a long way. I came from Sydney. That's where I live. With Tilda. Remember? She came after Mam got sick. Before she died.'

She'd been aiming for a short sharp shock, like the bang Dad used to give the TV when it was on the roll. Nothing, just that big wide smile. He'd always been a bit deaf though, by fault or design. And he wasn't wearing his hearing aid.

She moved her chair a bit closer, but not too close.

'Dad? Shandy said you'd had a bit of trouble.' Stupid name. Sounded like someone's horse. 'She said you'd been going walk-about.' Still smiling, Dad cocked his head. She was shouting now, her voice clamouring back at her from glass and tiles. 'Where were you going, Dad? Home? To Twenty Bends?' He shook his head fast, like a dog with a fly, and she remembered Winston, tied to the gate outside. Hoped he was all right out there.

'We sold it though, remember?' she said. 'And Mam's not there any more.'

'Twenty Bends. That old place.'

Where six months ago the mere mention of either Mam or the farm was enough to make him turn purple, now he said the name with an air of wonder, like it was something from a fairy tale.

'Haven't been out there in donkey's years.'

'No. You were there less than a year ago, Dad. Before we sold it. Then you moved to Frederick Street.'

He snorted, hands clenched on his stick.

'That bloody dump! Wouldn't put a dog in there. Couldn't even fit Eddie's car in the garage. Had to leave it out in the driveway. All madame's idea of course.'

This was more like it. Still, it rankled. Dad had chosen that place himself.

'Still going, that car. Remember Eddie's FB?'

How could she forget? Dad lavished more care and money and attention on that car than he ever gave his kids.

'Good as the day it was bought.'

'Dad. Forget the car. Look, I'm sorry I haven't been to visit for a while. I should have. But I didn't think you'd want to see me, after last time. I tried ringing, a few times. And I sent letters, remember? But you didn't write back.'

Useless. He was off somewhere, smiling vaguely, polishing duco, his arm out some remembered window as tyres ate Technicolour miles. She thought about touching him briefly on the knee, to get his attention. Lifted her hand then dropped it again.

'Dad, listen. About those letters. You remember the last one I sent, to Frederick Street? After we sold Twenty Bends?' His smile faltered, his gaze wandering off over her left shoulder, to where a tiny old lady was splashing around in the shallow end of the pool. 'Well, it's turned up. I mean, I found it. See?' She waved it in front of his face. 'But I'm not sure how.' She wasn't making any sense, she realised, not to a deaf forgetful old man, or even to herself.

'I'm hot,' her father announced suddenly, shrugging away his blanket. 'I need a swim.' To Ursula's horror, he started fumbling with his shirt buttons, white hair spilling out. Frightened he was about to start on his trousers, she looked for Shandy, but the courtyard was deserted, the people in wheelchairs having trundled off, or been spirited away. Just the little old lady paddling in circles, a flowered cap on her head.

'Dad. Wait. Not now. Later. When you've finished your drink.' She handed his mug to him and he sat back, draining it obediently, although the stuff must be stone cold by now. 'About that letter. See, I found it, in someone's pocket. But I sent it to you. I don't know how it ended up there.'

Her head hurt with the heat and the effort of trying to explain the hopscotch of clues and whispers and inklings and yearnings that had led her here.

'Ray got hold of it somehow, Dad. The letter.' He smiled back. 'Remember Ray?'

'Yeah. He ran off. Got lost.' Get lost. That's what Dad used to say when Ray was little and Ray was trying to help him, with fences or wood chopping or cleaning Eddie's car.

'Big secret. Delly won't let me tell.' Dad tapped his nose, a sly look on his face. Mug shaking, dripping the dregs of the chocolate all over his pants. Loose tracksuit bottoms. No belt. 'Ray was Eddie's you know.'

It was all she could do not to throw her own chocolate at his face.

'Yes, but that's not true is it? That's just what we told people. When I went away.'

He was grinning and nodding, enjoying some private joke.

'Good thing too. Taught you some manners, those old nuns.' One good kick to that walker thing he was sitting in and he'd be in that pool, clothes and all.

'You're Ursula.' He was looking at her properly, for the first time. Smile draining away.

'Yes. That's right. And I'm looking for Ray. This letter, see?' She held it up. 'I sent it to you months ago. But I found it in Ray's clothes.' The sun went behind a cloud and the courtyard dimmed. She tried to move herself into her father's eye line but his gaze was strafing left and right, looking everywhere but at her.

'How did Ray get hold of it, Dad? Did he come to see you, maybe here, or when you were at Frederick Street?'

'He came to lunch.'

Heart thudding, she leaned closer but her father reared back, seeming to notice the state of her for the first time.

'What happened? Did the nuns beat you up?'

'Forget that. Ray came to lunch, you said. When?'

'No! Not Ray. Eddie. I told you.' He looked furious suddenly, waving his cane in the air, slamming it against her chair leg, and she jumped. 'Just said, didn't I? He came for his car. But he didn't take it. It's still there. Someone nicked the wheels.' His face was swimming, waves of anger and sadness and confusion passing over it. In the shadowy light he looked thinner, the bones etched, the hothouse bloom fading from his cheek.

'Dad, Eddie died. You know that. Ages ago.'

He shook his head adamantly, eyes fixed on something over her shoulder. 'He was there. Had some little lout with him, and a mongrel dog. Made a mess of my front lawn. I told him, you gotta show 'em who's boss.' Fear in his eyes. Some hole of the past he was falling toward. 'Like I did with Ray.'

They like to be touched.

She reached out slowly, through air like treacle, to take his hand.

'That's not true though, is it? About Eddie? It can't be.' His hand trembled. No calluses, palm soft, the skin paper thin. 'It must have been Ray who came. And you gave him the letter.'

He snatched his hand away.

'Do you know where he is now? Where he went?'

'Get off. Go away. Mind your own business. Bugger off!'

She was still staring at his hand, at the wild trembling of it, marvelling at how soft and breakable it had felt, so she didn't see the stick coming until it hit her across the cheek. Not that hard, but in reflex and shock, her arm shot up, the stick bounced back and hit her father in the chest, before rattling harmlessly away.

He heaved himself out of the chair, his leg knocking her mug over, shattering it, bits of crockery tinkling into the pool. And she realised he was crying, chest heaving, face awash, gulping at air, like a child.

And then Shandy was swooping, settling him back, patting him down. Glaring at Ursula, who wished it was her shoulder someone was patting. Her forehead someone was smoothing, telling her it would all be OK.

'Right. That's quite enough for today. Come on, Jim. Time for a rest.'

~

She sat watching her father sleep. For an hour or two, maybe more. At some point Shandy stuck her head round the door, to check on Dad and to tell Ursula to come to the office before she left, to sort out the unit, the fire, the insurance papers, the money owing to the lady who lived above. Ursula nodded until she closed the door. Sat watching the sun decline over the Japanese bridge and the empty sand garden and the half-built villas along the town tip hill. And still he slept.

After a while she got up, looked around. Some shirts in the wardrobe. Mam's old copper sunburst clock on the wall above the bed. One of those panic button things hanging on the wall. The rest could have been anyone's, anywhere, impersonal and blank. On the windowsill there were three cards, for his birthday, months ago. None of them from her. One from the nursing home, a generic-looking waterfall on the front. One from Aunty Ada, whom Ursula didn't know was still around, who must be a hundred in the shade by now. The last, with an Australian bush print on the front, the sort of thing favoured in real estate calendars and doctors' waiting rooms, she wasn't even going to bother with, but as she went to put it back down, she saw the inside was covered with small, dense writing. Tidy, neat. Familiar. The old-fashioned copperplate cursive taught to her by nuns and rulers, which she'd taught to Ray.

Hey Dad. Happy birthday for tomorrow. You were asleep when I came. (Bit of a tartar, that nurse of yours.)

She whipped around, like Tilda, but the room was full of wet breathing, lurid sunset. Her father a dim outline in the bed.

Got some news since I saw you last. I'm getting married. Not for a while but I'd like you to come. We're having bit of a get-together at this property I work at sometimes, place called Ruby Downs, out Tibooburra way. Nothing big, just a few mates. I can pick you up and bring you back, if you're up to it. I'll ring soon as I have a date, clear it with the powers that be. Hope you're feeling better. See you soon. Ray.

She read it three times before she remembered to breathe. No love. No kisses. But he'd been here. He'd seen Dad. He'd met a nurse. Maybe it was the same nurse, the one with the name like a horse. Maybe he'd left his mobile number, or his address. But when she got back to the front desk, there was a closed sign propped on top and there was no one around, even though she rang the little bell again and again.

Didn't matter. She'd call later. Collecting Winston from outside, she hurried down the hill. She had a place. A map, a direction. A clue.

CHAPTER SEVENTEEN

The sand was heaving. Mick stared out at the picnicking families, the bodysurfing Santas. Made no move to get out of the car.

Something occurred to Ray. 'You been to the beach before?'

The boy shrugged, drawing a forearm across his ever-dripping nose.

'You can swim though, right?'

'Don't have any cossies. They're at home.'

'Just go in your daks. No one'll care.'

Mick gave him an incredulous stare.

Digging in his pocket, Ray held out a fifty. 'Here. Chrissie present. There's a surf shop down there. Don't spend it all at once.'

'It's Christmas *Day*. Everything's shut.'

Ray sighed, reached over, tucked the money in Mick's top pocket. Opened the passenger door.

'I dunno. Buy yourself an ice cream or something. Take the dog for a walk. I won't be long.'

He sat with the engine running, watching Mick stumble across the grass, almost pulled off his feet by the frantic kelpie. At the sand's edge, the boy paused, shifting foot to foot. Ray knew what he was thinking, the dreary circling patterns of it. The leaving, the being left, in a strange place, surrounded by other people's mothers, fathers, sisters, brothers. Even the dog not his own.

Rolling down the window, he shouted into hot exhaust. 'Be back in an hour, OK? Meet you right here. Tie that dog up if you go in the water. And swim between the flags.'

Mick took off finally, in a blur of leaping dog and curly red hair.

Heading into a world of hot asphalt, ticking sprinklers, clenched cul-de-sacs bathed in waves of cicada song, he envied Mick even that crowded city beach. No air here, even a few streets from the sea. Coming in, he'd driven across the bridge and back, just to see it, to show Mick, who refused to be impressed. Looking for fat ferries, creamy sand, sparkling water, all those stories that had spanned his childish imagination, Ray found himself stuck by traffic in the middle lane. Trapped by an iron lace of shadow between road and sky.

Number 50 was a little semi languishing in the shadow of the big white mansion next door. Ray sat in the ute, sweating, staring between the address on the back of the letter and the piles of boxes, bricks and rubbish on the front verandah. A rusted bicycle under the front window. A row of Buddhist flags tattering from the eaves.

Nothing spoke to him of the sister he remembered. But there, beneath the car port she'd noted in the letter, between what looked like a painting easel and a stand fan missing most of its blades, sat one of Mam's old carved-oak dining-room chairs. Along with a box of cowboy novels and the family Bible, it was in the list of things she'd given Dad, things she threatened to throw out if he didn't write back soon. Her name at the bottom in that familiar rounded hand. No dear, no kisses. No love.

He turned off the ignition. Thirty-five by the car thermometer. Mick's Fantales turning to goo on the dash. Because it was the only decent thing he had and because it would hide the tea stain on his shirt, he struggled into his coat. Then he remembered there was a stain on that as well. Swearing, he reefed it off and the shirt with it. Rummaged through his rucksack for his old blue work singlet, the only clean thing he had left, then turned down the visor mirror, got out his comb. Thinking as he scraped and flattened of a tall woman with hard rough fingers, tutting, spitting, trying to coax a curl from a little boy's dead straight sticking-up fringe. In the glare of the mirror, he saw someone pink, wet, featureless, blond hair dark with sweat.

He got out, collected his present, pushed the gate open against cracked and lifting concrete, went up the front path.

Nothing prepared him for it. He'd expected shock, tears, anger even. Waiting at the front door, hearing his knock echoing for too long down some hallway, he'd braced himself for someone frailer, slower, shorter. A woman gone soft at spine or middle, but unmistakeable. A square face, olive-skinned, the eyes steel blue. That same look in them he got when he knew he was up against it. When he'd made a mistake but wasn't going to admit it. No fear.

And it was a mistake. It had to be.

At first, all he could think was how could she bear a jumper in this heat? Heavy, long and black, it hung off her like she was made of wire. Bare feet, bare legs, a white neck rising like a stalk from all that wool. Blue vein at her temple. Blue eyes, like pale flat stones. He thought of curls, dimples, blondeness, a gap-toothed smile. Couldn't be. Wasn't possible. All that dead black, dead straight hair.

'Till?'

Nothing. She wasn't looking at him, seemed to be focused on the street, over his right shoulder. But there was something, wasn't there? Some line drawn between them, humming in heated air.

'Tilly? It's me, Ray. Remember me?'

He bent down, trying to get into her eye line but she just cocked her head to gaze past him again, out the gate and down the road.

He took a step back. Must have it wrong. But there was the letter, the address. Mam's chair, sitting right there in the car port. The letter was old though. She might have moved, left all her stuff here while the new tenant or owner moved in. What about this woman then, her spidery fingers picking at white and wasted forearms? Her jumper falling off one shoulder, revealing a collarbone like a chicken wing? This sick-looking stranger with his sister's eyes.

'Sorry. Maybe I've made a mistake. I'm after Ursula. Ursula McCullough? Does she live here?'

Nothing. Blue eyes in a death's head. That killer stare.

He was about to turn, walk away, get back in his ute, drive back to the beach then out of town as fast as he could, when the woman nodded, stepped forward. Taking the present, she shuffled off into the gloom of the house.

He had no choice but to follow, stumbling up a dark hallway with missing floorboards, skirting piles of paperbacks, more boxes, what looked like an amp for an electric guitar. Expecting Urs to appear at any moment, mop in hand. To explain that she was moving in, she was moving out. That she didn't really live here, in this place like an old man's boarding house, with its smell of mould, incense and cooped-up cat. But when he reached the little lounge room, he found only the woman who had to be Tilda, sitting perched on the arm of a chair, his present in her lap.

He picked his way across a floor covered in dirty mugs, full ashtrays, sleeveless LPs. Sat down on a leather lounge that felt fat, soft, overripe. It was stifling in there. Dark too, the curtains were closed. Wallpaper trailed above the fireplace, the rest of the walls painted bright new pink. Wind chimes tinkled somewhere, a curtain puffed in a stray breeze, revealing a fish symbol pasted to the window. A statue of the Virgin Mary on the mantelpiece.

When he finally worked up enough moisture in his mouth to speak, his voice sounded too loud in that little room. 'Till. It's good to see you, eh. Bit of a shock, I bet. Me rocking up after all this time.'

She went back to staring at the box on her lap. Since the journey and the car crash and its meeting with Mick's size nine boot, it bristled with torn reindeers and knotted clumps of sticky tape.

'You were only a little tyke last time.' Seven, going on eight, but she'd seemed younger. Throwing pig knuckles on the back verandah, chattering to dolls, stones, trees, drinking from an imaginary cup. 'We had tea together. Remember?' Bark tea, mud scones, blue dogs, hula hoops. On the back verandah at Twenty Bends, when he was barely nineteen. His one and only visit home since he'd left, five years before.

'You brought me a present.' A statement of fact, empty as her face. But she'd said something, and she was looking at him now at least.

'Yeah. I did. That dog.' Not a real dog, which she'd always wanted, but he'd seen how dogs got treated at Twenty Bends. A big blue toy dog with a sideways tongue and a goofy smile. He'd won it at the carnival where he was working, a travelling show which, by chance or fate, had settled for a two-week stint in a town a few hours from home. It had been a sudden whim, a summer homesickness, brought on by the smell of horse manure, saddle leather, swimming pool bush. Before he'd had time to think about it too much, he'd hitched a lift in the back of a truck. At a set of lights in town, a car full of teenagers had jeered at him, this boy tall as a man clutching a big blue dog. A stupid note, for Tilda, pinned to its front.

He'd crouched in the scrub behind the backyard for over an hour, on the lookout for a telltale cloud of tractor smoke coming up the track toward the gate. Hoping to see Mam emerging from the laundry with a basket of washing, or Urs heading up the driveway, on her way back from work. But there'd been just the little girl on the verandah, a plump little girl in a too-small pink dress. And he'd been so relieved by the sight of her, by the sheer busy blonde round-cheeked aliveness of her, that he'd failed to be surprised that she wasn't surprised to see him. Failed to be alarmed that she didn't speak to him or look at him, just kept up that cheery gabble while trying to feed the dog leaves and sticks, smashing them into the furry slit of its mouth. No words at all in that high-pitched noise she'd been making through her gap-toothed mouth. He should have realised. Should have known it wasn't normal, for a child of eight. Should have seen it might have something do with the scar on her forehead. Those missing teeth.

When she'd jumped up, pointing toward the driveway, still making those squealing, word-shaped sounds, he'd been so jumpy, all he could think of was to run. He'd been halfway down the path and hidden behind the wood shed before he looked. Expecting to see a big man stalking up the driveway, an olive-skinned woman walking up the driveway, he saw no one. Nothing there.

'Listen, Till. Is Urs coming home soon? I wanted to say gidday.'

Tilda shook her head, idly ripping at the wrapping paper on the present. His mouth went dry again.

'Oh. Right. Where is she then? Shopping or something?' Stupid, stupid. Who goes shopping on Christmas Day?

Tilda picked up a mug from the mess on the floor, started swigging something from it. Tipping up the opened box, she emptied the mess of plastic attachments into her lap. Sat staring at them, face blank. There was weird smell coming off her, he realised. Metallic, minty, mixed with something medicinal, like nail polish or aftershave.

'She's gone home.'

'You said she lives here though. Didn't you?' She hadn't. She'd just nodded. Could have meant anything. The sweat was running freely now, between his legs, into the depths of the sticky leather lounge.

'No. *Home* home. I wasn't allowed to go.'

Did she mean Dad's place, at Frederick Street? No one could think of that place as home. And the homestead was sold.

'Are you sure, Till? Thing is, I just came from out there.' But he'd lost her again. Her gaze had drifted past his shoulder, to the wall behind his head. A row of little paintings up there, soft hills, plump valleys, vague sweeps and blurs of colour, in dawn grey, cool blue. He longed to climb inside one of those paintings, find that plump blue valley, lie down in that river. Lose himself in a trawl of painted stars.

'Till? Do you mean Twenty Bends?'

There was the sound of a key in the front door. Before he could extricate himself from the womb of the lounge, heavy footsteps thumped down the hallway, and a man appeared in the lounge. A huge, blocky, musclebound bruiser in a baseball hat. Ray saw the pinprick eyes, the straining biceps covered in tattoos. He'd started calculating the distance from the man to Tilda, from the lounge he was sitting on to the doorway where the big bloke was standing, when a smaller, older man pushed in, his smile fading as soon as he spotted Ray.

'Matilda? What's going on? Are you OK?' The little man put a hand on Tilda's shoulder, which she promptly shook off. 'Who's this?'

'Ray.'

The man went pale. The big speed freak took a step forward, fists bunched, but when the smaller man shook his head, he fell back again.

'He's my brother. He bought me a present. But I don't like it.' Tilda swept the bits of plastic from her lap and they joined the mess on the floor. 'Can he stay for lunch?'

Ray stood up, put out his hand. Something about the little man seemed to demand it. The glasses, the prim moustache. The fussy little ponytail.

'Gidday. Ray McCullough.' The man just stood there. Didn't introduce himself, made no move to take Ray's hand. 'Tilda's brother.' Before Ray, nonplussed, could put his arm down again, someone else emerged from the hallway, a vast young woman in a flowered dress. Squeezing roughly past the bikie and the bloke with the ponytail, she plonked herself on the floor, right next to Ray's leg. Grabbing a remote, she turned on the TV. The bikie followed her, sitting hunched a few inches from the screen, staring and muttering, turning back to glare at Ray.

The little man still hadn't moved. He was just staring at Ray, red and yellow lights from a Christmas ad shining off his glasses, so Ray couldn't see his eyes.

He cleared his throat, tried again. 'Look, sorry to barge in. Christmas Day and all. I'm here to see my sister. My other sister. Ursula. Tilly says she's out.' The little man seemed made of stone. Ray thought about sticking his hand out again, but just wiped it on his trousers. Longing for a taste of whatever Tilda was knocking back from her mug. Or even better, an ice-cold beer. 'Sorry. Didn't catch your name.'

'That's Harry. He lives here.' Tilda took another swig from her mug, jerked her head at the bikie and the woman on the floor. 'Those fat cunts don't.'

'Matilda. That's enough.' The ponytail man took hold of Tilda's arm again, trying and failing to wrestle the mug off her. His fingers left pink marks on her too white, too thin skin.

'He's my brother so he can stay, can't he? For lunch? You said it was orphans' Christmas and he's an orphan, sort of, because he's alone, but you're not and you're not an orphan and I'm not either, even if Mam's dead, because Dad's still alive. And they aren't either.' She pointed accusingly at the bikie and the flowered woman. 'So can he?'

Ray felt dizzy. All that silence from her before and now all the words, fast and faster, in that strange hitching rhythm, too much like the speed freak for his liking, who was switching channels and talking angrily at the television, spit shining in his mutton-chop whiskers, while the fat woman hummed and rocked, plaiting her too-thin hair. Ray sat down again, and the woman's flowered haunch overflowed onto the edge of his boot. He shifted away and the leather made a sucking sound. Wind chimes again, what sounded like a rooster, somewhere. Rivers of sweat on his legs, sticking him to the leather. The corner of the poster on the wall, a rainbow with a bluebird, peeled and flopped in the heat.

'So can he? Stay?'

'No, Tilda. Not today.' Harry had managed to get the mug off her now, was sniffing at it, nose wrinkled. 'Might be time for you to take a shower. Before we eat.'

'Why not? You've got your stupid friends here. They're not my friends. Or even orphans. Just really fucking fat.' She aimed a kick at the flowery woman's ankle, who, without looking up from her plaiting, shot out a foot in return, her big boot connecting with Tilda's bare toe, making Tilda yelp. Then the speed freak was on his feet again, towering over everyone, swearing and spitting, and Ray was standing up too.

'Stop it! Gerald. Calm down.' For a little bloke, Harry had a loud voice. Tilda subsided, still kicking angrily at the mess on the floor. 'Give me that.' To Ray's surprise, the bikie handed over the remote and Harry turned off the TV.

'Take Dot outside. No, not that way. Out the front and down the side. You know the rules. See if you can find some eggs.' Eggs. Ray's head was swimming. Nothing made sense. But Gerald was stalking obediently back up the hallway, Dot trailing him like a large unfriendly dog.

'Matilda. Go and check if lunch is done. Then set the table, so we can eat.' And she did it, like she was a servant or something, disappearing in her somnambulist shuffle through a doorway leading to the back of the house.

Harry closed the door, turned to face Ray. Drawing himself up to full height in his little leather moccasins, chest all puffed out. Ray felt suddenly very tired.

'Now, listen here. I'm not sure who you are or what your game is, although I can hazard a guess.' Hazard. Something too crisp and fussy about the way he talked. Like a teacher or a priest. 'But you shouldn't be here. Matilda should never have let you in.'

'Yeah? Why's that? Like Tilly said, I'm her brother. And Ursula's. She lives here, right?'

'There was nothing in the paper.' Harry seemed to be talking to himself, fiddling nervously with his ponytail. 'How on earth did you get this address?'

Ray gave the man a good slow look, up and down. Old-man shorts, ironed to a crease. White T-shirt, *No Mining in Kakadu* in faded letters across the front. A protest button pinned above his breast. Plump little man breasts, budding out. Something girly about the T-shirt too. Too small, too tight around the arms.

'First things first. Told you who I was. How about you do me the same favour?'

'I beg your pardon? This is my house.'

'I thought this was Ursula's place.'

'It is. I mean, I live here. This is my home.'

'Oh, right. Thought you were the cleaner or something.' Ray nudged his boot at a dirty plate on the floor. The man's face turned a deeper shade of pink. Maybe this twerp with the pigtail was Ursula's boyfriend or something. Wouldn't have credited it but it was a long time since he'd seen her and, anyway, nothing here made sense. Fish stickers, prayer flags, grog-laced tea. The Virgin Mary up there on the mantelpiece, sorrowing away to herself in the dark.

'This is a mistake.' The man had braced himself against the door Tilda had gone through. Arms folded, legs apart. Socks with sandals, for pity's sake.

'I'd like you to leave, OK? Right now.'

Ray took his time getting up. Letting the bloke see the full scope of him, the broad shoulders, the big seamed hands, ready by his side. Fists easy, legs easy. A boxer's stance.

'Look, if it's money you're after, it's too late. The reward's been withdrawn.'

Bloke talked in riddles. Hard to get a handle on him. Just words and words and words, like Gerald, like Tilda, all piled up. Everything he said stuffed with some sideways smirking meaning, issuing from that pink mouth beneath that bum fuzz moustache.

'Haven't got a clue what you're on about, mate. I don't want money. I got money. I just came to see my sister. Simple as.'

'Well, you can't. She's not here. She's out.'

'But she does live here. We're getting somewhere.' He moved forward a step, and Harry moved back. 'Know when she'll be home? Or how I can get in touch? A mobile number would do.'

'You've got to be joking. I'm not giving you that.'

Ray took another step forward, the bloke backed up, until he could go no further, squashed hard against the door. Sweat was breaking out on his hairline, the little drops tinged brown. He must dye it, that stupid ponytail.

'I'm warning you, you'd better leave, right now, or I'm calling the police.'

'Keep your wig on. I just want to see her, that's all. Say gidday.'

'Well, she doesn't want to see you.'

'And what the fuck would you know?'

'More than you, apparently. This won't work, OK? You're too late. You've got it wrong.'

Bloke had balls, Ray had to give him that. He wondered whether he would have to actually do it, or whether the threat would be enough. Thing was, he was a bit keen by now. That coiling feeling in his stomach, spreading out, covering his skin like quick hot veins. One fast clean uppercut across that little bum-crack chin. The thought leapt out before him, acquiring flesh and heft. In for a penny, and he'd had a shit of a day. A sin in thought, according to old Father O'Reilly, in his billowing skirts, with his football face and his big ruler with pictures of New Zealand on it, his cracked leather hands. A hundred times on a blackboard, in a stinking classroom, all lunchtime, but when the priest came back, he'd made a mistake. Two words not one. Indeed, in deed, in O'Reilly's mocking lilt. The cane keeping time.

'You're not her brother. She's not looking for her brother. She doesn't have a brother. You'd know that, if you were Ray.'

Whatever had been brewing here, in the springing fur of humidity this little man seemed to be incubating, growing it like ivy, skin to skin, broke, and Ray stepped forward. Stepped up. So close now, he could smell the bloke. Sweat, musty clothes, a patchouli stink. That little protest button which had looked at a distance to bear an emblem like a nest of worms revealed itself to be a photo. Tiny arms, wrinkled legs. An addled baby eye.

Time to knock this shit on the head.

Ray raised his arm and the man flinched, but Ray just plucked his pencil from behind his ear.

'OK. Listen up. I reckon you're a lying mongrel but anyway. Here's what we'll do. I'm gonna leave my number, and you're gonna tell my sister to ring me when she gets back from wherever it is she's gone.'

Looking around for some paper, an old book or something, not finding any, just dusty records and dirty cups and crap all over the floor, he thought of arms, foreheads, the soft skin of Harry's white, plump, female-looking wrists. Instead he walked over and wrote his phone number on the half-stripped wall above the fireplace.

'There. You tell Urs to give us a ring. Now I'm going to go and say goodbye to my other sister, then I'll use your bog and then I'll be out of your hair.' He gave one last look at the dye-stained bald spot at the back of Harry's head, then pushed past, through the door.

Tilda was in the kitchen, standing at an old door which had been roughly rigged up as a bench. She was prodding with a fork at something black and wizened in a roasting tin. A smell of scalded nuts. Even hotter in here than in the rest of the house. Oven must have been on all day.

'What's that?'

'Lunch.'

Letting the fork fall, Tilda picked up a bottle on the counter, shook out a tablet, swallowed it down with a gulp from her freshly filled mug. The bottle had her name on the label. That weird smell was sherry he realised, mixed with a chemical fug.

'Yeah, but what exactly?'

'Tofu loaf.' She stabbed at it again. 'It's burnt.'

'It's OK,' he told her, although when he took a knife to it, the inside was like charred soap. No wonder she was so thin.

This was something he could do. While Tilda stood worrying the elbows of her jumper, he cut off the burnt crust of the thing, fried the inside up in some oil. Under the sink, he found potatoes, carrots, old and whiskery, but vegetables at least. He set Tilda to peeling them, while he put a pan of water on to boil. No time for roasting and he wasn't turning the oven on again.

Going in search of herbs or garlic, he found a tin of Gravox. In the fridge, a carton of cream. As he flipped the tofu in the pan, he saw Tilda was chopping vegetables without washing them or peeling them, big chunks of carrot top going straight into the pot. He said nothing. From outside, faint yelling, getting louder. Chickens squawking, what sounded like a car alarm. He put his head down, eyeing the cream, waiting for it to pip. The void between himself and Tilda strung precariously, their elbows meeting companionably as she chopped and he stirred.

'What's that?' She nodded at the stuff in his pan.

'Gravy.' He added more cream.

'Harry won't eat that. He doesn't eat dairy.' She sounded like a kid parroting the teacher.

'Yeah, well. What Harry doesn't know won't hurt him.' She giggled. And there, just for a moment, was that little girl with the cheeky grin.

'What it needs is a bit of wine. Or some of that.' He pointed at the mug she'd been drinking from. 'Reckon you should lay off it for a bit though. On top of those pills.'

That did it. She closed up, drifted off, to the step by the open back door. Sat drinking, staring out to the backyard. He could have kicked himself. Plating up some food and pouring himself some of her McWilliams, he went and sat beside her. Together they watched Gerald kicking at chickens, doing violence to the fence with a bit of wood. Dot was sitting cross-legged inside the coop, keening high and wild. Harry was attempting to wrest the wood off Gerald while glancing back at the house and dialling numbers one-handed on his phone.

'Here. Try some. Just a little bit.' He held out a forkful but she shook her head. Didn't blame her. It tasted like roasted surfboard. Ray took a swig of sherry to wash his mouthful down and the sweetness mixing with the cream made him want to gag.

Harry seemed to have got through to someone now. He was talking fast, looking frantically between Gerald, who was attacking the Otto bin, and Ray sitting on the step.

'I better go, Till. I think John Lennon's calling the cops.' No smile. 'Before I forget.' He fumbled behind his ear for his pen again. 'Will you do something for me? Get Urs to ring me when she gets back? I gave him the number.' He jerked his head at Harry. 'But I don't trust him.' When he reached for her arm, it was flaccid, skin on bone. He rolled up her jumper, wrote his number on her as gently and clearly as he could.

'Like a tattoo.' She turned her arm this way and that.' Like Gerald's.'

'Yeah. Sort of. But it'll wash off. So write it down somewhere else as well, OK? And don't tell old four eyes. Our secret, right?'

She nodded obediently. He left her there, on the step, with her warm sherry and her inedible meal, with a mad bikie in the backyard, and that fat woman screaming on and on. All he could do. Too little, too late. Like the day with the big blue dog.

CHAPTER EIGHTEEN

The luxury health retreat near the creek was for sale. Reining in her monster of a four-wheel drive, she lumbered to a stop outside the top gate.

Willow Waters, they were calling it now. Could you do that, change the name of a creek? No, on her map it still said Twenty Bends. Just the property then, but there was precious little of that left, if the diagram on the sign was correct. A bit of that poor pasture backing onto Tangello's, a wedge-shaped paddock down near the old stockyards. The denuded orchard, now an organic vegetable patch. The rest had been sold to the owners of the new golf course, those sausage-casing tycoons.

The historic homestead was still there, nestled in the bends of the creek. Things always nestled in the country, didn't they, when city people were involved. Weren't just plonked there, close enough to water, high enough for flood. Good enough, near enough, working or buggered, those were your choices. When something stopped working, bits were picked off the carcass, absorbed slowly to something else. When that died too, it was left to moulder, at random sunlit angles. Her whole childhood littered with them. Ex-sheds, ex-tractors. Ex-sheep.

Now, though, even the worst old outbuildings had been slapped with a thick coat of nostalgia, the word rustic liberally applied. The old shearing shed had been gutted, painted, hauled off its piers, plonked in the middle of the front garden. Reborn as a summer house slash yoga retreat. All part of the relaxing country lifestyle, according to the real estate sign. As if that was an option, like a sandwich filling, instead of something you were corralled into, ground down by, until you fitted the great sprawling fly-blown shape of it, not the other way round.

And it hadn't done much good, all this relaxing and retreating, not as far as she could see. Things had got so relaxed around her, weeds were crop tall along the driveway. The gate listing halfway off its hinge.

Not her problem. Chop it up, sell it off, burn it down. Graze bloody camels on it for all she cared. Yet even as she told herself this, she was giving the gate a tentative shove. Third go and the padlock fell off. Wind could have done that. The hinge was broken, the chain rusty. Everything in such tawdry disrepair.

She walked on, curving right then left, on long slow bends she could have navigated in her sleep. Up the ridge, down the dip, through the gully where the creek crossed the road at flood time, the causeway crumbled and potholed now, the old flood marker counting backwards to itself in the ditch. Not twenty bends, never had been, on either creek or road, she wasn't sure who'd come up with that. Seven on the drive, eight at a pinch if you counted that weird dogleg Dad had put in to avoid driving over the top of the septic tank. Up again and round again, the avenue of silver birch Mam had planted now just an honour guard of stumps. A pair of spindly Japanese maples there instead, trying tremulously to turn. They'd planted willows all along the water line too, to justify the name. Romantic weeds, Mam used to called them. Thirsty bloodsuckers, according to Dad.

At the driveway gate, she could hear the creek but not see it, a black burbling over rock. Her view of the water was blocked by the transplanted shearing shed. It looked silly and, yes, sheepish, hulking there in the front garden, with all its walls gone and what was left of it painted pink. Like a burly farmhand had been forced to come to Sunday dinner wearing lipstick and minus his shirt.

Rounding the last bend, she feared the worst. But there was the house, spreading low and ungainly in honey-coloured stone. Leaves scudding on gravel, a pear tree sat flattened into its own shadow along the orchard fence. The day leaching and silvering already, like something from a mournful Swedish film.

Climbing the front steps, inventing stories about dead mobiles and car breakdowns in case she met some woman in a hat, she saw that the blinds were drawn. A drift of leaves and real estate brochures littered the front mat. So she kept walking, past white crossed doors and weathered lintels, eyes half-closed, hand trailing. Telling rooms like a rosary, front parlour to back bedroom, sewing room to dining room, gold stone to silver shadow. Remembering everything, in her skin at least.

Halfway round, her hand met air. She almost fell down a set of steps that shouldn't have been there. The whole back of the house had been lopped off. That great mash of wooden extensions and tin lean-tos Dad had kept adding on out there like a never-ending sentence—Mam's pantry, Ray's sleep-out, the old laundry—all gone. Instead of the Hills hoist, the chicken coop, the old incinerator, a square of bright orange cobbles and some empty flowerbeds. The 'French-style kitchen garden' promised on the sign. Nothing growing but weeds and moss. Only the old pepper tree clung on, its roots already knobbling up the new pavers. Beyond that, the remains of the orchard, just stubble and stump. From this angle, without the generous skirt of its wraparound and the front verandah jutting out like a fake bosom, the house looked bald. Pimple on a pumpkin, Mam would have said.

And what on earth would she have made of her kitchen? All those windows, all those skylights. My giddy aunt. They'll fry like fish.

She leaned against the back French doors, funnelling shadow with her hands. A tundra of tile in there, waves of stone and chrome. No colour, no clutter, no handles on the cupboards. No bowls of eggs or faded farm calendars, no blackened, cranky, flap-sided toaster only Ray could fix. No appliances at all that she could see, just a black vase of poppies on a white swerve of bench. The ceiling raked so high now, the room looked taller than it was wide, a sort of coffin meets art gallery effect. You'd need to be scarily tall to inhabit it, like one of Harry's African art statues on stilts.

This was the sort of thing the architect had wanted to do to her place, before the money ran out. He'd stood in her back garden, sketching downlights and marble countertops, so excited, she'd thought his gelled hair was about to rocket off his head. To save money and while they waited for the loan to come through, she and Simon had made a start, ripping out some of the old cupboards, tearing up the lino, finding dead rats, old newspapers, ancient puppy bones. In lieu of the island they couldn't yet afford, Simon had rigged up an old door as a makeshift bench. Sanded it, but not painted it. Never got around to fixing it to the wall. And then he left and the bank reneged on the loan. The house had stayed that way, half-raw, half-old. Half-haunted, like this place, by what was, what might have been.

It was getting late. The pepper tree was casting knuckled shadows on the cobblestones. Couldn't tell the time by the clock in that kitchen. No numbers on it, just two silver hands measuring a desert of days and nights. The poppies dull smears of reflection in the stainless-steel fridge. Another flower had opened even since she'd arrived, that's how warm it was in there. Harry would find it symbolic, the mute clock and the frantic blooming. Found symbols in everything, Harry. Wealth in the arrangement of windows, spirituality in a bowl of fruit. When he'd switched from still life to pottery, it was God, inevitably, lurking in greasy chunks of clay. God made all things and all stories, according to Harry, and she'd wanted to ask him why bother then, when all your coffee mugs look like ashtrays and all your bananas turn out without a hint of bend?

Why things couldn't just be what they were. A house. A vase of flowers. A woman, waiting for her son to come home.

Heels on gravel, round the side. A tinkling laugh.

Diving down her old rat run, under the fence and along the creek paddock and through the orchard that wasn't there any more, she spotted a woman with a clipboard rounding the corner of the house, followed by a young couple dressed in black. Maybe they were going to buy the place. They would suit it. Taller, thinner, more modern people than she was, amid all those skimming, swooping angles, they'd be to scale. That kitchen would give them back to themselves, snug in their black geometry. They wouldn't feel like she did. Extinguished. Rubbed out.

After a night spent with Winston in the back of the car, she woke stiff, covered in dog hair, yet unaccountably refreshed.

At the last town before the big haul, she bought bottled water, sandwiches, a guidebook, a folding shovel, toilet paper and a box of muesli bars. For some unknown reason, a kilo bag of flour.

Plugging her mobile into the handy slot on the dash, she headed northwest on dead straight, brand new road. The phone blinked steadily, the map sat crisply folded on the passenger seat. The road she was following neat and black, as if cut with dressmaker's scissors, eating its way steadily toward the border, before joining that other, fainter road, looping up toward the left-hand corner of the state. It gave her pleasure, all that land cut from a pattern and staying where it should. It was the little roads you had to watch out for, the spidery, pinkish faint ones, hiccupping their way across empty slabs of green.

That was wishful thinking, for a start. Two hours out from the town where she'd done her shopping, all brown, as far as she could see. The guidebook called one section black soil, but she couldn't see that either. Just various shades of dun. A hundred k in, a switch from bitumen to white dust, then abrupt red flood-plain, flattening to long stretches of channel country, grey earth speckled with lignum, cane grass, mulga, gidgee. Leopardwood, beefwood, bimble box and supplejack, the guidebook intoned. Such delicious names for things so uniformly grey. From some neglected corner of her brain, she retrieved the facts that mulgas were edible by stock, dams were called ground tanks, and a dry sheep was a ewe without a lamb at foot. If she were a sheep, that's who she would be.

For two hours, nothing but grass, bleach yellow and bottle blonde. Silver cassia lined the lime-wash track. Dead roos, black goats, glossy as sin. An emu lay in the middle of the road, split and spread-eagled like something from a cartoon. Wedgetails lifted ponderously on her approach, barely clearing the bonnet, guts filled with guts. A lake, once, bobbing sea green and chimeric as she topped a rise. Emu on the shore, serene and legless in the shimmer. Then the land fell, the road turned, the lake disappeared. On the horizon, like a sideways thought, a kestrel hovered, wings spinning, as if to conjure something. Water perhaps.

Somewhere to the left of the track she was travelling, the famous old river. Now and again she crossed one of its smaller tributaries, called an anabranch out here. Below vast iron-laced bridges, a deep-gouged history, hoary with roots. On the banks, silver gums infested with mistletoe, herons stalking oily water. More goats, scrambling, hoofs clattering, to perch nonchalantly in the forks of drowned trees.

A patch of grass down there, tiny green for the eye to drink up. And then she was over, in a rattle of rust and dust.

After a while she forced herself to relax, stop gripping the wheel like she was about to fall off a cliff. Instead of checking the fuel gauge and the temperature dial all the time, she fixed herself on the horizon, navigating static until she found a local station on the radio. She warbled along, her tuneless hum underscored by Winston's snoring, the caramel thrum of tyres. Winding down the window, she stuck her elbow out, sculpting her face into the stare of the men she'd seen in passing utes. By late afternoon, she'd adopted the official salute. A nod that could be road judder or fly avoidance. A single finger lifted from the wheel.

When the radio died, somewhere in the middle of a vast dry floodplain, called, impenetrably, Dick's Dam, she punched recklessly at buttons on the console, as if in managing to steer this big black beast in a straight line for a few hours, she'd somehow assumed its armour, drunk its blood. Like the naming of trees and tributaries, a spell of sorts. She had no idea what most of those dials and levers accomplished, and for the first hour she'd driven in four-wheel drive on bitumen, wondering why the car felt so sluggish. But they calmed her, these shining ranks of winks and clicks. Floated her, cool and invincible, above a dry old world.

At dusk, fearing wildlife, as if roos crouched, commando-style, under every bush, she pulled into a roadhouse, the last one before the turn-off to that cobweb of tiny tracks on the map. It had a motel attached to it, steel cabins made from shipping containers, stained pink from the dust of passing trucks. Steel-toe boots sat lined up beside each door. But there was a restaurant and there was airconditioning and, according to the manager, dressed for safari behind his desk, dogs were allowed, just not inside.

She sat on her doorstep with Winston, eating bright pink Chinese, watching other travellers come to roost in their trucks and caravans. Feeling sun swept, sanguine, in control. When the manager passed by, well camouflaged for his trip to clean the toilets, she tipped her hat. Like her, it had acquired a satisfying patina of dust.

The illusion lasted until sunset, when yet another ute pulled into the cabin next door. It was drawing a trailer of barking, snarling dogs, packed so tight, their tongues and ears poked through the mesh. Towering above all of them, an unearthly black mastiff, its massive chest covered by a studded leather vest. Winston tried to melt between her legs, his blond bulk stuck there like a cork.

The driver, a rabbity little man in tiny shorts, came over and asked her for a cigarette. She offered him the packet, mesmerised by his teeth. He was on his way to Hungerford, to meet a mate of a mate, to go roo hunting, but he'd done his ball joint and then his battery went and then he'd hit a pig. Big fucker. Size of a horse. Woulda shot it, if he'd had a gun.

As soon as she could, she escaped inside, dragging Winston behind. Bugger the rules. Like her shiny pink bedspread covering a mattress vicious with springs, this place held only the thinnest veneer of civilisation. Lying there, wrapped in her pink polyester sheets, she thought about the owners of all those big steel-toe boots, the little pig man with the big dogs. Wondered what sort of man Ray might have become.

CHAPTER NINETEEN

N ext morning, at the turn-off from the highway, marked only by a boiled-looking lantern jaw of rock, she sat staring at the route drawn by the motel manager on her map. His biro line meandered uncertainly, coinciding only now and then with the dotted line of the track. Beyond her window, the track itself, thin, rutted, curling up through starved-looking hills. On the map, her path was overlain with a series of faint wiggles and squiggles, like the moth tunnels on a scribbly gum. Contour lines, according to the motel man. Or dry creeks. Or both. He wasn't sure. Sprinkled here and there, small dots with italicised names. Not places or towns, just properties. Some historic, mostly abandoned, even the homesteads gone.

Ruby Downs was there, in italics, but the motel manager had never heard of it. Near the border, where the line he'd drawn finished at a junction with another track, he'd put an uncertain-looking X and a question mark. Beyond that point, just desert, dingoes, the famous fence. Between the junction and the border, scoured yellow space. Even the mapmaker had stopped pretending anything lived out there.

She took a swig of thermos coffee, racked up the aircon, struck right.

~

For the first forty ks, the road was grooved and sandy, but firm enough. After keying herself up for battle, it seemed the place might defeat her with gates. Every ten minutes she had to stop, get out, wrestle with some new and elaborate variation on a wire loop, drive through, get out to close the gate, get back in again. Beyond the car, a watchful ticking silence, an odd bright singing when she touched the wire. Her journey travelling out before and behind her, sounding too loud, too foolish. By the eighth gate, she was wishing for a companion. Even Harry would do.

At the last gate, a goanna sat draped like yellow and white paint on the post. Remembering Dad's stories, how they'd run up any available leg in lieu of a tree, she hovered uncertainly, swatting flies. No trees out here. Just defeated-looking bushes and a little mailbox like a little house marking some house that was no longer there. A goat skull had been nailed, voodoo-like, to the other post.

In the end, she had no choice but to jump forward, wrench the loop off, jump back. The lizard didn't move. Might be dead. Might have been waiting there since the dawn of time.

An hour later and even gates and fences had disappeared. The road got steeper, rockier, all furrow, crest and dip. Those innocuous-looking contour lines on her map were flowering to a full set of hills. This was jump-up country, according to her guidebook, unique, ancient, geographically significant, but she didn't care, any more than she cared to know the name of the spiny dusty greyish plant that seemed to be the only thing growing out here.

Soon even that had petered out. Just gibbers, ridges, white circles of salt. Emu ran in packs, keeping pace with the car. Now and again, at some unknown signal, one would alter trajectory, the whole flock veering with it as if drawn on a string. On one curve, five of them headed in bouncing swaying arcs straight for her. After that, each time she spotted any she slammed on the brakes, waiting nervously while they performed their demented zigzags up ahead. Trying not to think what would happen if she hit one. Trying not to worry what might happen to this track if it rained. A few clouds tracked her progress, but they were fluffy, thready, far away.

Two hours in and she could no longer ignore the impact on her bladder of the juddering road. Outside the chill of the car, the heat was overwhelming, the skin of her face sucked instantly dry. Looking for a tree and not finding one, she squatted on leaves the colour of emu feathers, protected only by the tent of her dress. No one here to care or see but, even so, her trickling seemed interminable and far too loud. Leaves crackled as she shifted uneasily from haunch to haunch. She worried about snakes. She worried about dingoes, spiders, those looming, bustling birds. Another of Dad's stories, surfaced slyly, finding purchase in this lean dry space. Mate of a mate of his who'd chased an emu across a paddock, for a dare. Disembowelled with the flick of a claw.

Still dripping, she scurried back to the car, to the comforting thunk of its big black door. According to the car thermometer, it was thirty-eight degrees outside.

If possible, the road got worse after that, just two lines of gravel traversing a broken spine of rock. As she lurched up and down, she touched her supplies, partly for reassurance, partly to stop them falling off the seat. Her little bottles of water and cling-wrapped sandwiches looked suddenly stupid and puny against this place. On one particularly vicious corner, the car dancing sideways across the corrugations, the flour bounced off, exploded on the floor.

She drove on in a mist of white. What had she been thinking? Damper probably, in case of an emergency, cooked on a fire by the side of the road. She could make the damper but she couldn't light the fire. She'd forgotten to buy matches and that horrible little dog man had stolen her lighter. No lighter in this modern car, of course, despite all its clever slots and holes. She felt a sudden affection for Simon's old Volvo, even for her despised mobile, but when she checked, there was only a single bar of reception. On the next dip, even that flickered out.

After what seemed like a lifetime of jouncing up ridges and skidding clumsily down on the other side, she came to the intersection the motel man had marked on her map. Intersection was overdoing it. Just some tracks colliding at random angles in a moonscape of dust. But there was a sign. An ordinary yellow road sign, noting two destinations, looking silly and domestic, as if it had been beamed down here from a suburban cul-de-sac. The names on the sign matched names on her map, but neither of the names was Ruby Downs. One, Bald Hill, if her map was correct, looked like it was almost at the border, hours away. The other, Oak Springs, wasn't on the map at all. Probably derelict, like all the other stations she'd passed out here.

Even more confusingly, instead of two roads to choose from, as marked on the sign, there were three. To her left, the track to Oak Springs, which seemed to be indicated by the motel man's arrow and his question mark but which couldn't be right. It only continued for a few metres, petering into a rough patch of gravel before disappearing into the bed of yet another dry creek. No track on the other side, as far as she could see. To her right, the track to Bald Hill, which, if her map was correct, would take her back to where she'd come from, via a tour of an old copper mine and an abandoned limestone quarry and the restricted no-man's-land round the dingo fence. Straight ahead, shooting off at a sharp angle from the track she was on, heading straight up a steep, impossible-looking ridge, a road that wasn't indicated by either sign or map, if you could call a single stripe of rubble a road. The sign was no help, even if she'd wanted to go to either of the places it indicated. Some fool had bent both sides down so they pointed at the ground.

She sat there, aircon roaring, trying not to panic, turning the map this way and that. Ruby Downs was east, about an hour's drive from here, if it existed. But it had existed not that long ago when Ray left that birthday card. And the people who lived there had to get in and out somehow. The motel man must have got it wrong. That track in the middle wasn't a dead end. It must veer left again after the top of the ridge. She just couldn't see it from here.

Too late to go back. With all those gates, it would be past sunset before she hit the highway again. And anyway, there was nowhere to turn around, she was surrounded by rocks. And if she hit trouble on the way, rain or wildlife or a flat tyre, she'd be stuck, a long way from anywhere, in the dark. On cue, the sun went behind one of those innocent-looking clouds.

She checked her seatbelt, put her hat on, took a firm grip on the wheel. Breathing deep, reversing to give herself a run-up, she punched the accelerator, shot up the ridge in a spray of dust. She was just congratulating herself on getting to the top when she realised how sharp and thin the crest was, how steep the drop was on the other side. Rough loose gravel, when her front wheels started down. At the bottom, a dry creek bed, deep cratered and studded with rocks. And she was going way too fast.

When she tried to brake, her back wheels went out, skidding the car sideways, heading her straight toward the bank of the creek and the only tree for miles. She thought about steering into the skid but wasn't that in wet weather, on proper road? In desperation, she wrenched the wheel the other way, heading toward what had looked at a distance like firm red earth but was in fact deep red sand.

Her front wheels hit something solid, spun, and the car left earth. She closed her eyes. An age later, when she came to ground, the car bucked forward, smashed back, and she whacked her head hard on the roof. Then, inexplicably, she seemed to be going forward again, climbing skywards, bonnet tipping, horizon slipping. An awful grinding noise. Before she had the sense to take her foot off the accelerator, she had time to notice those fluffy clouds had overtaken her. They were massed above the ridge now, which was tilting slowly sideways as the car lurched up. Turning oyster, those clouds, with a deep hem of black.

She switched the engine off. Fell rather than stepped out of the door. Heat settled around her, pressing in. The car, still juddering, was tipped sideways like a black beetle. Without warning, it shifted suddenly in the other direction, making her jump. By the side of the creek, an emu watched. A scaly rufous eye.

Her bowels went to water and she grabbed the toilet paper from the boot. No time to find a tree.

By the time she'd come back, sky and earth had gone an infected-looking purple. A swollen hum to the air. She walked round and round the car, Winston watching from the back seat as she bent down and touched things, as if by stroking the shredded tyre, examining the big boulder the car had tried to mount, the right back wheel sunk almost to its hubcap in sand, she could fix something, achieve something. Lost for what else to do, she opened the boot again, got out her shovel, unfolded the dinky little thing. It still bore the shop sticker, a cartoon man with dizzy flies round his cork-swing hat. She folded it up again. A peal of thunder sent her scurrying to the front seat.

For half an hour she sat on her tilted bed of flour, eating muesli bars, grinding away with her defective teeth. Washing down the dry porridge with a gulp of water and about to drain the bottle, she stopped herself. People died of thirst out here. But she had lots of water. And lack of water wouldn't be her problem, not by the look of those clouds. Deep blue-black now, almost green. Stay with your car, her guidebook had advised. But what if your car was in a dead creek bed, so dry that ten minutes of rain would make it a creek again? She remembered that mate of Dad's who'd camped with his family in a dry creek, on a fine night, not a cloud in the sky. While they slept, a sudden roaring. Everything—tents, dogs, wife and children—swept away.

More thunder, closer this time. Winston whined from the back seat. He'd been so quiet since they left the highway, she'd almost forgotten he was there. She offered him water in her cupped palm, which he refused, and a sandwich, which he ate in one gulp. When she checked her mobile again, no bars at all. She was in a dip. If she could climb that hill on the other side, steep but she could do it, with Winston pulling on the lead, maybe she'd get a signal, and they'd be out of the creek at least. Out in the open, though, on an exposed ridge, in a storm. Lightning out there, elaborate tree shapes flickering to the west. She listened for thunder, started counting, was distracted by another griping pain in her belly, lost the thread.

She could head back, along the track she knew, on foot. It would take hours. Never leave your car. But it was autumn, not summer, and she had lots of water, and it was only midday, although it looked like dusk, and she'd been going so slow on the way in, almost at walking pace sometimes, and the track was clear, on foot at least. Unless it got dark before she got there, or the storm got worse. She thought of darkness and of lightning, of being on foot, dragging Winston through all those other dry creeks she'd crossed, running like rivers from rain to come.

If it did get dark, she could light a fire, for rescue purposes. Then she remembered she didn't have any matches and that it looked like rain. And if it didn't rain, the fire might get out of control, it was so dry round here. And if it didn't rain but there was a storm, there might be dry lightning, and a fire might start without any help from her. Heat, fire, flood or electrocution. Working or buggered. When Dad piped up with more of his stories, she told him to shut up.

Another crack of lightning. A snapshot of the creek. Gash, root and runnel, veined red and white. That stupid bird was still there. Flightless, motionless, as if dipped in ruffled silver. She punched the horn and it lolloped off, up the creek side and away.

Fashioning a sling out of her cardigan, she put three bottles of water in it, along with her phone and the rest of the muesli bars. She could see herself, from outside, doing these things, while her mind stalled and whirred. She was leaning over, trying to coax Winston out of the footwell, so she could attach his lead, when another flash of light made her glance up toward the ridge. A man at the top, backlit by the storm. Tall, standing easy, his long legs apart. A hat on his head, so she couldn't tell the colour of his hair.

As she struggled out of the oddly-angled door, her cardigan fell off and the water bottles rolled away. She let them go. Stood watching as the man came down toward her, surfing gravel on the sides of his feet. The car door beeped insistently, the inside light was on. But she just kept standing there, feeling old, helpless, hopeful. Winston in a morose huddle at her feet.

As he got nearer, she realised he wasn't nearly tall enough. Too slight, the shoulders too narrow. When he took his hat off, his head was bald and brown as a nut.

'Hello there. Heard your horn. You OK?'

She wanted to say does it look like it, but he could be anyone, and she was a woman, out here alone. She tried to pull Winston into a more dignified position and failed.

'Not really. I hit something, on the way down. I'm stuck I think.'

He cocked his head, surveying the car. 'Yeah. Think you might be right. Want me to take a look?'

As he walked toward her, she stepped back. But he just reached over and shut the driver's door. 'That's better. You don't need a flat battery as well.'

He took his time walking round the car, scuffing at the buried back tyre, bending down to inspect the wheel and the rock, clicking his teeth at the bent rim and the shredded rubber. Making vague disapproving noises, as men will. She was reminded of Harry, when he did that car maintenance course. Donning his spotless overalls and his accountant's glasses, sticking his head under the bonnet of Simon's ancient Volvo, tinkering and fiddling, until he'd taken the engine apart, the guts of it laid out neatly in the carport according to some diagram in some library book. Then he'd moved on to Spanish and the car had stayed like that, until she called a man who took the lot away for parts.

'You don't do things by halves, I'll give you that. I usually try and go round these things myself, not straight over the top.' An English accent, flattened with something else. Maybe

South African. Maybe just Australian with pretensions. He was annoying enough.

He kicked the wrecked tyre and the car trembled pitifully, shedding dust.

'Please. Be careful. It's not mine.'

'Rental?' She nodded and he sighed, settling himself comfortably down on his haunches, fishing in his pocket, bringing out a pouch of tobacco. He started rolling up, depositing tiny lumps, examining them, removing them, shaping and pinching, while over his shoulder the clouds turned blacker all the time.

'Not sure what they told you, but that's a city car. Not enough clearance. Road gets worse further along.' As he licked the rollie closed, something glinted in his mouth. He had a stud through his tongue.

'Yes. I'll make sure to tell them when I get back.' He squinted at her, looking amused. 'Can you fix it, do you think?'

'Maybe. If you've got a spare.'

'Of course.' She glanced uncertainly at the car. He tucked the unlit cigarette behind his ear and headed toward the boot.

When he opened it, she blushed to see her bag had upended in the crash. Flowery dresses, big bras, everything covered in dust and flour. Stacking them away neatly, he lifted up the carpet, started shaking his head again.

'Jesus. That'd be right. Your spare's OK but this . . .' He held up a jack as small and shiny as her shovel. 'Idiots. This won't even touch the sides.' Reaching for his rollie and lighting up, he leaned back against the car, smoking, staring at the wheel.

'I've got one in the Landy. Maybe if we use both together. Have to brace that offside wheel though or you'll end up deeper in.'

He waggled the Drum packet but she shook her head. If he started rolling up again, they could be here all day.

'Could we try?' She nodded at the clouds massing above the ridge. Thunder grumbling, long, low, almost continuous, like someone shaking a big sheet of tin. 'And soon?'

'Oh, don't worry about that. It'll head further south. Always does.'

When he grinned, she was relieved to see his teeth were all accounted for and the right sort of shape.

'I'm Max by the way.'

When she said nothing, he shrugged and walked off toward the ridge.

⌒

He was gone so long, she decided he must have given up. A loud crack, a sizzle of ozone, and Winston gave up trying to melt into the creek bed, crawled under the car.

She was about to head off in search of Max when a battered Landcruiser appeared on the crest of the ridge. It paused theatrically for a moment before slaloming down at such breakneck speed, she was forced to jump out of the way. At the bottom, he performed a dramatic donut, bringing the ute to rest with its back tray a scant metre from the front of her car. She turned away, refusing to be impressed. Collecting her cardigan and her water bottles, she dragged Winston out from under the car, in case he got squashed.

At least this man seemed to know what he was doing, heaving rocks to brace the back wheels, setting up the jacks, ratcheting them up and down with the same leisurely precision he'd brought to rolling his cigarette. Now and again he asked for something off the back of his ute. She delivered a chunk of wood, a set of spanner-type things. Standing there, swatting flies, watching him knock at the wheel rim with tidy punches of his wrench, she found herself wondering how old he was. Beneath the monkish skull, his face looked weathered yet smooth. He seemed carved from some petrified, airy substance, neither young nor old.

'Do you live around here?'

'For my sins.'

'On a farm or something?' She'd presumed he was a farmer but, if so, he was the strangest farmer she'd ever seen. The bald head, the tongue stud. Thongs not boots, no shirt under his overalls. His chest nuggety and hairless as his head.

'A property. That's what we call them round here.' As he leaned forward to wrestle with a wheel nut, a strap of his overalls fell back. A nipple, brown and silky, a ring through that as well. She looked away.

'How far is it?'

'About forty k. That way.' He jerked his head behind him, back up the hill she'd just slid down.

'Do you mean one of those places on the sign? Bald Hill? Or Oak Springs?'

'Second one.' He was breathless, tugging on the tyre, the muscles in his arms standing out like rope.

'Nup. No go.' Sitting back on his haunches, wheezing a little, he picked wheel nuts from his teeth. 'That rock's hooked right up under the rim. You couldn't have done it better if you'd tried. I can't jack her any higher either or she'll tip.' He sucked on an inhaler from his pocket, craning to look under the car. 'Could try bashing it, I s'pose. Hand us that crowbar.'

'Where?'

'Big iron thing. Next to your foot.'

She handed it over and he crawled under the precariously tilted car, only his horny feet sticking out.

'Where you headed, by the way? This road doesn't go anywhere unless you're deeply interested in sheep.' So she was on the wrong road.

'A place called Ruby Downs. I'm staying there.' In something called Rose Cottage, she added, which sounded completely ludicrous, out there.

'Ah. The spa room. If it does rain, you'll be in luck. That roof leaks like a sieve.'

She bent down to look at him but his eyes were closed against the dust falling from the bottom of the car.

'You know it?'

'Yeah. Told you. That's where I live.'

'You said it was Oak Springs.'

'Bald Hill, Ruby Downs, Oak Springs. Same diff. Bald Hill used to be a neighbour but we bought them out. Oak Springs is just the name of the B&B.'

The question was like a bubble in her throat. But for some reason, the same reason she hadn't asked the woman who'd answered the phone at Ruby Downs about Ray, just told her she was on holiday and needed a room, she couldn't seem to spit it out. Something about not wanting to jinx this journey before it had begun. Some dimly lit notion that in finding these clues, piecing them together and walking in Ray's footsteps, she was piecing herself together. Unpicking herself, back and back, toward some fatal flaw.

'I wouldn't get your hopes up though. Not an oak nor a spring in sight.'

'Well, why did you call it that?'

He laughed, the sound ending in a wheeze.

'Jesus, I don't own it. Thank God. That was Freda's idea. She reads too much.'

The crowbar slipped and he swore, crabbing out from under the car. Hopping round in a circle, he looked a bit mad. Maybe it wasn't Ventolin in that little inhaler after all.

'You all right?'

'Fine. Just cramp. That wheel's not though. You're not going anywhere without a winch. Sam's got one on his truck. We can come back tomorrow. For now though, you'd better hop in with me.'

She looked at the car, its helpless, shiny black bulk. At that moment it felt like the closest thing she had to home.

'I can't just leave it. What if it rains? And the creek fills up?'

'Listen, lady. If it rains out here, I'll eat your tyre.'

In the end she persuaded him to have one more go, with her help. Felt his eyes on her as she tucked her dress into her undies, squatted down and took hold of the wheel. While he crowbarred, she pulled, his arm right next to her face. A hot peppery smell coming off him, like fennel gone wild in the sun. Then the tyre gave and she fell back and the first few drops arrived, turning the dust she was sitting on to mud.

CHAPTER TWENTY

For the first two weeks he slept in the shed. Lily offered him the sleep-out but it was crammed with her husband's old home-brewing equipment, his work clothes, stacks of *Playboy* magazines. When Mick said he'd get wet out there if it rained, Ray said if it rained here, he'd dance naked in it. Then blushed when he realised Lily was in the room.

The shed was OK. After he'd pushed out the dead tractor, hauled out a pub's worth of empty beer bottles and swept the floor, he made a nest for himself in one corner with his tarp and his sleeping bag. Wasn't cold, despite the patchy roof and lack of walls. Forty degrees most days, and what remained of the tin roof held heat well into the night. And there was something about the way air tuned itself out there, a thin ragged fluting through all that rusting shambles, himself temporary and light-boned beneath it, that reminded him of the desert. Something fine as a hangnail between him, the earth and the sky.

He woke at dawn each day. No use lying around waiting for the heat. Brewing tea on the primus so as not to wake the house, he took his mug on walkabout, his eye roving from hill to ridge and creek line. Reading boundaries, touching only on what could be achieved in an hour, a morning. A day. No use thinking about the great big shape of it, you'd end up paralysed. Or paralytic, like Mick's dad.

Trick with a job like this was to break it into sections, like a long run of fence. Some floorboards here, a patched rain tank there. That big one near the house could be made to hold water, if he could get the tools. He'd spotted an old bore pump too, in one of the sheds. But it needed parts and he didn't have a drill. And even if he had one, there was nothing to pump. The bore had run dry. No access to the creek, according to Lily, even though it ran straight across the far paddock, a faint line of olive-green scrub in the dust. Some trouble between the husband and the neighbour, an illegal, boundary-hopping fence. Never got the gist of it, because in the middle of telling him about it, Lily had to go and lie down.

Climbing the ridge above the creek, he drank his tea, lit a cigarette. From here you could see the whole spread, such as it was. Even in the soft bloom of dawn, the place was a tragedy. Dirt, fleece, rust and dust. Sheds were strewn across the landscape like half-finished thoughts. The house itself looked like it had been through a prize fight, all scattered bearings and blackened outlooks. The land it sat on like a gnawed yellow bone. Three dams, all dry, every fence in tatters. In any case, there was nothing to keep in or out. Just a few chickens scratching round the front yard. Those bloody hens drove him mad at night. Yesterday he'd woken with one gone broody on his chest. Sitting there, all fluffed up, regarding him with its sad chicken eye.

A henhouse. Should be easy enough. Bit of iron from one of the sheds, a roll of wire he'd liberated from Sam's. Some of those palings he'd taken from the back door would patch the front verandah boards. They lapped up in places like the tongue of a shoe. Lily, on her rare trips outside, tottered dangerously, grasping at posts, like a woman at sea.

Wouldn't fix it properly of course. That whole verandah was an accident waiting to happen, as Dad used to say about Ray himself. Piers were shot, the earth receding from the foundations like bad gums. Looked at from here, in bald morning light, he saw that the whole left side was curling down and sideways, pulling the house with it, not a windowsill plumb. One good jump by Mick as he launched himself from the front step to achieve a skateboard wheelie in the front yard and the lot would peel away, take off the front of the house.

The foundations needed propping, at the very least. A few stones from the river, some bricks if he could find them. New joists, pack the bearers, try and level the weight between the posts. But he'd need fresh lumber and a decent screw jack and a second pair of hands. And Mick was worse than useless, lying around on the lounge, watching TV. He refused to either go back to school or go back to Sam's. Anyway, even with help, no amount of sweat would fix what was wrong here, not without money or rain. It would take six men six months and thousands of dollars to get a place like this going again. And he wouldn't be here that long. Another week. Two at the most.

⁓

He'd told himself that at least three times a day. He hadn't been intending to stay at all. Taking Mick back to his mother in the hospital, he'd seen himself pushing off from that car park toward another empty horizon, like a swimmer launching from a wall. Travelling to somewhere he could mourn Mam in peace and silence, to where he could wait for Urs to call. And if she didn't, if there was just more silence, well, he would live with that. He'd lived with it for over thirty years.

But when they'd arrived at the ward, they'd found Lily speech-less with nausea, half-lying in the waiting room chair. The chair, her brown dress, even her suitcase, looked too big for her. Cheryl had a work emergency. There was no one to drive her home. What sort of emergency you got in country town hairdressing, with your sister-in-law sick and your nephew with nowhere to stay, Ray wasn't sure. But he'd said nothing. Just walked them out, carrying Lily's bag, while Mick half-carried his mother toward the lift.

'It's fine, Mr McCullough,' she kept saying. 'We don't want to hold you up. You've done enough. We'll get a cab from here.' Those last few words seemed to exhaust her entirely and she had to sit down at the bus stop. No cabs in sight. When she'd stumbled in the car park and he'd caught her arm, she'd felt like a kite, skin strung on bone.

Getting back to the house, it was worse than he remembered. The tea towel curtains, the wrecked driveway and broken window, the boarded-up back door. The front door was stuck fast. When he'd put his shoulder to it, the whole thing splintered from the frame.

'I'm sorry,' she said, gesturing feebly. She'd said sorry all the way home.

Inside it was hotter than outside. The kitchen window was broken, the place billowing with dust and leaves. Glass and possum shit all over the kitchen floor. Somewhere, faint but getting stronger, the musky smell of mice. Lily flushed with shame, before Mick led her off to bed. A second later though, Ray heard him call out, high, panicky. Come quick. Ray? I dunno what to do.

When Ray went in, he saw there was a hole in the ceiling, above her bed. Right through the tin, the sky peeking through. The bed itself was covered with dirt and leaves, the pillow dusted with something white. Ceiling plaster, he hoped. He thought of changing the sheets but mice had got into the pile of dry washing in the basket and, anyway, by the time he came back in with the only semi-clean set he could find, she'd gone to sleep, in the middle of the mess, and Mick had scurried off into the living room.

Ray stood there, looking at the muck on the pillow. Could be anything. Asbestos even. Trying to brush it off, his finger caught in a lock of her hair and it came away in his hand. He stood horrified, clutching the glossy black hank. Unsure what else to do and not wanting Mick to find it, he put it in his pocket, crept away.

Mick was prone on the lounge, clicking irritably at the remote and swearing at the blank TV.

'Mate. Think about it. No electricity.'

Mick threw the remote across the room. 'Everything's shit.'

'There a broom somewhere?'

'Dunno.'

'Yeah, well, you won't find it lying there.'

After he'd set Mick to work sweeping up the broken glass, he foraged in the shed for a hammer and nails. He put the front door frame back together as best he could, then nailed a few garbage bags over the kitchen window, to stop the wildlife getting in. The washing he took straight to the incinerator, watched unflinching as tiny pink things wriggled in the flames. Back in the house, he tore down the boards nailed across the back door, noting again the frantic overkill, the boards lapping over and over. To keep things out, or in?

In the kitchen, with more light, he saw the extent of things. Bare shelves, holes in the lino, a burn mark above the stove. A fist-shaped dent in the fridge. On top, a stack of bills so old, dust had turned the envelopes pink. In the fridge itself, a half-loaf of greenish Tip Top and a carton of milk which Cheryl must have delivered a week ago.

The sun was getting low. He flicked at the light switch as he'd now done three times without thinking. No hot water either, of course. Lucky it was daylight saving. Lucky it was summer. Lucky they were on bottles and the stove was gas.

He found Mick outside chucking stones at the dog. Dog was trying to fetch them, like the idiot it was.

'I'm heading back to town. Need to get a few things. Be back in an hour.'

'Can I come?' Mick trailed Ray to the door of the ute. The look on him wary and hopeless, like when he'd been left at the beach.

'Nuh. Stay here. Look after your mum. It'll be dark soon. Try and get that going if you can.' He pointed to the old heater he'd found in the shed.

'We don't have any kero.' The old whine in his voice.

'I'll get some. Maybe go and find some wood while you're waiting. There's heaps of dry stuff near the creek.'

'Why?'

Breathing deep, Ray put his seatbelt on.

'To make a fire, Einstein. Keep an eye on my dog too. Until I get back.'

He left the dog there as hostage. The boy stood tall and still in front of the house, getting smaller and dimmer as Ray drove away.

⌒

In town he bought kero, refilled the gas bottle, got a bit of meat and veg at the supermarket. Just enough to last them a few days. At the post office he sweet-talked his way past the woman locking up, got her to open the till again so he could pay the bills. Didn't like to think of Lily and Mick out there, without lights or a phone, once he was gone.

On the way back, passing the sign to the highway proper, he was tempted but he was low on petrol and the only open servo was all the way on the other side of town. And it was getting late, roos would be out. And he couldn't just leave them there, without any food. And his tent was there, on the verandah. Not to mention his dog.

By the time he got back, it was nearly dark. Mick was a melancholy figure in the twilight, languidly collecting twigs. At that rate, they'd have a fire by next year. Too late to rig the gas bottle up now though, and the connection was rusted shut. In the sleep-out, Ray found some old hurricane lamps which he filled and lit and hung from the wonky eaves. There was a generator in the shed, ancient and spidery, but it might work. He could use it to power up his car fridge at least, leave it with them until the electric came on. Could always buy another fridge, when he was back on the road.

'Right. I've got sausages. Onions, potatoes. We'll have a barbie.'

'But we don't have a barbie.'

'Jesus.' Holding onto his temper with difficulty, Ray reached into the back of his ute, finding the dog in there already, perched on a roll of wire. Gazing nobly out toward some unknown horizon. He batted it off.

'Here. This is called a shovel. You dig. I'll chop some proper logs.'

While he set up his tripod and his griddle and his camp oven, he talked Mick through the mysterious art of digging a fire pit, not too wide, not too deep, gabbling like an idiot to hide the sounds of retching coming from the house. We'll eat alfresco, he said, and Mick, poking morosely at the flames, said Al who?

At least the place looked a bit better, in the forgiving glow of the fire. Lily's face when she came out and sat down, so close to the pit he worried she'd catch alight, had lost some of its greenish tinge. At least twenty degrees out here and even with the roaring fire and his old coat and the blanket and a beanie on, she was still shivering. At Mick's urging she managed a bite of sausage and bread. How's that, he asked. Wonderful, she told him, after the muck in the hospital.

'Better than Cheryl's Christmas dinner.'

Mick muttered, 'Shit, wouldn't be hard.'

Lily seemed too tired to tell him not to swear.

Kneeling down to stoke the fire, Ray saw the way she was baulking at the single mouthful she'd taken, her throat white and painful, like she was trying to swallow her tongue. Under cover of looking for her glass of water, she spat out the sausage and the dog gobbled it up.

⁓

The sun was twinging over the ridge now, earth growing warm beneath his boots. Another hour and it'd be too hot up on the roof. He drained his tea, set off.

Under the house there was an old ladder, missing several rungs. Setting it up against the wildly tilting chimney, he hauled his tarp out of the shed, kicking chickens from beneath him, then climbed the ladder hauling the plastic behind him, his mouth full of nails. He'd make do with the sleeping bag and the fly off his tent. Only a couple more nights.

The henhouse and verandah would have to wait. The roof was shot. The tin was barely held together by rust and a few rivets, half the battens were missing, one joist rotted clean away.

The gaping hole over Lily's bedroom was the worst. He could see right down to that little slice of her bed. She'd edged it so far away from the rain of gunk falling from the ceiling, she was almost sleeping in the hall.

When she slept of course. In the middle of the night, or before dawn, he often saw the kitchen light go on. Heard the toilet flushing, heard her retching, crying. Her gaunt shape behind the window in uneasy, flickering light.

Just until she was on her feet, he told himself again as he secured the tarp temporarily with stones. But she wasn't on her feet, was she? The night before, she'd barely made it from bedroom to dinner table before listing sideways and collapsing on the lounge.

'Mum! I told ya. Go back to bed. I'll bring a tray.'

'I'm fine, mate. I'm sick of lying around.' She tried to settle herself upright on the cushions, got halfway, slumped back. 'Don't think I could eat anything though.'

'You've got to. Or at least drink something. All that spewing. Ray says you'll get unhydrated.'

'Well, a cup of tea would be nice.'

Turning on the kettle with his elbow while frying curry paste at the stove, Ray noticed the boy's small attempts at grace. The sheet tucked into the lounge cushions, the pillow fetched from the bedroom, the little folding table set up ready for the tea cup. A Tim Tam on a plate. Then Mick started trying to find reception on the set, swivelling the rabbit-ears aerial this way and that. When that didn't work, he twisted a coat hanger into a question mark, stuck it on top.

'There's one of them David Attaborough things on later. After the news.'

'Oh. What's it about?'

'I dunno. Plants and shit.'

She was fretting at the blanket, her hair. Another clump had fallen out. She closed her fist on it, burying it beneath a cushion. Ray looked away. Mick hadn't seen. He was still wrestling with the aerial. Now he'd strung the whole contraption on an old coat stand from the verandah. Stuck the lot out the front window, where it rattled wildly with each puff of wind.

'Be careful, love. That sill's broken. It won't stay up.'

'I am being careful.' He banged the side of the TV and his leg knocked the table, splashing tea on the floor. 'Shit. Sorry.'

'I'll get it. Stay there.'

Lily smiled at Ray, a watery thing, but still a smile. Ray focused on mopping up the tea, then went back to the stove, concentrating on frying onions, not too fast.

'Ray? Let me help. I can do the potatoes. If you give me a bowl.' He didn't want to tell her that those were for his store, out in the ute, that he liked to keep it topped up. Ready to head off at a moment's notice, carrying everything he needed, like a snail. That it was curry tonight and he'd be serving rice.

Instead, he put the potatoes and the peeler in a bowl, arranged them in her meagre lap, then hurried back to the stove.

The news had ended and Mick's show had come on, black and white monkeys in a field of mist. Mick resorted to banging the side of the TV, upsetting the coat stand which plunged right through the window, turning the picture to a blizzard of snow.

'Fucking piece of shit.'

'Mick. Don't swear.'

'Well, we need a proper aerial, Mum. On the roof.'

'Yes, well, we need a lot of things. We can't afford it, not right now.'

Ray didn't say that to install an aerial you'd need to fix the roof in order to have something to attach it to. He just said, without turning around, 'I can have a look tomorrow. If you want. I'm going to town anyway, to get my mail.'

'No. Please. I don't want you to spend any more money on us.'

'They don't cost that much.'

She levered herself upright, looking serious. 'No, really. I feel bad enough about those bills you paid. I'll pay you back, though. When I get back to work.'

The idea seemed to exhaust her, and she slumped down, the peeler dropping into the bowl. Ray, unable to stand Mick's banging and swearing any longer, walked over, wrenched the remote off him, propped the window open with some books, secured the coat stand aerial inside it, adjusted the rabbits-ears to some knife-edge calibration where the picture was semi-clear. Went back to the stove.

'Ray? Why don't you sit down for a bit? You're making me dizzy, rushing around.'

'Yep. In a sec. I'll just get this on the pip.'

When he couldn't feasibly do anything more to the curry, when he'd wiped every surface and rinsed every dish and washed his hands, he sat down, choosing the furthest edge of the lounge, eyes on the screen. Eagles now, soaring through clouds of fuzz. The sound fading entirely, the aerial knocked off kilter again after Mick banged out the door in a sulk, fumbling in his pocket, saying that the show was boring and he thought he'd heard the dog bark, and he'd better check the chickens, there might be a fox. Ray had heard nothing, and his hearing was good. Lily sighed as they got a whiff of dope through the open window.

'I meant it, you know. About paying you back.'

'No rush, Mrs Jones. Wasn't that much.'

'Call me Lily. Mrs Jones makes me sound about a hundred and two.'

'Oh. Sorry. OK.'

He could smell the curry catching and in a minute the rice would boil over. He should get up but it seemed rude, after he'd only just sat down.

'It was a mistake, anyway, that big bill. You didn't owe all that. Another Jones. It's a pretty common name.' A feeble lie but she seemed to buy it, or was too tired to argue.

'My name isn't really Jones anyway. That's just Mick and his dad. All the bills, and the house, they're in Gary's name.' She went silent, picking at the dirt on a potato. He stared at a shark on the TV, longing for a cigarette. Not knowing what to say. Best he could come up with, a full five minutes later, was, 'So what did you do? For work. Before.' She didn't answer, just made a little noise. Stupid, stupid. He'd upset her, talking about before and after like that.

'Lily?' The name seemed too small and delicate for his big fat mouth.

When he turned to look at her, he realised she was asleep. Snoring softly, her head dropping toward his shoulder. He swung back to the TV. Some stupid game show now, the sound blaring suddenly as the wind caught the aerial, and he couldn't reach the remote to switch it off.

Slowly, she tilted, came to rest, first on his shoulder, then in the hollow of his neck. She smelled like flowers, or perhaps he imagined it because of her name. Sweet grease or something fruity, underlain by the faint smell of vomit and medicine.

When Mick banged back in, bringing with him a sultry waft of dope, his eyes widened at the sight of his mother sleeping on Ray's shoulder. Ray, manoeuvring himself out from under her, replacing his shoulder with a cushion, raised his finger to his lips.

She didn't wake up, even later, when he carried her to the bedroom. Inside her little nightie she felt like nothing at all. Just air and flowers. Skin and bone.

CHAPTER TWENTY-ONE

Dreaming of deserts, she woke somewhere hot, dry, volum-inous. The walls porridge coloured. The sky through venetians slatted swimming-pool blue. A sound like hail.

Hooking up the blind with one toe, she saw a cocky edging along a palm tree frond too green and limber to be real. It tapped its beak on the glass, screeched, flapped away.

Then she remembered. The crash, the storm. Limping along in her wounded car for what had seemed like hours, following Max's tail-lights through sheeting rain, wheels sliding through acres of dust turned to rivers of mud.

As they reached a gate and a mailbox, the rain stopped and the sun came out. Half an hour later, a clearing, a long low house, the patch of grass in front shocking green after all that red. A beachball-shaped woman bounded up, making a winding motion with one beefy arm. When Ursula opened the window, she stuck her head right in, as if to deliver a kiss.

'You got here then. Brought the weather with you too. Follow me, OK? Up there. Watch them trucks though. Don't park Sam in.' Clambering onto a quad bike, she spurted off through the mud, up another rut-filled track. Ursula turned to look for Max's ute but he'd disappeared.

By the time they reached Rose Cottage, everything felt hallucinatory, still lives carved from exhaustion. A bright pink house, a tropical palm tree, plastic flamingos by the front door. Freda trailed her up the path, saying something about pig shooters and white ants and leaking ceilings and how she hadn't had time to clean.

'Sheets are fresh, but, and if you want to head up to the big house for a bite, I can whip the Hoover around.'

To her shame, Ursula remembered shutting the door in the woman's face. Falling into bed fully clothed.

When she got up, she found her sheets were full of mud. Going in search of coffee and a washing machine, she found herself in a tiny lounge room stuffed with giant leather sofas. Beer cans in wobbling stacks, full ashtrays on the floor. Boot marks on everything, even the TV screen. A sauce bottle loomed at her from the coffee table, three times its normal size. That feeling of unreality again, the gaunt elongations of her desert dream. A man bearded, bald and feathered, with the bent back legs of an emu, tracking her silently from ridge to ridge.

Taking one look at the kitchen, she headed straight for the bathroom. The sink was full of pig shooter stubble, something white smeared across the mirror. She kept her sandals on in the shower. The whole place was probably ripe with athlete's foot.

Too late, with the water running, she realised there was no toilet in there. But she must have gone last night. She had a vague memory of stepping from a screen door into darkness, walking in bare feet across plastic grass covered in mud. As she'd turned on the light in a little outhouse, a rain of tiny white frogs fell from the ceiling, more frogs exploding in a hopping wave from the bowl as she flushed.

She stayed in the shower for far longer than the five minutes prescribed by the drought notice taped above the taps. Whatever was making her linger here in this pink water giving off its septic stink was the same thing that had made her scuttle inside last night without even asking that woman about Ray. Vanity, partly. If he was here, working or visiting, she hadn't wanted his first sight of her after all this time to be an old lady balding under rain. Fear mostly. Fear that they'd never heard of him, that he'd never been here, that she'd got it all wrong. That if he was here, by luck or chance, he might walk around a corner and fail to recognise her, or that she wouldn't recognise him. Grey hair not blond, teeth missing, head balding, one leg shorter than the other. A weak little chin. Shorter than he had been, time in going forwards somehow bending him backwards, toward earth, like her. Those footprints she'd followed all night, splayed, birdlike, disappearing among hollow rocks and failed water. The silent, stalking bent-legged prophet of her dream.

Something floated up through the fog of her exhaustion. An old saying. One of Mam's. One of those little, shamrock-infested needlepoint things she had tacked up all over Twenty Bends. Irish of course. Mam's sayings always were. Blessings, prayers,

curses, hard to tell the difference sometimes. This had been part
of some tediously scrolling, Gothic-lettered thing, rambling on
about lakes and pillars, by Someone McSomething or Other. It
used to sit above the fireplace, where Mam insisted no knitting
could be done, unless all the sheep were asleep, and how could
you tell? Spilled salt thrown over the shoulder and no cats in
the house, in case they turned their backs.

She tried to remember this particular saying, because it
somehow seemed important, in her fatigue. But it kept receding
into dream tatters and bathroom steam. Hills, valleys, roads
rising, roads falling, in lilting cross-stitch. There were a lot of
roads. A lot of walking went on. Dreams were cast and spread,
and God was always lurking, opening hearts and turning ankles,
seizing people in the great bleeding hollow of his hands.

Something about a ghost. There was always a ghost.

The drain was blocked with dust. The water was backing up,
forming a red brown swill round her calves. She got out feeling
dirtier than when she'd got in. Sullied by the sheer state of the place.

After she'd dressed, dabbed on some makeup and enticed
Winston from behind the lounge with half a muesli bar, there
was no putting it off. Gathering her hat and sunglasses, she
caught a glimpse of herself in the hall mirror. The powder had
been a mistake. In this light, she looked Elizabethan. Ghostly.
That was it. On the wall by the fireplace, at Twenty Bends. To
appease a ghost you must do what he wants.

As a kid, it had frightened her, the cosy, firelit tenderness of
the embroidery, against the idea. Some ruthless smoke-coloured
ghost, arriving down the chimney, making impossible demands.

~

Outside, the heat hit her like a wall. Between her cottage and what Freda had called the big house, a ramshackle thing tacked together by a flyscreened verandah, a vast expanse of dust. Yesterday's rain might have been a dream.

Walking across it, she expected at any moment to hear a footstep behind her, a man calling her name. But there was just the squeak of her sandals, dogs barking somewhere, the sound bouncing back at her from a row of yellowing needle pines, austere with drought. That brave little patch of grass outside the house littered today with a dirty casserole dish, a single galosh, a dog bone, red with gore.

'Hello?' Cupping her hands round her face to peer in at the flyscreen door, she saw a blue heeler eyeing her from the shadows of the verandah, its freckled belly heavy with teats. The pad of her finger itched against the wire door. That dog of Dad's had been pregnant too. That's why she'd tried to feed it. Because of the sad little bulge below its ribs.

It reminded her to get a grip. That she used to be a country girl too. Tying Winston to the outside tap, she went inside, edging past the bluey, which growled but seemed too exhausted to move. Emerging from the gloom of the verandah into a dilapidated yellow kitchen, she blinked in the sudden glare.

'Gidday. Sleep all right?' Freda was squatting beside a wood stove, bum wobbling as she poked the fire with a stick. 'Bloody thing. Why we can't just get electric like everyone else, I don't know. But no, everything has to stay exactly the same as when

Sam's dad was around.' Clanging the door shut, she heaved herself upright, wiping her hands on her shorts.

'You've missed breakfast, love. We start early round here. Can do you an egg though. Or cornflakes, if those termites left me any. Toast? Coffee or tea?'

She didn't wait for an answer to any of these questions, just kept bustling round the kitchen, breaking eggs into a frypan, clicking the kettle on with one rubber-covered elbow while reaching for a catering sized tin of International Roast.

'Coffee, thank you. And toast. If it's not too much trouble.'

'Jam or Vegie? I've got some marmalade somewhere.'

Pushing two slices of bread down into the toaster, Freda wrenched open the door to what Ursula had assumed was another room but was in fact a room-sized fridge. Still talking, Freda burrowed deep inside, her voice muffled by the legs of lamb hanging from meat hooks above her head.

'Only jam, sorry. It's home-made though.'

'Jam is fine.'

Feeling stunned by the sun and all the sudden activity, Ursula cleared a space at the table between a child's colouring book, a spanner, a drift of toast crusts, a half-drunk glass of Milo and a headless Barbie doll. Listened to Freda's muffled chatter about Sam and neighbours and bushfires while the kettle sizzled dry. Trying to think how to start, what to say. After yesterday's rudeness, she had amends to make.

'You've got kids, Freda? How many?'

'Eh? What?'

Ursula yelled louder, telegram-style, her voice sounding rusty and unused as Freda's front gate. 'Children? How many? What kind?'

'What *kind*?' Freda's face appeared between the lamb legs, puzzled and pink.

'Sorry. I meant, boys or girls?'

'Oh. Three. Of each. Two at boarding, eldest at uni, then the girls.' She pointed to a photograph on the sideboard of three blonde girls in descending sizes. 'All the spit of Sam, except for Marcus. He's the oldest. He's a ginger, like me.' She went quiet, diving back into the fridge, rattling through jars on a shelf. 'After the boys, we just kept trying and then we had Ronnie and then two at once. Never rains. Well, it doesn't usually. Not out here.' She poked her head out again. 'Max said you had car trouble. You want Sam to take a look?'

'No. It's fine. It's rented. I'll just call someone.'

A snort. 'You won't get anyone, not out here. Anyway, roads'll be closed. All that rain.'

The toast popped up, burnt black.

'Yes, it was pretty bad. Freda? Do you think I could I get that coffee now? I can do it myself.'

'Oh, sorry, love. Don't know whether I'm coming or going.' Hurrying out of the fridge without the jam but carrying another carton of eggs, she spotted the toast, swore, put two new slices in, cracked the eggs Ursula didn't want into a frypan, started spooning coffee into a mug. 'Milk? Sugar?' Ursula shook her head but Freda was staring out the kitchen window, spooning sugar idly while she looked at the dust out there.

'Gone already. All that water. See?' She made a zipping noise with her lips. 'Barely touched the sides. You know, our twins have only seen rain twice, counting yesterday. It poured for two weeks straight when they were one. Land couldn't take it, after all the drought. Sam nearly bought a boat.' She spun around. 'Shit. What's today?'

'What? Oh. Tuesday, I think.' Without dinner or breakfast, Ursula couldn't be sure. The last thing she'd eaten was that muesli bar, on the road, years ago.

'Forgot the sausages. If it's Tuesday, it's sausages. Written in ruddy stone.' Running back into the fridge, Freda re-emerged with a straining plastic bag full of pink meat. Stood, meat juice dripping on the floor, worry creasing her plain face.

'You're not one of them vegans, are ya? Last bloke we had here, that's what he was. All he'd eat was the bran we feed the horse. Sam reckoned we should just put him out to graze.'

Ursula was wondering whether to pretend she was a vegan when the smoke alarm went off.

'Shit. Excuse the French.' Freda grabbed a broom, jabbed the ceiling alarm with the handle, then scraped a lace of burnt egg onto a plate. Putting her fingers to her mouth, she let out an ear-splitting whistle. The blue heeler slunk in, giving Ursula the evil eye.

'There go, Lol. Your lucky day.'

While the dog chased egg scraps round the floor and while Freda stuffed pig intestines with bright pink pork, talking as she did so, in long looping stories, about Sam's grandmother and her secret sausage recipe, not so secret, and how she had to follow

it, to the letter, breadcrumbs, lard, thyme, pig's blood, from the
pigs Sam shot, or Sam would always know, Ursula drank her
coffee, watched Freda moulding, mixing, tying and squeezing.
While she should have been wondering how to start, how to ask
about Ray, she found herself thinking instead that a woman of
such heft and roundness as Freda should never wear a top like
that. Not with all those pleats and ruches and gathers, the little
sleeves strangling the top of her shoulders, her arms pink and
swollen as the sausage links.

Lulled by the capable milking motions of those square red
hands, she was busy redressing Freda, sketching her in something
floaty and solid-coloured, a mid-length dress perhaps, when she
realised Freda was staring at her, a sausage link dangling from
her hand.

'Well. Did ya? Or not?'

'Sorry?'

'See any pigs. On the way in.'

'No. I don't think so.'

'You'd know it if you had. Nasty buggers. Sam caught a big
pregnant sow a month ago. Brought it home, for a bit of meat,
and now the littlie thinks it's a pet. Rides the bloody thing. Of
course Marcus, my eldest, he always thought we should breed
them, like a sideline or something. He did ag, at uni, so he could
take over, when Sam retires.'

She went quiet, her face serious again. Ursula wondered what
it would be like to have a face like that. So sheer, her feelings
so transparent, like sun or rain on glass.

'Bit of a handful, our Marcus,' Freda sighed, tying a knot in her link. 'Touch and go there for a while. He's settled down now though, thank God. Got married. Got a good job, in the city.' The toast popped up again, was ignored. Didn't matter. With the smell of the raw pork, Ursula wasn't hungry any more.

'I told Sam, my girls aren't going anywhere near a sheep. School here first, if we ever find another governess, then when Marcie's ready for the boarding, they can all go up together. They're booked into that big Catholic near Orange, and then uni, probably just for the oldest, because Marcie's into hair and beauty, and with the littlie, it's all horses and bikes, but my Ronnie, she's sharp as tack.' She paused, staring at Ursula. 'You're not a writer, are ya? That last bloke, the vegan. He was.'

'No. I'm a teacher. Or I used to be. Retired now.'

As Freda embarked on a long ramble about teachers and Ronnie and governesses and how they couldn't get one to stick, not after that other business, years ago, and how if it was history she wanted, they had miles of it, always tripping over it, and she had some brochures somewhere, in one of those drawers, Ursula saw herself doing it. Telling the truth. To this fat, friendly stranger who'd dropped a sausage and was down on her knees, chasing it around the dirty floor, wrestling it off the dog.

She nearly did it. Nearly broke a silence of thirty-odd years. Something about that peachy guileless face.

'Put these together myself.' Freda had unearthed some yellow stapled photocopies from the sideboard. Was holding them out, shyly, with meat-speckled fingers. 'There's a mud map in back, if you feel like a drive. The old homestead is worth a look.'

'Thanks. Maybe later. I'm not really here on holiday, Freda. I'm actually looking for someone. I think he works here, or he used to.'

'Yeah? Who's that?' Freda was still busy twisting knots in the sausage links, looping them high above her head. 'We get a lot coming and going out here.'

'Ray McCullough. Do you know him? He's my brother.'

Freda went still, her face stiff. Dropping the sausages in a tangle on the table, she turned, went to the sink to wash her hands.

'He used to work here, I think. I just wondered if he'd been here recently or if you'd know where he lives.' Freda was uncharacteristically quiet, staring out the window again. Just the buzz of flies, the drip of the tap. Ursula started gabbling.

'You see, I've been looking for him for a long time. We lost touch. If you know anything . . .' She petered off.

A bad feeling in the air, undeniable as the burnt toast, that smell of week-old meat. Then a phone rang somewhere in the hallway, amplified and shrill. Freda shot toward the table, snatching up a brick-like mobile, her hat, a bunch of keys.

'That'll be Sam. We got fires. Gotta go.' Before she rushed out, leaving the meat on the table for the flies, she thrust the bunch of photocopied sheets into Ursula's hands.

'Here. Max can take you out if you want. He's down the shed.' And she was gone, the flyscreen banging in her wake.

Ursula found herself out on the lawn. Blinking, bewildered, reading Freda's brochures, taking nothing in. Densely spaced and boldly misspelled, they told her so many head of sheep, so many goats. An historic goldmine, an historic homestead, first steam-driven something or other. At the back there was a grainy photocopy of a page from a local newspaper, dated 1962. Something about a dead farmer, late of Ruby Downs, first to import some type of sheep. At the bottom, a story about Aboriginal people receiving the vote. A local said nothing would change. That their town had its own ways with blacks and whites. She bet it did.

'That your dog?'

She turned around. The voice seemed to be issuing from inside the wall of yellowing pines. Then a head bounced into a view. Blonde curls, a pair of bright black eyes, disappearing again. A twang of springs.

'What's its name? Are you the new governess? Are you gunna live with us?'

When she walked around, she found a little girl jumping on a trampoline while eating something from her hand. Her solid brown body was naked except for a too-big bikini top.

'Other one died,' the girl told her through a mouthful of scone.

'Sorry. Who?'

'The governess.'

'Did not. Don't fib.' An older, darker haired girl came hurtling from the treetops, hanging by her hands from a flying fox. Landing with a flourish on the trampoline, she bounced the little one right off. By the time Ursula had hurried around to check, the smaller girl had scrambled back up and was bouncing again.

'Did too.'

'Did not.'

Did too, did too, while shaking wild blonde curls out of her eyes. The older girl eyed Ursula stonily, reminding her of the blue heeler, which had appeared again out of another of the numerous verandah doors. Ursula tightened her hold on Winston's lead.

'Did too.'

'All right. I believe you.'

'Did not. She just went to Adelaide.'

'Did too.' The little girl finished with a decisive bounce, right off the edge of the trampoline. Fell over, bounced straight back up, still grasping her scone.

'What's your dog's name? Ours is Lolly. That's 'cause she likes them. She ate a whole box of chocolates once, spewed all over my bed. She nearly died. Is yours sick? Or just old? Dad'll shoot it if you want.'

Not waiting for an answer to any of the questions, her mother's daughter all right, she scrambled over to where the blue heeler lay sprawled and panting in the shade of the trees. 'Lol's having babies. See her boobies?'

She grabbed one of the dog's swollen teats, started squeezing it in a familiar milking rhythm, the dog not moving, just groaning, in and out in time with the child's fingers, like a set of old, mottled bagpipes. Feeling faintly sick, Ursula asked the child her name.

'That's Ellie,' the older girl said loudly. 'I'm Ronnie and Marcie's my other sister but she's not here. I'm the eldest. Who are you?'

'See, when babies come out, they come from there.' Ellie had lifted up the dog's tail, was preparing to poke in there with her jammy fingers until Ursula caught her by the wrist.

'Don't, dear. Not while you're eating.'

'She can if she wants.' The older girl folded her arms across her grubby pink T-shirt. 'You're not the boss.'

Ursula thought of Tilda, how she would like a T-shirt like that, all pink princesses and spangles, and then shut out the thought. She didn't have time to worry about Tilda right now.

Shading her eyes, she stared out toward the collection of tin buildings behind the house. 'Can you tell me which way to the shed?'

'Which shed?' Ronnie sounded scornful. 'There's lots.'

'Yeah! Lots!' Ellie was up on the trampoline again. 'There's the shearing shed and the feed shed and Dad's shed and the tractor shed and the dog shed and the other shed, and Dad's shed . . .'

'I'm looking for Max.'

'Cooking shed. Over there.' Ronnie pointed out toward a long low tin roof, rippling with heat.

Putting her hat on, Ursula pulled Winston to his feet, stepped out from the shade of the trees.

'You're not allowed down there but. Not if you're a visitor. Dad said. Because of the dogs.' Ursula became aware again of that frenzied barking in the distance. Realised it had been going on ever since she left the house. 'Some boy tried to pat one and he got bit. Fucking city kid.' Ursula had her hand on the gate but stopped. She was tired. But not that tired.

'Rhonda. You shouldn't talk like that. It's not nice.'

'My name's not Rhonda. It's Veronica. Don't you know anything?'

'I know that's not a nice word. Why aren't you at school?'

The girl rolled her eyes. 'It's smoko. English then reading, then smoko, then maths, then geography, then lunch.'

'Yeah! Smoko! Don't you know anything?'

'Apparently not.'

Halfway to the shed, Ronnie called out to her, 'Watch out for them dogs.'

'And the pig!' Ellie piped above the jangle of the trampoline. 'It got out. Dunno where it is.'

By the time she found Max, in a hot metal shed next to a cage full of snarling hounds, she was too tired to dissemble any more.

'Hi, Max. I'm looking for someone.'

He held up a finger, warding her off while he counted out cups of flour.

'Ray McCullough. Is he around?'

'Good morning to you as well.'

'Well, is he?'

A timer buzzed on the stove.

'Come in if you're coming in, but shut that door. Flies are getting in. Dog stays out though. Sam's rules.' She was getting heartily sick of Sam and his rules. But she tied Winston up in a bit of shade near the water tank, sending the curs in the cage into a frenzy. When she came back, Max had a mixer going and she had to scream above the din.

'Well? Do you know him or not? Is he here?' He turned the mixer off suddenly and her voice boomed rudely. Max was shaking his head.

'No. He used to work here. Not any more.'

She sat down on a stool. The day gone dull, even in the glare.

'Do you know where he went?'

He was shaking his head again, scraping batter off a spoon. 'Sorry. Wouldn't have a clue. He did a runner, that's all I know.'

She sat there for a long time, watching him work. He was making scones now, cutting butter through flour. All the wind knocked out of her. Sun rippled off water somewhere, finding all the gaps and mistakes and weaknesses between the tin wall and the iron roof.

'He must have left a number or something. An address. He was going to get married out here.'

A fuse of light, falling fierce on a knife, a metal bowl, and she closed her eyes.

'Don't know anything about that. Freda's the one to ask. She and Ray were pretty thick.' He moved across to the sink, his feet rasping on the rough plank floor. No shoes at all this time. No shirt, no overalls, just shorts. 'All I know is he left Sam in the lurch and they were getting desperate. Must have been, eh. They hired me.'

He was rubbing flour and butter to fine seed now with his long brown fingers, adding salt, milk, scattering flour on the table in a graceful arc. Tipping the dough out, bringing it together with slow gathers of his hands. Seemed to know what he was about.

'Ray was the cook here?'

Max nodded.

She thought of a small boy no higher than the old kitchen table, watching her knead pastry, sift flour, stir icing. Being good, so he could lick the bowl.

'Yeah. He did odd jobs too, I think. Fencing and stuff. But cooking, mostly. For the men.'

She tried to see Ray here, in this hot little shed. But like in the pub and, as always, he retreated to an outline, a blank left over from the spaces Max was moving between.

'He cooked in at the pub bistro sometimes too, in town, when I was working in the bar.'

She leaned forward, into the shadow cast by his body.

'So you do know him. You've met him, at least.'

Max shrugged. 'Not really. To say gidday, that's all. We were on different shifts most of the time.'

'What is he like?'

He looked at her oddly. Seemed about to say something, but just went back to cutting scone shapes from his dough.

'Hard to say. Pretty quiet. You didn't want to get on the wrong side of him, according to Sam. Although coming from Sam, that's rich.' There was a renewed frenzy of barking outside, stopping instantly at someone's rough command.

'Listen, to tell you the truth, I don't remember much at all from back then. I could have met the Queen and I wouldn't have known.' He went quiet, the table squeaking as he greased a tray.

'See, pubs and I don't mix.'

She watched him start on rissoles, shaping them from bread-crumbs, parsley, more of that bright pink pork. Only the wall holding her up. After that, more pastry, more butter and flour, Max wheezing a bit as he launched himself at the table, rolling the shortcrust out with an old vinegar bottle, pressing it into the fluted sides of a tin. Bluebottles hovering, green apples in a silver bowl. The sun through the window hacked him to crystallised parts. Nipples, pirate earring, the faint rough bubble of his lungs. When he offered coffee, he took her silence as a yes. Could have been a few minutes that she sat there, could have been an hour. Long enough for the scones to cook, come out of the oven, be set to cool.

'Ray. He a friend of yours?'

He stood holding out a mug of coffee. She stood up abruptly, knocking the stool over.

'Sorry. It's too hot for me in here.'

She was leaning down, untying Winston, brushing away her tears and the flies feasting at the sore on the dog's head, when Max came up behind her, so quiet on his bare feet, she jumped.

'He left some of his stuff behind, if that's any help. Must have been in a hurry. He even left his boots.'

'Where?'

He pointed out toward yet another shed, on the far side of a dam.

'Old shearers' quarters. That's where he slept. Bit basic for me. But I think he liked to be on his own.'

As she set off, he called out, 'Watch out for snakes.'

⌒

In Ray's cell in the shearers' quarters, she found another monastic single bed. Another pair of boots. Holes in the sole but the right size this time. The bedside table was bare. Just an old-fashioned alarm clock in a metal bucket on the floor. Above it, a little plywood bookshelf battered into the tin wall of the shed. A single book on it, the cover red not blue. Paterson's poems. There was curly writing on the flyleaf but she couldn't bear to look at it. She shut it with a bang. She checked under the bed, in the drawers of the bedside table, but there was nothing else.

She lay down on the bed, into the hollow he'd left, his book of poems clutched to her chest. Thought of him reading it at night. Thought of him waking here, seeing that same light at the same window, through the paltry curtains. Getting up in the morning, probably in the dark. Walking out that door, in his special bobbing lope. Away and away, into silence and dust.

She must have fallen asleep, because the next thing she knew someone was banging on the door. She scrabbled for her shoes. But it wasn't her father, come with his belt.

'Hello? You OK in there?'

She patted down her dress and hair.

'Freda said to say it's time for tea.'

CHAPTER TWENTY-TWO

By early February he'd put a new door on the back, a new flyscreen out front. The verandah boards were replaced with timber he'd got from the hardware in lieu of an hour spent shovelling blue metal and a few rolls of Sam's wire. He'd braced the foundations with an assortment of stones and ropes. But it was all temporary, without proper refooting. A bodge job. Bit like that husband, by the sounds.

Clearing the sleep-out to make way for his camp bed, searching through piles of old paperwork for farm deeds, a sale contract, some notion of the property boundaries Lily seemed so unsure about since her husband started selling off the land, he'd found, amid the piles of sticky pornos and unpaid bills, a photo of the bloke, sitting astride some brand-new bike he'd bought before riding off to Queensland, never to be seen again. Shortish, darkish, big toothy smile. As Mam used to say about Dad's brother, Eddie, all shine no shoes.

Up on the roof again, dragging up iron he'd liberated from the dismantled shed, it was hard to see anything he'd achieved, even after weeks of work. Place still looked like photographs of the American dust bowl he'd seen in his old Brittanica. Scoured boards, rackety dirt-humped fences. The dust was so mounded up in places that a tall man could just have stepped straight over. So long since rain now that when the wind blew, whole paddocks were on the move. At night, dust sifted through the flyscreen of the sleep-out, collected on his pillow. The same sere earth here as those old bad time photographs, red, dull glimmering at dusk, turning sepia as the sun went down. As if any future here was history already, a place nurturing its own drear climate, buried in its little hollow beneath a ring of hills.

As he battered at the roof, his mouth full of nails again, it wasn't the lack of water or money, or even the hole in Lily's ceiling, but those fences that worried him the most. Their frowzy disorder nagged at him like a missing tooth. They made the place look lax, uncared for. Like the woman in the room beneath him, sprawled on an unmade bed, arms and legs flung wide. He shook the image from his head, the dust from his hair.

Just as he went to hammer the last bit of tin across the hole, the flyscreen banged and the whole roof shuddered, the metal sheet skittering sideways and away, mocking him in the heat. Leaning out to catch it, he snagged his wrist on the edge.

'Ray? You up there?'

Where else would he be? He counted ten, sucking at the wound. 'Yep.'

'Kettle's on.'

At noon, heat had a hum, hollow as a gong. The brim of his hat divided the world to fence and road, dust and sky. Time fell to wilderness between them. The blades of the windmill etched a shadow like stopped clock hands in the dirt of the yard.

'How's the roof?'

'Getting there.'

'And the pump?'

The pump lay in pieces in his lap.

'You want something to eat?'

'Nuh. Too hot. A beer'd be good.'

She fetched it for him, sat down again, sipping at her tea. A little breeze got up, faint, wilful, riffling the dust, the brim of his hat, playing with her hair.

'Did you check the forecast? I meant to, on the radio. But I fell asleep.'

'Yeah. A bit down south. Nothing here.'

'That'd be right.'

The wind got stronger. Hot though, no moisture in it. The windmill groaned, clanked once, blades shedding dust, then stopped again.

'You know, I've never seen it this bad, not even in the drought. At least back then we had the creek. We had feed growing, too, did I tell you, in those paddocks near the road. We were even thinking of putting in some fruit trees. Limes and stuff, for the restaurants. Going organic. Gary reckons citrus does well round here.'

Gary reckons. Gary thinks. Organic. He thought of all those empty insecticide drums marked with skulls and crossbones he'd dragged out of the shed. Said nothing. Picked up his rag, dipped it in vinegar, started scrubbing at the rust on the pump.

'It's not all his. Along the creek. It can't be. Gary wouldn't have done that. No way.' She was leaning toward Ray, her thin brown leg poking out of her thin brown dress. 'Could we at least try and get the bore going, do you think? Until we sort out the creek?' Her bare foot on the edge of his boot. The need coming off her in waves.

'Yeah. I'm trying. I told you. We need a part.' An expensive part. And just yesterday, his money had started running out. He'd stood on the pavement outside the bank, staring at the receipt, Enough left for a few groceries, if he was careful, if it was just flour, sugar, tea, a tank of petrol to get him over the border. Enough to live on for a month. But only if he was careful and he was alone.

'Sorry. You did. I forgot.' She sat back sighing, fanning herself with her hat. 'I'm just tired. I didn't sleep very well. I keep having that dream. The one I told you about before.'

He opened his beer. His radio beside him, but he didn't turn it on.

'It was just like the last time, but more real. It was growing all over the bed this time and up the wall. So green, so lush. That proper English green. I could almost taste it, like a thirst or an itch. Like those people in accidents who dream they still have legs. Then of course I woke up.' She gestured listlessly, out toward the road or the ridge, or beyond that, toward the city and the sea. Some home he'd never seen.

'Yeah. Well. The doctor warned you. Maybe lay off those pills.'

'I know that, Ray. I did hear him. I was there, remember? If I don't take them, I don't sleep at all.' Jaw set, she stared out toward the creek. Something moving out there, at knee height in the steady blow of dust. A humming noise beneath the groan of the windmill blades.

Squinting out, he realised it was insects. Clouds of them, snipping, snapping, whipping through the air, sounding like a thousand tiny sprinklers going all at once.

Before he had time to wonder what they were or what they were finding to eat, a big gust blew up, and they were lost in a billowing wave of dust. She sighed.

'Jesus. Look at that. Bad as Ruby bloody Downs.'

Here it comes. He took a long swallow of beer, went back to his pump.

'You know, I think the only green thing when I got out there was me. I remember getting out of Sam's truck and the heat hitting and seeing Freda shovelling dust off the verandah, mountains of it, and thinking, Jesus, what have I done? They'd had this big storm, the day before. She was taking it out in wheelbarrows. No grass out there. Just rocks.' Her face was lean and anguished in the shadow of her hat. 'Those poor bloody sheep. What do they eat?'

'Saltbush mostly. It's why they taste like that.'

She sniffed, waving away a fly.

'Wouldn't know. Don't eat lamb. Don't eat meat, not really. Not unless there's nothing else.'

Dumbfounded, he reached into his pocket for his tobacco. All those stews and curries he'd been cooking. The Sunday roasts he'd slaved over, in that tiny oven, in forty-degree heat. Just last night, a casserole. He'd thought it was the pills again, the nausea, the way she'd eaten only a potato while pushing lamb shanks round and round her plate, watched intently by the dog.

'Ruby Downs sounds so pretty, doesn't it? It's why I answered the ad. I liked the name. How stupid is that.' She started picking at the arm of her chair, fretting at the cane, unravelling it, trying to stick it back. 'Don't know what I was thinking. Sunsets in meadows or something. What a joke.' Big hands on her, for such a thin person. Brown fingers, strong wrists. As if what was left of her had been stretched on the scaffold of some sturdier, more capable person, someone she might have been or might be again.

'Max told me later it was named after some farmer's wife. Ruby someone or other. Dead, of course.'

He drained his beer. Watched a chicken peck back and forth across the yard, like an actor crossing a stage.

It was always like this, in their conversations on the verandah, at midday, when it got too hot to work, or at dusk, when work was done. Her in the chair with her hat and her tea and the same book she never opened. Him on the step with tea or beer and whatever bit of machinery he happened to be working on at the time. Head down, hands busy. Listening, not listening, to her talking and not talking, to the long moments when she fell headlong and hopeless into a tense silence which was only the absence of the next story. Always the same story, over and over, in fits and starts and circles. Always fretting at the same dry little knot of it. The farm, the creek, the lack of water, lack of money. Gary. Mick. The farm. Lack of rain. Lack of green.

'I dream of green,' she'd say, or 'I'd kill for it.' Once, 'I'd die for it,' before catching herself, with a horrified laugh.

Maybe it was just the illness, the way she was. Her immune system was down. Maybe it was a good sign, this fretfulness. Meant she was getting better, like a child coming out of a fever or a scab itching just before it falls away. Still, hard to take when he was tired from work that was done but never over. Something always nagging at him here, persistent and hopeless, pointless as her worry, peaking at the day's tipping point, until hot and strung out, he felt like he'd been infected by whatever scouring illness was ailing this place. He wished for a straightfoward job, with a start and an end to it. Even a fence would do.

'Shouldn't they at least have some grass on them?' she was saying now, leaning toward him again, face cross with glare. 'If they're called downs?'

Maybe he had it all wrong. Maybe the way she was at first, soft, shy and uncomplaining, was the illness, and this was how she really was, all the time, underneath. He wouldn't know. Had nothing to measure it against. All he knew was that if he just kept sitting here, working away at whatever broken thing was in his hand, if he didn't talk too much, didn't look at her, as if she was a high-strung horse and he a steady point at the end of her rope, she'd stop picking at things, the chair, history, her own skin. Settle into some story or other. His job was to weather her, like a rock or a tree.

'It's an English word, after all.' Her father was English, she'd told him. There was a photo of him on the bookshelf inside. A bald man with big-knuckled hands, playing golf with his new and much younger wife. There was a photo of her mother too, at the opposite end of the bookcase, a small dark woman sitting alone on the verandah of the harbourside home Lily had grown up in, where she'd learned ballet and nagged for a piano and had big plans to visit England, after school, after her year off in the outback, working as a governess. Where she'd met Gary and had Mick. And that was that.

'I always meant to go,' she'd told him. 'Meet Dad's new family, then go round Europe or something. Before uni. You know.'

He didn't know. He'd left school at fourteen. He'd gone travelling too, but for work, pivoting away from home in wide parched circles, heading to places containing more sheep than people, always on his own. Ballet, ponies, uni, England. It was all as alien to him as Ruby Downs had been to her.

'Why don't you go now then?' he'd asked, more than once. 'Just sell up. Go and see your mum.' In her nice house on the harbour. But the house had been sold, after her parents' divorce. And she didn't get on with her mum's new husband. And there was Mick, in school, and the farm, which couldn't be sold until she found the papers, which may or may not be in her name. And there was Gary. Who might still come back. And there they were, again.

'Ray? Someone's coming. Down there.'

She was pointing out toward the dam. Fear or anticipation in her voice, he couldn't tell.

'See?' A little puff of dust, heading cross-country, up toward the house. He thought of the feral neighbour, the husband and his beer bottles, the scar on Mick's arm. Had started clearing his lap and thinking about his own gun, still locked in the ute, bullets wrapped in their pillowcase and hidden in the strongbox under his bed, when he heard the sound of the engine, high and whiny, like an overburdened sewing machine.

'It's just Mick. He must have got the bike going.' Although where he'd got the petrol from, Ray didn't know.

'What bike?'

'You know. The one I found in the shed.' Gary's old trail bike, which Ray had fixed up, new tyres, new sparks, new fuel line, all on the proviso that before Mick rode it or even touched it, he'd make a start on the henhouse, with all that new lumber Ray had bought with the money he didn't really have.

'Oh. Yeah. That old thing.' She frowned at her watch. 'It's really late though. Shouldn't he be at school?'

'It's Saturday. And anyway, it's the holidays.'

'Oh. Yes. I forgot.'

Mick had reached the driveway. Together they watched him doing donuts, ploughing his front wheel through the blue metal Ray had lain across the entrance, to quell the dust and fill the holes.

'He needs a haircut. Before school starts.'

Ray, who had his own ideas about what Mick might need, relit his rollie. Mick was off the bike now, leaving it running, petrol chugging away, while he used Ray's shovel to scoop and gouge at the metal, mounding it up to form a ramp between the cattle grid and the drive.

'Should have a helmet on at least.'

'He's got one, Lily. He won't wear it.'

'I know,' she sighed. 'He's just like his dad. There's no telling him.' She could give it a go.

Revving the little motor to breaking point, Mick embarked on a long wobbly wheelie past the house.

'Gary loved that bike. He was on it when I first met him, you know. Out at Ruby Downs. He was helping Sam with mustering or mulesing or something, whatever new and awful thing they were doing to those sheep.'

Ray checked his watch, then the shadow of the windmill in the dirt. Still too hot to get back on the roof, but he could work on the henhouse. Mick had left it barely half-built.

'He was really nice, back then. About the only nice thing that happened out there. I needed to post a letter, see, and he gave me a lift into town. Way Freda went on about it, you'd think we'd eloped. She left me this note. No *fraternising*. She kept going on about it. Couldn't spell it of course.'

Lily drained her tea and made a face, either at Freda or the tea, which had to be stone cold by now.

'They'd had some trouble or something, with the one before. I guess that's why they put the governess quarters so far from the house.' She snorted, kicking away the chicken, which was trying to peck her toes. 'Governess. What a joke. Mum said it sounded Dickensian. I said, you want Dickens, you should see my room. I don't think that bathroom had ever been cleaned.'

Ray thought of the state of her own place when he'd first arrived, but said nothing. Went on shaving rust off a part that would never work, not without another part he couldn't afford.

'Don't know what I was expecting. Latin and shady hats or something. Instead it was heat and dust and sheep poo and frogs in the toilet. And those boys. My God. Freda let them run wild.'

'Yeah. She's got a lot on her plate. With the kids. And Sam.'

'Yeah. Right.'

'Boys have settled down a bit now. They're at boarding school.'

A long silence. Ray heard the motorbike again, faint, growing louder in tune with Ray's irritation. He thought about getting up, despite the heat. If Mick came back down the driveway, he could head him off.

'And Marcus? What about him?'

'The eldest? Don't think I've met him. Before my time.'

'Oh, you'd remember if you had. Big, fat, red hair. Looks like Sam. Always killing things. Pigs, mostly. He looked a bit like a pig.' The words bitter, sharp, spat out. He glanced round but her face was hidden by her hat.

Relighting the stub of his rollie, he heard a clicking sound. She had her hand out, snapping her fingers. When he hesitated, she raised an eyebrow, as if to say, what difference could it make? So he rolled her one and lit it for her, not meeting her eyes, focusing instead on her wrist, the freckles there, like flecks in brown gravy. Her big teeth snagging on her bottom lip as she picked shreds of tobacco out of her mouth.

'He was the worst. Those younger ones, they were just naughty, stealing shoes or putting lizards in my undie drawer. But Marcus. You know, I found him with a cat once, out behind the shed. It was horrible. I told Freda. She did nothing of course.'

'Yeah. Freda does her best.'

'He put a snake in my room, Ray. A *snake.*' A stream of blue smoke, and then a coughing fit. She threw her half-smoked fag into the yard, where the chicken pecked at it hopefully then wandered away.

'A big brown one, right in the middle of my bed. I spent half the night locked in the bathroom. How was I to know it was dead?'

He got up to stamp the butt out, really to hide his smile.

'I would have spent the whole night in there, if Max hadn't come along. Do you know Max? The artist guy, with the long hair? He still there?' Ray nodded. He knew him, although the artist part was rich. He was the accountant come temp cook come hippie backpacker who'd arrived at Sam's years ago, looking for a few weeks' work, then never left. Did odd jobs for Freda, bit of cooking, bit of bookkeeping, this and that. Freda called him her artist in residence. Grog artist, more like.

'What did he want?'

'Max? Nothing. Just being friendly, that's all. He'd bought me some books, because he knew I'd run out and all I had were Sam's old ones, and they were all about sheep. Had enough bloody sheep during the day, thanks very much.'

She had her hand out again. 'Ray. Can I have another one?'

'Sorry. No papers. I've run out,' he lied, hoping she'd give up, go inside, have a lie down. But she kept on talking, into the glare, as if vomiting up something she had to get out.

'It was my fault, in the end. Such a stupid thing to do, after all that fuss about Gary. But Max asked me if I wanted to come for a drink, with the others, down at the dam. And it was Friday night, and I was lonely, and he was nice. Different. I liked his accent.' Her teacup now empty, she picked up Ray's beer, draining the last few drops, putting the bottle back down with a bang.

'I didn't realise. When he said the others, I thought he meant the B&B people. Some of them were women. Girls.'

Ray concentrated on peeling the label from the bottle of beer. Didn't want to ask. Didn't want to know.

'What did he do?'

'Who?' She seemed lost out there again, beyond the creek and ridge.

'Max.'

'Him? Oh, nothing. He wasn't even there by the time I went over. They said he'd gone off to do some painting. Although it was pretty dark by then.'

She cocked her head toward the track. That tinny whine again, faint but growing louder, heading up the road.

'It wasn't his fault, not really. It was the place. The whole set-up. The feeling out there, you know? And I was such a twit back then. They were only kids really, barely older than Mick is now. But they were pretty big. Well, Marcus was. I should have just gone back to my room as soon as they started. But I was a bit freaked out, I guess, and angry at Max for leaving, so I stalked off. On my own. Exactly what you're not supposed to do.'

Spitting stones, a flurry of crows startled from the fence. Mick, at full throttle, heading toward the ramp he'd made.

'You know how dark it gets out there. I didn't even have a torch. I didn't think I'd gone that far but I must have been walking faster than I thought, because by the time I calmed down and stopped, I couldn't see the house lights or even the fire any more. And there were all these rustling and cracking noises, probably just animals or something, but I thought they were footsteps. So I started running, like an idiot. Thought I was heading back to the house but I must have got turned around in the dark.'

Mick had hit the metal, mounted it, the bike airborne, twisting sideways, sailing too close to the fence. Amid the dust, a glint of silver, flaming red hair.

'By the time Gary got to me, I was way out, past the dam, near that old quarry thing. He said I was lucky I didn't fall right into it. He said it had happened in the fifties, to some girl, and they'd never found her, not even her body. Lucky.' She broke off, panting, as if she was still running. Ray sucked at the dead stub of his cigarette. Wanting to get up, walk away. Wanting to put his fingers in his ears.

'When Gary found me, he said I tried to run off. Scratched up his face. I don't remember. Good thing, I suppose. Lucky. Like he said.' Ray felt sick. 'I must have thought it was Marcus, see, back again. They'd been shooting together, see. Pigs or something. In the dark, they smelled the same.'

They watched Mick reach earth again, in an ungainly spin of dust and gravel, wheels skewing wildly side to side.

'Silly sod. He'll break his neck.' And still she made no move to get up.

Ray threw his beer bottle at the drum. It missed, smashing on the tap, making Lily jump. The hen squawked, fluttered wildly. Glass everywhere. Another mess for him to clean up.

'Better get those chickens in. There's been a fox around.'

He walked fast and furious toward the gate. On the way he saw the petrol flap on his ute was open. The cap was missing, a bit of garden hose sticking out of the tank. The rest of the hose had been cut to pieces, lay scattered on the ground.

He kept on walking, past the henhouse, built in the wrong place of course, right out near the tank, where there was not a scrap of shade. Wonky, wire flapping loose. Wouldn't keep a rabbit out, let alone a fox. He just walked on, faster and faster, out toward the gate, where Mick was still mucking around with the blue metal, driving fresh ruts into Ray's new track.

'Oi! Your mum wants you. Up the house.'

As soon as he spotted Ray, the little bugger roared off in the opposite direction, toward the creek.

Ray turned on his heel. Time to check his phone. He strode up toward the ridge, the only spot he could get reception in this place.

Wind was getting stronger. Dust rising, the far paddock relocating itself to the banks of the creek. Not his problem. Organic. What a joke. This place would never be organic, not in a hundred years. And you'd have to grow something first. For that you'd need to get the bore going, and for that you'd need to hit the aquifer, and for that you'd need a new drill and a new submersible, which would cost a lot of money he didn't have. Six months, six men, six inches of rain. And who was this you, exactly? Not him, that was for sure.

He panted up the incline at a punishing pace. Two more weeks of treatment and a hospital visit every other day. Three days until Cheryl was back from her Gold Coast holiday, having topped up her terracotta tan. The only reason he was still here, he told himself. Lily's lack of a car.

At the top, the air was fresher, the pain in his chest slowly ebbing away. Not a cloud in the sky now. Hard, hard and endless blue. Three black cockies flew across in an arrow shape, their mewing desolate and mournful, on their way to somewhere else.

No messages on his phone when he connected. Nothing from Urs, and it had been over a month. Three more days.

Putting his phone back in the pocket of his overalls, his hand met something dry and soft. He looked at the hair, still black and glossy, before letting it drop and blow away.

CHAPTER TWENTY-THREE

She didn't get up the next day. Taped a note to the door, saying she had a cold. And she was cold, despite the heat and the mothy rattle of the airconditioner. She watched a scourge of light from the venetians travel across the floor, window to door. Like her skin, the light worn thin by the day's great expanse.

Now and again her mobile beeped from the depths of her bag. Six messages so far, all from Harry. All about Tilda, with exclamation marks. No details but she could imagine. She'd stopped taking her pills. She'd caught a train, to the coast or the country or to some blighted outer suburb where buses rarely ran and where taxis refused to go. She'd been caught shoplifting. A man had attacked her while she was sleeping on a bench. She'd burnt down her room and the house and garage with it, along with the box of family photos, Harry's guitar, Harry's African art statues, all Mam's old clothes.

The last message just said Urgent. She kicked the bag under the bed and the bleeping died away.

At dusk, a knock on the door. Freda, asking how was she feeling and did she want Panadol or dinner on a tray. Ursula lay doggo until the bulky permed shape behind the glass moved away. After that, she got up, closed the blind entirely, sank back into oatmeal-coloured gloom. Lay labouring against it, heart beating slight and fast, like some tiny wingless bird.

Night came but no sleep. Too many hours and they were hers alone to make and shoulder, despite their sly weight and muffled purpose. A heavy swathe of useless and unnavigable time. It had always been like this, she realised, ever since Ray.

Before dawn, a storm, dry and violent. Lightning sheeted at the window, roof tin took sudden flight. She listened to it clatter on fake lawn or fake palm tree, the bonnet of her car. She lay there, willing destruction entire. When it didn't come, she got up, went to the outhouse, moving slowly in brilliant electricity. Smell of ozone, sewerage. Things leaking, bursting, giving way.

At first light, she found a frog on her pillow. Tiny, albino, it lay curled like a baby's hand.

⁓

She was woken later by another knock at the door. A tall shape behind the front door glass. Not Freda. Not Ray.

'Hi. How you feeling?' She stood looking at his feet. Boots today. 'Sam's going to take a look at your car, but he had to head out to the neighbour's first. There's a fire. Don't worry. It's a long way away.' She wasn't worried. Didn't feel anything at all.

Max jangled his keys, shifting boot to boot. 'Listen, no one's around much today. I thought, if you're feeling better, you might like to get out, go and see something. The river and the old homestead. We could camp out there. If you'd like.'

~

They drove in hot silence, along no discernible path, across hurtful stones, cracking mud, drying already to dust. Little mailboxes lined this track, the Gilberts, the Shaughnessys, the O'Riordans. All gone, according to Max. Now and again her mobile beeped piteously from her bag.

'You might want to get that. Before we lose reception.'

'It's just Harry.'

'Oh. OK.'

More bumping and skidding, more silence and dust.

Half an hour later he asked, 'Who's Harry?'

'No one. Someone I live with.'

She went quiet and Max didn't ask and she didn't say, just sank gratefully into more hot, grainy silence. A solitary hum in the car as Max got out to open a gate, got back in, got out to close it again. At some point, off the main track, they passed a tiny town, with a wooden pub, the world's smallest RSL. An old dog lay sprawled beside a water tank. Looked like it might have been there her whole life. Something wet dripped on her shoulder. Winston, panting in her ear from the back seat. She'd forgotten all about him. She wondered where he'd been, who'd been feeding him. He looked better. Glossier, brighter-eyed. Leaner even.

'His head looks better. His sore.'

Just disinfectant apparently, a dab of some ointment from Max's overall pocket. She wished for some mysterious salve for herself, something to heal the puckering hole in her heart.

Silence again, for another hour, the ute bouncing along invisible ruts in tall silver grass. A stalky murmur, like some dry old sea. On the map, which she consulted with not much interest, she saw they were heading toward the famous river, the historic homestead, marked by a big circle on Freda's map. Nothing there, of course. Half a fence, some old machinery, a row of white-anted piers. Far below, the river itself, deep, brown, thick, shrunken between high steep banks.

While she sat in the car, Max got out to poke around, kicking sheets of iron, banging inside the drum of the steam engine with a stick, as men do. She put on her glasses, reading without interest Freda's photocopies. Steam paddles, wool yields, wide-toothed shearing combs. In the end, all that endeavour, all those statues and photographs, all that bewhiskered boasting, for this. Old brown iron, dry wind riffling through dry grass, gutted bits of life. Right then, it felt like nothing might ever run green or true again.

'What's he like?' Max asked after he got back into the car, handing her, for some reason, a rusty bolt. She put it on the back seat. Winston gave it an experimental lick.

'Sorry? Who?'

'Well, not the dog. This Harry. Bloke you live with.'

Where to start? With his faith in angels? Or his non-belief in microwaves? That little cavalier beard he'd affected lately, the sort middle-aged men grow to cover a weak chin.

'If you ask him how he is, he tells you. In detail.'

'Oh. One of those.'

An hour later, and the road ran out entirely, Max aiming the ute at what looked like a solid wall of bush. Where are we going, she was forced to ask, as they jounced through, undergrowth cracking against the windows. A famous creek, Max told her, wrenching the wheel to avoid termite mounds tall as cows. It would be cooler there, he said.

No water though, when they got there, just more red dirt. Up ahead, in a shallow indentation of stunted trees, amid a swamp of tiny pink flowers, a procession of pigs, in descending order, like they had been arranged by a child. A big hairy one, a mother with swinging teats. A brindled baby bringing up the rear.

'Why is it famous?'

'One of your explorers camped here once.' On his way to being dead no doubt.

What from a distance had looked like shaded green grass turned out to be a field of prickles, host to a million ants. While Max dug a hole for the fire, the idea of which seemed insane in the heat, she tried to pick the worst of the burrs from Winston's fur. When Max asked her to unpack the tents, she did so badly, ungraciously, sweating and swearing, tangling ropes, losing pegs, high-stepping skittishly through long grass, worrying about snakes. Not hot enough, according to Max, who was digging a pit for the fire, his pile of sticks flaring almost before he touched them with the match. Going back to the car for her nail scissors, to trim away Winston's snarled undercarriage, she saw by the temperature gauge it was forty-three degrees.

They sat in deep hot shade under the mulgas. Not a breath of air. When it got too hot even for that, Max suggested a swim. She followed him up a steep bank of earth. Below it was a dam, tannic and algal, slimy with more of those little pink plants. All around it, tracks like little emblems and Max deciphered them lovingly. Emu splay, roo arrowhead, the molar shapes of goats. One he didn't know. Feathery, sly, the heel just a witchy wisp.

While he squatted down, pondering it from all angles, she took her sandals off and tested the water, worrying about what might have swum and died and defecated in there. But he just stripped off and waded in. She followed gingerly, T-shirt ballooning behind her, until she took it off, watching it float away. Even that slimy, tepid water a relief, after the heat.

Later, as he foraged for wood, she sat in the taut shade of a bush. Noticing things, despite herself. The intricate hairs of those little muscled plants. The fine shadow they cast against the red. For a long time, she watched a trail of ants build a world around the drip of sugary tea on her sandal strap. Wondering, in some tiny corner of herself, about the owner of the hairy-winged heel. Wanting to see it. Expecting not to. Telling herself she wanted and expected nothing at all.

Finally, toward sunset, a cooler breeze through the mulgas, little pockets of desert night. They sat on a log eating sausages, and she stopped worrying if the crunch on them was chilli, dirt or ants. When she got out her hip flask and offered it to Max, he shook his head.

'Nah. I'm good. Don't do that any more.'

And he said nothing more and she didn't ask, just drained the whiskey, watching spindled shadows, silver grass, the torn lace of trees. A full moon, yellow and hazy. Perilous-looking stars.

In her tent, at midnight, when she heard something scrape and scuttle against the canvas, she lay rigid, telling herself a snake wouldn't make a sound like that. When she heard it again, feathery, insistent, closer this time, she called out and from the next tent Max told her it was just a moth.

In the early hours, when that fluttering started up again, right by her ear, she picked up her sleeping bag, blundering out of her tent and into his. They lay together, chastely separated by nylon and zips, hands clasped. Listening to the distant mourning of ewes and lambs, caught in their separate pens.

CHAPTER TWENTY-FOUR

'I told you, Ray. Nothing that's going to die.'

A singed smell of cooling earth through the open window. They'd had a bit of rain a few days ago, just enough to put a fuzz of green on the home paddock. Not enough to settle the dust.

'Everything dies,' he said, not unreasonably, then regretted it. She went quiet, tugging at her nightgown, trying to free it from the sheet.

'Come off it. You know what I mean.'

'There's only seven.'

'Yeah. Exactly. So what's the point?'

He couldn't see her face. So black and thick these autumn nights. But he knew she was looking at him, one eyebrow quirking up in that way she had. They were still black, her eyebrows, thick and dark against the yellow shriek of her skull.

'I dunno. Felt sorry for the bloke.'

⌒

When he'd seen the notice in the local paper, he'd just thought fertiliser, lumber, maybe some poly pipe for the drip-feed watering in Lily's vegetable patch. For anything more permanent, for the orchard she kept going on about, they'd need proper irrigation and there was still no sign of that missing paperwork showing who owned the land along the creek. That left the bore, and for that he'd need a drill.

Could rent one though. Maybe even buy one, second-hand. They could afford it, just about. Two months' fencing work on a neighbouring property, navvying three days a week at the hospital building site, pay from his new job, cooking weekends and Thursday nights at the local Chinese and now they had money in the bank. Even after servicing the loan Gary had taken out to feed dying stock, they'd be ahead. Cash in his pocket, for the first time in months.

To celebrate, he'd bought himself a new shirt, new boots, lunch at the pub. Sitting at the bar, he'd leafed through the local classifieds, looking for hire equipment, maybe a second-hand drill, finding instead a rash of auction notices and farm clearances. Cheap stock, small acreages for sale. More land. His thoughts circled yet again to the neighbour and the creek. Lily was adamant the man was lying, that if they could just find the contract, they could prove the water was theirs. Even if it wasn't, it might still be possible, in six months' time, if they were careful, if he kept working, kept saving, if Lily kept getting better and the jobs kept up, to make an offer, for water rights or even for the land itself.

Driving out, heading deeper and deeper into the poor red country west of town, for the first time he'd dared to see a future unfurling, steady, rich and orderly as the rows of fruit trees Lily dreamed about. Farm clearance, the real estate sign promised him, and he turned left. Might get a bargain, he thought, turning up a driveway as wrecked and rutted as their own. Might even have a drill.

When he saw the place, he felt ashamed of himself. Tattered fences, bare paddocks, dry dams. The word foreclosure hung everywhere like thick, red fog. Here and there, a bit of green pick. Worse than nothing, because it offered hope to man and beast. No beasts here anyway except for a couple of horses tied to the verandah post. One was old and ribby. The other, young, nervous, too thin for its height, pranced nervously at the end of its rope. Outside the sheds, their doors swinging, shiny padlocks hanging off, their empty interiors floating with hay and dust, the only things worth selling, lined up in rows. A tractor, a harvester, drums of fuel and bales of feed. Next to a truck piled high with furniture, the family, in faded blues and weathered greys, standing shoulder to shoulder against the crisp-shirted men from the bank.

He got out, scuttled round the back. He was checking out a cage trailer—rusty, unregistered, suspension shot, but could be useful, for hauling supplies or firewood—when the farmer came over, planting his worn-out boots next to Ray's. They stood in awkward silence, looking at the trailer. Ray offered him a cigarette, but the man waved it away.

'Four-fifty. Cost me two thousand new. Cash in hand only. Extra hundred and I'll load it up with those.' The farmer jerked his head toward some sheep bunched near the fence. Thin, silent and wool-heavy, they had the dull eyes of the recently starved.

'Yeah. Thanks mate. I don't run stock.'

The man folded his arms, squinting at him. Ray realised he must look like some sort of hobby farmer in his shiny new boots and his packet-fresh shirt. He bent down to look at the trailer again and a missed pin from his collar stuck into his neck.

'Good dorpers, those. Worse places to start. Don't look much at the moment, but they'll be OK when they get some condition on.'

'Yeah. Not sure what I'd do with seven sheep.'

'Eleven. At least. Probably more.'

Jumping the fence, the man waded through the bunch of sheep. Grabbing a ewe, hauling it over the backs of the others, he flipped it easily, the animal hopeless and placid under his hands. Ray saw a firm bulge beneath the sunken flanks.

'This one, those two, old girl at the back. All in lamb.' Dad's voice in his ear. Them lambs'll go like smoke when they hit the ground.

'Cash only. Like I said. To me, right here. Fucked if I give those bastards another red cent.'

Together they turned to watch the bank men trying to load the young horse onto a float. The colt was baulking, frantic, white-eyed. The man at the front was hauling too hard, the one behind standing far too close. Halfway up, the horse pig-rooted, scrabbled, lost its footing on the ramp. It came down hard, bashing against the float. Stood trembling, a big gash on its leg, while a young boy watched from the verandah, arms by his sides.

'Listen, I'll take the trailer. OK? Four-fifty, you said.' Ray counted out from his wad of notes. Even his money, straight from the bank this morning, looked too new and crisp. 'Not sure about the ewes.'

The man spat, just missing Ray's boots.

'Suit yourself.'

The farmer stalked off toward the house. A woman waited for him behind the flyscreen. White legs, white apron, her face in shadow. Giving only her body to Ray's assumptions before her husband slammed the door.

⁓

When he got home, towing his sagging trailer stuffed with pipes, feed bags, an old sprinkler system and seven half-dead sheep, he found his own front door hanging open. Mick's skateboard was lying halfway up the steps, as if trying to mount them all by itself.

'Hello?'

'Mick, please. Take it off. Right now.' Lily's voice was high and echoey, on the edge of panic or laughter, or both.

'I can't. Not yet. You'll look weird.'

'I do already! I can't believe I let you do this. Must be mad.'

'Just wait. Trust me, OK? I done this tons of times. Well, once at least.'

Following a trail of discarded clothes—Mick's school trousers, Lily's bra, her yellow dress—he found them in the bathroom. Mick was wearing Ray's washing-up gloves and Lily's pink cooking apron and not much else. Lily was crouched in the bath, dressed in her swimmers, great dollops of white stuff all over her near-bald head. Hanks of black hair all over the toilet seat.

'How much longer? It really stings.'

'Twenty minutes. Half an hour, tops. You'll see. It'll look really cool. Like that singer. That blonde one you like.'

'Annie Lennox?'

'Who?'

Lily and Ray exchanged a look in the mirror, until Mick slathered on more of the bleach and Lily clenched her jaw and closed her eyes. Wincing along with her, Ray unplugged his clippers, which were dangling precariously from a power point above the half-full sink.

'Jesus, how much of this stuff did you use?' He picked up Mick's big black bottle of bleach. *Not For Domestic Use*, in red letters on the side. 'You could do an Olympic swimming pool with this.'

'Don't worry, Davo showed us. You know Davo, from school. His hair went green from swimming training, so he bleached it but then he had to shave it off anyway, because it makes you go faster, but he left the top long, like a mohawk. It looked cool.'

As he talked, Mick was twisting what little was left of Lily's hair into scrubby little hillocks, like you do to a kid in the bath. With her tufty head and those poor brown ribs, she looked like a woodcut of some medieval saint.

'And what did his mother have to say?' Lily asked, eyes still closed. 'That's what I'd like to know.'

'Nothing. She's dead.'

A long moment, the boy frozen, crouched there above his mother in his silly frilly apron. His face blanched to the old sandshoe colour of the bathroom tiles. Lily still and quiet, a nerve ticking in the skin between her shoulderblades. Then the dog erupted into a volley of barking, there was some startled bleating and she cocked her head toward the window. Saying what's that, splashing at the water in the bath. Wondering idly whether this stuff might work on the shower grout.

Ray took the bowl from Mick's hands. 'Go and see what that dog's on about. I'll finish up in here.'

Mick just kept standing there, his rubber fingers dripping white stuff. Ray slipped the gloves off him and pushed him out the door.

'While you're at it, fill up the trough in the paddock.'

'Why?'

'You'll see. Go on.'

As he cupped and rinsed Lily's head, feeling the poor egg shape of it under his fingers, the way the little bulge at the back fitted so neatly into his palm, she lay sighing, rubbing her skull across his hand like a cat. Flakes of raw-looking skin in the water, but she had her eyes closed again and he scooped them away.

'Mum! Come and see what Ray got.'

'Yeah. In a minute, love.' Emerging from the towel, she blinked up at Ray, her hair hot yellow, her scalp bright pink.

'How do I look?'

'Yeah. Not bad.' Once it grew out.

He was in the yard, trying to coax the reluctant sheep out of the trailer with a handful of feed and no help from Mick or the dog, when he heard the back door go. A sharp intake of breath.

'See Mum? What you reckon? There's not many but all those ones over there are in lamb. I separated them out. Ray says we could put them down there, near the creek, where Dad had that other lot. Should be a bit of feed down there, if we get some more rain. I'm gonna fix the fence.'

Ray waited for it, the slam of her feet on the boards, the slap of the door. Nothing. She must be in shock. Feeling shame-faced, he kept herding ewes off the trailer and through the gate, carefully, slowly, as if it required great skill and concentration. The sheep were so exhausted, they put up no resistance as he heaved them around. Just woolly bags of bones.

When he finally got the courage to look, he found Lily kneeling next to the trailer, stroking the flank of the oldest, skinniest, most pregnant ewe.

'What's the matter with this one?'

'Nothing.' A lie. He cleared his throat. 'What do you mean?'

Lily flipped her ear over. The underside was a mash of flesh and flies.

'Oh. Probably just caught it in a stock gate or something. It's not deep or anything. I'll put some stuff on it.'

'Flies are getting at it. I can do it, if you tell me how.'

While he went to work on the fence, footing posts, fixing the gate catch, restringing wire, she stayed kneeling by the old ewe, painting the ear with antiseptic. Scratching and fondling the sheep like a dog. Murmuring, 'Poor old girl.'

⌐

'They look pretty sick. Is that why they were so cheap?'

A gust of wind, hitting the bedroom amidships, shivering the window frames. Roof tin chattering and groaning, but his rivets held.

'They'll be OK. Just need feeding up.' He remembered the man's harsh voice, his empty eyes. The words he was echoing, said by rote.

'That last lot Gary bought? Before he took off? When they gave birth, the lambs were all too sick to feed. Something wrong with their mouths. And then something started getting at them, dogs or foxes or something, and we had to shoot the rest and burn the carcasses, just in case. I'll never forget the smell.'

'I can take them back.' He couldn't. 'Or sell them on.'

'No. That's worse. They'd be dead then for sure.'

More wind, harder this time. A storm was on its way. A dry one though, from the feel of the air. Something whispered down from the ceiling. In the morning the bottom of their bed would be covered in a scree of white.

'We've got to do something, Lil. Sell something, grow something. At the moment all we grow is dust.'

'Yeah. We will. The citrus, like we talked about. And we're doing all right, aren't we? You got those jobs. And after next week, when I get the go-ahead, I'll get one too.'

'Doing what?'

She picked fastidiously at the bits of plaster on the sheet, throwing them on the floor.

'I don't know. I always wanted to teach, but I'd have to go back to uni for that. But I could do distance learning, maybe. I read about it. And I could work for Cheryl at the hairdressers in the meantime. Or cleaning. They're looking for cleaners at the hospital. I saw an ad.' The thought of it, Lily in a plastic apron, lugging buckets down shiny corridors. Pausing at doorways to rooms containing women like her, sitting small and thin on the edge of beds.

'Yeah. We're not that desperate. Not yet.' He took her hand in the dark.

'I might even like it. I'm sick of sitting round here, I know that.'

She shifted closer, hooking herself under his arm. Still thin, her body swimming in the flannelette nightie, ribs clear under his fingers, but there was a little of plush of fat now on her hips and thighs.

'Or what if we just sold up, like you were saying before? Just do it. Just piss off.' He could feel her tense with excitement at the idea. 'We could go to the city. Not Sydney, I know you hate it, but Adelaide or something. I've got relatives there. Or we could live on the coast. A house by the sea. Imagine that.'

'What about the orchard though? I thought you were keen.'

'Yeah. Not really. It's not a big deal.' He thought of all the work he'd done, that poly pipe he'd bought. 'It was always more Gary's thing, this place, not mine.'

'You'd have to find the bugger first, if you want to sell. Isn't it his name on the deeds? And Lily, face it. No one's going to buy this place the way it is. You'd have to show it can pay its way. Another thing, too. The rates are due.'

As always, at the mention of money or bills, he felt her glaze over, drift off, her body gone soft and heavy under his arm.

'Yeah. Grow something. OK.' Limes, lemons, vegetables, she murmured. Almond trees, for the blossom, apples and apricots. Her voice rose and fell on waves of greenery, tides of sleep. Beneath the smell of the dust, a faint scent of apricots, from the body lotion she used. Peaches, nectarines, her voice conjuring them, ripening them, hoisting him high up a ladder, her below in her yellow dress, plump and brown as a nut. Walnuts, sitting on the back step with his father at Christmas, cracking them with a hammer, his lap full of nuts. At the moment, that lap of hers wouldn't hold much at all.

He lay awake for a long time, swallowing at the scour of dust in the back of his throat. Quietly thinking, against Lily's snoring, the glow of the alarm clock. Planning things with pumps and pipes while his body lay rigid, trying not to wake her up. Pale glimmer now at the window, dawn coming through the curtains she'd run up from an old tablecloth, or the marital bedspread, he couldn't remember which. Both pink. Lily liked pink. She liked little things. Lambs. Earrings. Baby vegetables. Baby carrots, baby eggplants. Micro herbs, for the restaurants. Organic, of course, and he thought about the frozen bags of cheap crinkle-cut veg he stir-fried every Saturday at the local Chinese. Finger limes, she countered, or jojoba, and he almost asked what's that into the dark, forgetting she was asleep. She'd read about it, and that clinched it. Lily had this strange unshakeable faith in anything she'd read. And some of it might happen but most of it wouldn't and it didn't matter, because it made her happy, and at that moment, with the apricot smell and the sun coming up, tinting everything in the room dull pink, everything seemed possible, even a house by the sea.

He fell asleep to sheep bleating somewhere, faint as gulls.

CHAPTER TWENTY-FIVE

By mid-morning, sorting pipe and checked gradients, running hoses between tap, tank and vegetable patch, the dream was receding. Instead of bright fruit, white blossom, brown skin and spangled trees, it was Mick forking through half-digested compost, a grid of dry black plastic on bare red dirt.

There'd been some rain in the night, enough to flood the septic and turn the dust gluey. Not enough to grace the tank. By lunchtime, grubbing channels and jimmying rocks, just the bare shoulders of what he'd imagined last night, dipping lower. A faint smell of apricots on his fingers. Slick of grease on his belly skin.

When the hoses snarled for the third time and the connectors broke, he allowed himself one short sharp kick to the pump. Then he headed down to check the sheep.

He smoked a cigarette, leaning against the wobbly fence. Mick's repairs weren't up to much. Then again, those ewes weren't going anywhere. Once the feed he'd scattered was gone, they stood in an aimless huddle, looking down toward water that was just pools of mud. Above it, stuttering across the bank in a way that could accord to no legal boundary and bristling with barbed wire, the neighbour's fence. Crooked, mad and brutal as the man himself. Nailed to a post, a new sign, in that same lunatic hand. *Privet Property. Keep Out.*

Looking for tools in the shed this morning, Ray had finally found the sale contract. It fluttered out like a dead flower from between the pages of an old porno magazine. Two years ago, Mr G. Jones had sold Mr A. Ronson five acres of pasture along the creek. No mention of water rights. At the back, a diagram showed the shorn boundaries of Lily's place. Ronson's fence was a good ten metres from where it should have been.

He was heading back up the slope to finish the hoses and maybe get his wire cutters from the ute when his boot kicked up something half-buried in the dust. White feathers, tinged with red. A bit further on, a yellow claw. Following the trail—more feathers, a shorn wing—he found the head of the old boiler which used to go broody on his chest. Dead chicken eye.

He was digging a hole, going much deeper and wider than it needed, determined that neither the dog or Lily, on one of her walks, would come across it, when Mick wandered up.

'Shit. Not another one.'

'What?' Ray turned mid-grunt. Mick had given himself a brutal go with the clippers too. His ears were sticking out like pink oven mitts.

'Yeah. Forgot to tell ya. I found the rooster this morning, out behind the dam. You reckon it's a fox?'

Not unless it was a fox wielding an axe. Ray collected his hat and shovel, headed up toward the ute.

'Come on. Let's go.'

'Where? I'm meeting Davo. In town.'

'I'll give you a lift. After.'

'After what?'

When Ray turned right not left at the mailbox, Mick went pale beneath his freckles.

'Nuh. No way. This bloke's feral. Last time Dad went over he took a pot shot at him. Said he'd kill us if we went up there again.'

'Yeah. Well. I'm not your dad.'

As they crossed the bridge, Ray saw water welling beneath the boards. Heaps of water down this end of the creek. Snarls of black plastic hose all along the bank. As they got closer to the gate at the top, they saw more signs lining the track, all red dripping variations on *Piss off.*

'Ray. Deadset. This bloke can't even spell.'

'Yeah, well, that's what happens when you don't go to school.'

At the end of the driveway, there was no house. Just a collection of old caravans, most of them missing wheels and up on blocks. Ray had half-expected that, along with the jumble of broken motorbikes, the car trailers piled with fuel and garbage, the Australian flag tattering from an annexe pole. What he wasn't expecting was the crude pulley rigged from a tree branch, which he told himself was for car or bike repairs. Metal hooks hung from it, with what he hoped was more red paint staining their ends.

Next to the pulley, cage upon cage of birds. Rosellas, galahs, cockies, all crammed in together, even a bedraggled crow. Wire-ridden, their wings all crushed. Flight bent out of shape.

As he got out, a dog barked faintly. He scanned the empty distance. He shouldn't have brought the boy. Didn't know why he had. To teach him something? And what would that be?

'Stay here, all right? And lock the doors.'

For once, Mick didn't ask why.

Ray had chosen the largest caravan and was knocking at the door, steeling himself to see some mad furry face appear at the grimy windows, seeing only himself, when he became aware of a faint sweetish tang in his throat. Realised it had been there since he got out of the car. Almost algal, getting stronger, forming a fur on his tongue. It was coming from a forty-gallon drum near the pulley. An oily slime on top of dark liquid. Something white and clean poking through. He'd turned away, stomach lurching, intending to drive off, when he heard Mick calling.

'Ray! Come here.'

He was down near the creek. Too much to hope he might have done what he was told. Dark shapes, strung along the boundary fence. Dogs, Ray realised, as he got closer, or used to be. Ten or so, if you reassembled the parts.

They'd been arranged by size and level of decay. Some were noosed to the wire, some spread-eagled, paws nailed to posts. Spotted ones, dun-coloured ones, a blue heeler speckle, some wolfish thing. Grey fur, a cracked yellow cranium rotting through. A red kelpie, like his. Mick breathed too loudly beside him.

A fucking puppy, for God's sake. The fur of its haunch and belly peeled up and over, revealing cords of red muscle and blue vein, a cowl of skin mercifully covering its head.

Ray grabbed Mick by the shoulder, marched him away.

As they got closer to the ute, more barking, growing louder, from the direction of the creek. Mick scuttled round toward the passenger door but Ray made himself walk, steady, measured, thinking of his empty gun in the ute tray. Even the sight of it might be enough.

Before they left, as the barking closed in and Mick mouthed something at him through the window, his face white as a sheet, Ray got his tyre iron out and, one by one, bashed the locks off the bird cages. The crow stumbled, hopped, then took off, blue black and elegant against the sky. The cocky just sat there, one wing useless, until he went to pick it up and it bit him hard and flapped awkwardly away. As they drove off, an explosion of rosellas, high and bright against the grey horror of the place.

⌒

At midnight, when most farmers, even mad ones, should be asleep, Ray drove his ute into the home paddock, bumping across the ruts and stones of Lily's unborn vegetable patch.

At the top of the ridge, his headlights found the sheep, huddled together against the fence. Parking up and leaving the lights on, he donned his head torch, strung a series of hurricane lamps along the bank. Set to work.

There was a grim, fierce satisfaction in the wire giving under his snippers, the old rotten posts lunging out under a series of vicious kicks. Barbed wire caught him between glove and sleeve, a bracelet of blood on his wrist. He thought of broken flight and red feathers, a peeled puppy skull. Worked on.

By dawn, the evil old thing was gone, leaving churned and bitter earth. Under lamplight, the raw crust of mud, crumbling off, rising steep and red up the other side, looked like something from the Somme. Carefully he stepped out the distance between the neighbour's other fence, then laid his string line and checked his level, stopping every so often to consult the diagram in his back pocket and realign holes for the posts. Wondering how much of his life he'd measured out like this, with string and steps and wood.

With the sky greying, he worked faster. Starting with the old augur at the eastern boundary, he dug post holes but they were too wide for the sleek modern posts he'd bought in town after dropping Mick off at Dave's. So he went back along the line, patiently tamping and refilling. When the headlights started to dim, he turned them off, working on in the dim glow of the hurricanes. Three times, checking the boundary on the contract, he found he'd wandered off course, waylaid by rocks or humpy ground. There'd be no mistake, no comeback. In answer to wavering greed, violence and madness, he would bring good workmanship. A cold slow calmness as he pulled out a two-metre run, unstringing, restringing, altering the trajectory of the fence by two steps either way. A job worth doing. A few feet of ground. Men had died for less. He thought of old Grandad with his medals, Dad and his stories, all that mud, blood and bullets, as he tackled the next post, the next hole, his miner's light carving home out of frosty air.

As the sky turned pearl along the ridge, his new fence finally met the other fence to the west. Settling the last post, testing the tension, adjusting the strainers and then tying off, he leaned panting against his new boundary. His defiance ran straight and true, on the right side of the creek.

Before gathering up his tools, he took the photocopy he'd made of the contract diagram out of his back pocket. Stuck it to the middle of the fence with a twist of wire. Left it fluttering there, a declaration of war.

~

When Ray drove Lily to the hospital for the results of her last check-up, Mick refused to come.

'I should finish that henhouse, eh. With that fox around.'

As they drove off, he saw that Mick was putting the henhouse door on backwards. A chicken would have to be Houdini to get in. He let him get on. He understood it, the need for all that hammering and sawing. A way to reduce the world to governable details involving hammers and nails.

In the car park Lily asked if he was coming in. He pleaded errands in town but in truth he couldn't face the antiseptic, gleaming indifference of the place. He sat in the ute watching her walk away. She was wearing old jeans cinched tight with a belt and a shirt he liked, pale blue with faded yellow teapots on it. Her figure dwarfed by the shining new hospital wing he'd helped to build.

An hour later, when she emerged from the sliding doors, he squinted through the dazzle of the windscreen, trying to read what had happened through her body. Too far away to see her face and she had on those big black sunglasses that made her look like a junior owl. Maybe just the autumn light, maybe wishful thinking, but it seemed some grace had returned to her, flowing through those narrow hips in their faded denim, the silver stubble softening the bird shape of her skull. The jut of her collarbone appeased now by a tan.

He got out of the car, arms already making a circle toward her, but she stopped short, and he was left executing a strange step in brittle mid-air. Wondering why his body felt so disjointed, so not his own.

'Lil? Everything good?'

Her black, blank sunglasses. He wished Mick was here, rattling around on his skateboard, or even the dog.

'What happened? What did they say?'

She stepped forward, taking off her glasses, her little crow's-feet crinkling up. 'All clear. Nothing. And there's something else.'

CHAPTER TWENTY-SIX

At dawn, blue, calm, shining soft yellow through the canvas of the tent, a bell-like cry. The noise of something small and simple making itself known. As she unzipped the fly, a quick tremble of ears, fur, a liquid black eye. And it was gone. Just one print, as if whatever it was had touched down once, lightly, then blown away. Quoll, Max thought. But he wasn't sure.

By the time they were in the truck, heading back, through that dry wash of grass, she knew what she had to do. As soon as they were in range again, she'd call Harry, tell him to move out. She'd borrow some more money, somehow, finish the renovations, or maybe just sell the house the way it was. There'd still be enough to buy herself something smaller, more modern, with a little courtyard and an electric oven, a place out of the city and well away from cliffs and the sea. Enough left over to find a place where Tilda could get some proper care. Ursula would visit, twice a week. She'd try and listen this time, try to hear whatever truth Tilda had been trying to tell her for all these years, in all those mad, sideways stories of hers.

Or perhaps she wouldn't buy a house at all. Just put the money in the bank, buy a big black smooth-sounding car all her own. Go travelling, and when she was sick of it, end up somewhere like this, teaching English and manners to children like Freda's wild little girls. Make sausages on Tuesdays. Go camping with Max. Find the owner of the hairy-winged heel.

By the time they got back to Ruby Downs, the sky had turned black. Smoke on the horizon, thick and choking, and the clearing was crowded with trucks and tractors. Their owners, exhausted and dirty, sat slumped on the verandah. Wind like an oven when she got out of the car. That unmistakeable bushfire smell.

Max melted away, stripping off his shirt as he went. As Ursula mounted the steps, Freda rushed past, her hands and hair stark with flour against the black faces and soot-streaked clothes of the men. Dry lightning, she barked. Fire to the east and south and behind as well. Ursula followed her gaze to a wall of smoke on two horizons, far away, but in this wind, not far enough. A hundred acres gone, two hundred maybe. How many sheep, nobody knew. The flyscreen banged behind Freda, and as if it was a signal, all the men got up, slinging overall straps back over their shoulders, putting on hats and goggles, heading out toward the trucks.

The afternoon passed in a flurry of cake and sandwich making, big smoky male bodies angling through the female flurry of the kitchen. Endless cups of tea. Freda was everywhere, flipping meat patties and carving lamb from a bloody-looking shoulder while barking orders into her brick of a satellite phone. Even the little girls were cooking, making scones and Anzac biscuits, until there was enough cake and salads and ham sandwiches to feed an army. If you could fight fires with food, Freda would have won.

Ursula, deemed too slow and helpless by Ronnie to do anything else, was assigned to buttering bread and refilling urns. The girl sat cross-legged on a bench, bossing her younger sisters in the art of scone-making while keeping a beady eye on Ursula. They set up a rhythm, Ursula cutting, filling, spreading, the little girls arranging the food on plates and whisking them off, the smallest one eating icing as fast as she could make it. Freda stirred a pork and pineapple curry to sludge. And still they came, men and other women now as well, black-faced and wild-haired. At one point, Freda, running past with a bucket, a length of hose and another huge bottle of tomato sauce, thrust her chin at one of the men, a man almost as wide as he was tall. He was coated in smoke layers, circles of white on his face where his goggles had been.

'Sam. That's Ursula. Lady with the car.' Ursula stuck her hand out, covered as it was in flour. The big man regarded it stolidly. Then the phone in his hand went off and he rushed out the door.

Early evening, when she stepped outside to catch her breath, she could hardly breathe or see. Thick yellow smoke pressed in, tumbleweeds racing past in hot bright wind. As the sun set, she heard the thunder of hooves. A white horse arrived at full pelt on the ridge above the dam. Tail high, eye wild, a ring of fire springing from the darkness up there, before the horse galloped off and the sun went down.

At midnight, Ursula sat with the girls on the trampoline, feeding them stale trail mix from her car, until even Ronnie went to sleep. A while later, a red pinpoint bobbed toward her through the darkness. The trampoline rubber heaved, there was a deep sigh, a big bounce, and Ursula only just managed to grab the ankle of the smallest girl before she fell sideways into the night.

'Wind's changed. Thank fuck. Oops. Sorry. Didn't know the girls were here.'

'They're fast asleep.'

The red tip glided toward her and Ursula accepted it, along with a mug of sherry so sweet it made her molars ache.

'Thanks for your help today. You worked like a dog.'

'I didn't do much.'

'Still. You didn't have to.' She clicked her fingers and Ursula handed back the cigarette.

'I'll head off tomorrow, Freda. If the car's OK.'

'Yeah. Don't think Sam had time to get to it, love. And the roads will be closed, with these fires. They're not out, you know.'

Silence from Freda, just her coarse black knuckles illuminated as she lit another cigarette.

'Listen. I have to tell you something. Would have said it earlier but with everything else going on.' A long silence as she sucked, the ember of the cigarette glowing and dulling again. 'About your brother. Ray, I mean.'

Ursula felt her face start to burn, and she turned away, looking for landmarks, something to anchor herself with, even though it was pitch black out there.

'Though I'm pretty sure Ray doesn't have a sister. Not as far as I know.'

Nothing to see, not even the moon, which had been so full and white last night.

'Get the feeling you're his mum. The way you are. What confused me, see. Why you'd lie. And Ray told me his mum was dead.'

High above the roof, threads and scuds, an orange glimmer. Just the tip of the moon, swollen and painful, balanced on steep tin, before smoke or clouds streamed across, obscuring it again.

'Listen, none of my business. And I understand. Not why you lied, not really. But you must have your reasons. And I'd do anything for my kids.' Freda pinched her cigarette out and threw it away.

'I'm sorry,' Ursula managed to get out.

'Yeah. That's your lookout, as I said. Why I didn't tell you, yesterday or whenever, is the last time I heard from Ray, he asked me not to ring him, and not to tell anyone where he was. God knows why. He's an odd fish, your son.' Freda hoiked in her throat, spat into the dark. 'Bloody smoke.' When she stood up, Ursula felt a great weight lifting, their rubber raft floating free in the dark.

'Freda? You know where he is?'

'Well, I did, a while back. Last time I heard, he was living with a cousin of Sam's. Not a cousin exactly, cousin-in-law. Second cousin? I dunno. Anyway, her name's Lily. She worked here for a while. Wasn't much chop as a governess, but nice enough. She was married to Sam's cousin, Gary. Before he ran off. Good bloody riddance too. Real ratbag, he was.'

Ursula fought the urge to get up, grab Freda's round soft black shape in the darkness, shake it out of her, before they got lost in some unravelling family connection or the fires roared back.

'Where do they live?'

'Outside Bourke. Little run they got out there. On its last legs, according to Sam.'

Not very far. Not after all the distances and years she'd travelled. Ursula tried to remember where she'd left her handbag, in the kitchen or in the cottage, the location of her keys. Then she remembered the fires, the roads, the darkness. The wrecked wheel of her car.

'I'll leave tomorrow, if you could lend me a car. I'll bring it back. Soon as I can.' She got up, feeling the need to do something quickly, even if it was just to go to bed and make the morning appear.

'Men'll be back soon. I better go put some more beer in the fridge.'

Freda started moving in her fast little trundle toward the house, Ursula hurrying behind.

'I won't even mention you. OK?'

'Yeah. Look. I dunno. Ray said . . .'

'Freda? Please?'

Freda paused, hands on hips.

'Yeah. Well. Getting a bit sick of Ray and his bloody secrets by now, tell the truth. Thing is though, he might not even be there any more. When I spoke to him last, he was heading off. Wouldn't say where.' She sighed, scuffing at dust with the toe of her boot. 'Don't blame him really, after what happened. They were going to get married, see.'

'Why? What's wrong? Is he sick?'

Ellie murmured something in the darkness, crying out, and Freda turned, headed back to the trampoline. A twang of springs as she picked the little girl up.

'Not him love. Lily. She died, you see.'

CHAPTER TWENTY-SEVEN

In May he embarked on one of his long, looping, once almost rudderless journeys, up to Queensland, across and down to South Australia, working his way from sheep to cattle, cotton to grain, back again. Crossing borders, time zones and seasons, he worked on roads and fences, dug ditches and ground tanks. Went anywhere, did anything, as long as it paid cash in hand. Once, he travelled three thousand kilometres in two days. Nights were for driving, days for grafting, an old rhythm with new purpose. Watching the white line unravel by the glow of the dashboard, he thought about how his compass had always been work taking him closer to money and further from home. But everything was different, now there was Lily and home was somewhere else.

A week before his father's birthday, he headed for Bourke, stopping at Sam's on the way for the autumn shear. He'd rung Freda, looking for Charlie. No news but that English cook had taken off again and Sam was in hospital after a fall from his bike. Just a fracture, but they needed help. Sam would come round eventually, Freda reckoned. Now Ray was part of the family, or almost.

After a day cooking in the shed, Ray would come to rest at Freda's big scratched kitchen table, cradling one of Lolly's never-ending puppies, playing jacks with the girls, eating Freda's rubbery scones. Listening to her grand plans for spit roasts and marquees and napkins folded in the shape of swans, he wondered who would eat all those pavlovas and trifles she intended to make. Lily had only one relative in the country, some sister from Perth he'd never met. No friends to speak of, unless you counted Cheryl or that woman from the clinic she met for coffee sometimes. As for him, there was only Freda. And Ursula, who had never returned his message and he'd been too angry, then too frightened to call again. And Dad of course.

On his way back, the ute tray stuffed with Freda's old baby clothes, aching to drive through, get home after his long absence, he forced himself on one last detour. He kept thinking of Dad in that awful little house, cremating slowly by the fire. He'd get him out of that chair and into some clean trousers, take him out for a birthday meal. He'd listen to his stories, he'd smile and nod. He'd be Eddie. Be anyone Dad wanted him to be. He'd tell him about Lily and not care if Dad forgot about her the moment Ray left the room, laying out his sleeping bag in the looming shadow of all that old furniture from Twenty Bends. For just a moment, as he said her name, she would exist. He would exist.

A man, not an unwanted boy. A man with a future, a wife and child. Two, if he counted Mick.

But when he got to Frederick Street in the late afternoon, he saw the creeping disease in the rest of the street had reached the little stone house. Rubbish on the verge, beer bottles scattered across the front yard. The old Holden was still in the driveway but someone had nicked the wing mirrors and two of the wheels. The place was stony-faced with blinds. Even as he rattled the front flyscreen, he knew from the sound that the house was empty, and not just of furniture. A house left for an hour had a different silence than one abandoned and no longer home.

Walking around the side, steeling himself to find a body spread-eagled on concrete or wedged between a pile of fallen logs, he found more broken glass, more overflowing rubbish bags. The back door was locked. He was turning to go, wondering what to do with the card he'd bought, whether to leave it in the letterbox in the hope that someone, some new tenant or real estate agent, might pass it on, when a grey head popped above the back fence, then bobbed quickly back down.

'Hello?'

Stepping on the rung of the fence and peering over, he saw a wiry old lady glaring at him from her own neat backyard.

'Oh. Thought you were them kids again. You see what they done? Bloody disgrace.' She gestured, and he turned to look again at the piles of empty longnecks and flapping pizza boxes, the scorched earth behind the shed where a fire had been set.

In the middle, a bit of Dad's garden hose and one of his dog-defying Coke bottles, fashioned into a home-made bong.

'You from the council? 'Bout bloody time. Little mongrels nearly burnt down my fence.'

'No, I'm not from the council. Sorry. I'm just looking for the man who lives here. Or he used to. Mr McCullough?'

'Jim? Oh, he's gone. A while ago. He'd never let those louts get away with that.'

Ray braced his body against the fence. 'Gone?'

'Yeah. Moved out.' Ray's heart settled down. 'Don't blame him. If this keeps up, I won't be far behind.' Still muttering, the old lady started taking dry clothes off her line. 'Told the council. We'll get rats next, if someone doesn't clean that lot up.'

'Do you know where he went? Jim?'

She pointed up toward the town tip hill. 'That flash new nursing home.' She turned to squint at him. 'You that Eddie he was always on about? One with the car?'

Ray nodded, then launched himself back off the fence.

~

At the nursing home front desk, a crisp woman in a pink uniform told him visiting hours were two to three, that his father was resting, that he'd been found wandering out toward the highway the night before. That he'd been sedated and wasn't to be disturbed.

'Family only at the moment, I'm afraid. Are you a relative?'

Ray nodded. She waited, fingering an earring, looking doubtful. So he showed her his licence and then the phone started ringing and she pointed up a corridor, saying he should sign in first and leave his details for the doctor, who would like to speak to him if he was a relative, but Ray was already halfway up the hall.

'Just for a few minutes,' she called after him. 'And don't wake him please. He needs the rest.'

~

He sat beside his father's bed, watching him sleep. Remembering everything, but as if from far away. His mind spare and calm as the little off-white room.

Nothing much there. A vase of flowers, a pair of plastic clogs. A birthday card on the windowsill. But it was clean and large-windowed at least, after the fusty darkness of the house on Frederick Street. On the bedside table, a pair of glasses, a copy of the *Herald* opened to the crossword, clues half filled out in shaky writing. Spit stringing the hollow of his father's open mouth. His dentures sat in a glass of water beside the bed.

Ray sat vigil in the half-light, watching the shrunken figure breathing slowly under the tight white sheet. The sound of his own breathing tuned itself to that of his father, a whistle then a wheeze. The room darkened from pink to oyster to the blue glow of the night-light. And still Ray waited, his own birthday card clasped in his hand.

Past midnight, there was a knock on the door. When the nurse popped her head in, she gasped, shocked he was still there. He checked his watch. The highway would be quiet but the roos would be out. He'd risk it. Lily waiting. He needed to get home.

As he left, he thought about touching his father's hand, lying with its familiar dinosaur skin on the sheet. Instead, harangued by the nurse's sharp whispers, he put his birthday card next to the other one on the windowsill, and closed the door.

⁓

He saw the lamb as he reached the last bend before the front gate. It was sitting folded in the middle of the track. At a distance and except for the crow bobbing up and down on top of it, it looked snowy, compact, untouched. When he got out, he saw the missing head, the heart neatly beside it, as if bedded out on parsley. A tiny kidney, jewelled with dew. At the sound of his horn, the crow lumbered off, jelly trailing from its beak.

Something wrong. Not just the lamb. The front gate was hanging open, one side listing, the other torn off completely, lying buckled in the dust. Wind could have done that though. Mick was always forgetting to shut it. But there was no wind. Dust sullen and listless. The dark eye of the dam.

He drove on, pushing faster up the furrows. Even the air felt heavy, not verging but dwindling, more like dusk than dawn. A muffle to it, like a small child with a hand clapped across its face. And it did look childish, this place, after his long absence. The crooked chook shed, the stillborn vegetable patch. The house lopsided, windows fuddled with sun. The roof tin was licking up again, like stubborn hair.

Mick's skateboard lay on the verandah steps, just like last time, like a dream he was being forced to re-enter. Taste of metal in his mouth, a crawling on his scalp. Everything in slow motion.

Something looming. Something he was trying and failing to outrun.

Drawing up, he saw the boot-shaped hole in the front door, and he'd known it would be there, somehow, and he was out of the door before the ute came to a stop.

'Hello? Lil?'

The living room was dark, the curtains drawn. The room hard to navigate, the air fraught and he ran toward the bedroom, never fast enough. Something puffed underfoot. Flour, mixed with smashed crockery and broken glass. He tried to say her name again but his mouth wouldn't make the shape. Part of him was noting the capsized sideboard, the kitchen window smashed again, the TV upended, the screen cracked as he tried to make his body work, swimming it toward the bedroom. Leaning near the door, Mick's new cricket bat, a present from Ray for going back to school. Great gouges out of the willow and the handle cleaved in two.

Thinking of the neighbour, the husband, the scar on Mick's arm, he stopped at the doorway, afraid to turn on the light. Dark in there too except for the slice of uneasy dawn coming through the pink curtain. The glass in that window was also broken, he noted, as if from far away. A pair of boots sat in the middle of the floor. Gary's boots, from the sleep-out. Had she been mooning over them? Had he come back to claim them? Had he worn them as he rampaged through the house? Then Ray's eyes adjusted, and he saw the big stain on the bed and he touched it and his hand was wet and he wanted to be sick.

When he switched the light on it was pitiless. The bed was soaked. The bloodstain wide, brown, deep, something fibrous in the centre. Fabric from the bedspread, he told himself. Boot prints everywhere, and paw prints too, red, white, ticking and avid, circling the bed, across the pillow on the floor. Stalking him sideways, arriving from a dream.

As he picked up Lily's jeans, soaked with blood, he heard a shot, kicking dull against the sky.

Fear and anger sent him full pelt toward the verandah, where he stopped, swivelling frantically. Nothing, nothing. Just dawn light gleaming like dusk across the dam.

He scrabbled through the ute tray, looking for his own gun. Found the old pillowslip he used to wrap it in. Empty. He hadn't thought about the gun all the time he was away. Just assumed it was there.

He started throwing stuff around, Freda's garbage bags spilling tiny woolly pink and yellow things as he tried to find his strongbox, the bullets. Yellow mittens, a white bootee, curls of fencing wire. The arm of something, bright blue, impossibly small. The box wasn't there, just the old padlock from it, and then he remembered, he'd left it in the sleep-out, under the old camp bed. Forgot to take it with him in his early morning rush, all those weeks ago. A second shot rang out and he spun around. Birds flushed up from the trees along the creek. Down there, near the boundary fence. A flash of blue.

He started running, vaulting the fence, stumbling across the rough paddocks, too slow and clumsy in his big boots, in that poor sly light. Another shot, much closer, stifled by something, earth he hoped. He dived behind the water tank.

Peering round, he saw nothing but those bird shapes against the sky. He was reaching behind him, scrabbling for a rock, a stick, finding only a bit of poly pipe left over from when he'd done the irrigation, a lifetime ago, when his hand met something cold and wet. The shock set him back on his haunches and then the kelpie was licking him all over, before bounding off toward the creek.

Ray gathered himself, measuring the shape and weight of the pipe in his hand. Might look like a gun in this silvery light. Then, with one swift action, he stood up, stepped out, high on his toes, like a dog. Like Old Alf had taught him, long ago. Try and look bigger than you are.

He was ready to hit, shout, run, feint sideways, but there was only Mick in his blue school shirt, Ray's rifle held one handed above his head. Something loose and wrong about his other arm. Whirling, swearing and shouting, the boy was kicking out at the dog, which was leaping up and play bowing, thinking it was all a game.

'Mick! Stop. Put it down.'

The barrel swung unsteadily toward him but Ray was ready, stepping sideways, and the bullet pinged harmlessly against the tank. The kickback sent Mick sprawling, the gun flung clear. Ray picked it up and cracked the barrel before going over, heart beating hard.

'What's wrong? Where's your mum?'

'Wasn't me.' Mick's face was puce with the effort of holding back tears. 'Wasn't my fault. I wasn't even here. I shoulda been, I know, but I went to Davo's and then it was too late to ride back and the bike was playing up, and when I got back this morning, I couldn't get in. Something was up against the door. I think it was Mum. I tried to break it down. I hurt my arm. But I broke the window and then there was blood everywhere. And the bed . . .' Behind them, birds wheeled and wheeled, casting black shapes across the sky. And Ray knew it would always come to this. Dogs, guns. A light like dusk.

'Where is she? Is she okay?'

Mick nodded, then shook his head, going round and round. 'Ambos took her. They wrecked the gate, Ray. Just drove straight over the top of it. They told me to come but I couldn't. There was the dog.' He looked pleadingly up at Ray. 'Ray? Think I broke my arm.' He burst into tears.

CHAPTER TWENTY-EIGHT

They found it finally, on the edge of the rough acres designated for the new hospital. For half an hour they'd jolted through paddocks clotted with ruts and demountables, circling that red brick box on a hill. So small and squat and eaveless, he'd thought it was a toilet, haloed by bogongs and a fluorescent pall.

Mick didn't move when he stopped the car. Just sat staring past the smashed insects on the windscreen, as if they were still travelling. As if there was still somewhere to go. Grief was passing over him in roils and tempests, and he'd flattened himself beneath it. Found a small pocket where he could breathe.

'Just forget her, mate.' He'd been about to say Cheryl hadn't meant it, but the lie died on his tongue. 'She's a silly bitch.' He undid Mick's seatbelt for him. 'Come on. Let's get some sleep.'

Three rooms, three plywood doors. Some joker had put a boot through theirs, in anger, grief or despair. The bare lightbulb revealed two beds, a plastic kettle, two cracked mugs. The place stank of damp carpet, old air freshener, stale drains. The odour of charity, scant and dour. Inside the drawer of the old oak highboy in the corner, donated by some do-gooder probably, someone like Cheryl, some woman of upright morals and flint-cold heart, a little card told him how the Rotary cared for those in distress. The other drawers were empty. No blankets, no towels.

Mick was asleep almost before he hit the bed. Ray, unwilling to commit himself to another day ended, to another night where nothing and everything might draw to a close, sat outside on a garden bench dedicated to some dead person. He drank warm beer from the ute tray, watching lights in town wink out, one by one. Somewhere, a cow bellowed. In the lumpy, torn-up darkness, the plod and rasp of grazing sheep.

When his phone went, he expected Cheryl, but it was Freda. Offering shock, fear, condolence. God-flavoured hope.

When she stopped asking how he was and what she could do and when he still hadn't said anything and he was about to ring off, she pleaded, 'Ray. Wait. Just one more thing.' He sighed.

'I know it's bad timing but I thought you'd want to know. I found Charlie, through that church friend of mine.' Charlie. A name, a person from another life. In a pub, about a hundred k from here. 'He's pretty bad, Ray. He's drinking again and he's off the pills. Maybe if you gave him a ring. He listens to you. Or I could give him your number, he's probably lost it . . .'

'No. Don't. And don't ring again. I'll ring you, sometime, soon.' In some afterwards he couldn't imagine. When she started crying, he turned off the phone, then switched off the blue glare of the insect light. Sat in darkness, cradling a cigarette. If he closed his eyes, he could almost pretend he was safe in the little orbit of his camp fire, his outline simple against the sky.

It was freezing out here but at least it was properly dark. In the hospital it was always endless, lidless, fluorescent day. It had only been forty-eight hours but he felt he had been walking those corridors for a lifetime, following pastel lines running at chest height on moth-coloured walls. Pink for emergency, blue for palliative, yellow for something he couldn't remember. Green for exit, he knew that way by heart.

Every hour he'd walked from Lily's room to the kitchenette for coffee then back past the nurse's station and the hard chair waiting room, passing a room indistinguishable from all the others except for the old lady in the second bed who kept pulling her nightie up over a bald, bandaged skull. He'd tried not to look at the bags of flesh hanging on her rib cage, the little head brown and shiny, fighting for air. The last time he'd gone past, maybe an hour ago, a nurse had been wrestling with her and Ray had winced at the sight of those big beefy forearms bearing down on that little bag of bones. A relief to push through the swing door to the little courtyard provided for visitors, planted improbably with ferns and palms.

He'd cowered out there as long as he could, adding butts to the little alp he'd created under the No Smoking sign. And all the while, the door creaked back and forth on its invisible current. Waiting to breathe him back in.

The room seemed to contain more and more women every time he returned. Cheryl. A nun from the local convent, who'd arrived unheralded, homing on grief with bat-like instinct, in the middle of some night. The sister of Lily's he couldn't remember the name of, looking in her sturdy shoes and grey cardigan more like a nun than the nun herself. Nurses, of course, short, blonde, wide, plump and freckled, handling that little body he knew so well, but already it seemed to belong to everyone but him. Her neck lolled under their fingers as they propped, wiped, smoothed, jabbed and bustled, murmuring greeting-card bullshit about passing on, finding peace. A better place.

Once, briefly, sidling in, hovering uncertainly, pressing his hand once, hard, before sidling out again, a woman as thin and pale as the woman in the bed. The friend from the clinic Lily had coffee with sometimes. Lily herself, of course. But he couldn't look that way. Like those first few weeks at the farm, he could only manage her in glimpses. A hand. An eyebrow. A white blank around which others scurried, throwing shadows, muttering prayers.

A vigil, Cheryl was calling it, plucking the word from some hospital pamphlet and bestowing it like a Vaseline halo as she rocked herself to the nun's rosary incantations, the tap of the nun-like sister's foot. Performing grief. Constructing it. They'd been doing it for hours, the women. With ritual and small repetition, casting the room adrift. Pushing him and the boy further and further, to a chair by the door, a mattress in the corner, put there by a nurse, so people could sleep in shifts.

No one slept. Rituals like this required an audience. Even Mick, slumped on the mattress with his earphones in and his death metal turned to high, had picked up on it, this silent conversation they were excluded from but somehow scaffold to. A busy chatter of eye lines, knitting needles, strategic cups of tea. It made Ray jumpy, this secret language, the way it flourished in clammy undergrowth. Made him angry, in the small blue reaches of the night. The nub of things always sideways and elsewhere, in the space between strangers and the shadows they cast.

Sitting there, lapped by waves of rage and sickness, anchored only by the same things that were uncoupling him—Lily's eyelids, a vein in her forehead, too thin and close to air—he tried to steady himself on the calm horizon of the older sister. She wasn't praying. Armed with thermos, pen and newspaper, she was doing the crossword. Sitting so prim and upright, she looked like she was about to rodeo.

She reminded him of Ursula of course. Like her, Ursula would have been scornful of this humid confederacy, the way it fixed everyone in some general mid-distance of sorrow. Ursula would have refused to submit.

The thought had made him push back his chair yet again, startling the women, who frowned, fingers to lips, enforcing this mute religion of which they had become the priests. Resume his eddy of pacing, wading greenish air, past the kitchen and the nurses' station and the topless lady in the second bed, now being fed breakfast or was it dinner, some brown pap from a plastic bowl. The courtyard sucked him in once more until it breathed him out again. And when he returned, a feeling, faint but unmistakeable, that everything that had ceased in his absence was gently sighing, rearranging itself. Waiting only for the sound of his boots to seamlessly resume.

At some point, in the middle of this night, or maybe earlier, who could tell, in that soupy air recycled by the click of needles and beads, some darker thing had risen up. Beneath the bright scent of the cream they kept smoothing on Lily's face, as if even now rejuvenation might be possible, the stink of something shameful. No amount of air freshener or roses could disguise it, the lush, soiled scent of her dying. As if through the alchemy of her illness and his knowledge of her body, he could smell the rot at the heart of each infected cell.

For the last hour in there, he'd fixed himself on a smiley face some nurse had drawn on the whiteboard above the bed. Below it, Lily's face, collapsing toward zero. The imprint of her head on the pillow as they lifted her to rearrange her, yet again. How heavy even that little bird skull seemed on her neck. And all the while, the women's penance billowed on and on. Every prayer, each smoothing of the sheet, pushing him further and further, until he found himself standing by the door once again.

'Jesus. Just go if you're going. And take him with you. This is all his fault.'

⌒

Christ, he was cold. Long slow grief had washed through here, eating holes in the bedspread, wearing the lino to a gleam. He clicked his fingers at the kelpie, to coax it up for warmth. Rotary could go fuck itself, place was a stalag. But the kelpie stayed on high alert by the door. As if it knew this place was just a way station to somewhere worse.

Too cold to sleep, he got up again. A shower might warm him up. No cubicle, the tiled room awash with water and yellow fluorescence and then he remembered. No towel.

Drying himself with his clothes, he put them back on, then got into bed. A deep chill from the rubber-covered mattress, his teeth clicking, and he lay wishing for hard ground, a pure clean desert cold. Getting up again, he emptied his rucksack, put on all his T-shirts, two flannies, a jumper. At the bottom of the bag, Lily's pink poncho. She'd been wearing it the day she'd come in. He stood fingering it in the dark. Too small for him of course. Too small for Mick. The neck gaping from where he'd stretched it over Mick's head and the plaster cast on his arm, that night when he took him out for some food. Was that only yesterday, driving out from the hospital looking for pies or pizza, slaloming around endless roundabouts? Ray speedy from no food and too many cups of coffee, Mick silent, staring out at the road ahead.

In the stadium light of the servo, the only place open at three am, Ray had joked feebly about the way the pink of the poncho clashed with the red stubble of Mick's hair. Mick didn't laugh. Didn't move. They'd stood in silence, watching two plastic hamburgers go round and round in the microwave. By then, the only thing holding Mick up was his music and the bit of food Ray managed to shovel into him twice a day.

The boy started up suddenly in bed, arms flapping, then sighed deep, settled back down. In the faint light growing from the window, a little tic in his cheek, feeble and fluttering, like a rooster after the chop.

For Ray, sleep just wouldn't come. When he pulled the curtains shut against the greying light, the dark was impenetrable again. He felt thin as the fog of his breath, taking up no space in this hyphen of a room. Reaching down for the poncho, the dog, alive even in sleep to the memory of a brutal puppyhood at the hands of a man like Sam, snapped out, caught his finger. Should get up and wash the bite but he was too cold.

Lily's poncho was so small, it barely covered his shoulders, but it was a comfort. It smelled of her. Sweat, sickness, apricot oil. The bottom was all stretched and loopy, from Mick's shoulders, and there was a big hole in the back, from where they'd had to cut it off. He turned it over and over in the dark, telling each broken connection and nubbly carelessness, each slapdash square. On the front, a stiff patch. Blood, or chicken grease, from that last picnic they'd had, down by the creek, the day she'd told him about the baby and she'd got the all-clear. On the fringe, a crawling stain of creek water, brown topography of what he'd dared to call home. The pink of this poncho, thrown on a bush. On the bank, her jeans and yellow teapot shirt. The brown of her skin, a silky terrain.

He got up to have another shower, feeling hot and ashamed.

CHAPTER TWENTY-NINE

There was only one photograph of himself with his father. Even then, his father wasn't in it, Urs having cut out Dad, the dead pig, the tree it hung from, the rifle, leaving Ray stranded by himself in the little silver frame. A ghostly hand on his shoulder. His own face a shocked white blur. The one bright thing the blue of his shirt. Dad's shirt, Ray's own having been soaked with blood when they gutted the boar.

The day he left home, he'd stood for a long time in Urs's bedroom, looking at that photo on her dressing table. Trying to decide whether to take it with him, whether to write a note on the back and leave it on her bed. Trying to imprint on his fourteen-year-old mind the image of his thirteen-year-old self. The light in the photo different, against the other times he'd seen it, against his memory of the day itself. The gold haze of a winter afternoon gone droughty and unearthly from the relentless sun pouring through his sister's bedroom window, and it had seemed to him as if his image had been worn out too soon by the bright regard of her relentless yearning, even before all the looking and longing she would do in the days to come.

He'd left it there in the end. It had seemed right somehow that she would go on remembering a boy taller, blonder, broader than he ever remembered being. Yet never bigger than his father, a man who filled any foreground even in absence. His shadow pitching forward into the yellow desert of the photograph, outpacing Ray, the tree, even the wolfish shadow of the pig.

No shirt or frame could fit his father. A mountain of a man.

In the end, he took only the money from the pantry, his dog and his rucksack. Dad's shirt, which he'd worn for years, the blood on it fading slowly, becoming a map to memory he wanted to forsake but could never quite leave behind. Tilda's blood on the collar, until the collar too fell away. For years he tended his memory of that day and of all the days between himself, the photograph, the day it was taken and the day he left, puzzling over them even as the past receded and the shirt itself tattered into an old blue rag. Half of it made into a bandanna, half torn up and tied round a sheep skull, left fluttering out there in the desert as the sign of a job well done.

In this way he kept himself tied by the sheerest skin to a hole in his past. A thread of blue drawn across the years.

⌒

When he got back home, the lamb was gone. Following a gut-stained trail into the scrub by the road, he found a flurry of feathers. Under a bush, two more chickens, bloody and gutted, and the missing head of the rooster, looking cranky even in death. Near the dam, a pile of scat, rank and thick as his arm.

Behind the pump house, his first clear prints, narrow, deep, strangely splayed. More prints around them, smaller, ticking, rabid, legion, leading down toward the creek and his new boundary fence. He squatted over the larger prints, wondering what could make a mark like that. What sort of jaw could rip a hole in brand-new steel mesh. He almost looked up, to see something crouched above him in a tree, before remembering he didn't believe in those old stories, told by his father at dawn over camp fires. The evil in them laboured, gloating, cartoonish, compared to the sins of ordinary men. Men with dogs and guns. Men like the neighbour or his father. Men like him.

Heading back up the creek bank, he smelled rot. A mound of leaves, marked by a haze of flies. When he nudged the dead sheep with his foot, it fell apart as if he'd undone a zip. An old kill this one. He saw an ear, torn, barely healed. Lily's dry ewe, the one she'd fed by hand. The rest unrecognisable. Hollowed of organs, she'd been ripped limb from limb.

By the time he got back with the shovel, it was dusk. It fell quickly out there, on those poor boundaries, flowing fast up the creek gully, striking down sharp from the ridge. Out there, on the edge of night, a grown man with a dog and a gun, he felt small and afraid.

⌒

Next morning, he counted over and over, trying to make that huddle of ears and tails come out right. He'd found two more dead at dawn, a lamb in the far paddock and one of the pregnant ewes, opened breast to hind. Four gone all up, including the old ewe and the first dead lamb. Five ewes left in the home paddock, one still pregnant, three with lambs at heel. But he didn't know how many had lambed while he was away up north or at the hospital and if they'd been singles or twins and where the other ewe was and whether it was the mother of the dead lamb. How many he'd have to find or bury before all this was done.

Dawn and dusk was when they hunted. He started getting up well before the sun, moving sheep between creek grazing and home paddock three times a day. Almost as soon as he got them there, he moved them back, like a man shifting piles of lumber from here to there, with a wall of bushfire on its way. If a paddock was more open with less scrub for stalking and hiding, it was also more badly fenced, with less feed and further from the house. Back and forth he went, the poor sheep following, exhausted. Couldn't settle, couldn't decide what was worse. Sheep starved, sheep missing. Sheep torn apart.

For two days, nothing. He chopped wood for a hundred fires, fed his five remaining chickens, herding them back to the coop as soon as they'd finished pecking the grain. In the long middays, he jumped at every sound. The dog scratching. The windmill sighing. A tic started up in his eye. A dead hen the third morning, headless and wingless, but she was old and broody. Could have been a fox.

He did the rounds again anyway, patching wire and checking gates, shoring up rotten posts. When he was done, too jittery to sit still, he went back to clearing the already empty shed, hauling out the leaves and rodents that had collected there in his absence, even sweeping the floor. In a dark corner he'd missed, inside a rotted hessian sack, he found a few of the husband's old traps. Small, blackened, flimsy, meant for fox or rabbit, but he buried them in a childish necklace around the house.

By the end of the three days it took Lily to die, he was rising at first light, going to bed with another dawn in the sky. Sometimes between last round-up and morning head count, he felt he had barely closed his eyes. When he did, sitting on the verandah, or lying in his little sleep-out bed, he felt himself pitched always toward various shades of darkness. Brown, brindle, dun-coloured. His whole body an unpeeled eye.

The last night and day, he didn't go to bed at all. Just sat on the chopping block by the shed, gun in his lap, facing the direction of the coming sun. At midnight he felt frost forming in wrinkles of earth, between the joints of his toes. Before dawn, in the deepest dark, shadows of leaf and branch turning to tail and claw, he heard a high howling. Jumping up, he fell straight over. An old cold man lying in darkness. Peering sightlessly toward the sound, hearing only the growl of a possum. Sheep shuffling against the greying sky.

⌒

The morning he got the call from Cheryl, the worst so far. Two lambs at the far end of the home paddock. Half-eaten, but still alive.

After he'd shot them, he set to work, hauling, digging, burning, burying. Except for Lily's old ewe, which he dug up. So ripe by now a nudge of his shovel made what was left of her head come away. He held his breath and closed his eyes, hacking blindly, metal breaking hide with a buttery hiss.

Shovelling the flesh into another hessian sack, he hauled it up toward the house. From the shed, a sprinkle of mice bait and weedkiller. From Lily's empty vegetable patch, handfuls of blood and bone. He followed the dog for half an hour, waiting for it to lift its leg, then soaked the bag and its contents with kelpie piss. Old Alf in his head this time, that summer they were losing sheep to wild dogs at Twenty Bends. The old man outside his bush shack, scratching shapes with a stick in the earth. Square house like a child's drawing, fat wiggle for the river, ribbed lines for fields. Here the sun, here the moon, both rising together in Alf's universe, his secret duskless topography. Then bang bang bang with the stick, deep, hard, vicious. Dot dot dot on the ground, the man's little face drawn up in a snarl, waiting for Ray to nod at something he hadn't understood.

When Ray shook his head, Alf leapt up on those old chicken legs of his. Mimed digging, then hopping, then growling and howling, cocking one skinny leg above a bush, pointing urgently toward Ray's blue heeler puppy and then back to himself. Grinning his toothless grin. When he'd started undoing the rope that held his trousers up, Ray had backed off, thinking the old man was mad or bad or both.

Old Alf knew things though, beyond the shape or sound of words. How to grow the best tomatoes, with little water, in rabid frost. How to mend a wound with spider web, laying a fine cocoon to drown the blood. How to milk a bruise with leeches then pale it with parsley, leaving only the faintest imprint of belt or fist. How to hit a man twice your size and weight so he went down and stayed down, a dark bruise of your own blooming in the hollow of his throat.

Stripping off his clothes now, knotting his old blue bandanna round his throat, Ray rubbed himself with dirt, leaves, blood, chunks of rotten sheep. Set off to walk Lily's boundaries, laying bait as he went. After a while he forgot the smell, the scrub flaying arms and thighs. The grief that was making it hard to breathe. Under his bare feet, hot dust, sharp gravel, broken wire, a map of his own, blooming against his skin. Coiled snake for the creek, three lines for the fences. Squashed egg for Lily's orchard. A double noose of dots, bang bang bang, for where he should lay the bait, just beyond their killing highway, within sight and sound of home.

See what they see. Think what they think. The old man on all fours, sniffing and pawing, his yellow neck stretched to howl. Be snout and tooth and claw.

Crawling naked through hot tunnels of scrub, the world was hot, sepia, intricate. Himself a yellow eye.

⁓

Too much blue sky.

He sat on the verandah step with his back to Lily's chair. From here he could see all directions. Creek, ridge, both sides of the track. One arm flayed and potholed, bumping toward the front gate and the grave of the lamb. The other side lined with trees and pooled with shadow, disappearing toward the neighbour's hill. In between, brown paddocks, the henhouse, Lily's orchard, where the last of the sheep butted at yellow stub.

Beyond that, the ridge, circled by hills. In front, the burnt scar of earth where he'd made a bonfire of carcasses, dousing and lighting, adding bits of the shed he'd torn down, a splash of petrol and Lily's clothes, until he had a line that, in his mind at least, nothing could cross. Anything breaking cover from bush or creek would be outlined at sunset against the ridge. Geometry, that was all. Two sides of a triangle and those killers didn't know it yet but Ray and his gun formed the third.

'Too much blue sky. That's what did for Len.'

At noon, a silence so deep, he could hear ice cracking in the empty freezer, a blue chink-chink. No radio, no burble of weather or stock prices. No sound from her as she stood behind him in her teapot shirt. Her hair dark and full again, her creamy throat obscured. Fading even as he turned, the house absorbing her to its old seam of darkness. The wind picking up. That hinge loose again.

'He said that, just before he died. It was like the sky was choking him. Like he couldn't breathe. Like someone was squeezing his throat, a little more each day.'

When his mind started to wander, becoming rootless as the dust blowing along the road, Ray brought the tip of his smoke to rest on a tender part of his arm. When his eyelids started to go, he told himself stories, the old comfort, childhood tales of mutiny, shipwreck, empire cannon. His hat a pith helmet, casting brave shadow along his boot. His enamel cup of beer a sailor's ration of dark rum. Raising the gun, sighting out, he saw, amid the tracery of bare winter trees and flickers of shadow, a horde of Zulus storming the neighbour's hill. His sheep a huddle of redcoats, flanked to defend the fort. Another swig, another lift of the gun, and the shadows muscled to the vicious shapes of men on the swag. Grandad's tales of the Depression, hobos and robbers, cutthroats all. His cup filled again and he drained it again and Dad was laughing now, his smoky chest rumbling, coughing deep and throaty, and Ray could hear the clink of frypans, smell camp smoke rising. See branches shuffling through shadowy hide.

'Mate of a mate, you know, out west. While ago. He had four hundred head ready for market, but they were too thin to hold themselves up in the truck. Had to shoot them all. Then he shot himself.'

His father, a man of such long silences, such sudden stories. Words etching deep as acid. Never going away.

'Pity of it is, this place would have been OK, you know, if we'd got rain. Down at the creek, there's red box, belah, pine and white gum, and up there, in the rough, leopardwood, bimble box, bit of pasture. Sandy loam toward the river, some red soil, and edible timber. You tell them that Ray. Put it in the ad. Don't let them rip you off. Stony mulga, high mulga, here and there, heather brush. Further out, just on the boundary, ironwood, rosewood, supplejack, beefwood. Sounds good on paper at least.' A big laugh, ending in a croak, a spit, drying in the dust.

'Dad? What do you mean?'

'And the bore. Don't forget the bore. We got the windmills, and the ground tanks, not to mention that bloody wool shed. Nearly killed me, that shed. All timber framed. That stockyard, it's bugle style, three-way draft, water laid on. If we had any of course.' Another long-parched swig of beer, his cigarette butt flicked sideways in disgust, out to where it might have caught something, if there'd been anything left to burn.

'Green drought. That's what we got here, Ray. That's the worst.' Dad staring out from inside Ray's head, speaking to some blue and heartless sky. 'Bit of rain and you think, we'll be right, for a while at least. But there's no bulk to it, see? No moisture. No heart to it, deep down.' Dad thumping the earth with his boot, then his chest with a fist.

'Dad? What's wrong?'

In some future, his father had said. In the light at the end of some tunnel Ray didn't know about. At the end of some day.

'Right. Can't sit around here all afternoon.' His father slapping his palms down on his trouser legs, springing up from his thighs. As if he'd decided something, drawn himself to some sticking point.

'Gotta go check the dam.' Dams were dry. Creek was dry. Had been for months. 'You keep an eye on that fire.' He jerked his head toward some plume of smoke on some other horizon. 'That wind changes, be here before you turn around.' Halfway down the verandah stairs, he'd turned back to look at Ray, the old glare in his eyes. 'And watch those sheep Ray. I counted 'em,' Dad tapping a finger on his iron-grey temple, leaving a dusty mark. 'All up here.'

'But Urs isn't here. What about Mam? The toilet and everything. Her pills.'

'She's not your mam, son. Your mother's a slut.'

And leaving Ray reeling, he'd walked off, rocking through heat haze, drunkenness, waves of dust. And Ray had been so busy putting those words together, feeling the shock settle in him like cancerous grit, that he didn't hear what lay in the silence between and behind. Didn't notice the gun missing from its place in the wood box. Failed to see the dusk was coming in.

Gun, dusk, landscape. So deep in that old puzzle, even now, that at first he didn't see the low shadow detach itself from the shadows along the road. Only when the screen door banged, once, hard, into the old sore dent, did he jump, pick up the gun, sight out through it. See the shape outlined against the ridge. Slinking at belly height, heading for the home paddock and the ewes. Other shapes flaring out behind it, smaller, more ragged, a dirty mottle flickering through spent seed heads, spun dust, smoke from his funeral pyre.

He leapt the steps, vaulted the fence, going at a loping crouch through what would have been Lily's orchard. Head bent low beneath a vault of remembered trees. Those big old gnarled apple trees at Twenty Bends. The ground a carpet of rotting apples the day he left. Something crunched beneath his foot now, and as if memory could conjure it, he smelled rotten sweetness but it was meaty, not fruity. A possum head, jaws snarled with rot. Next to it, a hank of fur, coarse and peppery. In a flattened hollow near the fence, more fur, brindle, blue-spotted, white and fluffy, and scattered here and there among it, yellow bones. Possum or joey, too small for sheep. Prints led away, up toward the creek. A sound behind him and he spun, half-expecting to see a little girl, blonde, curly, milk-smelling as a lamb. But it was just his kelpie, feinting at shadows. He thought about tying it up or taking it back. No rope. No time. He ran on, carrying the gun like a spear.

For an hour he trawled the creek boundaries, following wombat paths and roo tunnels, losing the trail in pebbled shallows, finding it again in the soft earth beneath a lattice of fallen trees. Taking his boots off, tying his bandanna round his head, he waded into the water, became part of its brown rippling glare. That noise behind him again, but he didn't turn. Knew who it was. Wasn't afraid.

Sharp stones ahead, he warned her. Glass here, barbed wire there. Together they walked the shallows, her bare feet on his big white ones, losing scent. Tadpoles darted, pretty pebbles of light under an overhang of rock. Fish shapes in the deeper water, footprints minus the toes. At some point he left his shirt on the bank, his trousers in the mud. Her shirt fluttered yellow from a tree. Time slowed, spread to a shining line between them, her before and behind him, seeing that fringe of old scars on his thigh, his skin singing with the notes of his old bravery, in puckering light. He told her all about it. The horse, the fence, the wire, the chunk of flesh with a horseshoe stamped in it. The leaping firelight making something primitive of the kitchen as Dad stitched shadow to skin to blood to memory.

She brushed it with a finger, a touch soft as a leaf, quick as a fish, and he was turning to look, to see and welcome her, when up ahead, from the corner of his eye, he noticed the kelpie freeze.

Wind had changed. Bark scuttling up the bank, not down it. Saplings along the road straining like young white bones.

He dropped to his belly, smashing his chin on the gun. Another noise, and the kelpie fled, a quick red curve into undergrowth. Ray stayed where he was. Stones in his knees, water soaking his crotch, bullets sleek moulded to the bone of his hip. Swallowing blood from a bitten tongue, his mind going fast and pure. Calculating distance, angle, trajectory, the time it would take to load, stand, brace, take a sighting, against failing light, an unoiled trigger, the size and scale of the thing.

An outline bristled up in his mind, in grainy light. Coat of a wolfhound, from the fur on the branch. Skull and jaw of a mastiff, from that hole in his fence. Craven hindquarters of an Alsatian, from those strange deep prints he'd found near the pump. The rest of the pack smaller, slyer, more dingo-like. Rust, sand, butter-coloured, curling through stands of white gum, messy silver light.

See what they see. Think how they think.

Closing his eyes, he parsed the breeze. Leaf rot, sheep shit, water must. Preen smell of someone burning fence posts. The neighbour perhaps. Old bushfire stink, dark and sour. Just smoke from his pyre probably, drifting on the wind. Just his imagination, the past rising up, that old frantic circle of his on the verandah, when Dad walked off and he knew something wasn't right and when he realised about the missing gun. Urs not there, Mam sick, Tilda calling, his feet slapping, smell of smoke rising, and all those doors locked against him. Dad missing. Fire coming. Dusk coming. Sending him spinning off in a panic, at the wrong moment, the wrong angle, a boy falling through a blur of sky, earth, paddock, into a new and faltering geography, out there where the creek met the river. Finding something he had no equation for. His father, sitting propped against the old white gum where all their names were carved. A big man leaning like the broken upright of a name. The only thing holding him up the muzzle of the rifle braced inside his mouth.

The wind shifted again and now all Ray could smell was himself. Sweat, mud, bait. A carrion tang. From his bandanna, so old and weathered it had gone from the rich indigo of history to something the colour of weak kerosene. Below it all, the stink of fear. Dad sweating, crying, pleading, holding out the rifle. Ray. You do it. I can't. Come on. Do it for me. For once, do as you're told. Be a man.

From the coiled ache of his crouch, he cast himself forward now, out of the mud of the present and the dusk of the past, into a different history. Instead of a boy lunging wildly, desperately, a shot ringing out as he wrestled the rifle off his father, the bullet bouncing off something, finding his little sister, grazing her temple, knocking her over, a rock knocking her teeth out, teeth which he'd picked up and put in his pocket, as if in doing this, he could hide what had happened, erase his crime in leaving Tilda lying bloody and unconscious, his father sobbing and helpless under the tree, he saw himself doing as he'd been told. Saw himself rising, slow and steady, disentangling himself from a seethe of scents, shadows, false history. Finding height, will, clarity, some hard cold fact to brace against, something to bring to bear against the enormity of it. A hat, a shoulder. A cold geometry of eye and gun.

Afterwards, he noosed the thing to the tree. Left it hanging, shredding and boiling, bones and teeth rising from a snarl of rot. Saw himself standing beside it, like a photograph. Growing taller, blonder, harder, muscling out to fill the frame. A mountain of a man.

CHAPTER THIRTY

He'd never hit a woman. Came close, once or twice. A barmaid at Pete's pub, screaming hysterically at blood not her own. A woman he'd slept with once, who'd tried to steal his wallet in the middle of the night. But she'd hit him first.

'I don't want them. What am I going to do with them? Or that little lout. You seen what he done to my shed?'

There was Tilda of course. A girl not a woman, a gun not a fist, and he neither man nor boy but something dangerously verging, caught between.

'Oi. You listening to me?'

Looking down at Cheryl, her face snarling to gargoyle shapes beneath her shelving poodle perm, he wondered if once again, as with Harry, the looming threat of his big body might be enough.

As he moved forward, Cheryl fell back, and he savoured her little grunt of surprise. He was longing for it, the old simplicity. Knuckle on bone.

But he just kept walking, round behind the ute, unhooking the trailer, watching as sheep wandered across Cheryl's front lawn. One headed right through the cricket bat-shaped hole in the side of her shed. Cheryl herself had retreated to the safety of her patio, clutching her phone. She wasn't to know that since that day near the dam and the nights at the hospital, the fists at his side held nothing but air. Cardboard man, hole in his heart.

As he got back in the ute, a curtain twitched at the front window. A freckled wrist, a flash of red hair. By the time he'd backed out, Mick was gone.

It wasn't until he stopped at the garage for petrol that he realised the dog was still in the back of the ute. He'd meant to leave it with the boy. Too late now. It was along for the ride. Before that though, one more veering journey. One more debt to pay.

At Charlie's pub, the threat of his big useless body worked one last time.

'We're closed,' the landlord said, jerking his head toward the front doors.

'Not after a drink. Looking for a friend of mine. Old bloke, called Charlie. I heard he's staying here.'

The man shrugged, went back to polishing a dirty glass with a dirty towel.

'Wouldn't know. Wife does all that. She's out. Come back later on.'

Ray placed his palms flat on the bar.

'Yeah. You'd know him if he was here. Old. Bad teeth. Drinks a lot.'

'That narrows it down.'

Ray took his time walking round behind the bar. As he moved forward, the man moved back, and Ray saw himself in the mirror behind the bar. Broad shouldered, hard fisted, in a sweat-stained hat. A white blur of face. When he took his hat off, his blond hair shone ghostly in the gloom. 'Talks religion. Dresses like a priest.' He was so close now, he could see the sweat beading on the man's forehead. 'Little bloke. Even smaller than you.'

'Look, it's cleaning day. Everybody's out. House rule.'

'That's all right. I'll wait upstairs. Which room's he in?'

When the man started gabbling about no visitors upstairs, Ray raised his arm, pointed to the board of keys hanging above his head. 'Which one?'

~

He took the stairs two at a time. The door to number 22 was half-open, so he didn't need the key. From downstairs, he heard the landlord calling, 'Oi! Mate! I told you. There's nobody home.'

Home. What a thought. A single bed, a cock-eyed crucifix, brown dentures in a dirty glass. Empty bottles, food scraps, old newspapers, dry insects. A hepatitis light.

At first he thought the landlord had been telling the truth. Could barely see him in the bed, the old man was so small and thin. He'd thought the newspapers spread on the bed, for warmth he guessed, were rising and falling in the breeze from the window. Then a corner fluttered up and he saw stubble, a slice of toothless mouth.

Wake him up. What to ask. What to say.

He sat for a while on the room's only chair, watching the old man sleep. Keeping vigil. Mouse droppings underfoot, scraps of paper. He picked one up. Dead people, in shreds and tatters. He picked up another, then another. More people dying, more people grieving, from Mudgee to Murwillimbah. He thought about getting down on the floor, scrabbling through, finding the bit with Mam's name on it, the message Charlie had tried to give. Then he thought about the old man startling awake, amid yellow scabs of paper and insect husks. Finding Ray empty hearted, empty handed, with not even a mouthful of something sweet to give. Couldn't do it, couldn't face it. Couldn't bear the scope of what might be needed by a man like Charlie, against what a man like Ray had to give.

When the light slanted to some white no point between the curtain folds, he cleared a space on the floor. Laid it all out, such as it was. His one spare shirt, one of Gary's he'd taken to wearing for dirty jobs round the farm. Miles too big. His good watch, his book of poems. His wallet, containing all his money but minus his licence, in case he got pulled over before he could do what he had to do. Lily's ring, still in his trouser pocket, still in its little velvet bag. He'd meant to leave it for Mick, along with the dog and the four half-dead sheep. Then he imagined Mick unwrapping it, its hard little sparkle carving a fresh hole in fresh grief, in lost future. In memory. Better for Charlie to have it, to see God in its miraculous facets, before he magicked that little twinkle into beers and bets.

The old man shuddered deeply in his sleep, the newspapers covering him fluttering away. Looking around for Charlie's coat to put over him, once Ray's old coat, which had seen better days, he thought of his good suit, still at the drycleaners, meant for the wedding, and how Charlie would have liked it, all that nice warm tweed. Too late now.

As he placed the coat carefully over the old man's shoulders, something fell out, clunking on the floor. A hanky, not one of Charlie's. The old checked one with Tilda's teeth. He'd forgotten all about that. After keeping them safe for years, carrying them with him like some sort of reliquary, wearing them on his body like a tiny hair shirt, he'd just handed them over with the coat. Didn't matter. Tilda had new teeth. He'd seen them. She'd survived, after a fashion. That old guilt was nothing against what he felt now.

Standing at the door, ready to leave, he wondered what Charlie would conjure from these gifts of his. Heaven, hell, a vengeful devil under the bed. Might send him off the deep end. Should leave a note, try to explain.

Instead he went back, put the little beer coaster on the pillow near Charlie's softly breathing mouth. An omen, speaking sideways and backwards, in some tiny secret language only Charlie would understand.

The afternoon was hour after hour of grey-blond grass. Fire to the west, a pale billow, but the road he was on kept angling away and away. He stopped only when he had to, when his bowels turned to water, leaving him stranded at truck stops raucous with birds, in tin toilets greedy with flies. The last time, his body empty of everything except grief and cramp, he turned away from that hot vintage stink. Left his thin glossy greenness against the old brown of lizards, dry leaves. Ahead, a single chimney marked the place where a home had once stood. Sheep huddled round it, as if remembering being owned.

Soon even grief was just a far-off shimmer against starved old hills. When a lake bloomed over a ridge, impossible, unbearable, that cool holiday turquoise against hot red earth, he struck left, on ruts not a road. Where there was water, there might be caravans, radios. People. He took a long detour to avoid them, veering and fretful, waiting for some other nameless tiny track to loop him back down to the road again.

So intent was he on that old animal numbness, the lulling concert of hand and eye, that he didn't notice the thunderclouds up ahead. The sky gone plum, a ruined, pulpy light. The track turned to slime as the first rain came down. Lightning behind and before, confounding geography. A land all knot and knuckle. Two roos, purple furred, stood sentinel on a ridge. He felt the strike rippling over the roof of the ute. In the rear view, a smoulder of wood, tree. Maybe flesh and bone.

He kept going, faster and faster, fishtailing through mud, stone, scrub and hollow, tipping himself through skidding arcs of earth and sky. Telling himself it was so the wheels got traction while all the time he was waiting for it, something to break the skin of it, all this nothing, which kept happening, over and over. A wall of mud or water. Some lightning to the head.

There. Across the floodplain, an artery of froth. A newborn creek, crossing his track. Getting wilder and deeper even as he watched, until there was no track, just water, raging, carrying all before it, dirt, rocks, trees, branches like bone.

He threw his last cigarette out the window, wound the window up. Taking off his seatbelt, he steadied breath, will and his accelerator foot. From the corner of his eye he saw the dog sitting upright on the passenger seat. Still in shock at being allowed inside the ute. Still certain there was something to do and somewhere to go. All that love and certainty coming off it in waves. A cancer, love. Something grafted on.

As he punched the pedal and the ute leapt forward and sideways, he was tempted to close his eyes. Swim through red air to red water to black nothing, fill his veins with mud and sleep. But he thought it cowardly, so he fixed his gaze ahead. Now or never. See what you're made of, you little shirker. If he was good for anything, good at anything, it should be this headlong rush into nothing. He'd been doing it most of his life.

His last thought, as the bonnet hit water and his wheels hit rock, was the poor dog.

⌒

When he opened his eyes, earth was purple. A tree grew sideways, the rain fell up. His face left the dashboard with a leathery suck.

Something wet, harsh and slow against his cheek. With lazy, calm determination, its golden eyes half-shut, the kelpie was licking his face. Slowly, doggedly. He thought about the word as he watched its tongue advance, move away, return. The tongue pink and pimpled, streaked red. He wondered whose blood that was.

Then its teeth snagged his collar, catching flesh, and he hit out, hard and blind, and the dog bounced up, scrambling through the open passenger side window. Where the roof should have been, a square of sky.

He sat there for a while, head wound stiffening, water pooling feebly round one ankle. He would die of boredom here before anything else. Hauling himself upright, he followed the dog out of the window of the wildly tilted ute. When he jumped down, the water came to his knees. The sun was breaking through, the new creek already drying up. The sky above, blue and blue. On and on.

Leaving everything in the ute, even his shoes, he took the old knotted pillow slip and the gun out of the tray. Walked off in no direction, the dog close at heel. Above a ridge, a gravy-coloured house. Just as he was pivoting away again, thinking people, farmers, unwanted cups of tea, sun snagged on a broken window and he saw the big hole in the roof. A lost place then, hunkered down against land and sky.

He followed the remains of a concrete path leading to a gate connected to nothing except its posts. Levering it open against tall swards of grass, he spotted something dark, winding, rust coloured. Brought his bare foot down hard but it was just an old radiator hose. There was something else though, some older deeper danger, brewed here in this sullen triangle of outhouse, water tank, ancient Hills hoist. An imminence, a fester just before the bleed.

Even the dog could feel it, its wry little body straining toward the weedy darkness under the house. A shape in the window of the outbuilding, sketched by wind and cobweb. A squat man, one arm flung out. Just an old mangle, boiled and grey. On the broken flyscreen door of the house, a bellied imprint, from someone who must have stood there, day after day, waiting for life to come home.

The front door gave with a shove. The dog paused again on the threshold, one foot cocked, all its hackles up. Snakes, mice. Perhaps some skittering, yellow-eyed notion of what he was about to do.

Stepping in, he stood swaying between glare and gloom, waiting for his eyes to adjust. A laminex table. A Bakelite phone. An old wood stove, like Mam used to have. He passed through, vague and tender as a ghost. Pantry fly wire crumbled at a touch. Everything in the cupboards left from some frozen moment in the 1970s. Lyle's Treacle, Parisian Essence, Keen's Mustard, labels unreadable under rust and drips. A museum to his childhood, as if the place had been waiting here for him, slumbering in golden syrup haze. Near the sink, a tin of creosote which hadn't won its battle with the ants. A feather duster, a wooden spoon. A leather belt. Ordinary things, fat with old fear.

Beyond the kitchen, a tiny lounge room, hot and dark. The windows were boarded up. In the far corner, a bulky shape complete with head sat in a chair. Maybe newspapers, maybe just the missing shade from that broken lamp. He backed off, angling through gloom to the bright bedroom, a hot and private space. Two single beds, with orange covers full of holes. Laid out on one was a man's suit with wide lapels, complete with a fat blue tie. The clothes had rotted away, revealing a mice nest in the mattress, weaved with leaves and droppings, mouldered to the texture of hair. As he walked away, a shirt arm fell in a clump to the floor.

In the last room, a sleep-out made from what used to be the old wrap-around verandah, all glass and sun, he found a wardrobe, overturned, like a shot elephant. Nothing else. Wind rattled the louvres, scouring the space with heat and light. He kept walking, as if he must complete the circuit, obedient to the strange electricity of the place. As if this house was a map to somewhere, a room as yet unseen. He found himself back where he'd started, at the bellied wire of the front door. Nothing. Nowhere else to go.

The dog seemed to know it. It sat in the middle of the sleep-out floor, all that love in its eyes. And he understood it finally, all those men in the newspapers and on the radio and in family stories, all those wives and children, the axes, the knives, the guns. How impossible it was to leave love just sitting there, pouring out with nothing to catch it, and nowhere for it to go.

'Sorry,' he told the dog, and its ears pricked up. 'Stay.' And for once in its life, it did what it was told.

He raised the gun. Breathing deep, squinting along the sight. Determined not to shut his eyes or look away. To receive this fully into his empty, useless heart.

As he squeezed the trigger, a wet sounding click, there was a loud banging on the front door, and the dog bounded off with a joyful bark.

'Hello? Anyone home?' Home.

A bearded man was peering in through the flyscreen, his big belly pressed against that old sag in the wire.

'Hey mate. That your ute out front? Saw you go over. I was coming through ahead. You all right?'

The man started pushing open the door. Seeing the blood on Ray's face and shirt, the gun in his hand, he stepped back, making settling motions with his hands. 'OK. We're good. Just came to check you're OK.'

Ray moved forward, but his legs went on him. He sat down on the top step, the wire door propped open against his body, his arms cradling the gun.

'Want one?' He was being offered a packet of Drum. 'Looks like you might need it.' Ray shook his head.

Leaning back against the Hills hoist, the man started rolling up, eyeing the gun in Ray's lap as he licked his Tally-Ho. Something steely and keen about him, despite the big belly and the little shorts, the Father Christmas beard.

'What's all that about?' The man jerked his head at the gun. 'You after pigs or something?' Ray stared at his hands. 'Roo then. Whatever it is, don't reckon you'll find it in there.' He nodded back toward the house. The dog was frisking and play bowing before him, the man idly holding his hand out, the dog leaping up to lick his horny palm. Both of them seemingly immune to the evil of the place.

'Might be stuck, eh. Look of them clouds.' He squinted up, tobacco sprinkled in his big white beard. 'Bloody river up ahead. Gail and I only just got through.'

'How far?'

'Eh?'

'The bad bit. Ahead. How far?'

The man made a creaky sound that was a laugh turning into a cough, buried in that long white beard. 'Geez. Wouldn't have a clue. Mileage has gone round so many times on my old girl, we're back at the start.' He scratched his head, staring up again. Clear sky above, thunderheads before and behind. ''Bout three tinnies ago?'

⁓

Name was Bandy. Wife was Gail. They'd been travelling together, all over. South Australia, West Australia, the Strzelecki, the Stony. Walking out of the front yard, Bandy ticked deserts off on the four remaining fingers of one stubby, mangled-looking hand. Ray let the stream of talk tip him off the steps, down the path and, through the gate, into bright and ordinary air. A top-heavy camper sat at a slewed angle to Ray's fallen ute. Bandy walked round and round it, shaking his head.

'Gotta hand it to you. You don't do things by halves.' He squinted thoughtfully at Ray through rollie smoke. 'You were going like the clappers when I saw ya. Where's the fire?'

When Ray didn't answer, he shrugged, sighed, stubbed his butt and flipped off his thongs. 'You'll have sucked water for sure. Plugs'll be fucked. Lucky for you, I got a winch. Chuck us that rope from the front.' Ray went over to the camper. The cabin was empty and he wondered dully about Gail, the wife.

'Mate. You'd better be right behind me. I'm working up a thirst.' Holding up the hem of his little shorts daintily, Bandy was already wading in.

For half an hour there was just the meaty smell of the other man's singlet as they dug, heaved, grunted, dumb flesh against rock, metal, mud. Something to do. The old animal thing. The dog splashed between them, throwing up glints of water. The sun shining, harsh and ordinary. The dense power of the place draining away.

Afterwards, he sat in Bandy's camping chair, drinking Bandy's beer. Watching as the man worked some jerry-built lever on his home-made camper, showing how the tent popped out, his own invention. How the little cupboards were built above and behind, with a dinky sink below. A fridge, a stove, an ironing board. The whole thing tinny and compact as a home-made aeroplane.

'See? Place for everything. Even Gail.'

Ray looked around. Just the empty camper, the old blackness of desert, the fire Bandy had built.

'Where is she?'

Bandy's face looked suddenly old in the fire glow.

'She's good. She's ready. Sitting tight.' He clapped his hands together, started clattering frypans, moths gathering around his lamp and his little pull-out stove. 'Right. We got snags, steak. Chicken. That lot's been marinading since Bourke.'

While Bandy cooked, Ray sat and drank, listening to stories about the man's time in the army, his stints as an oil driller, a mining engineer. Bandits, black snakes, blood diamonds. Closing his eyes, tipping his head back, Ray let the stories swim him up and out, to where the moon was rising. Stars popping, sharp as bone.

A cry from the back of the camper made him open his eyes. A little noise, like a bereft-sounding owl. Gail perhaps. But when Ray got there, it was just Bandy, swearing, shaking his head, sweeping at some grey stuff that was all over the stove and the sink. Looked like spilled spice.

'Forgot to bloody tie her down.'

Ray saw the loose ocky strap on the shelf above, the over-turned urn.

'She'd kill me. Hates a mess, does Gail.' Bandy continued scraping her up, returning her to the urn along with a hoard of toast crumbs, piles of dust, old burnt food from the top of the stove. She'd gone everywhere, all through his labelled cups and plates, sifting in a fine screen through the cracked lid of the water tank. After a while, Ray found a dustpan and helped, thinking as he did so of Bandy, travelling alone across deserts, partaking of his wife in small communion, in endless cups of tea. Love entering him, over and over. A slow grit in heart and bone.

CHAPTER THIRTY-ONE

He walked toward her out of land brown and creased as an old photograph. The old lilt to the knees, that easy grammar between hip and thigh. Her father's walk, she realised now. Grace translated, the body remembering, despite it all.

She got out of the car, clutching Freda's mud map. Stood listening to the creak of the sign, the wind singing in the fence.

Before she'd seen that sign—on old roof tin, neatly hand-painted, *Twenty Bends Farm, Organic Fruit, Pick Your Own*, pointing up a track red as blood and straight as pin—she'd been about to give up. Nothing on her map, those tiny hieroglyphs scrawled by Freda on a serviette, showing a forked road, a dead tree, a spindled blob which could have been cow or rock or house, accorded to anything outside the car.

As he reached the gate she saw he was just a boy. Red hair, not blond hair. Tall, too thin. Not grown into his shoulders yet, his body all joint, knuckle, Adam's apple. On his freckled cheek, a receding tide mark from a black eye.

'No fruit today. It's Sunday. We're shut.'

When she didn't answer, he walked closer, a dog wending between his feet.

'You deaf? Come back next week.'

Trying for gruffness, his voice ended in a squawk. Face crimson, he aimed a kick at the kelpie twining between his feet but it danced away. She remembered it, that age. The body rebelling, the body betraying, all the flushed, musky yearning of it. All those long hot afternoons she'd spent in classrooms, wrangling bristled, blushing, gangly bundles of fear and anger like this. Her only defence some boring photocopied poem.

She'd never seen Ray at that age. He'd stayed small, gold, shining, an agile brown boy emerging from brown water, the coin she'd tossed into the shallows of the creek clutched in his teeth. Afterwards, riding on her shoulders at dusk toward bath and bed, his neat ankles anchoring her hands, he'd told their path home in Egyptian Pharaohs, Latin names for fish. His voice a bell in the dark.

'Sorry. I'm not after fruit.' Her voice sounded dry and high as the boy's. 'I'm looking for someone. But I got lost. This map . . .' She fluttered her silly napkin at him. 'I'm Ursula. You must be Mick.'

He frowned suspiciously, the bruise on his eye crinkling up. 'You from the school?'

'No. Why? Should I be?'

Idiot. Not the time for spit and vinegar now. He'd rammed his hat back on, turned on his heel, was halfway across the paddock before she called out again.

'Wait. Please. I'm sorry. I'm looking for Ray. Ray McCullough? He lives here, doesn't he? You know Freda. She gave me this address.' The boy had stopped. The dog dropped a stone at his feet, looked expectant. 'I'm Ray's mother.' So easy after all this time.

The boy turned to stare, his face burnt brick red under that shock of curly red hair. A fly explored the faded terrain of his bruise, crawling toward the edge of his mouth. She wondered who or what might have made that mark.

'He's not here. He's out.'

Not again.

'But he lives here?'

He shrugged.

'He's fencing. All day. Won't be back till later on.'

'I don't mind. I can wait.'

He stared on for a bit. Then he walked back, with bad grace, slipped the chain off the gate and whistled up the dog.

'You'll have to walk. Front gate's locked and I don't have the key.'

He was gone so fast, on those long legs of his, that he'd almost disappeared over the ridge before she had time to ask what she should do about her car. As she hurried behind, stumbling along in her plastic sandals, she saw it wasn't memory or distance that had conjured it, that familiar articulation of his body, his puppety lope. Like the hat pulled low, the rollie held between thumb and forefinger, it had been borrowed, badly translated, his raw lankiness trying to contain some coiled menace it hadn't earned, didn't own.

'This is your mother's farm, is that right?' she asked, panting, when she'd managed to catch up. She was about to correct her tense, to say sorry about what had happened when he whipped around, face bright with rage or embarrassment. He seemed constantly on the verge of both.

'Not a *farm*.'

'Oh. The sign . . .'

'That's just for the tourists. For the fruit. It's a property. See? All that land over there, past the dam? And down there, right along the creek?' She followed the proud wave of his hand, nodding, taking in the sparse rows of trees, the dark still water. Something grazing far away, blobs that might have been sheep or very small cows.

'All ours. We got goats, and pigs as well. And that new pasture across the creek, when Ray gets it fenced, we're gonna get some sheep in again. If the water pans out.'

The words sounded borrowed as well. He turned his back, smoking furiously as he strode. Over the ridge, a shed, some skinny chickens, the dog herding them with little skill and great enthusiasm, turning mindless circles in the dust. At the bottom, in a bowl of earth, a little house, grey and famished looking. She saw the skew-whiff verandah, the cracked windows, the eaves scoured back to lime. Saw too the scrubbed, swept boards, the tidy woodpile, the neatly paired work boots outside the door. The boy was levering his off already, heel to toe.

'No shoes inside.' She heard her own voice, echoing back at her down the years. He slammed in, the screen door almost catching her in the face.

Inside, she had time for a quick impression of a small room, bare floorboards, a little bookcase made of bricks, before he pulled out a kitchen chair. Stood over it, glowering stonily, until she sat down. She wondered what Ray had told him about her, if he'd said anything at all.

She waited for Mick to turn the kettle on, ask about tea, but he was getting down canisters from the cupboards. Flour, sugar, bowls, a rolling pin, all lined up neatly on the table, so she had only a small corner to call her own. As he took a pink frilly apron from the back of a chair and tied it around his waist, he stared at her hard, as if daring her to laugh.

'What are you making?'

He gave this the silence it deserved. Shook yeast from a packet, measured flour, added water from a jug, his tongue poking out from the side of his mouth.

She sat in silence as the boy mixed and kneaded and grunted, his big red knuckles vicious against the defenceless dough. Closing her mind to thirst and a thousand questions, aware of the barely controlled rage the boy was giving off, she tried to take in, from what she could see, the little bits and pieces of the place Ray called home. A rusty fridge, a dent in the freezer door. A pot bubbling on the stove. Torn laminex, a cream-coloured clock, some monastic-looking shelves. The little brick and ply bookcase, the scanty spines on it old and worn. Too far to read what they were without getting up, and the boy was thumping the table so hard with the dough, she didn't dare. The only other door in the place was firmly closed. No pictures, no photographs. No sign of a woman here except the boy's pink-frilled hips.

She turned back, to the only reading matter she could find, a copy of the local newspaper on the table, two weeks old. As she pulled it toward her, the edge of it contacted the boy's hand and he threw the dough down harder, puffing flour all over her arm. She just wet a finger coolly and turned a page. Read intently about local elections, the death of a town worthy, the grand opening of a new hospital oncology wing.

After what seemed like hours but was only fifteen minutes by the clock, she felt rather than saw the tension leave the boy's body, poured out into the now-sleek dough.

'That's coming along.' He said nothing but threw the dough down with a milder thump. 'Mick? Would you mind if I made myself some tea?'

He shrugged. The little pink frills going up and down on his big shoulders made her want to laugh. Instead she got up, filled the kettle. The room silent except for the water drumming, the clock ticking, the boy grunting, but differently now, more companionably. A cooking silence, clouds of flour floating in late rays of sun. While she waited for the kettle to boil, she lifted the lid on the pot. The smell was rich with fat and meat, earthy with turnip and swede. So redolent of childhood, so intensely and privately familiar, it almost made her blush.

'This smells good. What is it?'

'Soup.' From the corner of her eye, she saw he was creaming butter and sugar now, folding flour with airy curves of a wooden spoon.

'What sort?'

Oxtail of course, with the bone left in. Secret was to make it the day before. While she listened to her own wisdom retailed back at her—long slow brown of the onions, skim the fat, only beef stock, home-made—she drank her tea and looked out the window, at earth the colour and texture of string. Sun was lower now, glinting off the dark hole of the dam.

'That's a lot of food you're making. Just for two.'

He was tucking dough in a tin, placing the tin on a tray.

'Might as well. The oven's on.'

Her rule. Her mother's rule. An old country rule, from the days of cantankerous woodfired ovens and no money for shop-bought biscuits and cake.

'What happened to your eye?'

The dog barked then, a single yelp. She heard the screen door go as the boy slammed out and she looked out the kitchen window again. The sun was twinging sharp on the ridge, slicing up past the curtains, forcing her to shade her eyes. Someone moving out there, amid the glitter of dust and stones. A tall man walking toward her, unfolding from some tender crease in her mind.

At this distance, through glare and shimmer, curtailed, foreshortened. A boy again, after all this time.

ACKNOWLEDGEMENTS

S pecial thanks to Annette Barlow, Christa Munns and Julia Stiles, and as always to Andre van Schaik, for all his support.